AN AGE OF LIONS

CHASE BOLLING

CHASE BOLLING

An Age of Lions

Contents

Chapter 1   1

Chapter 1: Camino   3

Chapter 2: Hunter   10

Chapter 3: Miryam's Way   18

Chapter 4: The Square   32

Chapter 5: Thicker Than Water   47

Chapter 6: Fuming   57

Chapter 7: Children of Twilight   69

Chapter 8: Oathborn   76

Chapter 9: Great Expectations   88

Chapter 10: Road to Bobastro   99

Chapter 11: Nuevo Bobastro   111

Chapter 12: Way of the Ancestors   121

Chapter 13: First Contract   133

Chapter 14: Old Ways   145

Chapter 15: Despeñaperros   157

Chapter 16: Las Navas de Tolosa   171

Chapter 17: Only Family Can Stab You   186

Chapter 18: Fangs of Betrayal   201

Chapter 19: Phantasms of Strife   216

Chapter 20: Bone and Blood   234

Chapter 21: Dawn of Darkness   252

Chapter 22: Interwoven   272

Chapter 23: Ard Allam   292

Chapter 24: Hour of the Lion   312

Chapter 25: Lord and Commander   334

Chapter 1

In the time of Noah, the Almighty chained the Watchers to the low valleys and begat the flood to destroy the nephilim and wickedness upon the face of the earth. The rainbow was placed in the sky a promise to the children of men to never again destroy the world by flood. But this world has never been solely the dominion of men, and to the beasts and the creatures of the earth the rainbow was also a symbol. A symbol of a covenant all their own, and as night fell and Noah and his descendants slept, it was decreed unto the other survivors of the flood that they would be given the places which sheltered them. As the tongues were divided at Babel, so were the children of Samyaza and the children of Noah divided. The children of Samyaza the giants, the djinn, the fae, and the nephilim and darker things yet were free to survive and thrive as they could, outside the light and Grace of God. And so a peace between the two houses was born and to man the world of light was given to stride and prosper upon the earth as the others we given to the hidden, the deep, or the high places to do the same.

As for the Watchers, the cythonic gods of men, who have always been the echoes of the ancient ones calling from the deep. Their avarice and lust remains ever undimmed, ever ready to reach out from the recesses of the shadows to touch souls where they may, and where men follow gods of darkness, so follows the heart. Even after the light of Our Savior these are dark days, confusion reigns, and surely all the world is Babylon. If men knew what hungered for them in the darkness, they would be loath raise arms against one another. They would know the cost of senseless loss of life. Men would forgive each other, love each other, and spare each other for fear of one less blade against the tempest. If the children of the Midnight Covenant were to come against us now, we would be as feeble as a candle in the wind.

There have been stirrings that disturb these old bones. A howling from my ancestors that haunts my sleep. There is a boldness to the others that should grip the heart of every prince of men with fear and trouble the intuition of every queen. The seers of every nation should tremble. When Tariq sailed north to conquer in Europa it was to secure a bulwark against what was to come. Now Al Andalus and the kingdoms of the Franks will not stand. The Ismaili are broken, their mission has failed. The Crusades to secure the Holy Land have failed. The Ayyubid's, God curse them serve the enemy and they know it not. The time has come old friend. In the land of the blind the man with one eye is king. We must do what must be done. The time of defending the light from the shadows has ended. The time of the wolf and the fox must end. Now is the age of lions. May our roar resound in the darkness.

-Letter to Leon Alfiere from Moses, Court Magi of Makuria

Chapter 1: Camino

"Beg pardon sir knight?" Sweat seemed to pour from the man's doughy brow as he huffed along. July in Seville was hot and the climate and this gentleman were in obvious disagreement In Cazador's opinion too much heat was adverse to anyone's health. Even when one's skin was a healthy brown of the Bilad al Sudan. Cazador looked down from his horse a white Arabian sired from a line brought from the Sahel." I hope I'm not being rude, but I must admit to a fair bit of curiosity. A occupational hazard as a scholar you see." Cazador looked down at the man. He certainly had the look of a scholar or scribe about him and Cazador wondered what had brought him on pilgrimage. With his mop of dark red curls combined with the iron grey eyes, adorning his handsome albeit plump features, Cazador could guess. From his own experience women didn't mind a man with a bit of substance to their constitution. "What brings a Moor to become a guardian of Christian pilgrims? Pray tell!" Cazador spoke Arabic, Latin, Spanish, Greek, English and a bit of the tongue of the North men he'd picked up among the Danish traders in Grenada. His aunt Miryam had paid for his education and the nominal civilization that went with it. Because of this, he did most of the talking as they traveled. This invariably made Cazador the target of every curious pilgrim. And their questions. "That's a long story messire..." Cazador paused. The sweaty young man stammered a bit. " Oh ah em I am Merfynn ap Merfynn of Powys." He said sticking out his hand. Cazador leaned down from his saddle and shook it. "As I was saying Messire Merfynn...it's a terribly long story. Merfynn smiled." Well sir knight, its a terribly long journey." Cazador smiled. That it was.

Preparing for the speech he'd given a thousand times. "My name is Cazador Al Takruri Alfiere of Monts des Maures. In 1086 my grand father's grandfather Saif and his brothers came with with Yusuf Ibn Tashfin to battle against Castile and Aragon in the name of the Prophet and the caliphs. Together they fought all across Al Andalus and against the Christians amassing wealth and glory. But in 1118 at the age of sixty six, old Saif was expelled from Zaragoza after the Moors were defeated. Disheartened by the fighting and animosity of Muslim against Muslim and disenfranchised by the cruelty and lack of tolerance exhibited by the rising Almohads he lost his faith in Islam. Bereft he wandered with his son's and younger brothers to Seville where he received a vision from the Lord compelling him to the true faith of Our Lord and commanding him to go on pilgrimage. With his kin he walked the Camino Santiago intent of taking the Via Francigena to Rome. On the way to Nizza the Takruri clan was discovered on the road by a patrol of men with faces as brown as their own. Saif learned that they were men at arms of knights holding a manor in the Monts De Maures.

Thrilled to meet other Christian Moors, Saif met Sir Alexandre, whose ancestors had been high ranking men of the town of La Garde-Freinet and the fortress of Fraxinetum. The Saracens of Fraxinetum had terrorized the area raiding churches and preying upon pilgrims. Sir Alexandre's family had held land in the area for sixty years until the fortress was razed. Those who did not flee were forced to convert and became serfs of the land. Due to their war craft and knowledge of the area Sir Alexandre's forbears were taken into the service of Ramon the Great, Count of Provence. He charged them with protecting the pilgrims on byways they once raided as penance. Given peonages and eventually knighthoods, the Moorish families of Monts Des Maures attended their duty and in time grew wealthy trading goods and operating hostels.

In 1114 my grandfathers father Esteve Ibn Nasr was born on the day Alfonso the Battler defeated the Almohads at Calamocha. He like his grandsire Alexandre, was a guardian of pilgrim's, protecting those traveling from Canterbury in England to Rome. In his time in England he was drawn into the service of the house of England fighting at Lincoln. From there he went on Crusade as a squire serving in the siege of Ascalon then fighting among the Normans who knew him as Steven the Moor and a puissant man at arms. He joined an expedition to Egypt where in the confusion the Normans turned their blades upon Coptic Christians.

Appalled by the slaughter of his Christian brothers he left their service. My aunt's and mother tell me of a time when he wandered Ifríqiya spending a time in the household of the King Georgios IV of Makuria. There he fought waves of Arabic raiders until God called him west. Joining a caravan of Fulbe kin he traveled toward the homeland of his forbears to see it with his own eyes.

As he journeyed near Gao his caravan met a group of Taureg whom they engaged in trade. Their he met the daughter of a Taureg chief who's grandfather lived as king among the Akan. This woman became my grandfathers mother the lady Dyhia. They lived as wealthy traders bringing gold to Marrakush in exchange for weapons and armor. It was during this time in Morocco that my grandfather was born. Seven years later in the year of our lord 1164, when the Caliphs signed a trade agreement with Marsielle my grandfather Hamza Ibn Esteve Ibn Nasr Al Takuri his parents, and retainers traveled to Marsielle, and from there returned to the Monts Des Maures.

Against his father's wishes my grandfather went on Crusade as one day my cousins may." Cazador added with a wink. "Rather than fight in the Holy Land he led retainers from Monts Des Maures to join Nubian forces in the fight against the Kurds in Upper Egypt. He fought there for three years before traveling back towards home. It was 1174 when he landed in Grenada. With the Almohad retaking many of the Taifas in Al Andalus the brown skin of my grandfather and his retinue caused nary a stir. Flush with coin from fighting Kurdish Mamluks in the east he corresponded with his brothers to build a fleet of ships and purchased the land and ruins around Bobastro making himself lord there.

In those days many of the pilgrims my family escorted came from the lands of Nubia and Abbysinnia and found it much safer to take the Camino entering Al Andalus than taking the short trip to Jerusalem from their home. Despite the promises of safety from Saladin many good Christians from the lands south of Egypt had ended up enslaved in the markets of Zanzibar. The Almohads had viciously begun to persecute Jews and Christians making the Al Takruri and other Monts Des Maures families a valuable asset. It was a simple thing to don a jibbah and tagelmust and greet others in Arabic or Hapullar often protecting travelers without ever drawing a blade. Generations of family connections among the Arabic and Christian worlds of Europa, Andalusia, and the Sudan had created and access to Templar banks from his father's service my grandfather sought to build wealth for our family. That wealth attracted many marriage offers. "Cazador swept his eyes across some of the comely young women that had drifted close enough to overhear he and Merfynn speak. He loved to tell this part of the story. He eyed the swaying hips of a woman from the party from Abbysinnia as she passed. They were a large group almost forty in total. Her flawless tawny brown skin and bright smile had caught Cazador's eye and he hoped she kept listening. With a small smile he continued. "Many rich and powerful families sought to tie him to their house but they all failed for my father had already fallen in love. One day he passed a stall where a woman and her daughter sold spices that were rare even in Granada. He met her eye across the square but he couldn't bring himself to approach for her beauty and the heady scent of exotic spices had unmanned him. In time he learned that he had fell in love with a daughter of the Iznagen called Xenobia. Her father was a educated man and a captain of the garrison. His family had been in Al Andalus since the first Almoravids and her mother ran a fine trade in spices. One day when Xenobia's mother was not was not there he managed to make his way to her to visit. My grandmother's mother Adina arranged for my very nervous grandfather to meet her daughter. A year later my father Guillermo Ibn Hamza ibn Esteve ibn Nasr Ibn Saif Al Takruri Alfiere was born.

They say he was a good fighter and a prieux chevalier who fought in England escorting pilgrims to and from Canterbury during the anarchy. He spend a time as a mercenary knight and sometimes Adalid for Aragon against the Almohads who my family has come to despise.

Unbeknownst to my grandmother Xenobia, my father met and married my mother born Zaida bint Aryad, a wealthy, educated widow who's family had been in Spain and traded in England for generations. However my mother Linda of Seville had made her life in Italia. My father left on Crusade to Outremer in 1191 in May just three months after I was born. He was never seen or heard from again, leaving yours truly. Humble Cazador Ibn Guillermo Ibn Hamza ibn Esteve ibn Nasr Ibn Saif Alfiere of El Bobastro and Monts Des Maures. Before you." Cazador bowed in his saddle like the finest knight. "And that is how a Moor comes to be leading a party of Christians on Camino!"

There was a smattering of applause led by the beaming Merfynn. The year was 1212 and the march of Christian armies and Andalusi fighters made life in España tense. Smiled had been rare. Cazador and his party traveled north from the city of Seville and were perhaps ten miles of El Ronquillo where there was a hostel run by the Alfiere. Sweat ran from under his simple round bar nasal helmet the steel protected from the sun by the indigo tagelmust of Cazador's Tuareg ancestors. His black jibbah was adorned with shining steel plates stitched into fabric was all that protected his body as it was too hot for his good lamellar. A round dish like plate protected his stomach, with two rectangular plates covering his flanks, and another covered his chest. Each was heavily engraved along the borders and bore the same Kufic inscription as their banner in argent on a black.

So fight you against the friends of Satan.

Family legend had it that they were the words that woke old Saif to the worship of Christ. He made them the motto of his household. When they crossed over into Christian lands Cazador would store the Arabic banner and raise the banner of their order even as Cazador covered his armor with his black and purple surcoat emblazoned with the coat of arms of his ancestors. He could still remember the notes taken by the counts armigers. *Per bend sinister meandering sable and purpure in first quarter a gauntlet clenched purpure in fourth quarter a lion head sable.* Next they would fly the Thebeai banner of Knights of Saint Attillo, and hoist the lesser banners. The group Moorish families who held estates in Provence collectively called the Du Maurmonts had been given lands in Provence by Count Hugh back in 953. As they moved through the Christian and Muslim worlds his grandfather would often joke that they changed coats but never principles. To supplement his jibbah Cazador had an ayar shield he and his kin favored in Al Andalus strapped to his left arm. On his hip hung *Tempest* Cazador's heavy bladed Damascus steel sword. He also carried a *tagheda* short spear and short fighting axe, and a double handful of throwing knives from the lands south of the Sudan. If it came to a fight he was a ready as a man could be for such things. Killing bandits and fighting off raiders and cattle thieves was something Cazador had been raised to do. After campaigns in France, Byzantium, and Morea he considered fighting a personal specialty no matter how often his grandfather cautioned Cazador to never delight in being a killer. Pride is a sin like any other he would say and he wasn't wrong.

The land around them was dotted with trees and sun parched scrubby grass rendering the landscape various shades of brown and green. Hills rose steadily to the west just beyond the heavily wooded banks of the Arroyo de la Parrita. Ahead the a oak, beech, and hazel trees thickened into a dense stand on either side of the track. It would be a good place to rest for a bit and water the horses. The shade would provide a welcome respite from the sun and heat and Cazador resisted the urge to increase his pace. He could almost feel the sweat cooling on his body as he entered the dappled shade. Eyes firmly trained on the wood ahead, his spirits plummeted when a glint of sunlight on steel caught his eye.

Cazador tipped his head back as if his eyes were searching the cloudless blue expanse for divine intervention. Praying he didn't see what he thought he saw. Failing that a cloud or ten to break the relentless onslaught of the sun would have been a kkndness. This is my first command. Simple trip, established routes. Easy. As much as he liked to fight, fighting wasn't on his itinerary. Cazador quit beseeching, grandfather always said, God empowered man to make his own miracles.

Chapter 2: Hunter

Cazador blew the small horn he carried and the other guards used to signal the pilgrims and each other. A single note meant stop and Cazador blew it truly hoping it was simple paranoia. His cousin's looked to him, eyes puzzled above their veils. Usually this deep in Al Andalus they didn't need forward scouts although his grandfather often insisted upon them. Cazador cursed himself for not sending any. He'd defended many caravans like this since he was thirteen years old, but at twenty two this was his first as captain of one. Not even two full days from Seville and he had led them into trouble." Is something wrong Sir Cazador?" Merfynn asked. Cazador looked at the man and shrugged. "I hope not." Cazador had six knights and eight archers and twelve light men at arms called almogovars.

A man of Monts Des Maures approached my position at the head of the column. He was named Idris ibn Idris al Sanhanji who's ancestors had been familia knights and me at arms of Cazador's grandfather's grandfather Saif. He served as my Adalid or leader of the almogovar light infantry. Idris was as bald as an egg with smooth skin as dark as rich earth. His defining features were his enormous bushy beard that hung like a shovel from his face to his stomach.

He carried no fat, and stood no more than shoulder high to most men, but was one of the fastest fighters Cazador had ever seen. Nobody not Cazador's grandfather nor any of his cousins knew how old Idris was. The man hadn't seemed to age, and rumors had it he had trained Cazador's father as he had trained Cazador and his cousins. The fact that he had come to Cazador now meant that his instincts hadn't been wrong. "Lord?" Idris said bringing his horse alongside Cazador's. "Take the horses and the folk to the arroyo to have a drink." Cazador said loudly and nonchalantly to a chorus of relieved groans. Quieter he continued, "I want the pilgrims off the road in the cover of trees by the arroyo. Have the almogovars form defensive circle around them. Take no more than two archers with you. We will pretend to watch the road for a time join you. " Cazador said imbuing the orders with confidence he wish he felt about the next part of his plan. Idris bowed in his saddle and rode back down the column.

With him was Alcazar al Thawr, an Almohad warrior who had denounced all faiths yet swore an oath to Cazador and his grandfather.

Found, fourteen years old and sorely wounded, he had been with them for years now. That day his large frame was bleeding from a dozen gashes and he'd been dazed from a head wound half dead with a broken sword still in his hand. Old Hamza noting his size and apparent ferocity, had declared the young man must have fought like a bull and so he was called Alcazar al Thawr or the bull. He had recovered and he and Cazador been friends and partners in mischief ever since. If not for his grandfather's coin, Cazador was sure they lot of them would have long ago ended up as slaves in a mine or galley. The other young men with him were little different. Cazador's cousins Izan, Jaime, and the twins Pedro and Pablo sat their horses with Maurice and Kaleb of Dongla, Makurians who had arrived for fostering. Last was his sister's son Leon, only a handful of years younger than Cazador.

All were well trained, each schooled in war from the time they could walk. Countless times they had bested bandits, littering Spanish plains or Alpine passed with corpses, to return to Monts Des Maures communes or the Alfiere /Al Takruri stronghold outside of Malága called Bobastro Nuevo. The only thing for Cazador to lament was that each of those times he hadn't held the command. Now the lives of his kinsman and more than two score pilgrims were in Cazador's admittedly sweaty hands. He had failed to send out his very capable scouts and now he had nine knights, and he was about to spring an ambush.

Idris had sent two men to scout the area near the arroyo and was already chivvying the pilgrims. Cazador was about to turn away when he noticed three men two mounted and one on foot emerge from the huddle of pilgrims. Cazador was surprised to see Merfynn among them. Of the other two men, one was clean shaven with olive skin. His hazel eyes seemed alert under the straw pilgrim hat that contained a mane of dark hair. Cazador could see the telltale hint of maille under his brown rough spun robe. The other had the piercing blue eyes of a Norman with a short trimmed blonde goatee, bright against his sun darkened skin. Each bore the sword and spurs of a knight. "I'm Alberto of Castille, said the dark haired man and I took his arm in the warrior grip favored among the Franks. "Roland of Palermo." The blonde man introduced himself and Cazador thanked God and Saint Maurice the patron Saint of Alpine warriors for the addition of two more trained fighters. Merfynn smiled sheepishly. "Y'already know who I am, all I need it to borrow a horse, a shield and maybe an axe." He said grinning confidently. Everyone laughed and Cazador felt the tension lift.

Cazador and his party of twelve worked their way into position. He had instructed the pilgrims in his care to take their leisure by the cotton and almond trees lining the arroyo as his almogovars kept a hidden vigil. Some of the pilgrims were making an early camp in the clearing. The area was beautiful, wild yet bearing a certain domestic quality. It would make a lovely homestead. Examining the layout of the clearing and the presence of the trees Cazador wondered if once there had been a farm here once. If there had been, it was washed away generations ago in a tide of war. It was a great spot for a home, but also a perfect place for an ambush. The steep western bank of the arroyo rose behind them like a natural barrier protecting their flank but leaving nowhere to run. Had Idris not had an idea of what he was up to he would have likely murdered Cazador for stupidity. If things went well his comrades would be buying his wine for a while. If his plan failed then it wouldn't matter because dead men didn't drink wine.

Cazador's grandfather had once told him that of a lion hunt in the Sudan as a boy. He had ambushed the beast when it attacked an antelope at a watering hole, and Cazador sought to implement that same principle now. Aunt Miryam would kill him if she knew he was using clients as bait, but he had little choice. Dead was dead reckless plan or no. Idris had given him a sooty substance which his party had used to conceal their metal accouterments. Cazador didn't want to compound his numerous mistakes and give away their position as their enemy just had. The plan was simple enough. Cazador didn't know if Merfynn and the other two men could fight, but he hoped it wouldn't matter. They had stepped up when they saw the party might be threatened and to Cazador that meant something.

If I tell anyone about this, it will sound like the opening of a bawdy joke. One day, nine Moors, a Sicialian, a Spaniard, and a Welshman hid in the woods. But instead of a witty phrase, Cazador was about launch himself into a storm of steel and bloodshed. It was truly the height of comedy. If his throat could hand summoned the ability to resist constricting he might have chuckled. Instead he waited, sweating into his armor in grim anticipation.

Cazador could smell the scent of wine and unwashed bodies before he ever heard the grunted Norman French mixed with Aragonese curses on the breeze. They broke cover. Their faded and filthy surcoats had once matched but now only shared a uniform dinge. The unarmored men among them showed they were being led by Aragonese almogovars their Adalid prominent with his red and yellow sword baldric slung almost arrogantly over his bare chest. *So trained raiders rather than common bandits then.* Soon the enemy van were overtaken by a conroi of men in trail stained white tunics of Templars. There seemed to be a moment of conference before the apparent leader amongst the Templars drew his sword. It's shrill rasp loud in the afternoon air waking screams from the throats of the women among the Pilgrims. "Deus Veult!" The Templar roared and the Normans followed suit. The Franks and their allies charged filling the clearing that before the tree lined arroyo with terror. Cazador waited long enough to say a Hail Mary giving the fastest a chance to make it to the rough middle of the clearing. The closest no more than a short five paces from the point of Cazador's spear poised in his left hand behind his shield. "Saint Atillo and Du Maurmont!" He roared. It was the signal his archers led by Constantin of Aksum we're waiting for. On the opposite side the clearing from of Cazador's party, arrows ripped into the Christian raiders. The first wave faltered with cries of shock and dismay as powerful Nubian recurve bows blasted heavy bodkin tipped war arrows into their maille. As the enemy momentum slowed Cazador's almogovars clad in plain undyed aketons with falchions, axes and Takouba swords and round black bucklers seemed to melt out of the landscape and coalesce into a loose cloud. They launched their javelins in unison, their darts lancing into the enemy ranks . "Alfiere for Christ!" Cazador barked. It was the final signal and he was off like he took was shot from a bow, leading his small band of men at arms in a wild charge.

The reinforced rim of Cazador's ayar slammed into the Frank's great helm stunning him. Wasting no time he unleashed Tempest, chopping into his enemy's unarmored leg. Heavy like a good cleaver, the old Viking style blade destroyed whatever it touched. The keen edge laid open cloth hose and flesh exposing bone in a wash of blood. Cazador followed up slamming his pommel into the helmeted head.

His enemy fell spewing dark arterial blood into the thirsty Adalusi earth. All around him Cazador's fellow shock troops exploded from cover forming a wedge with him at it's point. "He maketh my fingers for battle and prepares my hands for war!" Cazador growled emulating his grandfathers battlefield bark with all his might. Their formation rolled forward and Cazador fired a high thrust with his spear with body tight behind his shield. His target a wild eyed Templar, raised his own shield and Cazador used the lugs behind his spearhead to yank down on the boards. Launching a high cut with his sword Cazador clenched his lips tight as the Damascus steel blade shattered the maille coiffed head like an overripe fruit in a spray of blood. With a yell he shoved his shield edge forward to cover his left handed thrust as his spear's slim head punched into the haubergon of a big blonde man at arms. Cazador yanked it free with a savage twist and used his shield to block a wild slash from the Aragonese adalid. Shoving a the blow aside with his ayar Cazador drew the man's buckler high with a spear thrust, and aimed a disemboweling blow for his foe's unarmored stomach.

The man had not gained his rank for being without skill, and skipped lithely away. Almogovar adalids were chosen by their peers and known lovers of battle leading some of the most effective infantry in Christendom. This man was good, but he had never fought Cazador Alfiere. Battle was his calling, his birthright. Cazador and his forebears had killed men on three continents. "Venir I morir" Cazador bellowed in Catalan stepping forward and slashing low to high from his left hip opening the adalid's defense for his spear which took the man's throat out.

Beside him Izan broke a Frankish knight's shield arm with a mighty blow from his mace leaving him defenseless to his follow up blow that collapsed his helmet. The twins Pablo and Pedro fought with short spears and grim efficiency overwhelming stubborn foes in tanderm. The archers were picking their shots, and kill by kill Cazador and his men cut deep into the raider's formation.

Sheltering beneath his ayar against a flurry of cuts, Cazador crouched and hacked into the agressive fighter's ankle. He fell with a scream to reveal the Templar leader. He roared and cut at Cazador who parried his sword with his shield, flicking his spear at his enemy's face. The Temlpar's shield forced the blow down and away opening his guard for Cazador's thrust which took the man in the eye slot of his pothelm. He fell and Idris picked that moment to charge with the almogovars. The Franks and their Aragonese allies had come for loot and slaves, instead they found only death.

* * *

Later that evening Cazador sat by a fire an hours walk south of the battlefield. He reclined against his saddle sipping a hard cider from a flask with Merfynn and the others. The dead knights had been rich pickings and only belatedly did the thought arise that maybe they should have spared ransomed the knights. He could already hear grandfather chiding him.

Idris and the almogovars had found the enemy camp and plundered it finding food, wine and weapons. If any of the good Christians among the Pilgrims had a problem with our looting they didn't raise a single protest. In the morning they would go back to Seville. Cazador would bring in more men and restart the journey for any who wished it. He hadn't lost a single soul and more than fifty enemy corpses had been left for the wolves. To Cazador's mind if they'd wanted a Christian burial they wouldn't have accosted pilgrims.

Richer and flush with victory Cazador and his men held court among the pilgrims they had so valiantly defended. A young boy with the accent of Greece on his lips asked approached. "Pardon me sir knight? I overheard you speaking earlier if the birth of your forefathers, but what of your own?" Cazador smiled. "Ahh young one, my uncles and aunts tell me a story even I fail to believe." There was this fanciful tale starting with my mother deciding to birth me on in the land of her father's. A storm blew in from the coast of Ifríqiya that tore our the ship leagues across open ocean. My uncle's say the ship wrecked in a strange land where the trees and birds were unlike anything they had ever seen land the only familiar thing was the muggy heat. They were saved by a hunter from this strange land. He brought them food, fresh water, and a healer from his people. I was born in that land for which I have no name and for that man's kindness and compassion my mother and aunts named me Cazador the hunter. After a time my family sailed back to Takrur. It is a hard to believe story that I would not repeat if not for three things that make me wonder." Cazador said fishing beneath his surcoat, maille, and gambeson to produce a rawhide necklace with a disk shaped medallion depicting a black cat like beast similar to the leopard on a brilliant red and blue field made from hundreds of dyed beads. He took it off and handed it to the boy who's dark brown eyes and dark hair and accent hinted at Greek ancestry like many of their clients. The boy took it reverently and turned it over turning carefully in his overlarge pilgrim's robes to had it over to his mother and father for inspection. "I have had this since I was born and I have never seen it's like anywhere I have been. I have asked the people of a hundred nations and none could place it." The crowd of pilgrim's looked on in genuine interest. Smiling Cazador continued, "One day I met some northmen from Hebedy, who told me of a place called Vinland where men with copper colored skin and coal black hair they called Skraelings lived. They told me that there in that distant place the folk made things like this. Lastly my uncle made a fortune selling a map of their return journey to some traders from Djenne. If not for the fact that I still help him spend this coin even now, I would not accost your ears." Cazador took a moment to delight in the wonderstuck expressions of the pilgrims. They were good people who loved God. Cazador and his cousin's offered them not only protection but entertainment as they made their way to the various shrines and holy places. It was a good life. It was the life he and his cousins had imagined as they were forced to study at Cambridge by their aunt's as boys. Still it rankled Cazador to have to return to Seville on his first journey as captain. Part of him wanted to forge ahead but as he thought about his charges he knew it would be a grievous sin to risk their lives for his pride. Their crushing victory and loot and captured horses would have to be enough to soothe his battered ego.

Early the following morning when the mist was heavy and the air still cool they packed up and rode for Seville. This time Cazador had Idris ibn Idris and the *almogovars* out ahead of the column sent ahead almost four hours earlier. He still chided himself for not having had scouts out the day before, but he was wise enough to realize the outcome would have been the same. Those men had been waiting there on a family route and something about that felt off. Less emotional today he could spot the oddness. Not mastering his emotions could lead to trouble more often than glory. A lesson Cazador had learned as a boy in Kent.

Chapter 3: Miryam's Way

Miryam signed the charter that detached an English estate and from a trust held by La Vénérable Compagnie des Protecteurs et Avitailleurs des Pèlerins de Monts Des Maures, simply called La Compagnie and bestowed it on its newest owner. Next she took out the charter lordship for the castle of La Marche, and the commune of Le Cannet des Maures once property of her brother one of several freeholds in Provence granted by Hugh of Arles to her ancestors. Now it would belong to his son.

The English estate was established by their ancestor Esteve or Steven the Moor, and called Moorhouse in northern England not far from where Libyan Emperor Septimus Severus had his famous camp. She was happy to give Cazador his patrimony it was as though she could finally close the door on Guillermo's absence. Wherever he was his shadow had lingered over the son he abandoned long enough. Cazador was young and warlike but he would lead the commune of Le Cannet Des Maures well and it would gentle him. It was time for her nephew to take his place. Next she reviewed the contracts that would allocate those with feudal ties to the the Du Maurmonts families and assign them to a new accompagné or comitatus. Cazador's recent success boded well for what Miryam and her father Hamza Alfiere called the Old Lion were planning.

King John of England had come calling for fighters in his Welsh campaign. The Old Lion had come up with the idea of negotiating a lower scutage payment in exchange for arming and supplying mercenaries. They would send seven mensies under her nephew, each consisting of a knight, man at arms, two archers and two almogovars. The combined force would field a retinue almost fifty strong, complete with a Chaplin, a djali and a blacksmith. Miryam was calling them the Company of Saint Moses and with Cazador being made Lord of the Manor at Moorhouse as captain, not only would feudal obligations be met, but they would be paid as a mercenary force.

"You did well to recommend me Diallo when you did." She said to the statuesque woman sitting beside her. Linda of Seville smiled happily, the cloth of gold fabric of her head wrap and matching afetek glowing against the bronze of her skin. "I am putting the finishing touches on assigning Cazador's household. Some kind and a promising crop of young men from the hills around Nuevo Bobastro and from the du Maurmont communes. Diallo will be a good fit, and although Idris ibn Idris is retired I've attached him to keep an eye on them." Linda nodded looking pleased and thoughtful and Miryam beamed. When Linda was silent it was often her loudest praise.

Her big sister was her hero and Miryam had dedicated herself to employing her sisters philosophies on business and statecraft when she founded La Compagnie. In the early days her unflinching support had been vital introducing Miryam to the right people and helping her establish her credibility. Soon the Old Lion had taken notice and together the three of them had changed generations of tradition. Miryam looked at her willowy elder sister. It had been some time since they had seen each other and her visits were rare thanks to the the rare circumstances of their sisterhood. With her kohl lined eyes, high cheekbones and freckle dusted nose men still courted her, but she would have none of it. Even though her fingers and wrists dripped with gold and her estate in Italy made fine wines and honey, Linda was most proud of her education, the sword belted about her waist, and her children. As a girl Linda had chosen to become an adība or woman of letters spending time studying in Al Andalus before spending time in Salerno and traveling to Rome. Fearless and intelligent she had secured the patronage of Aldruda Frangipane, after she distinguished herself fighting in armor with the Bertinoro against Barbarosa in '73. She had returned in '77 with three children married to a wealthy Sonninke trader scandalizing her family. Despite years in Al Andalus they still held to the ways of the Sudan. Caste was caste and a trader was beneath her as a noblewoman. Shunning Al Andalus she remained in Italy.

Angry and more hurt than she could admit, Linda couldn't even be bothered write when her first husband passed. Perhaps if she had things would've been better, or at least different. The estrangement and subsequent silence were why Linda had never learned that her own mother Kahina, a wealthy well connected widow in her own right, had married Hamza or Leon ibn Esteve in 1174. A year later their union produced Miryam. Linda had returned to Spain in 1190 after eloping with the brash and handsome Guillermo ibn Hamza Al Tekruri who unbeknownst to either of them had become her brother by law. Embarrassed and furious Linda had purchased a ship intent on sailing for Takrur. With her were Miryam, her older brother Yvain, and their brother Antonio. She would never forget the fury of the storm that saw her nephew born on far flung alien soil. After their return her sister spent most of her time in Italy, or with her eldest son Tomas in England, and visiting her daughters in France. It was a rare occasion that she would come to Al Andalus, and Miryam was determined that her sister would enjoy herself. Despite everything they had always been friends and allies and Miryam hoped that maybe she would even thaw some of the ice that stood between Linda her and her youngest son.

Miryam had loved Cazador from his first breath. She had seen greatness in his eyes from the moment he opened them, and watched the lively, irrepressibly intelligent boy grow into a fine man. Like Linda Miryam had thought he might be a doctor or scholar, perhaps a priest allowing his God given mind to shape the world. Instead he was too much like his grandfather and her lost brother Guillermo. They were bred from the warrior nobility of the Sudan and tempered by the Fula ways of pulaaku. War and restless feet were the heritage of the Al Takruri and Du Maurmont yet as glorious as it was, it made her sad. Linda sighed beside Miryam as if reading her thoughts. " Your nephew reminds me too much of his father and maybe my own father." she murmered, wistfully eyeing the documents.

Miryam reached out and squeezed her sister's hand. Pride and vanity were chief sins of the Alfiere and other Du Maurmont men. "The same things that make us strong is a sword with two edges." She replied. Linda nodded. "The fools would rather die on battlefield in blood and shit on behalf men who care for naught but their own gain. Is it better a glorious death? Is it more fulfilling than a long humble life as a scholar, tradesman, or servant of the church?" She tutted. "Glorious fools! They never live to have to deal with the aftermath of their foolishness." Linda spat, her tone laden with disapproval as if she were not the same. As if the sword at her hip had always been idle. Miryam shrugged, "All things work together for the glory of those who love the Lord. If he lives and I truly think he will, he will inherit all I own, even if your family has stricken him from your inheritance. If not through me then through my father. Cazador will never be a simple soldier." Miryam said reassuringly. The hostility in Linda's eyes softened. "Good," she said. "He deserves to be more than just another killer with a trimount, or Thebeai on his breast." Miryam nodded and completed her work with a signature and a wax seal. She placed the patents and charters in a leather script and an aide appeared from an alcove to whisk it away to be notarized and copied. Miryam had already sent riders to recall Cazador and his party. News from the north of a new Crusader offensive had forced her to delay contracts. War would make the pilgrim routes dangerous compromising Miryam's carefully crafted supply chain. Cazador's battle at the arroyo was all the proof she needed that she and been correct to delay.

The Via Miryam was their nickname for the route from Seville to Santiago de Compostela, from there pilgrims would be led east towards France, or a bit farther north to the port at Crunia then on to England making port at Dover or Milford Haven in Wales. In truth the route had was older than Miryam twice over having been developed by the forebears of the Old Lion transporting goods for monks from Canterbury or the priory near Hubberston Pill.

Miryams meandering thoughts were interrupted by an outburst from among the low chatter of the ruling elders. "We must increase dowries, that way we don't have to increase the tolls we charge on the passes we control. We have over forty young women with offers. If we set the minimum dowry at three livres, we make up our losses with minimum effort." Miryam was hardly surprised to see uncle Rudolfo at nearly a hundred, shouting and pouting like a boy of fourteen summers. A relic from the time of her grandfather's father, he stood with a wooden walking staff held high in a bony fist. His facial tattoos jiggled from sagging cheeks as he continued his impassioned speech. "We have only increased the price of cattle and the tolls we charge in the passes twice since my grandfather's day! And for good reason! We are lucky our neighbors didn't burn us out then! Already they complain about our wealth, and look towards our lands with avaricious eyes. To raise prices is to invite their ire. Look to the Cathars, and ask them if I lie." Miryam longed to shout him down. Rudolfo was the worst kind of old fool, at the best of times. He had only managed to become an elder by nature of age, having been too stubborn to die with his contemporaries. He was usually loud, and almost always obnoxiously wrong. If Miryam were less of a Christian woman she might have hired a young whore to fuck him to death years ago. Rudolfo's only saving grace was the fact that he was easy to control. Under his bluster he was a coward, utterly terrified of his great nephew Hamza. This meant he would vote whichever way Miryam told him to for fear of upsetting her father. However, it was a sad day when Rudolfo was actually making sense. *I have to stop this before the old goat gets on a roll.* Miryam thought.

She made to intervene but was stopped by Linda. Who prompted her to listen. "Let this play out a bit." She whispered, and Miryam forced herself to listen. "The prices of livestock are the business of no man here. Worry after your horses, sheep, and goats!" Their mother snapped. Rudolfo shut his mouth. Miryam suspected if he had teeth they would have clacked together. By the ancient customs of their people women owned the cattle and camels and the rights to the herds passed through the women. "But you are right, something must be done. If we sow saffron, ginger, and pepper plants for the last of the growing cycles, by harvest we can have a lightweight yet high value crop. We can then send the men that would be guarding pilgrims to guard pepper as we ship it north for markets in Denmark and beyond." The gathered elders seemed to stew on this.

In the old days each manorial family ruled independently with little if any cooperation outside limited trade and times of war. It wasn't until the Al Takuri arrived and Nasr Ibn Saif married Xenobia Maurard that the first changes were made. The elders under their manorial lords still wielded power but now each community functioned as part of a greater community. Generations later La Compagnie was born allowing Miryam to coordinate their considerable manpower and resources marshaling them and expanding by buying more farms and opening hostels and commissioning mobile traders that catered to the wealthy travelers her family was feudally bound to protect. With her managing La Compagnie and her father leading the family they had all flourished. Good service, hard fighting, and shrewd trade had brought her kin to the courts of great magnates and kings. She and her father had been good vassals to King John of England while secretly supporting the rebellious barons of England who's cause the Old Lion sympathized with. England wasn't the only place they straddled a line. In Al Andalus they played a dangerous game as well accruing allies of both faiths. In Provence deep in the Monts Des Maures they were safe, or at least safer than anywhere else.

As the head of La Compagnie she had almost as much power as the family elders who guided many aspects of the family from what crops were planted on what farms and estates to how their descendants would be educated or which trade their descendants would take up. Miryam used her power to protect her kin. Forming powerful alliances was a necessity now more than ever. With success and wealth came the growing target on their back. One day avarice and jealousy on behalf of their fellow Christians would escalate from raids and slander, to spill into all out war. Her family was strong with knights, castles, walled towns and dozens of fortified farms and manors. *Even our womenfolk train at arms.* Miryam thought. But would it be enough to stop a crusade as had befallen the Cathars? It was exactly that question that enforced their generations long policy of humility hiding themselves behind the cross or the cresent and assimilating where they could, and being useful. Very Useful.

* * *

Miryam's steward Marco caught her eye giving her a hand signal. Rising from her seat Miryam slipped into a partitioned area at the rear of the dais. The grand tent was actually a collection of tents within a larger shell allowing for the warren of passages Miryam now employed. Not only did they allow Miryam and her agents the ability to vanish just to reappear elsewhere, it also gave the brilliantly color Kufic scripted silk walls ears. This time she used them to enter a separate reception area used for problematic visitors or those who required special handling.

Miryam found Marco waiting, his features drawn in a scowl of annoyance. "What news?" She asked not quite sure she wanted to know. "It would appear that a handful of the bandits Cazador's party slew had powerful kin. Now I have about thirty angry Danish huscarls and a priest screeching to the high heavens about Black devils creating martyrs. He has about a hundred idiots under his sway ready to burn the farm and storm the camp he's an aggravation of note." Miryam wanted to laugh. Shakedowns were common requiring a show of force or a show of coin. It all depended on the situation. "How much do they want to go away?" Miryam asked and Marco suddenly found the need to study his sandalled feet. After a moment he took the deep breath common to all men about to deliver unwanted news. "A thousand English pounds in weregild. Two hundred pounds a piece for the five kinsmen of the king of Denmark killed in the fight." Miryam's cheeks flushed with anger. "Anything else? A piece of the true cross perhaps, maybe a vial of Christ's blood?" She snapped voice rising in time with her aggravation. Marco barked a nervous laugh. "They want the leader of the expedition, meaning they want Cazador too." Miryam shook her head. "Where are they?"

* * *

Wigberto Grimaldi reclined in his camp stool enjoying fine Spanish wine. His surcoat and maille still reeked of smoke from the farms and small town he and his men had torched. It had been a good week. The raiding against the Moors in Spain had made him rich and he was about to become richer still all while striking at his family's hated rivals. It had cost him a few shillings but from his father's du Maurmont spy Wigberto had managed to get a copy of the latest itinerary from La Vénérable Compagnie des Protecteurs et Avitailleurs des Pèlerins du Monts Des Maures.

After studying it Wigberto picked a perfect place for an ambush. Next he campaigned in the camp of the allied Christian forces for volunteers. Most didn't want the distraction, or wheedled about permission from their lords. Wigberto didn't dare risk involving some of the more powerful or influential crusaders. Instead he stuck to the scum and the zealously stupid. He succeeded in finding some silver hungry Danes, wool headed Templars and a few random men at arms and Aragonese almogovars who were raiders by trade and always game for coin. A simple attack on an enemy supply column laden with women and food. Everyone's favorite target. Wigberto left his Danes under their kinsman Hunlaf to lead the expedition, while he took a small warband and did the devil's own work around El Gobo and El Alisar. The ruins of ugly little Mozarb churches and shrines were a small price to pay for striking at the heathens who profited off of God's people. His father and his du Maurmont connection had been working for years to undermine their accursed influence. They had planned the scheme together.

Wigberto had no idea that his Danes were anyone important. He had met them on them in Calais, traders out of Ribe carrying furs and amber south to Spain after a faire in Northumbria. Wigberto had paid them to transport he and his men to Spain. Along the journey he managed to convince a handful of the younger Danish knights to join him in raiding Al Andalus as hired men. The leader of the Danes was called Hunlaf. A lively green eyed brute with more beard than brain readily agreed and had been good company on the voyage.

Wigberto was sad he was dead.

It turns out that Hunlaf was the son of none other than Erik son of Canute who was king in Denmark. As nephews to the current king Valdemar, they were engaging on a trading mission for their uncle's war chest before they had all been killed with the exception of the youngest of their party, Bjarne Ingveson. It was Bjarne who made his way back to Seville where he informed his lord.

Now their principal of their expedition a charming fellow named Gorm Grimgundison who had come to Wigberto for weregild for his fallen kin. Unwilling to part with his hard stolen loot Wigberto had simply blamed the Moors. "You think these Blaumen will pay?" Wigberto shrugged extravagantly, his maille clinking as his shoulders brushed his lank dark hair cut in a bob just below his ears. As living men Hunlaf Erikson and his brothers were potential threats but as dead men they were worth good hard silver. Silver Grimgundison wasn't leaving Spain without. "They have the coin, and they have a history of reconciliation through coin. They'll fight like demoms if you force them but they don't like trouble these Moors. Anything that threatens to put them before anyone with authority greater than their own, they pay them off." Grimgundison nodded. Seeming pleased and lumbered away to speak with his countrymen.

Wigberto allowed himself a satisfied grin. The man looked like a finely groomed bear stuffed in nobleman's clothes. His dark brown beard was oiled and his hair brushed and hanging loose, neatly falling to his shoulders. Wigberto noted the maille under his red surcoat and the long axe he carried like a baton, and wondered what manner of ferocity allowed a man to lavish such care and attention on his hair. It struck him to ask, but he shook the thoughts away. Wigberto didn't wonder what it would be like to on the recieving of his Danish friend's wicked looking axe.

Du Maurmont was the collective name given to the twelve Moorish families that ruled the former domains of Fraxinetum. The greedy Black devils had been neighbors in the the Grimaldi of Grimaud since the Moors had been granted their allodium. For generations the Grimaldi's of Grimaud had sought to drive the du Maurmonts from their mountain perches and back to whatever sandy hell that spawned them. When the Al Takruri called the Alfiere arrived rejuvenating the Monts des Maures bloodlines bringing scores of knights and retainers with them. Seasoned from fighting in Al Andalus Al Takruri and his brood of sons effectively ended the Grimaldi du Grimaud's lucrative raiding policy.

With their charter charging them with the upkeep of the Knights of Saint Attillo and entitling them to regular donations and the support of clergy they became virtually unassailable. The priests had fallen in love with the Moors who were once high ranking Mohammedan warriors, turned warriors of Christ. This meant Wigberto's family had lost military supremacy in the area settling for targeted, small scale raids by mercenaries the du Grimaud could easily disavow. Wigberto's father and grandfather had even begun to foster a very public friendship with the du Maurmont families. In private the Grimauds coveted an end to tarrifs across du Maurmont lands and access to the port at La Londe Des Maures and Wigberto's family's recent policy of friendship and intermarriage was to that end. It worked for the most part, and Wigberto had even spent time at feasts and tourneys among them.

Only once in his lifetime had the men of Grimaud attacked the Moors in force. At first Wigberto had struggled to understand why his father Roger was planning an attack on men he had been hunting with not a sennight prior. It hadn't taken him long to learn that his father had sworn as a donat to the Templars who were hungry for coin to support efforts in Outremer and therin lay the Grimaud's justification to attack their neighbors. As crusaders with a familial knightly order dedicated to Alpine pilgrims the du Maurmont families should have been untouchable. Generations of shrewd manuevering had faltered when they had distanced themselves from the Knights Templar in favor of the Hospitillars in Nizza, incensing a heated rivalry. With a few well placed whispers about heathen rites in the forest and the continued use of the Al Takruri name hinting at secret Mohammedan loyalties was all it took for his father to be ordered to raid. It had all been set. The lords of Bormes would sack the monastery near Collobrières while Wigberto and his kin would push into Fraxinet.

Leon Alfiere was supposed to have been away with his retainers and their lands lightly defended. That had all turned out to be a lie told by a grinning trader making his way to Cogolin. They had decided to invade the Moorish commune through the mountains just west of Vallon de Reverdi. Wigberto had cast the occasional glance to the thick late spring foliage to his left knowing no attack could come from the sharply declining hillside to the column's right. It was a beautiful but warm day. Already sweat soaked his aketon and by midday he'd be able to

The first sign of trouble had come when a head complete with helmet and ventail had sttuck Wigberto's kinsman seconds before a storm of arrows flayed their column. Before an order could be made a party of knights in the purpur and argent favored by the and the other Al Takruri spawned houses blocked the narrow track. Wigberto had drawn his sword and tried to wheel his mount to meet the enemy when it collapsed under him arrow buried to the fletchings in it's throat. Everything was chaos as men and horses screamed in shock and pain. Wigberto managed to clear his saddle, and hunkering behind his shield as his eyes desperately searched for his father, brother and uncles.

A rough line had formed facing what had been the columns left hand side Dozens of men in the gold tower on the red field, quartered with red and white checky surcoats were down. Arrows slammed into his shield the shock numbing his arm. "INTO THE TREES! AND AT THEM!" Hearing his father's battleground roar seemed to give life a sense of balance. Wigberto's terror and confusion finally started to abate as shields overlapped his own. With his brother Raoul and his cousin Benino beside him they rolled forward toward the foliage lining the track.

Benino was the first of their clump to reach the steep earth embankment. Using it's strap he slung his heavy kite shield over his back, he grasped a small tree and made to hoist himelf up onto the embankment. Other knights and men at arms were working their way forward while another band battled against the knights holding the road.

One moment Benino was scrambling up the hill, then suddenly he was pitched sideways. At first Wigberto was confused, then he saw a Moorish knight in a purple surcoat He wore a bar nasal helmet with a matching torse. The Moor's dark eyes blazed with a combination of malice and glee that turned Wigberto's bowels to water when his goateed mouth twisted in a hate filled snarl. Benino fell with his pothelm stove in, proving that although the Moor wasn't an overly massive man, he possesed great strength. Raoul and the others men of Grimaud roared. The Moor roared back in defiance beating his beautiful Wootz steel sword against his large kite shield bearing a purple and argent field divided per bend bearing broken lance in the first quarter and a clenched gauntlet in the fourth. Many sections of the embankment had proven to be impassible. To stop the archery they would have to get through the Moorish knight.

Raoul threw himself forward, breaking through the undergrowth slightly to the right of where Benino's attempt failed with Wigberto and a half dozen other hot on his heels. The Moor in purple and white met Raoul shield to shield with a thunderous crack. Wigberto watched as his brother attacked with his axe, only for the Moor to flick it aside and thrust with a spear he held in his left hand with his shield strap. Wigberto screamed as his brother's shield failed to intercept the thrust and it punched it into his throat with a crunch.

Rage. Pure, hot, and simple flooded Wigberto's heart as the Moor kicked his elder brother aside like so much trash. Two men of Grimaud fouled by Raoul's corpse followed the son of their lord in death. The Moor parried a wild slash, riposting so fast Wigberto almost couldn't track the thrust that killed the man on the enemy's left. The man at arms is on his right struck with a spear. The

Moor slapped his point into the earth, stepping forward and reversing his blow into a rising cut that sank his blade into the soft tissue just behind the man's jaw below his ear. His rage fled replaced by fear and Wigberto had backed down the path. Visions of his own body among his kin leaving his mind fraught with terror. I cannot fight him and prevail. Wigberto's mind had crowed as hot urine soaked his maille chausses. His brother and cousin had been some of the finest warriors in Grimaud and he had laid them low like children.

Wigberto felt numb. He could hear men massing behind him but his body seemed to take his commands as mere suggestions. Still he raised his sword, his mind pondering the merits of throwing the blade at the Moor and running. "If we attack him together lord he cannot stand against us." Came a voice at Wigberto's side. It was Henri, the butcher's son turned man at arms. Wigberto turned to meet Henri's eyes. He tried to speak. He tried to tell them that this was madness. That the devil himself stood before them and they should flee and hope he did not follow them. But he had said nothing and only nodded. As the men of Grimaud formed around him, his feet seemed locked to the earth. "I will break you all!" The Moor roared slamming his hateful weapon against his shield rim. The men of Grimaud shouted their fury in reply as a wedge took shape. In moments the huddle of men went from shouting to the relentless forward press of men desperate for respite from an arrow storm. He had tucked into his shield, and averted his eyes. The last thing Wigberto wanted to do was charge up that hillside again but the pressure was as inexorable as was the the killer blocking the path. Wigberto looked away from the hateful slayer only for his gaze to fall on his brother's corpse. Raoul's eyes seemed to glare at him in mute accusation and something in Wigberto, something human and godly broke. Fear evaporated and with a cry of anguish he threw himself at the Moor.

Wigberto attacked with a blinding series of cuts that the Moor simply blocked with annoying ease using the haft of his spear, and then his shield face. Then the Moor moved, Wigberto tried to void his leg. He sensed the low strike more than saw it. The Moor's blade clipped his leg, and instead of losing a limb,

Wigberto was pitched sideways and knew nothing more.

He awoke stripped of armor and weapons in a humble canvass tent with a throbbing head and a fracture in his shin. Some fourteen nobles worth ransom and several hundred men at arms and infantymen had survived to surrender. A special camp had been built where he learned later they would reside for parole. As far as captors went the du Maurmonts were gracious and civil. They were fed and watered and even provided luxuries adding the cost to their ransom. It was almost like being on a hunt except with more wine, and they weren't actually allowed to leave the leather walls of the camp. Their captors for the most part courteously ignored them other than to pass letters and process requests. Although he had suffered no ill treatment, nor had the du Maurmont families raised their banners and invaded Grimaud and still Wigberto had found himself hating them. The shame of his cowardice stung and he knew then that it was that black skinned devils fault. Who could fight such a hell fiend. The Moorish knight in the had taken more from him than kin. His pride and belief in the supremacy of his family had been shattered on that field along with his shin.

Wigberto shook the painful memories away. That battle had been the turning point of his young life. Wigberto now second rather than third in line for the lordship of Grimaud had chosen the life of a mercenary leaving his father's lands for England. He and his men had fought in at least five countries since then. Wigberto had done all he could that he would never be the same scared boy who had pissed his maille again, and now he had a du Maurmont in his power to punish. With the silver hungry Danes involved he didn't have to worry about the fragile peace back home. Wigberto's hands would remain clean while striking a blow for his family honor. Asking for the commander of the warband had been a genius move. Wigberto didn't know what the Danes had planned for him but he was sure to be delighted.

Chapter 4: The Square

Cazador had been riding in the van with Izan, Jaime Constantine, and Alberto of Aragon who was an accomplished scholar and a knight who had been as far as Ghazni in the empire of the Ghaznids. He had been explaining the ways of Turkish mounted archery. "Sir Cazador!" One of the almogovars under Idris Ibn Idris came sprinting towards him interrupting the conversation as the scout shouted jogging down the track. Cazador broke away and followed the scout to where a robe swathed rider waited. "Well met cousin!" The rider called pulling free his tagelmust revealing the hearty grin of his cousin Roberto Ibn Roberto Ibn Hamza. "Aunt Miriam sends her regards," Roberto called, setting Cazador's nerves on edge. He had sent Maurice on a fast horse back to Seville after the battle. He could already see her henna dyed finger pointing at his chest for being reckless and felt himself cringe. "She had sent me to recall you, I thought my task was done when I met your brother on the road." Roberto said grinning and Cazador rolled his eyes. Maurice had arrived with a group of pilgrims from Makuria, sent to foster with their grandfather. From the moment Maurice had set foot in the keep at Bobastro, the speculation and jokes had begun.

While it was true Cazador and Maurice were close and bore a resemblance. And it was true that few could tell their voices apart and they were often mistaken for one another. But that didn't make Maurice a bastard of Cazador's father. Roberto saw his kinsman's annoyance and laughed all the harder at his own stale joke. One would think after over a decade they would all be tired of it. Cazador mused. "Does aunt Miryam know of the attack?" He asked changing the subject. "Indeed she does, and she is pleased with the results too, said you did the right thing turning back and she's happy as a kitten in the cream that she made you captain of the guard." Cazador smiled and nodded, hoping to hide his sigh of relief wasn't too obvious. Their aunt Miryam was like a force. She along with Cazador's mother had helped transform what had been a band of dusty hedge knights with a few trading vessels into a thriving multinational company with a string of hostels, warehouses and trading caravans with connections to the exchequers through the military service of her kinsman in the Holy Land. She employed the Knights of Saint Attillo based out of Fraxinet and Collobrières as guardians for merchants and Pilgrims alike. With the vast wealth she used the coin to invest in churches and almshouses for both Christians and Muslims and was a vocal advocate for muwallad and mozarb communities. This and more made her an expert at dressing him down when she deemed appropriate. "That's not why she sent me to find you though. She feels like Seville is unsafe and wants you to escort your pilgrims to sanctuary. She told me to lead you to a rendezvous outside La Alagba." "Excellent, lead the way." Cazador replied.

* * *

Two days later they met with the main caravan. Miriam's almogovars had found them an hour previously leading them across a farmers land to where the baked leather walls that marked her camp sat in a crook of the Guadalquivir River. Cazador led his party to the wagon that sat parked in a gap in the walls to form a gate. Seeing the Thebaei, or the bisected concentric circles in oche and tenne that formed the banner of the Knights of Atillo, Cazador's party was admitted immediately. At the gate Cazador's uncle Yvain Alfiere watch as captain of the guard. He might have drank his weight in wine but he was a brilliant carpenter and mason and a capable veteran fighter. He had worked in Sicily and Normandy for years before retiring to work for La Compangnie. "Heard you boys ran into some into some real work." Yvain growled in the Provençal French spoken around Monts Des Maures behind an easy grin. Cazador bowed from saddle. "All for the glory of God and the honor of Saint Attilo," he called as dismounted and took the older man's arm in warrior grip. "Its good to see you in nephew, heathen garb suits you. The very image of the fierce Saracen." Yvain said chuckling looking every inch the Provençal knight in his head to toe maille covered with a argent and indigo surcoat. As long as he wore a closed helmet, nobody would know he hailed from the Sudan.

Resting his hand on the hilt of his sword Cazador struck a pose, before joining his uncle's laughter. "Go bathe and present yourself to your aunt and mother they've been waiting for you to arrive." Still beaming Cazador turned to go, but his uncle shouted, "Maurice said you looted some Italian wine so good you could taste the sunlight on your tongue and I expect a taste or five myself!" Cazador waved and proceeded towards the heart of the camp. "We'll see you after you make your report Capitan!, I will take our party and find them a spot to call their own" Izan called, rounding up Merfynn, Alberto and the other pilgrims. Cazador nodded and made his way down the orderly lane of tents.

Although he had never been to this particular camp, the layout was always the same and he found his way easily. Within the circle of it's walls the camp spiralled like a sea shell around a central road. At regular intervals smaller avenues branched off, straight as an arrow creating neat blocks of tents around the open central space. As if to defy the uniformity of it's layout, the tents came in an array of colors from muted browns and tans to vibrant saffrons, warm greens, and deep indigos. He could hear priests leading prayers in Latin, Greek, Spanish, Coptic, and Nubian as children of a half dozen nations raced between the tents at play. Cazador smiled, he and his cousins had been caravan brats just like this once. Bobbing his head to a group of Egyptian priests with their dark robes, full beards and bronzed features Cazador let his feet carry him to his destination.

Although his family hadn't been Muslim for generations the tradition of gusul had stuck. Cazador like most of his family took every available opportunity to maintain good hygiene, even on the road. Reaching in his belt purse Cazador drew out a few coins and paid the attendant, before making his way to an unoccupied partition in the large tent. Ringing the small bell to alert the attendants he began to strip. His sweat sodden tagelmust and jibbah were first. Next Cazador set to peeling off his maille hood, coif, tunic, boots, and padded chausses. By the time he was down to his shirt and hose a large trough filled with steaming water was pushed into his partition from a small flap on the opposite side. Cazador eyed the hot water and the small basket of aromatic soaps hanging from the side. No matter how sinful some of his fellow Christian said bathing might be, the way Cazador smelled was surely a sin as well and he climbed in.

Luxuriating in the hot water Cazador took a moment to let the stress of his failed pilgrimage melt into the water with the dust and grime. The fact that his aunt had recalled him days prior meant he had not failed, that didn't mean she would pay him for it though. Knights of Attilo were not required to take vows of chastity or poverty, therefore they were expected to equip and provision themselves and any retainers from their own purse. Horses, tack, food, armor, weapons and the means to repair them could prove ruinously expensive. To that end patrons would often commission them covering the cost of the pilgrimage and make a donation to the knights and men at arms that protected the pilgrims. It had been aunt Miryam who had combined her family's diverse interests into a single smooth machine. Her tactics had taken hundreds of years family tradition and turned it into profitable trade that made them a regional power.

The farms and vinyards of La Garde Freinet, Collobrières, and La Londe Des Maures were productive sending wine, milled grain, cheese, wool, and livestock to markets in Marseille and Toulon. The men of the du Maurmont clans protected the passes and patrolled the roads as part of their feudal duties and collecting tolls. So it had remained this way for generations, supplemented by trade through family contacts in Ifríqiya. When grandfather had brought his first ships things had begun to change. The ability to ship goods from

Ifriqiya directly to the lords and ladies of England, France and Spain. Where grandfather had begun to move goods from Ifriqiya with pilgrims from the scattered churches not swallowed by Islam. Grandfather had been a fighting knight that dabbled in trading. Aunt Miryam had intergrated the family's business with Knights of Saint Attillo.

Food and animals from Monts Des Maures supplied caravans and hostels alike while good from the Sudan, Egypt, and Ifriqiya arrived with pilgrims and routs were carefully crafted so Al Takruri and Du Maurmont traders could now cross no fewer that four international boundaries. Whoever held military command of the expedition gained a bonus of ten percent of the expeditions profit and to be named Captain was sign of honor and trust. If the family elders decided Cazador had bungled his expedition then it might be the last time he was chosen for a while. "If I'm going to be shamed before the family elders, I'd better look my best." Cazador muttered finding a razor, scissors, and small mirror along with a comb in a second basket. With a sigh he took up the scissors and began to trim.

Clean, barbered and smelling of myrrh and vanilla Cazador dried, dressing in a clean dark lavender tunic that ended with cuffs stitched with a swirling silver brocade. Next he pulled on a set of black Hausa riding boots that rose to his calves. Topping off his ensemble with a sleeveless black knee length, tunic bearing his paternal arms on the breast. Cazador bucked on his belt and attached his sword on his left hip and an ornately decorated black buckler to his right. Wishing he had a bigger mirror to give himself a proper once over. Cazador set off to face his elders.

His aunts tent was a lavish affair of red silk larger than the homes of at least three prosperous farmers. As he approached he was greeted by guards in du Maurmont livery and slipped into the prodigious foyer of the tent. A young man in a black silk coif a sat working busily at a desk, his golden brown features screwed up in a grimace of concentration. Marco was his aunt's steward and personal secretary. Only slightly younger then Caz, he was handsome and well built, but no warrior, for all he might have the temper of one. No, Marco was a scribe, a man of learning and politics with a keen mind. His family had lived in Al Andalus from the time of the Fatamids and he had been educated in the great libraries and universities of Córdoba. "Welcome oh mighty slayer! Hunter of men and glory!" Marco said without looking up. His wry smile soothing the sting from his acerbic tone. "Maurice told us how you trapped and destroyed that force of raiders. Aragonese and Normani scum. Savages" He spat. "Word has it you did well and your aunt and mother are proud, but it's best not to dawdle. I'll let you but me a cup of wine and I'll finish congratulating you later." Cazador laughed and ducked throught the heavy flaps into the chamber beyond.

To call it a court might be a bit too grand considering the audience halls at La Baroud, Fraxinet, La Marche, and Nuevo Bobastro, but it was close enough. Sumptuous rugs from the Levant covered the floors in swirls of gold, cream, and crimson matching the drapes and the large pillows that adorned the floor. The walls were hung with tapestries commissioned to reflect the martial history of his people. The first depicting his great ancestor Saif leading the Sudani contingent at the Battle of Sagrajas under the famous Yusef Ibn Tashfin. The next showed Esteve Ibn Nasr better known as Steven the Moor fighting at Lincoln and another depicted his subsequent knighting. Every man of the Al Takruri or and Du Maurmont family was coveted a tapestry of their own.

Behind what Cazador could only describe as the dais where his family elders sat was a tapestry depicting his grandfather Hamza called Leon fighting in Outremer. His mother aunts and an assortment of senior family elders sat upon low stools chatting quietly. Their clothing like their shades of their skin reflected the range and might of his kin. The reddish browns of the Sanhaja, and the Pullaar of Tekrur mixed with the walnut and almond shades of Abbysinnia and Makuria. Yet others bore the pecan tones of Mali and the wine dark shades of the Fezzan. There were many with the tawny or tea and milk skin of the Greeks and Arabs marking their Muladi or mixed heritage. Through marriage and military service Cazador's kin had established trade networks from the jungles of Zanj to the Cinque ports of England with hundreds of farms, and a number of fortified manors and two towns and castles. While aunt Miryam ran the business with absolute authority, the elders governed the joint affairs of the family, and Cazador's grandfather was the military leader functioned as the nominal head of the Al Takruri family as a whole and the Du Maurmont clans. Aunt Miryam and elders decided on everything from what crops were sown on what estates to which trades the youth would learn, and where they would live and work. They would say, *"We are all fingers of the hand and each finger must do it's part if we are to grasp our blessings."* Alongside the tenants of pulaaku this was taught to every child in their family fold.

Cazador l would rather face a charge of heavy horse then to bear their scrutiny. Bowing low before his elders, Cazador willed his churning guts to stillness. His mother smiled broadly. "My son it is good to see you whole and healthy from the road. God is great" Cazador beamed back. "Its good to be seen mother." He replied. His aunt Miryam rose in a cascade of of bangles and jewelry. Her deep indigo robes seemed to shimmer against her sand colored skin even in the low light of the tent. Flipping her braided light brown hair over her shoulder with an imperious tilt to her chin, she pinned Cazador with a basilisk stare. "Word had reached us of your success protecting your charges nephew. I have spoken to Idris Ibn Idris as well as Maurice. You showed bravery and battle skill but more importantly you put together a good plan and exercised caution and prudence in choosing to return." She smiled broadly.

"I'm proud of you!" She said beckoning him to approach the dais.

Cazador embraced his mother and aunt warmly in a wash of lavender and lemongrass. "We have a surprise for you my son." Cazador's mother Linda murmured happily. Her dark eyes danced with genuine pride and Cazador took a moment to soak it in. It wasn't every day his mother hugged him or greeted him with kind words. The surprise he was less enthusiastic about. Cazador liked his surprises in the form of new books, weapons, horses, or armor. Casks of wine and pretty women were also perfectly acceptable, however Cazador didn't see any of these things at hand. His mother was incredibly intelligent and valued education above all things. She would have rather seen Cazador a scholar, or even better a priest than a knight, which was exactly why Cazador prayed silently her surprise didn't entail a semester at one of the universities or worse still a rotation as a clerk to some bishop or abbot. "Meet Diallo Kouyaté of Djenne, he's been in training as a djali, and I have commissioned him to your retinue." Cazador felt a warmth hit the pit of his stomach and a smile split his face. Similar to a skald of the Norse, a djali was a singer, poet, herald, and a storyteller who would record Cazador's deeds in verse adding his exploits to the history of their family and this one was teasingly familiar. The man stepped forward and bowed.

Diallo was of an age with Cazador and bore honey colored skin and aquiline features set in a full face. His head was bare and his wooly curls oiled in the way of the Afar. He wore a flawless white surcoat over a dark green shirt with matching pants and shoes so heavily embroidered that Cazador wondered if it had been made for a man. "Baron de Moorhouse,"he said conspiratorially offering Cazador a leather scrip with courtly bow. "Its a pleasure to meet you again and to be a member of your household." Cazador beamed. The script contained patents confirming him as lord of a small manor in England and lordship of his father's castle called La Marcha at Vallon De Cinqé Sedés. It was the the ancestral home of the Alfiere and Al Takruri families, granted when they first settled in Provence. Their lands beginning in the mountains and foothills between La Garde Freinet and Les Mayons stretching north to encompass Le Plaine Des Maures all the way to the Vallon De Pey Coucu. It was called Cannets Des Maures or canes of the Moors. The Al Takruri who had taken the name Alfiere in Europa had ruled there since from Saif's days, holding the northernmost of the territories once held by the powerful Fraxinetum Moors. The Al Takruri under the name Alfiere had held it against raids from Lorgues and all comers for over a hundred years.

Cazador felt a lump form in his throat and felt his eyes drift to his mother and aunt who looked on beaming. He reviewed the ledgers portraying his accounts and suddenly found it hard to breath. From wine sales alone for the last two months his accounts had accrued twenty pounds, on top of the one hundred and fifty pounds he had accrued from the sale of cattle and tolls on the roads. The estates in England were far less impressive but the truth of the matter remained unchanged. He was a lord, and captain of a mercenary company, and he was rich. After nine years as a dirt poor hedge knight, Cazador found himself struggling to accept it all, and breath at the same time. After all the years of being taught to be a lord, it had finally happened and Cazador was equal parts elated and terrified.

Diallo reached out and patted his new lord on the shoulder. He had already reviewed Sir Cazador's accounts. As a djali of the Du Maurmont clan it was his job to advise his jatigi, and to learn as much as possible. Whether it was local legends, and family histories, to which wines and fashions were in style it was Diallo's job to know and to use it to his lord's advantage. He would sing of Cazador's exploits and act as his proxy and ambassador if need be. His status was tied to Cazador's. A glorious and successful lord could make even a mediocre djali pre-eminent amongst his peers. Diallo smiled, already he'd heard the makings of a good song with Cazador. Rumor had it that he'd fought in France for the king of England and in the lands along the Black Sea. Diallo had resolved himself to getting the story from Cazador.

After all djali was not a djali without a jatigi was not a jatigi without a djali. By attaching Diallo to Cazador's comitatus his aunt had made him a true warrior scholar and nobleman among the du Maurmont families. "Does it feel unclean my lord, to be so filthy rich?" The wordsmith asked Cazador laughed long and hard at that and Diallo took an instant liking to the man. Raising his fingers he signaled the serving staff that supplied the elders and their guests with food and drink. Rather than a liveried servant it was lady Miryam herself. "Gentleman, come wit me if you please." Cazador met his aunt's eyes finding them cold and steady as a mountain lake. With a nod he rose and together he and Diallo followed Miryam as she slipped into an partition in the tent.

* * *

Izan reclined next to Jaime enjoying the ghawazee female dancers from Egypt. The air in the large pavilion tent of his cousins mobile tavern hung heavy with the scents of jasmine, sandalwood and vanilla. In short it was heaven for a man at arms fresh from the road. The wool stuffed silk cushion was like a cloud after days in the saddle. "Thérèse could have given us more of a discount." Jaime muttered tearing his eyes from the dancers to contemplate his empty cup. The establishment was run by their cousin Thérèse, a skilled merchant who brought not only goods to her customers, but entertainment. Her troupes included troubadours, actors, dancers and djali while her wares included silks, furs, ivory and precious jewelry. Her expeditions always turned a profit and she was in many ways aunt Miryam's successor. Admittance to her tent cost two pence, and the wine started at one pence a cup for anything worth drinking. Another pence if you wanted lamb stew and flat bread. He signaled and a decanter bearing server refilled both cups silencing his kinsman's protests.

Jaime grinned raising his cup in salute "To kin, glory and Christ!" Izan grinned back. "Speaking of glory, do you think we'll end up fighting this season rather escorting pilgrims. Jaime shrugged, busy eyebrows climbing up his bald brow. "Better that than be bored to tears holding passes in the Alps eating ourselves poor. Maybe we'll get lucky and draw garrison duty. But likely we'll end up fighting for Aragon or against Aragon and do it looking over our shoulders the whole time." Izan grunted. He had a point. Technically the king of Aragon was their feudal lord, but in deep in Al Andalus it meant nothing. More than once du Maurmont knights had fought for Muslim emirs as expedience dictated. His thoughts were interrupted by the arrival of Pablo and Pedro who arrived at the flaps of Thérèse tent. The twins were both helmeted and in maille with their axes at their hips and shields slung over their shoulders. Izan took a longing look at his wine and nudged Jaime and rose to meet them. "What news?" He asked. "Caz is in some shit." Pedro the larger of the twins answered. "Apparently some of the lot we killed in the fight at the arroyo had important kin." Continued Pedro, the younger of the two by five minutes. "Now a score of Danish huscarls and a armed rabble are demanding weregild and Cazador." Pedro finished. "Merda!" Spat Jaime. The twins nodded in unison. "Let's go before Caz starts a party without us." Izan muttered.

***

Cazador looked up to see his kinsman enter. "Caz you must listen!" His mother hissed. What are you going to do attack them?" Cazador ignored her. "I will not stand for it mother. Pullaku demands that I–" Lady Linda turned on her son with such fury Cazador wondered if she would draw her sword on him. Technically she could challenge him as a belted knight, a dame of Rome in her own right. "I will not see you pervert the code of your ancestors with pride boy!" Cazador felt his temper flare but clamped down on it hard. Hefting his looted Byzantine curiasse, it's black lacquered steel lames trimmed in purple dyed boiled leather was just prize loot from Eastern Rome. Heaving it over his head, Cazador offered a gratified nod to Diallo who wordlessly helped him with the buckles. Next he fitted on a matching set of lamellar tassets to a thick leather belt. Over that he rebelted his sword and buckler. "Mother, my men and I committed no crime. We were attacked and defended ourselves. We never attacked anyone we never burned any farms nor looted any chapels and I refuse to go with those men for ransom that will bleed my estates or a trial that will be little more than a rope and a tree." Her eyes flashed with anger but she was ominously silent.

Cazador was cut short when aunt Miryam stepped forward carrying a set of beautiful plate shoulder armor with lamellar sleeves. Each shoulder cop was worked with the head of a roaring lion, they were beautiful and must have cost a fortune. His aunt met his eyes, and her look said volumes. She was angry, but she trusted him. Which was more than he could say for his mother. "Thank you auntie." Cazador murmured past the lump in his throat. Miryam nodded. "You would condone this?" His mother screeched. Cazador made to speak but instead pulled up his maille coiffe and pulled his round topped bar nasal helmet onto his head. "Milady, Sir Cazador is an annointed knight and charged by God to defend his life and his name. What choice to any of us have but to honor that." Diallo said smoothly. The look Linda of Seville turned on her son's djali made Cazador glad of his armor. Diallo busied himself with attaching the spaulders to his liege and said nothing more.

Cazador strode from his tent with Diallo and the rest of his comitatus in tow. The shakedown for weregild was bad enough, they had demanded he submit himself as well, and that Cazador would not do. *They can take me from beneath a pile of corpses.* He thought grimly. His aunt had seen his logic from the start but his mother had not. Her vocal protests had shamed him in front of his men and it still burned despite his attempted composure and his armor rattled angrily with each step.

As he approached the camp's gate with his retinue he noted the increased security. A squad of knights loitered on either side of the gate and almogovars and archers crowded the platforms. His uncle Yvaine approached eyeing Cazador's armor with a low whistle. "Brought yourself a little trouble with that loot huh? Now your back here and dressed for the ball I see." Despite his foul temper he felt a smile crack his face. He rarely wore the lamellar suit outside of special occasions as he'd previously been too poor to get it properly repaired if it was seriously damaged. Today that wouldn't be a problem. The thought made him smile all the broader. "No good deed goes unpunished uncle." Yvain chucked seeing the barely restrained fury in his nephews eyes. "Give them hell nephew." He growled. Cazador nodded he planned to do just that. He'd spent enough time around Danish traders to have an idea. His uncle had the gates opened and Cazador could see the bored looking Danish knights and a frustrated looking mob of armed peasants being haraunged by a wild haired priest. Jaime came to his shoulder. "We're with you cousin, although I have a question." Puzzled Cazador nodded. "If you die, can I have this armor?" Jaime said hopefully. Cazador snorted "As long as you clean my blood off it first." He muttered shaking his head. "I call dibs on his horse. Alcazar chimed in causing a ripple of laughter. Page boys brought their horses to them and they mounted and rode towards Caz's accusers.

As they neared the clump of Danes Cazador raised his voice in a shout. "Gorm Grimgundison! Show yourself and make your accusation!" From the group of Danes a man with a wild mane of dark hair and prodigious beard with glittering maille stretched over his enormous frame. "D'you think the feed him the smaller Danes?" Jaime asked and Cazador shrugged, "He's not so big." He said with confidence he didn't feel eying the large axe Grimgundison carried as casually as a lady with her fan. The Dane tromped to within fifteen paces of Cazador's party. He had come alone but Caz had already spied the crossbowman covering their leader. Brave but not stupid.

The Dane eyed Cazador as though he were a new species of shit found on his favorite pair of boots. "I am Gorm son of Grimgundi knight of king Valdemar of Denmark and I charge you with the murder and robbery of my king's kin at The Arroyo de Las Parritas after commiting atrocities against houses of God and his childre–" Cazador leapt from his saddle and stood before the northman shocking the man and ending his little speech. "I am Cazador Alfiere knight of Saint Atillo, lord of Le Cannes Des Maures and Baron of Moorhouse and I say you are a liar and a thief. The kinsman of your king attacked a caravan of pilgrims and died in the attempt." The wild haired priest had joined the Dane ready to lend his support. Cazador met his eyes and continued. "I have over a score of good Christian folks including priests and nuns who can vouchsafe for my actions and those under my command. You and your pet here are bearers of false witness seeking nothing more but larceny and violence against fellow Christians." Both the priest and Grimgundison began to flush shades of crimson. "We have witnesses ourselves!' The priest roared defiantly. Cazador smiled wolfishly and drew Tempest from his hip pointing it at the Dane and the priest. "I say you lie and that we shall make the square here and now and may God almighty be my judge and jury in trial by combat!" The priest paled but the hirsuite Dane smiled, "

"Accepted blauman!" Grimgundison shouted with feral growl. "I will piss on your corpse, slave!" The word hit him like a slap. Cazador looked at the large man and for just a moment allowed himself to imagine what the Dane's big axe might feel like hitting his body. Then he poured every ounce of his fear inspired spite into a single withering glare and said in the best Danish he could muster "I will break you with my sword, and sail to whatever shit hole spawned you and burn it to the ground. Before I leave I will shit on your father's hearth and piss on the graves of your ancestors." Cazador looked at Grimgundison deciding where he would put his sword like a butcher eyes a side of beef for his first cut. The Dane simply reddened.

The priest intoned a prayer inviting God to express his divine will through the combatants. Next Cazador and Dane were both shriven in as few words as possible. The tension of the moment would allow for no more. Cazador looked across the paltry dozen paces separating him from his enemy. The Dane spun his axe in a dizzying array of arcs. Cazador stood in a warrior stance, his buckler strapped to his left arm with a small axe in his left hand and his wootz steel short sword in his right. "Are you going to stand there playing with your shaft all day?" He shouted to the Dane. Grimgundison's axe froze consternation clear in his clenched jaw and then he launched himself at Cazador with alarming speed. It was like facing down an armored horseman. Cazador stepped offline meeting the haft of Grimgundison's axe with the strike of his own smaller axe hooking the shady behind it's head. Yanking he pulled his enemy's axe down and away, stepping forward to slam the point of his blade into the rings over Gorm's neck crushing the Dane's throat. With a ragged gasp his enemy's mouth fell openining and closing in impotent gasps Cazador fired a second thrust, skating past Gorms teeth to punch through his vertebrae tenting his maille coif behind his head. Cazador ripped his blade free and the corpse that was Gorm Grimgundison coughed spasmodically sending a bright spray of blood that forced Caz to dance aside to keep his armor pristine. He hadn't meant to kill the man so quickly, but he'd made his point.

"God had spoken! Not guilty!" Cazador screamed at the priest who had gone paler than parchment. He nodded, crossing himself as he uttered the verdict voice hoarse with shock. Cazador was already wiping his blade on the dead man's surcoat, checking the edge of his pattern steel blade before mounting his horse. His blood was up, and he struggled to resist the urge to charge the remaining Danes. Before he could act Jaime had spurred forward and putting himself between Cazador and any potential quarry. "I suggest you run along now priest and disperse your rabble before we ride them down, and do tell the Dane's to pick up their countryman immediately or join him." He spat imperiously.

As they rode back to camp, a crestfallen Diallo looked at Cazador. "My lord is a puissant knight. But perhaps, next time he will leave his poor *djali* with a longer song to sing?" His question was met with a string of guffaws and a sheepish grin from Cazador. "Caz is a brawler Diallo, best get used to it." Maurice said to a second round of laughter. They road into camp to the applause of the almogovars archers and the knights that had seen the fight.

Chapter 5: Thicker Than Water

Wigberto had saddled his horse and made to make a hasty escape. The efficiency with which the Moor had dispatched Grimgundison was nothing short of perverse. It wasn't the first time that he had seen that level of skill. All the du Maurmonts could fight but he had only seen such butchery once before. *That blade.* Wigberto had only seen it when he lost his kin on a blood soaked field in the Massifs Des Maures. Terror or it's very close cousin filled Wigberto's veins. He had been the first man to the horse lines terrified that the Moor he now knew to be Sir Cazador of Mont Des Maures would come finish the job he started years ago.

Wigberto hit the road at a gallop. He was a full quarter mile ahead before the Danes fled, followed by the priest and his rabble. Terror of his family being implicated thus sending du Maurmont knights into Grimaud would have been ample enough motivation. Seeing the man that haunted his darkest dreams and helped impoverish his kin was enough for him to risk killing his horses. He had to find the Crusader forces and safety quickly. Only then maybe would he reach out to his father's spies among the du Maurmonts again. Wigberto's only saftey lay in numbers and superior authority. If the du Maurmonts sent riders they could destroy his small force. They would haul his body back to Grimaud and accuse his father of breaking the treaty. With such thoughts dogging his heels like devils he took his mensie and fled north as fast as the horses would carry them.

* * *

Cazador knelt before the dais he had sat before in triumph not hours earlier. His mother's silence was deafening as the elders and the more mouthy of his older cousins took turns berating his recklessness as though he were not there. Taking deep breaths in through his nose and plout through his mouth Cazador resisted the urge to rage against them. "Cazador should be punished. He could have avoided that fight at the arroyo prioritizing the lives and the safety of his charges like a true captain. Instead he played the butcher and now he's executed a knight of the king of Denmark! He is dangerous and taints us all with his actions!" Screeched his elder cousin Genovova. Cazador felt his cheeks flush hot. Stinging tears prickled the back of his eyes. His elder by more than ten years, his cousin Genovova could be arrogant, opinionated, and high strung when the mood took her. Still she been like one of his elder sisters doting on him while he was growing up. The coldness in her eyes now stung deeper than he could imagine. Several elders nodded in silent agreement while his mother glared daggers at him. His aunt Miryam looked annoyed and sad but said nothing in his defense.

Taking a deep breath Cazador cast a gimlet eye around the room. Richard de Caen smiled smugly beside his wife. "Let there be no mistake. Sir Cazador is a brave knight, a crusade.r" He said, his mocking smile evaporating into a somber mein. His tone was too smooth by half. The bastard of some Norman knight and a distant cousin of the du Maurmonts Sir Richard had no lands of his own but plenty of ambition. " He is well educated but young and more used to the battlefield and the rugged roads and Alpine passes. Our young lord is perhaps less so used to the unique rigors of diplomacy and trade. In light of this perhaps it would be prudent for the elders to appoint him a steward to help him oversee his lands and show him more...courtly means of problem solving." He finished bowing to the elders who nodded thoughtfully. Cazador felt bile surge in his gut and resisted the urge to spit in Richard's face. This bastards wanted his lands because leaching from his wife was no longer enough.

If the elders take this bait they should be flogged. Cazador raged from the safety of his thoughts. With a deep breath he made to speak when Diallo cut in, "I take it Sir Richard would be keen to show his worth to the family by aiding Sir Cazador in this task no doubt? I mean it only right you should enjoy and enrich yourself his birthright while my lord continues to sweat and bleed for the glory and wealth of the du Maurmonts? Perhaps you can distribute some of my lord's wealth into failed ventures and fine clothes as you have proven so adept at doing in the past?" Diallo finished with a grin as deadly as a blade. Cazador grinned. *Oh but I like my new djali*, he thought. The best of his caste were always allowed a certain amount of leeway for a vassal that made the impudent when the mood arose. Cazador wondered if Diallo could truly use the sword at his hip. Sir Richard had the grace to allow a bright red flush to creep up his heart shaped face until his normally olive skin burned all the way to the roots of his tight sandy curls. Sir Richard glared at Diallo's portly form with his beady eyes as the nostrils of his aquiline nose flared indignantly. It was common knowledge that he had gambled away Genevova's dowry and personal fortune within years of marrying her. "Be that as it may," Sir Richard said his voice clipped with anger. "Your actions could potentially bring upon us the fate of the Cathars if it provokes the king of the Danes." The gathered elders broke into a cacophony at that. Agitated they resumed bickering about what should be done.

His mother and aunt continued to sit in stony silence. At first Cazador was content to wait and let it burn itself out, until he heard the words disowned, and stripped. Suddenly the air in the tent felt charged. Cazador's head began to ache and his pulse beat at his temples. He understood that he elders feared reprisal from the Danes regardless of whether or not Cazador had proven his innocence. But to strip him from his recently granted lands or to disown him was far too much. *They can't. They wouldn't. I've done everything they have asked! Would they cast me aside so easily?* Cazador stood no longer willing to kneel before the people he had loved and respected his entire life. He was not some irresponsible boy but a man grown who had dedicated his life to his family. The elders divided themselves into camps as the elder warriors lent their support to Cazador, while those more concerned with trade were split down the middle between those who wanted to disown him and the others who thought that he should pay a fine that could be used to placate the Danes before any trouble could start. With anger and betrayal tearing at his heart Cazador didn't trust himself to speak. He looked to his aunt Miryam but there was no kindness in her dark eyes and his silent plea for her to end the madness died.

Genevova smiled at him triumphantly, her dark brown eyes alight with something Cazador couldn't place. When his aunt Miryam stood he felt a wave of relief. "I will hear no more talk of disowning or stripping titles from my nephew. He is a man of honor." Miryam said in a tone as cold and hard as ice. "He will submit a years incomes from Le Cannet Des Maures as a bereavement gift to King Valdemar. I've already drawn up the paperwork." Cazador's relief faded, replaced by a sense of profound hurt. Miryam met Cazador's shocked stare. "He will approve the documents or he will be forced to submit to the judgement of the elders, whatever they decide." Ashamed and angry Cazador did as he was told. Scratching his name on the parchment, with his left hand.

* * *

Cazador packed his tent, spare gambesons, surcoats and armor into panniers on his packhorse. A train of mules was loaded with fodder for man an beasts. Rather than celebrate a victory he had been attacked and shamed and although his eyes were dry he could barely swallow for the lump in his throat. His aunt had told him that the men of his company had been quartered at Bobastro Nuevo awaiting his arrival. Cazador could see no further reason to tarry and resolved to retrieve them. He wanted to get to Nuevo Bobastro ahead La Compagnie and planned to leave before they arrived.

After that Cazador wasn't sure. Sure the money hurt but the reaction of his elders was a wound. Rather than rally around him too many had been ready to cast him down. Perhaps he would sail to the Holy Land and seek service. For all the fighting he had done on Crusade he has come no closer to Jerusalem than Syria. Maybe he would go and sit at La Marche and spend the fighting season blind drunk and useless.

The idea appealed but the castle he had coveted and the land he loved no longer appealed to him. *Fuck the elders, fuck the company and fuck this family.* Cazador didn't care where he went so long as he did not serve La Compagnie or enrich the elders. He was done, all the years of service and praise were nothing more than manipulation. He had done no wrong yet the elders had been sure to remind him that he was lucky not to be exiled from the family. Cazador would save them the trouble.

* * *

Miryam had watched the scene between Cazador, Genevova, and the elders unfold with with something akin to disgust. Cazador's gambit with the Danes while overbold had been good strategy. In demanding judicial combat he not only avoided a larger bloodier conflict but had shifted any and all guilt from himself and the family by winning. Miryam tried to think of what she would say as she briskly stalked toward the main gate of the camp. Cazador was understandably angry but with the challenges ahead their family had to remain united. A rift like what she saw forming tonight could not be allowed. She had ordered Jaime and Izan to slow Cazador down and sent a message by birds telling Yvain's men at the gate to hold him until she arrived.

Miryam sighed. The birds were descendents of those who had been bred by agents of Sultan Nur ad-Din over forty years ago. Hopefully they were fast enough to beat her nephew to leaving. Access to the Al Takruri pigeon post was one of the many boons of her position, but it wasn't without it's drawbacks. Her heart broke for her nephews but as head of La Compagnie she was forced to maintain public impartiality. Now she had hoped to have an opportunity to speak with Cazador privately and now she feared she was too late. The loss of a years income was a heavy blow, and unfair one even. Cazador was a good knight and a loyal son of the du Maurmonts. He had done nothing to merit punishment, but Miryam had to let the elders feel like they had done something that would get the situation under control.

While the King of Denmark was not an enemy they could afford to make, he would never see a single pence of the money she had taken from Cazador. Before her nephew had even been apprised to the issue Miryam had sent a fine horse to king Valdemar explaining that his kin had been killed when they had mistakenly attacked eastern Christians under their protection believing them to be Mohammedans. Instead Miryam would use that coin to ensure the loyalty of certain elders and kinsman. A lifetime around merchants, lawyers politicians and churchmen had given Miryam a nose for treachery. Something about her niece's reaction didn't sit well.

The entire thing stank, growing ranker the further she thought about it. Genevova had been orphaned young and had lived with Linda and her children for years as a child. She and Cazador had been close and this sudden enmity felt wrong. Miryam had no children of her own, and so all that she had acquired would be split between her god children and her nieces and nephews. It was possible Cazador's new titles might have ruffled her feathers. Miryam scoffed, Genevova had to know that she wouldn't be inheriting everything by herself. Cazador was young but he had proven he could not only fight but lead and most importantly think. To lose him would be a blow to her heart and to the family. The Old Lion had plans for all his grandchildren and had molded them educating them while enhancing their natural talents to that effect. Miryam refused to allow pettiness to destroy a generation of planning.

Huffing she arrived at the gate still manned by a clump of Knights of Attillo. "Has Sir Cazador left?" The guards nodded the negative and Miryam let loose a pent up breath. Heartbeats later Cazador came trotting up the main path with Diallo beside him at the head of his followers. Miryam noted that three of her pilgrims had joined his party. Alberto of Aragon, Merfynn ap Merfynn, and Roland of Palermo had shed there brown robes for rode with him.

Upon seeing his aunt, Cazador halted his column and dismounted. "Auntie I love you and I thank you for all you have done, but I must ask you to step aside and let me leave." Miryam crossed her arms over her chest and summoned the same look that had cowed her nephew since she had caught him stealing in the market at five. Much to her satisfaction he stiffened and hung his head. "I can't force you to stay," she continued. "But I will make you listen now pick up your lip." Cazador looked up obviously displeased to be called out for sulking. He met Miryam's eye with a steady gaze. "Genovova and the elders were wrong." Miryam continued in a softer tone. "The Abesingian Crusade has them all petrified that our neighbors will unleash a crusade upon us, but I am convinced there is more to it than that and you have my word I will get to the bottom of it." Some of the hostility left Cazador's face but his tone was still heated. "Why punish me at all when I have proven my innocence?" He spat. Miryam smiled. "Tis but a feint dear nephew, I assure you." Cazador snorted. "The worlds most expensive one I daresay!" Miryam giggled at that. "So much like your grandfather." Cazador pulled a face making her laugh all the harder. Pulling her still armored nephew into an embrace. "I fear your cousin and her husband have sown the seeds of a dark design. I will uses the stripped revenues to thwart it and to build your power in Le Cannet Des Maures and ensuring you have allies in places you need them, otherwise I fear your first night in La Marche may be your last." Cazador nodded stiffly, shocked at the implications of what his aunt had said. "Gather your men at Bobastro and go to England. There's fighting to be had in Wales or a long the Scottish marches. I know Moor House is poor in comparison to Le Cannet Des Maures, but it will be safe and it still produces a few pounds a year." Miryam could see the disappointment in her nephew's face but she could tell he understood. She knew the set of his jaw, the coldness in his eyes. Cazador had never met his father but Guillame was there in the hard expression on her nephews face. He rode off into the settling dusk and she wondered if she would see him again.

* * *

Richard opened the cage and tied the tiny note to the creatures leg and sent the bird to his agents. *The die is cast.* He sat at his folding camp desk, propping his elbows on its mahogany surface and steepling his long fingers. This tent he shared with Genovova was as much his home as anywhere else in the world. He served as a seneschal of La Compagnie a position he thought would bring him dignity. A position of honor he's thought placing him above the other du Maurmont brutes who seemed to love nothing more than chasing and fighting ragged assed bandits and playing the nurse maid to pilgrims. Instead they treated him as if he had some sort of malady because he didn't ride about hitting things with weapons. It wasn't that he was opposed to fighting, he was simply opposed to fighting for anything but a tidy profit, pilgrims rarely paid and bandits weren't exactly known for their rich baggage trains.

Worse still was how they ignored the fact that Richard had sprung from the line of the de Hautvilles. He had spent a fortune of Genevova's money securing the services of Michael Scot and his coterie of students. Both he and his wife had been present at dinners in Toledo where the dishes had been served by hands unseen, and knew his power. From that point on Richard had made himself a loyal customer. Cantrips, curses, charms and wards had been instrumental in his rise to his current position. As far as Richard was concerned it was coin well spent, especially now that Le Cannet des Maures was his to command. After Cazador had stormed off like an angry child and Miryam had disappeared, it was all too easy to convince the family elders he was too young and unpredictable to be a ruler, and that his talents best served the family as a military asset.

The only issue was, once Cazdor learned this Richard would have to spend his days looking over his shoulder. His wife's cousin was likely to challenge him to a duel, or worse still he might raid Cannet des Maures and set himself up as a bandit lord terrorizing the area. If it came down to a seige Richard would be loath to trust the men at arms of Cannet Des Maures to stand firm against the commune's rightful heir and favored grandchild of The Old Lion. Despite his youth Cazador's intellect was legendary amongst the family and his skill with the sword and spear style of the blue veiled heathens was respected even by the warlike Du Maurmonts. Simply put Richard could not allow his party to live. With a handful of men behind him he would be an even greater threat. That simply could not be allowed to happen.

***

Miryam steeled herself for the storm of her sisters ire. Linda had many skills but holding her tongue had never been one. She had been admirably quiet during the proceedings but now she was thunderous. "What grudge do the elders bear my son." She asked indignantly as if Miryam had an answer to what lay in the heart of others. She did have some insight, but to offer such now would mean to literally poke an angry bear. It was why her sister was a knight and she the politician and merchant. With a sigh she met Linda's eye. What had been done to Cazador was unfair. She had argued vehemently with the elders that to deny Cazador the lordship of Le Cannet Des Maures would be a waste of talent. Nevermind the fact that it was his patrimony. Her nephew had been fighting since before his eighteenth birthday, and was praised by every captain as a capable leader. The fault didn't lie with Cazador, but with the greed of others. The Old Lion's sons had shown no desire to lead. Even some of his elder grandsons had chosen quiet positions within the family showing little and less desire or aptitude for the games of trade, war, and power. Her nephew Cazador was a different matter, he was much like the Old Lion, and had entirely too much of his mother in him to comfort the elders. Leon Alfiere called Hamza Al Takruri in Al Andalus was easily as powerful as any of the great lords of Europa commanding troops in the Maghreb, the Sudan, and small castles and ribats in the Holy Land. Simply put the ruling elders sought to curtail the power of the Old Lion by denying Cazador his birthright. They had stripped him of everthing but the barony in England. La Marche, the ancestral home of the Alfiere family since their partiarch Saif al Takruri first took the name Alfiere when he settled in rugged western marches of the former territory of Fraxinetum.

Now that snake Richard had gotten himself appointed as lord of Cannet Des

Maures, Miryam could see nothing but trouble. He was smart, competent, charming and utterly untrustworthy. He was perfect for his role within La Compagnia, part diplomat, part trader, part spy. There his ambition could be harnessed. *But now?* Miryam wondered if she had made a mistake by not letting Cazador challenge and kill him. Richard would be the first outsider to hold a major family seat, a single act of duplicity could undo generations of careful work. Her niece Genovova was little better but she was family. Rather than rant, Linda said, "Warn the Old Lion." But Miryam was already writing.

Chapter 6: Fuming

His kinsmen knew him well enough to not question it. The dark mood that sometimes crept upon Cazador like storm clouds. It was an uglier, meaner, cousin to anger that like frost could kill everything it touched. They knew that for some anger was a flash flame in a bonfire. Terrifying but gone in a moment. For Cazador it was enduring like the cold of a bad winter. It took all his self control not to ride back to the camp and make a bloody spectacle of his so called kinsman. The only things that truly held him back were God's love, the look in his aunt's eyes, and the fact that he was no longer a penniless hedge knight. Instead he was a nearly penniless baron and for reasons he couldn't quite explain that made him feel better. He was smart enough to realize that any violent reaction would prove his enemies to be correct. Even in the grips of the frost where there was no forgiveness and even less mercy, Cazador understood a simple truth. Anger is no reason for poor strategy.

Merfynn knowing little and less of Cazador's bleak moods spurred his horse until he drew level with his new friend.

"Family can be trying. It is for such things they say the blood of the covenant is thicker than the water of the womb. Eh?" The Welshman said earnestly. Cazador tried and failed to summon words for Merfynn. He marked the Welshman as a good sort. He turned and met Merfynn open look and managed a half smile and a nod. "Not many men would have acted with grace as you did. Your a good man and a prieux knight. I salute thee." Cazador smiled a heartfelt smile of gratitude. "Come," he said lifting his voice. "Let's find somewhere free schemers, and scum." Meryfynn rode on wondering exactly where such a place could possibly exist.

A few hours ride brought them to a small nameless trading town on the banks of the Genil River. Merfynn did his best to ignore the rumbles of underfed stomach, stifling a sigh in memory of his interrupted repast. His new friends seemed to know the way, and the night was pleasant. Town may have been a generous word for the ramshackle collection of mudbrick buildings and dilapidated mosque surrounded by a semi-circular palisade of timber and adobe. Even calling it a ribat would strain the imagination. Cazador halted their column and dismounted striding a few paces to speak with the watchmen loitering near the rude gate. Usually a party of armed men arriving in the night would be cause for alarm, or at least suspicion, but Cazador gestured to the the Arabic inscribed banner they rode under and the guards visibly relaxed. Merfynn marveled at how simple traders and bodyguards could generate so much influence.

Cazador remounted an they rode into a deserted market plaza. Merfynn felt an eerie oddness as they plodded past the empty stalls and a silent forge down a well trod path toward the wet mud smell of the river. "The best delights are always nearest the water!" Jaime said excitedly, but there were no sounds of music or merriment. "Perhaps there might be a place to procure something to eat as well?" Merfynn asked hopefully. Jaime beamed, his white teeth flashing in the moonlit darkness. "We will not allow you to starve Merfynn. Last time I was here I ate a wonderful lamb stew." Alcazar spurred his horse closer, "I remember that stew. The one with the eastern spices?" Jaime slapped his leg, " The very one!" "The bread was good too." Alcazar added, "Nice and fresh it was, and it hasn't been that long since we've been here last." Merfynn sighed contentedly at the thought. "Shouldn't be far now." Cazador called over his shoulder. They turned off the hamlet's main thoroughfare onto a lane that was smaller and equally well trodden. To their left adobe hovels intermixed with larger buildings that exuded the telltale metallic mixed with rotten meat stink of butchers combined with the acrid smell of tanneries. The smells were muted, somehow stale. The result was a miasma that fought an unseen war with the smell of the river. Merfynn hid his features with the tagelmust he had been given to wear blessing whoever had thought to scent it with mint. To their right wooden warehouses loomed like sentinels in the dark, alleys between them offered occasional glimpses at the river that shone like a silver band in the moonlight.

The groups idle chatter died away leaving breathing of man and horse with the creak of harness to compete with the distant river and the clop of hooves. Although there was sound the genral silence was tomblike, a comparison Merfynn didn't appreciate. "Something is wrong." Cazador growled softly from the head of their column. "I do remember this town being a fair bit more lively." Izan murmured. "Even the caravansarai are quiet and I smell many things but no wood smoke." He continued. Merfynn began to despair for his chances of a meal. Something was decidedly off. He knew that the world was large and full of terrifying things he would decidedly rather not think about. It was the reason the trade in relics and magic trinkets was so brisk. Like mint is thought to repel mice, relics and blessed objects repelled the various nefarious forces that stalked the world. Having a priest around made things a sight better. Lacking those a strong will, prayer and a weapon would have to do. But just as man can not live by bread alone, steel on its own merits would not suffice. Growing up in Wales Merfynn knew of the Adar Llwch Gwin the great raptors who could understand the words of man and follow the commands of the worthy, or the Cath Palugs the giant cats as large as horses that had been the bane of many a herd. Then there were the Pucá who were like djinn the Moors and Saracens were familiar with. The branches of the Tylwyth Teg or fairy family that shared this world with men and beasts were many. There were folk who didn't believe, but the wise knew the tamer the land the more firmly the hegemony of man stood. But in the wild places where man held little sway such conceits were stripped away.

They pressed on to the taverna, finding it dark and altogether uninviting. There was no light or music and other sign of life coming from the large two story L shaped building showing lofts above the empty stables. Cazador looked as though he would dismount before shaking his head violently. "No," He muttered, "For all the gold in the Sudan I won't sleep in this place." Cazador said before leading them back the way they had come. "Where are the people of the place." Alberto the Spanish knight pondered aloud, breaking heavy silence. "The better question is, who pays men to guard a dead town." Said one of the twins whether the bulky Pedro or the slim Pablo, Merfynn could not tell. "Let us make for the river. I would purchase passage a barge and be away from this place." There was a round of nods and grunts of assent. Cazador led them onto a track that was pitted with wagon ruts running parallel to the street they had just traversed.

The glare of moonlight off the Genil did little to alleviate the gloom. The bulk of the warehouses leered on their left reminding Merfynn uncomfortably of barrows and the shabby wooden wharf on their right was deserted along with several barges moored against the current. Further down the track the wharf ended and a series of adobe enclosures with walls twice the height of a man began. If there were any signs of life Merfynn could discern none. "We must leave this place my lord." Diallo said, his voice a harsh whisper. "The darkness stalks us." As if to punctuate his point the breeze freshened bringing with it the iron tang of blood and the unmistakable scent of rotting corpses.

The horses began to whinny and Merfynn could feel the tension in his own mount. It reminded him of days in his father's paddock breaking stallions. He could sense it's readiness to throw him and bolt. Cazador grunted, dark eyes distant in the moonlight. "Jaime, you and the other's head to the wharf. I will cover our retreat. Find a boat that accommodate us and give me the whistle." Idris nodded, discomfort written plain on his face. He led the column towards the wharf as his kinsman moved aside.

Dismounting Cazador drew a spear and Byzantine kite shield from his saddle and remounted his skittish horse. He patted the animals neck whispering soothing sounds. He liked nothing more than solid earth beneath his feet in a fight, but horses made a body mobile in a hurry and he knew he may have sore need of such speed soon. *If* the animal didn't throw him and run for safety first. Thrusting his spear in the earth near at hand he checked his brace of

Tebu throwing knives each was two feet long, and their slim curved blades were bifurcated like a bill to give the weapons a forward curving point and a forward facing fluke. Wickedly sharp and weighted they could be hurled to devastating effect but also made excellent weapons in the melee. Times like this they would serve him better than the recurve bow in his saddle. His eyes scanned the warehouses and the deeper darkness of the alleys between them. Cazador could feel the gris-gris at his chest vibrating faintly with energy as it repulsed the malevolence of from whatever evil eye lay beyond.

Chancing a glance behind him, he saw that Sir Alberto had remained, a short bow like those found among the Turcopoles strung in his fist. "I will cover you." the Asturian said softly. "I stay as well," said Izan hefting a spear. Cazador nodded. Glad for the presence of his cousin and new found ally. Cazador cast his mind back to his youth where many an hour was spent at study of nations, their people, and the various beasts that stalked them. All manner of things preyed on men in this world no different than men hunted the beasts of the wood. The only question was what? He knew that the talismans he and his kin wore would only respond to forces of darkness. Who paid men to guard a dead town? Unless... Cazador slid free a throwing knife cursing himself for a fool. Ghûls or ghouls were known to thrive in places of misery and death, delighting in vile trickery in order to gorge on human flesh. "Tell me Sir Alberto have you faced ghul before?" Cazador asked his ally. Alberto made as face as if to say he didn't believe in such things, but shook his head to the negative. Before Cazador could speak again, Izan said, "Sunlight and the words of the Holy Books weaken them, often forcing them to flee, but a ghul must be slain with a single blow. You cannot wound them, to do so is to invite death as it drives them into an unstoppable frenzy. Crack the head, scramble the brains, or break the spine, or don't strike at all." Izan murmured, quoting

Idris ibn Idris's childhood lessons verbatim. His voice was calm and Cazador felt himself steady. As knights of Saint Atillo they had been trained to fight all manner of foe, from simple spearman to dragons. Cazador reminded himself of this as he screwed up his courage. "Pray, or recite the Bible as you fight," Cazador m iumbled to Alberto, "It slows them." He smiled reassuringly at the man even as the overwhelming urge to piss attacked his bladder.

Listening intently for Idris' whistle, Cazador could hear the others scuffing and cursing colorfully as they herded the skittish pack animals along the worn wood of the wharf. It was Cazador's horse that warned him first. The tense animal, sidestepped at some unseen movement in the impenetrable darkness to Cazador's right. "Bollocks!" He spat as he fought for control of the animal. "Be calm you beast before you get us both eaten! Cazador hissed in singsong tones known to parents of fractious children worldwide. "It's too dark and our kin take too long." Izan said reigning in his own mount. "Agreed," Alberto stammered equally beset. Unable to control the skittish animal, Cazador cursed vehemently. "Fine have it your way you dumb beast, piss on me for thinking we'd survive this together!" He spat. Unable to abide either the skittish horse or the darkness Cazador tore free a piece of his tagelmust and wrapped it tightly around the haft of a javelin, before daubing it in a bitumen from his tinder box. Using his flint and throwing knife he soon had a makeshift torch that he hurled into the summer dry thatch of the nearest warehouse.

The roof caught blazing merrily, lifting the veil darkness. Almost immediately any relief at being able to see faded as no fewer than a score of humanoid shapes materialized. Cazador could remember reading that ghul could appear very human if well fed. The treatises rumored some lived amongst men keeping their activities secret. Others, those less clever Cazador supposed haunted desolate areas eating carrion from battlefields, and plundering mass graves. For ghul as much as for men, you are what you eat, except ghul drew on the appreance of their meals. Lesser ghouls where said to bear an animalistic aspect like dogs, hyenas, or jackals. The Codex of The Knights of Saint Atillo said that the educated might tell a Umm or Baba the greater ghul by their corpse like pallor, long arms, overlarge hands and with fingers wider and flatter than is normal. An overdeveloped lower jaw, and elongation of the teeth could also be in evidence. Lesser ghouls could be hairy, or even scaly, with a hunched back and elongated body more adept at scrambling on all fours, than walking upright. All ghul carried the stench of carrion, which now filled the air.

All that and more passed through Cazador's mind as the ghouls charged as one. He launched his first throwing knife cleaving the upper face of a charging ghoul. Throwing a second and a third finding his aim true, Cazador was forced to cease his barrage and take up his spear.

"Let not your heart be troubled, neither let it be afraid. For God hath not given us the spirit of fear; but of power, and of love, and of a sound mind. Be strong and of a good courage, fear not, nor be afraid of them: for the Lord thy God, he it is that doth go with thee; he will not fail thee, nor forsake thee." He heard his djali shout. The ghul reacted as if stung and they hissed in fury as the holy words struck the oncoming fiends like a shock wave, slowing their charge a half step.

Ser Alberto's arrows fell among the ghouls like rain drops. "Are you sure your not a Nubian?" Izan barked with a laugh even as his barrage of javelins arced to meet the horde. Cazador couldn't help but laugh. His horse lashed out with its hooves pulping the skull of a slavering lesser ghoul who'd ducked the barrage. Leaning forward in his saddle, Cazador punched his spear into the mouth of a maille wearing ghoul before the creature could strike his horse with it's falchion. Turning to his left Cazador got his shield between a spear and his horse's neck but got his own spear around to slow. With a curse he stabbed out. Rather than kill the ghoul outright Cazador's spear took the ghoul between neck and shoulder. A killing blow for a man but for a ghoul Cazador was unsure. With a growl he continued driving his spear leaning on the weapon until it was deep in the beast's guts, pinning it to the earth. The monster thrashed and snarled but was held fast. Cazador drew his Tempest and struck it's head from it's shoulders.

Arrows spent Alberto drew his sword and charged trampling two of the beasts as they sought to flank to Cazador's unshielded side. That was enough for Cazador's horse to launch a frenzied series of kicks. "Bugger this!" Cazador roared, rising in the stirrups. Before he could stop himself Cazador stood in his saddle and leapt. Sword scything, with a formless battlecry on his lips he met the nearest ghul. The blade laid open the creatures skull like a cracked egg. The remaining ghouls closed on Cazador like hunting hounds to cornered quarry. He could feel the gris-gris humming against his chest as he flicked a thrust at a charging ghoul, scraping along the beasts cheekbone and into it's eyesocket. Whipping the blade free, he cut at a new foe charging from his right skating across it's maille collar to bite deep into the creatures neck to crunch into it's vertebrae, using the ghouls boneless weight Cazador freed his sword.

Seeing his cousin's plight Izan hurled his spear, the long weapon seeming to snatch a speeding ghoul by its neck, clearing Cazador's left flank. Alberto spurred his horse forward leveling his spear like a lance and charged for Cazador's vulnerable side his spear punching through the skulls of two ghul and the throat of a third. Dropping the weapon, Alberto's horse lashed out at two more slavering foes with it's hooves cracking skull and bone. The spanish knight used the time brought by his mounts vicious kick to draw his sword. His eyes swept the area but there were no living ghouls in evidence. When he rejoined Cazador and Izan the former met his eye nodding. "Outstanding work sir. You saved my life." Alberto nodded back, unable to speak still shocked that he had crossed blades with the undead. Before anyone could say anything else a whistle cut through the night from the wharf behind them. "Come we must tell the others, we cannot leave until we have purge this place. Our duty as Knights of Saint Atillo demands it!"Cazador growled.

Jaime eyed Cazador carefully checking to see if his bold cousin had taken a head injury. He wasn't wrong but it didn't stop him from sounding crazy. *He has a crazy look in his eye too.* Jaime thought grimly. The scramble on the wharf to find a barge that hadn't been holed, or caked in liberal amounts of blood, whilst keeping the animals from bolting had been enough to fray his nerves to snapping. They had eventually found a high sided river cog with room for both the men and animals and only minimal bloodstains. Its hull had been lined with prayers in beautiful flowing Kufic that rode just below the waterline which explained why it hadn't been damaged like the others. "How precisely do you propose we eliminate an unknown number of ghul?" He heard Idris ask. Cazador grinned, "We start burning the town until they come to us." He gestured with his chin, "We make the boat ready to set off at the moments notice, and hold the wharf as long as we can. If we pull in some wagons from the park to protect our flanks we should be able to reduce the town and their numbers. Eventually the emir's men will see the smoke and investigate." The grizzled old almogovar smiled and nodded, his white teeth a flash in the moonlight. "It's what your grandfather would do." Cazador clapped his hands, obvious pleasure evident on his face as he rushed off to prepare.

Cazador gripped Tempest and ensured his shield was tight against Pedro's who held his one handed axe high, where moonlight glimmered from the inscriptions across the half moon blade. Behind him was his twin Pablo, beside him was Jaime, with Izan anchoring their right flank. Together they formed the front rank of an eight man shield wall. Sir Alberto, Caleb of Dongla, Idris ibn Idris, and Merfynn ap Merfynn stood atop two of the abandoned wagons they had dragged to protect their position and protected by Diallo the djali and Roland of Palermo. They would use their bows thin the enemy ranks. Makeshift torches lined the wharf behind them even as fires burned merrily in the town beyond. A wall of fire and brave souls, it sounded like poetry. But when Caz looked around it all seemed paltry before the great darkness set before them. The smoke grey swirls of his wootz steel sword seemed to absorb the night around it even as the lighter whorls in the steel seemed hold the moonlight and torch glare as close as a lover. The emanations from the gris-gris around his neck seemed to build in intenstity with each passing moment. "Nothing like torching a town and waiting for an entire clan of ghul to attack to soothe the nerves." Jaime crooned in a sing-song voice, and was rewarded with a round of nervous laughter. They all knew after Idris, had taken to the mast of their pilfered ship and used it's height to set most of the town alight with fire arrows, that the beasts would come. "Don't think you won't be buying me new arrows Lord Cazador." Idris muttered darkly, none too pleased with the waste of good shafts. "If we live through this I will make the next fletcher we find a wealthy man on your behalf." Cazador quipped. Idris ibn Idris grunted, followed by the telltale thrum of an arrow leaving the bowstring. When the scent of carrion hit them like a physical blow, they knew the ghul had come.

The charge was unlike anything Cazador had witnessed before. Men screamed or bellowed but the ghouls came forth with a sibiliant snarl. A vanguard of lesser ghouls charged, their four limbed stride allowing them to avoid the worst of the arrow storm. Within moments there was a wall of corpse pale flesh and patchy dark fur. Cazador punched with the rim of his shield connecting with a leaping ghoul, forcing its head to an obscene angle with an audible crack. Chopping over the corpse of his first kill, he shattered the head of the next. Pedro screamed a battle cry beside his kinsman and buried his axe in the skull of the ghoul facing him. As he worried the blade free his brother Pablo thrust over his shoulder taking a ghoul in the eye Izan's mace rose and fell like the arms of a woman churning butter. Each of the lesser ghouls who stepped into his range fell with it's skull stove in. Another weaponless lesser ghul threw himself at Cazador grasping at his shield with its strange shovel like hands. He had to check the urge sheer the overlarge fingers away, instead he let the beast tug his shield down and plunged the tagheda through the creature's gullet and into it's brain. Flicking the spitted ghoul from his spear Cazador managed to get his shield up just in just time.

The axe threw sparks from the boss of his shield numbing his arm from fingers to shoulder. The ghoul was clad in maille and gambeson with an aventail protecting it's face and neck. It was instinct alone that brought Tempest around to plunge the point of his sword into the ghoul's eye. Silently thanking God and every ancestor for the ghul overbalancing itself with the strike. Shoving with his shield he freed his blade and knocked a spear off line. The ghoul struck again, it's spear held overhand and a round shield well forward. Cazador refused to be pulled out of line and was rewarded as an arrow punched into the creature's mailled face. With alarming speed their thin line was pressed by well armed and armored ghouls fighting like experienced men at arms. With a trill of fear Cazador began to wonder if he had made a terrible mistake. Blocking strikes Cazador weathered blows as the arrows fell, he could feel the pressure and hear Leon grunt as he thrust over his shoulder. Peering over his shield rim, he raised it to deflect a sword blow from its curved top, and planted his sword in his opponet's open mouth. With a savage twist he yanked his sword free and shoved the body aside. Motion caught his eye and he turned in time to see Merfynn leap from the wagon swinging his axe in a mighty arc cleaving the heads from two ghul before his fee touched the earth. With a roar he jammed a rondel dagger into the eye of a third. The pressure on their tiny shield wall immediately lessened, and Cazador charged unsure of where to strike the heavily armored ghouls. Protected by helmet and coiffe the ghouls could only be taken down in a few choice places. Landing a killing blow was no easy task. Slinging his sword in a mezzano slash he connected with the base of the nearest ghouls neck hearing the crunch of bone beneath maille. The fiend fell, and Cazador released a breath he didn't know he'd been holding. "For Monts Des Maures and Saint Atillo!" Cazador bellowed emboldened by relief. Stabbing with his tagheda he took another ghoul before it could react.

With Cazador turning the ghouls flank and Merfynn wreaking havok to their rear Idris Ibn Idris entered the fray his takouba like a trail of silver vapor in the smoky night air as he swayed between the ghouls, his lithe form slipping away from attacks only for his sword to reach out and take eyes or dart into snarling mouths. Cazador saw that the wagons were clear and a staggering amount of ghouls lay downed. Shoving his sword in his scabbard Cazador took up the small horn that Knights of Saint Atillo bore to warn of danger or give instuction. Three short blasts. A signal trained into them from childhood gave the order to retreat. As one the human fighter scrambled for the gap in the wall of carts. While the others made for the boat, Roldand, Jaime and Cazador stopped. The Sudanese hurled throwing knives at the on coming ghouls and as the fiends reeled with split skulls, or crouched behind their shields, Roland had time to push a cask of pitch and lamp oil into their midst, task done the trio turned to flee with fear winged feet. Kaleb, Idris, and Alberto fired a volley over their heads as Izan hurled a flaming javelin at the cask. The wheels of each of the wagons and the ground beneath had been liberally soaked int the same mixture as had the killing field beyond their cart wall. With his cousins and the Sicilian aboard Pedro needed no urging to cut the line tethering them to the smoldering quay. The hot wind created by the inferno and the current of the Genil carried the little cog away swiftly and the eyes of the twelve men remained glued to the flames.

Chapter 7: Children of Twilight

The phosphorescent red purple light of inner earth's ubiquitous luminescent lichen glowed on Oberon's tawny brown skin and made his silver eyes glow a brilliant shade of lavender as he stared from his balcony at the vast underground sea. Wine colored waves crashed upon a shore of sand that eons past had been black diamond studded granite cliffs. The freshening breeze carried familiar scents of salt and wet stone to his thin nose. Gazing at the ten million myriads of glowing stones and wondered about the yellow fabled yellow sun. He had never seen the sun, and wondered what it's glow would feel like. Warm he supposed. Some of the elders told him tales of their time spent in the world of men. As the descendants and kin of the Bisimbi, the Tuathe De and the Aos Si the elvish kind were once worshipped and revered in the world of men. Some like his great great great grandsire's half brother Wotan, called Odin, whose name means frenzy supplanted Freyr. Together with his kin the Aesir had established themselves as a pantheon and grew powerful from sacrifice. Oberon could only imagine the days after the flood when weapons like the great Gungir, or Claíomh Solais the irresitable shining blade were wielded as The Elder Remnants, the Elioud, Nephilim, and the Gibborim fought for supremacy amongst themselves. Human contact, was addictive. Reverence brought a certain sublimity that Oberon had only heard poets hint of.

Such worship would bring doom to most in this age. A few Samyazan rulers had managed to find a new synchronicity within Christianity. Although the church of Inner Earth frowned upon such things, it mattered little. Even still as mighty as they were, even *their* power was diminished. These days the fair folk didn't stray far from the bases where their power waxed. Gone were the days of his forefathers shrines and fairy circles dotted the land where his kind might draw from the mana that fed their magic like wells from hidden springs. The light of Christ shone and what power the Children of Samyaza had waned like snow before summer sun. Man however stood ascendant. Like a stain they spread across middle earth, their industry crushing the memory of what once was. But soon the day would come when the Samyaza's children would stride supreme on middle earth once more.

Oberon sighed and returned to his chambers, a smooth organically curved expanse of mother of pearl inlaid with platinum softened by silk and cashmere tapestries and rugs. Beside the four pillared alabaster bed the size of a peasants hovel stood his armoire and kit rack. Oberon wasted little time pulling on a long kaftan of layered silk he them busied himself donning a coat of made of thousands of interlocking orichalum plates, before belting on the electrum plaques that held his mace Sebarī the smasher. Forged from a mixture of bronze, stone, and thokcha in the earths fire by the great dwarven and Mouros smiths of Vulcan's school. Bred from by Azazel from the seed of the first men and demons as a race of miners and craftsmen the dhvaras or dwarves and their kin the Mourous weapon and armorcraft surpassed even that of the elves.

For generations immemorial the Children of Samyaza had been helpers and sometimes punishers of man as was the will of the Creator. It had been part of the covenant that gave them salvation. That aid had allowed the Samyazans to glut themselves from human mana. Where mankind had dominion over the surface of the earth, the children of Samyaza were given the elements. Some rose to call themselves gods as mankind forgot their power. But then came Yeshua and after him the Prophet Muhammad turning the faces of mankind from the powers of the wild to a higher instrumentality altogether. Now however with humanity's protection of expiring, the time had come to choose. Would they war with the human world as the children of the Thirteenth Angel and the Giant kin, or would they rule their twilight halls in peace? After all

Humans were not without their own protections. Their iron weapons were anathema and the magic of humans while a far cry from their own, was potent enough. *What would war bring?* Mused Oberon. Doomsayers and war mongers had made their rounds to the high halls of the elvish tribes harbingers of a greater call heralding the restoration of the old power of their people.

Oberon wondered if they had made their way to the gleaming halls of the Ljósálfar. Like all elves they were descended from the children of watchers and the first humans called the Mourous, but they were marked by God as punishment for being the first to serve the morning star in rebellion. Their shining skin was the mark of their arrogance and vanity before the Creator. Since the coming of Christ they were no longer able to abide the sun. Theirs were the voices shouting loudest for war. Perhaps they were the ones who sent the macabre missionaries in the first place. It wouldn't have surprised him. Ljósálfar had once allied with the the House of the Thirteenth, they had never fought woodwose or ghouls in the squalid blood tinged half light. They never flown their griffons into the dragon fire as Oberon's father would say. Fighting the organized battle hardened humans would be a different matter all together.

Oberon examined himself in the mirror and found his visage suitably warlike. An honor guard of five hundred elves from his tribe would be similarly attired. Although the parlay was meant to be a peaceful affair, it was also a show of force. For the first time in his lifetime the entire Seelie House of Samyaza would meet. They would weigh the merits of war and peace. Fully dressed Oberon descended the grand staircase, passed through the gallery and into his throne hall. His five hundred griffon riders snapped to attention. The eyes of his captains gleamed with anticipation. He knew that in the courtyard beyond their mounts would be preening themselves, impatient to take wing. Bred in ancient times to lay low the dragons, griffins were to elves as horses were to men. Although they couldn't breath fire or match the sheer size their draconian foe, griffins were immensely strong and fast. Each also harnessed the power of the storm bringing thunder and lightning upon their enemies.

Griffins were imperious creatures the eldest able to connect psychically with those around them. Some of the great creatures had seen generations of riders and the pressure of their anticipation beat at him like a strong wind.

It would be a long journey much of it through the Twilight Ways, the system of roads deep beneath the earth of men that connected the House of Samyaza in trade, fellowship and often war. Other parts of the journey would take place into the moonlight world of man. The Seelie Court sat at the direct center of the earth's south pole. For nights to come tales of wild hunts would stalk the land as hosts of elves, dwarves, fae, Mourous, encantado, and Djinn converged on their destination. This would be Oberon's first journey to the hallowed halls of his ancestors where the survivors had gathered to outlast the great flood. The hearths of the court had been cold since Christ had harrowed hell and the high kings and their lines all perished. The war with Lucifer's elves had left the house of Samyaza a divided patchwork of armed camps, crossed loyalties

Decried by their light touched kin as Christ kneelers, the dark elves, dwarves and fae has to defend themselves from an onslaught of violence and forced conversion to the cult of the Thirteenth. Somehow, after enough blood was shed, they were beaten back. Oberon had been born into a world where some of the light Elves even converted to Christ, but the golden age of the House of Samyaza had ended long ago. With the high kings gone the Seelie Court had been abandoned and the great councils to determine the fate of Samyaza's children naught but echos of a glorious past. But now all that was about to change.

Oberon with hundreds of other clan or tribal kings would would sit in congress like their ancestors and cast their votes. From the terms of the agreement Oberon and the others had signed there would be no high kings or queens appointed. Instead they would vote, lay out treaties, and exchange hostages. Wardens or generals would be named to enforce the treaties and lead contingents. Proponents of the invasion of the human world or middle earth highlighted the corruption in the Church of Man, and the perversions of the veneration of Christ. Assuming direct suzerainty over human kingdoms was seen as a holy mission. Not only would they improve the human condition they would improve the condition of their souls and stand with man against the servants of the Unseelie Court. Opponents of the crusade said it was naught but a trick of the enemy to weaken their forces for the Unseelie Court. Oberon suspected the truth lay in between the two.

He looked into the expectant faces of his honor guard and the gathered nobles. "For the first time since my grandfather's time a son of Oberon the first will speak for the elves of Penume's Reach," he said. Letting a tidal wave of applause break over him Oberon paused. He had spent little time considering his vote. Above his underground demese were thick forests and rolling hills north of the great plains stretching as far south as the Dnepro river. The descendents of the ancient Sklabenoi still left their offerings in the wild places, honoring pacts made long ago with the elves, dwarves and fae of the land. To the south and west lay the lands held by the children of the Nameless Angel, servants of the Unseelie Court who the elves of Penume's Reach had battled from the time of Oberon's first ancestors. *Would the ghul, vyrlokas, light Elves, and woodwose also rise to strike at middle earth?* Oberon looked out at his people and wondered how much of their blood would be worth a place in the sun? For what purpose? Would he claim lands from the humans and lose his patrimony? Was the mana to be gained from ruling human subjects worth a war? All questions he had no answers for. With a deep breath he let the applause die, " I am no great diviner or sooth sayer to tell you what the future will hold. But I can promise to uphold the honor and best interests of our people. All of the house of Samyaza will march upon the surface or none. There can be no middle ground, to hang back is to assure our destruction. Therefore we must be bold and hold to our covenants! It is the Will of El that we

reclaim the grace and majesty of our ancestors. The kingdom of Penume's Reach will glow once more in the light and glory of the Creator and His son Yeshua the Savior for Blessed are the keepers of oaths!" The crowd roared once again and for the first time Oberon thought that things might go well.

* * *

After the grand procession of elvish king, fae high lords, djinn princes and dwarvish chieftains each contingent huddled by the tall alabaster thrones of kings hundreds of years dust. Each contingent strove for a level of pomp and circumstance that boggled even Oberon's royal threshold for ostentation. There was enough cloth of gold to pave the silk road ten times over and the are was so heavy with hauteur that it was a wonder the continent itself didn't buckle under the weight. Most of the elves were like Oberon and the elves of Penume's Reach, ranging from rich shades of gold touched browns to tawny honey, but even the Ljósálfar clans who had bent the knee to Christ had come. A people apart, setting foot for the first time in the Seelie Court since before the fall of the high kings. The flint hued eyes of the stocky dwarves peered from above their bearded faces. They, the most taciturn of Samyaza's children they sparked like jewels in their iridium alloy armor. Like the elves they were of the seed of the first men of the golden age kissed by the sun but here and there Ljósálfar ancestry a legacy of their enslavement showed in the paler shades, fair hair, and more elongated frames. The dwarves were a solemn people, their culture seeming joyless to the casual observer. That is until you saw their artistry. Craft was joy to a dwarf. Where elves gloried in art and the fae in music, the dwarves of Inner Earth expressed themselves in the carving of metal wood and stone to such an extent that it sang to the eye.

Not to be outdone the gossamer winged fae enrobed in gauzy silks bare arms and legs flashing. Precious stones suspended in aromatic oils graced their nubile frames making them shimmer in the light that poured from the high windows. As the the fae had the most contact with humans, their mana reserves were staggering and they bled magic into the air like fire belched smoke. Each fairy was surrounded in a nimbus of ethereal energy. As capricious as they are beautiful it was said to never offend a fae. They had fought wars with the elves and dwarves winning far more battles than they lost with their incredible speed and shapeshifting ability more than negating their small stature. Though they may not be larger than a tall child, they were old in war and wickedness.

The great procession took most of the morning and by the time afternoon rolled around Oberon was hungry and ill tempered. When the Megas Didáskalos, or Great Teacher head of the church of inner earth ascended to the dais at the center of the throne hall and began to intone her prayer, Oberon could swear the gathered nobles could hear the angry growls of his stomach reverberating through his armor. The Megas Didáskalos what what the humans called a Mouros, kin to the elves and dwarves. In a way they were their ancestors of all but the fae and djin, the humans of the golden age. Her dark hair formed a halo around he head, and her simple brown robes seemed like violence amid the riotous color of the rich gems and sumptuous fabrics that surrounded the dais. She offered up a prayer to El the Creator whom the children of Samyaza had worshipped since long before the flood. It hadn't stopped their ancestors from using their magic to turn the reverence and respect of humans to worship. That arrogance had led to the Harrowing of Hell after the coming of Christ. After the crucifixion, Yeshua appeared in The Seelie Court and all Samyaza's children and even some of those of the Thirteenth bent the knee in worship declaring Christ the king of all kings. The Army of Christ marched with great splendor to righteous war led by the son of El himself. The ensuing battles left the false pantheons broken alongside the high kings in a battle at a great underground plain called Ragnarok. Since that time the Church had been the only thing to unite the fractured shards of the Seelie Court. The Megas Didáskalos finished her prayer, imploring El to gift them all wisdom in the coming proceedings. Oberon felt that they would need it.

Chapter 8: Oathborn

Merfynn looked around at the men he was traveling with. For all he knew there were strange things in this world he still felt like he had lived through a bards tale and not something from his real life. He could still smell the corpse stink in his nostrils and their haunting dead eyes stalked his nightmares. The Italian, Roland had been in a state. Rolling fits of ranting shock and silent prayer. Although the wind had been moving the boat they had all lent their arms to the oars, tensely watching. Each of them scanning the shore for signs of other fiends in the night. Cazador Alfiere and his kin had fought like lions and Meryfynn was pleased of their presence. Usually full of banter and smiles, the Moors were subdued. The bags under their dark eyes and the grim lines of their mouths telling their own story of exhaustion. They had rowed through the night, and part of the following day, putting as many miles between them and the town of death as possible.

Roland aside, none of them had spoken a word that long night, and each seemed loath to break the silence other than the rhytmic splash of oars. "A thousand thousand priests and clerics in Al Andalus, and nobody knew about the devils own spawn, eating an entire town." Jaime said. Finally voicing everyones thoughts. "Never been attacked by none but the living in Wales," Meryfynn muttered into his oar. "Went on Pilgrimage to honor and find God, didn't quite expect it to be this way though." He continued. It was the elder warrior Idris Ibn Idris who answered. "Spain is at war, and war will always bring ghul1 although I have never seen an entire town in a settled place fall to them. Mayhaps the kings of Spain have resorted to darkness as a path to victory." He shrugged from the steering oar. "We have no way of knowing, we did our duty striking down the darkness. No need to worry ourselves about the problems of prince" Suddenly the old warriors dark brown face split into a feral grin. "First time I can say I put a town to the torch for God and it been the whole truth!" All the men aboard the ship laughed at that.

As if the some dark spell was broken by their laughter, the fear of the previous night dispersed. "Lets see if we can't anchor this craft and rest and let the animals gaze." Cazador murmured. An hour later they sat in a rough camp. He hurt everywhere. At some point in the fight he'd taken blows and now his ribs along his left side ached and he could feel a spectacular bruise forming stretching from his side to under his shoulder blade. His lamellar had saved him from the worst of it and Cazador counted his blessings. He had a vague memory of an axe trying to loop under his shield. *Apparently I only blocked some, rather than most of that one.* He thought gingerly. *Fucking ghul.* Pedro produced a skin of wine and Alcazar busied himself at the fire. He sliced an onion and fed it along with hunks of dried meat to a simmering pot of ale and olive oil. Cazador smiled at the delicious aroma and suppressed a laugh as Merfynn's stated at the pot as though it were a naked and comely woman.

Turning at the sound of booted feet, he could see Jaime and Pablo return leading a laden mule. "The farmer was more than willing to sell us some oats and cut grass to feed our animals and smoked beef and bread for us." Pablo rolled his eyes. "Was that before or after you pretend you would ride the man down in his own field?" Cazador cocked an eyebrow as Jaime's dark beard parted in a deep chuckle. "Well he did nearly shit himself but that's not on me." Cazador noted his cousin wore his sulke or maille armor over his gambeson and kaftan. His bald head gleamed like his maille as Jaime kept both kept meticulously polished. Eyes twinkling he shrugged. "Never hurts to make an impression." It was Cazador's turn to roll his eyes. "The last thing we need is to be accused of banditry...*again.*" He tried to be angry but all he could see was the poor farmer falling victim to his cousin's wicked sense of humor and he had to suppress a smile.

Jaime snorted and settled down by his cousin. "Calm down. Once he saw the glint of my silver he was all smiles. It was nearly as good as the time we rode with the tax revenue in England!" He said with a conspiratorial wink and Cazador and the other Du Maurmont men laughed aloud. Merfynn, Alberto and Roland looked on confused. "What's so funny about collecting taxes?" They said almost in unison. The laughter erupted again and Cazador tried and failed three times to explain. Finally Izan saved him. "We were squired to a knight of Dover and one day we were sent to help bring in the taxes. With us was an older knight called Sir Jacob. When we neared the first estate, he looked at us and said to follow his lead. He rode like a madman spurring his horse up the lane, yelling at the top of his lungs for the lord of the manor. We were so taken aback that we had to struggle catch him. By the time we caught up he was busy telling the lord that indeed he was being chased by dark spirits sent by God to punish those slack in their tasks and unfaithful to their lord." Izan pointed to Cazador, "This rogue starts screaming, waving his spear all about before hurling it into the door of the manor. The baron pissed his braes and his lady fainted. They ended up paying what was due and then some. The folk in those parts had never seen Moors before and despite our handsome faces and livery we were foreign, and they were afraid. So we went across the shire Caz waving his Afar sword chasing after the reeve like some devil out of hell scaring the living shit out of all and sundry. By the time we returned to the castle it had been the largest tax yield in living memory. The excess was split between us as reward for our mummery." Izan finished with a grin and a fresh round of laughter.

It was Cazador's turn to shrug. "It seemed the more tasteful option." He said before breaking into a feral grin. "I also charged a copper penny to let them touch my hair or try to wash the brown from my skin." The fond memories were bright in Cazador's mind. Simpler times, he thought. In his younger years his family seemed like an ancient tree. Solid with deep roots and far reaching branches. After recent events he could now see the rot thinly concealed beneath the surface. It sickened him, and it saddened him. The elder's he had loved and obeyed for a lifetime turned their backs on him.

Without his estates in Monts Des Maures he was left with few options and less money. Except for his estate in England which might as well have been on the moon, Cazador was homeless. He would either be forced back into working for La Compangnia or fighting as merceny. He knew his grandfather would retain him should he ask but Cazador wanted to be his own man, with the power to ignore the strings and machinations that always seemed to tug at his life. The anger born in his aunt's camp returned. He could already hear the whispers that he was just like his father. That at the first sign of adversity within the family he had fled. The pain of the thought stabbed him in a place years of armor couldn't protect. Suddenly his anger evaporated in a sea of self loathing. He'd told himself that he was riding ahead of the family to petition his grandfather. Now that this anger had faded, the excuse was thin. The fact that they had faced the ghul and he was honor and duty bound to report it made it little better.

With the once happy memory soured, Cazador remembered something else from their time as muscle for the tax collector. The lesson he and his cousins had learned that they all had tried to drown in silver and wine. To be a Moor in Europa was to inspire fear, disgust, suspicion or hostility among the ignorant and hateful. Even in their lord's livery, the peasants and barons us. That was the lesson. That was why what the Du Maurmont clan existed. Bound by blood they stood strong together. With the kings of Spain marching, a crusade to the northwest and now ghul taking towns, unity was survival. But unity and treachery couldn't sleep in the same bed.

They spent a lazy day by the river eating and resting before rounding up the animals and herding them into stable amidships. They returned to the fire as the sun began it's descent. Alcazar had set a leg of lamb on the coals earlier and it's aroma set Cazador's mouth to watering. All thoughts of food were dashed when Idris asked, "So after we see the Old Lion, then what?" Cazador sighed and the rumble in his stomach turned from hunger to anxiety. Itching at the top of his turban he gathered his thoughts. "Maybe England. I have an estate there and there will be good coin to be had with war brewing. But

I have a mind to pay one last visit to Le Cannet Des Maures first." Idris and the others looked thoughtful. "Not a bad plan." Idris replied stroking his beard eying Cazador like an instructor would a student giving a correct but incomplete answer. "After I have fulfilled my knight's service to King John, we can organize an expedition to the Sudan. English wool, and salt for gold. Use the money to raise some troops and... " Cazador's eyes went far away for a moment. So many of his steps had been ordered by others, his life dictated by the ebb and flow of trade, escort duty, and patrols through the Monts Des Maures. For the first time ever he realized that he had choices rather than orders. There was a moment of choking panic clawing at his throat. Cazador swallowed it down. An entire lifetime spent glorifying a clan that has rejected him. With his anger gone Cazador was left with the pain of the betrayal with full force. For many years he had wanted to raise a force and wage a crusade against the Ayyubids, but those were the goals and hatreds of his clan. All Cazador knew was combat, and commerce. There had always been plans to execute and goals to achieve. Now is life felt umoored and angst beat at his chest again.

Idris met his eye drawing Cazador back into the moment. "And what?" Cazador took a slow breath to steady his nerves. "Depends on how good the trading is." He finished lamely trying to smile but Idris had known him since boyhood providing a rough sort of love and a steady flow of support and wisdom. He could see the turmoil in Cazador's eyes. " I know that the events with that snake Richard and the elders chars your meat boy. No need for dancing around the fact and no amount of dead ghuls, trading voyages, or any other type of running will change it." Idris said rebuking Cazador as gently as he knew how. Idris ibn Idris was a man of stone and steel. He loved Cazador and his cousins like sons but he was first and foremost their weapons master, and these young men were weapons. Sometimes the rasp was needed to sharpen them.

Cazador sat up straight looking into Idris's smooth dark brown face. With its canted eyes, and high cheekbones set above a hawkish nose and grim slash of a mouth. If not for the nine wrinkles around his eyes, the old man seemed to not age. Cazador nodded, acknowledging his ancient teachers point. When he was sure the he had Cazador's attention. Idris spoke the truth as he saw it, tempered by fifty-five years of service to the Alfiere family beginning with the father of the Old Lion when he was just twelve dry seasons old. "Never in all my time among the clan have I seen what I witnessesed. The elders stripping you of you birthright and exiling you from the clan was wrong and shameful. You have a right to be angry." Cazador released a breath he didn't know he was holding. "Thank you." Idris inclined his head and continued. "The Bible says be angry but sin not. The minute your too angry to think clearly Caz you become stupid and stupidity is a sin." Cazador felt heat rise to his cheeks. But Idris ignored the angry flash in the young warriors eyes. "Think about it! Why? Why does Richard want Le Cannet Des Maures? Look past the money. Past your pride. does it mean? What's the end goal and how do you fit into it?" Cazador froze, eyes widening in shock.

Izan cleared his throat. "It is strange that we were framed and ambushed." Jaime snorted. "I think it's down right fucking odd they came right to the camp. If we were followed we would have known. It was a trick the entire time." Cazador nodded, then hawked and spat into the flames, his thoughts swirling like the spark and smoke. He was angry, but rather than the cold fury of Le Gel, Caz was inundated with needles of self recrimination."Its a coup." He muttered. "How!? Richard is a silver tongued jackal but he's only one man." Caleb of Dongla asked incredulous. Like most of the other men from the Christian kingdoms on the Red Sea coast he had come as part of the trade agreement between those kingdoms, The Knights of Saint Atillo, and the Du Maurmont families. Cazador shook his head. The lordship of Le Cannet Des Maures makes him singlehandedly one of the most powerful men in the clan. My grandfather is also my Lord Commander, bequeathing the seat to me is no threat to his power. But now all that's changed. Richard is no more a Knight of Saint Atillo than I am King of France."Cazador explained as his mind worked through the new landscape of clan politics.

Idris ibn Idris stood. "Its time you all learned the truth of things." He skewered each of them with his gaze as they sat by the fire settling in Cazador last. "This is the truth you would have received Caz, and although what's done is done you are the rightful lord of La Marche and Le Cannet Des Mauresand a true born son of the Alfiere family and it is your right to know."

Looking to the others he said "If you don't plan on giving your oath the Cazador go wait on the boat. This conversation is for the ears of the lord's of the Al Takruri line and their retainers." Idris' eyes drifted to Merfynn, Alberto, and Roland before roaming across the faces of Alcazar and Cazador's kinsman. "Since your all still here kneel and say the words with me." Cazador rose feeling distinctly uncomfortable. He'd always known the day might come when oaths would be exchanged but seeing his oldest and newest friends kneeling before him made him want to order Idris to stop. Cazador exhaled a shaky breath feeling as though a shield wall worth of men stood on his shoulders. There was a pregnant pause and a fat lump sat in his throat when Idris began. "I make known before these witnesses that I am the liege man of the Cazador Alfiere , Lord Captain of the Company of Saint Moses, and Lord of Moorhouse against every creature, living or dead, saving my allegiance to God the Creator. I become your Man from this day forth, for life, for member, and for worldly honor, and shall owe you Faith in war, peace, and trade and for and Lands, or castles that I hold of you." They intoned the words in unison, slowly, without stumbling or faltering.

When they were done, it was Cazador's turn to speak the words he had learned long ago. Suddenly the pressure lifted and his soul felt lighter as the time came for him to return the fidelity his companions had shown him.

"I Cazador Alfiere swear on the most holy body of the Lord and on the holy gospel that I will aid my liegemen in good faith, as their liege lord, against every creature, living or dead. Rise as my brothers in arms, friends and liege men." He embraced them all, nearly overwhelmed by the emotion of the moment. Idris even favored them with a rare smile. "Pedro, break out another one of those skins of hard cider you hoard and toast to your lord!" hes shouted to a raucous cheer.

When they had toasted and Idris sat them down and turned to Diallo. "You know the songs of Kusalia and Tin Hanan do you not. The reason the Hapulaaren and the Kel Tamsheq revere the Cross of Agadez?" Diallo nodded. "But do you know the tale of Pemba and Faro?" Diallo looked perplexed and the the blush on his sand colored skin was evident even in the firelight. Although Diallo was soft compared to Cazador, Izan, and the other sons of the Monts Des Maures, he was wise in the ways of people and well schooled in Pulaaku. "Enlighten me, teacher." He murmured as he bowed his head. Idris looked throughtful for a moment and then began. "Among the Mandenka it is known that the Creator Mangala formed the egg of the world and split it into twin parts that they might procreate. He then formed three others which became the elements and the pillars of creation. These The Creator folded within a hibiscus seed and these male and female pairs are know as the egg and placenta of the world. Within were a final two pair of twins one male and female who became the forebearers of people.

Within the number of the creations was one called Pemba, who craved dominance. In his bid to achieve it he tore free from the womb of creation prematurely, ripping free a part of the placenta as he plummeted through the heavens. This piece Pemba tore free became the earth." Idris paused to sip slowly from the skin of cider. "This reminds me of the beliefs of the Mandeans and Coptics." Alberto said, mirroring Cazador's own thoughts. Idris smacked his lips and smiled indulgently. "Nobody ever asks where the sons of Abraham were before Egypt." Idris said with a wink. Alberto who was better read than two monasteries of monks looked as though he would argue, but apparently thought better of it settling for a stiff nod. Cazador and his clanmates laughed knowing more than a few Jews from the M'Zab, Siwa, and Abbysinna with skins as dark as their own. When Pedro's twin Pablo said as much, Alberto's frown softened with thought. "My apologies he said pensively." Alberto of Coria was a man of rare and spectacular intellect and singular martial prowess but he was could hold his peace and admit his wrong. A rare combination of traits indeed.

Idris continued telling them of how Pemba finding the placenta turned earth barren tried to return to the womb from whence he descended, but could find it not. With his twin lost to him Pemba stole male seeds from the clavicle of holy Mangala. But when he planted them he found that only one would thrive. This seed had been in the blood of the placenta where it grew red and tainted because it was stolen. Indeed it was very much like the creation story of the Mandeans of Jordan who told of a prideful angel who tried to create his own heaven in imitation of The Most High and the flawed world they all inhabited was the result of this. Idris went on to teach them how Faro, the other twin took the form of twin fish and was sacrificed to atone for Pemba's perfidy. Legends say Faro fell to earth in sixty pieces that became trees. Eventually Mangala would restore Faro to life and a human form, allowing Faro to descend to earth in an ark made of Faro's placenta. Upon this ark came the ancestors of humans and the plants and animals of the world. Idris' measured tones continued. "The Hapulaaren beliefs were similar before Islam. Rather than placenta, the world was forged from a drop of milk. Then God who they called Dondari formed earth that became iron. The iron begat fire, which begat water that sired air. Dondari came again to create man from the five elements, and when man grew too haughty he punished them with blindness that defeated them. Then Dondari sent sleep to smite blindness and worry to strike down the pride of sleep. When worry became overmighty Dondari the fearless one eventually sent death. But in victory, death succumbed to insufferable pride. Seeing this Dondari came again as Gueno the Eternal One who defeated death. Gueno also set forth the great serpent Caanaba. The same serpent is called Nininanka by the Mande which might be familiar as not so dissimilar to the knowledge bestowing serpent of Bible." He went on to tell them of Sile Sadio, called Solomon and taught them of Njeddo Dewal, who learned the seven magical sounds from the six points of space who was sent to test and punish humans. Idris watched as each of the men before him digested the information.

After a time Cazador look at Idris and asked, "What does the knowledge of the ancestors have to do with me our the family?" Something he couldn't define, danced in Idris' eyes. "Understand this my lord and all you gathered here. The priests, and clerics will tell you that the ancient faiths of the Sudan are pagan idolators." Idris spat into the flames face contorted in anger. Eyes distant relieving memories likely older than Cazador's father. "I tell you they are not. All the dieties are emanations of the One Supreme creator. They see the Lareej or the Suudiibe, and get confused. As good Christians of the Most Holy Church we know that there is God, Christ, and the saints that intercede on our behalf we revere Solomon, John the Baptist, Moses, and the prophets." All the men around the fire nodded. "How is it different then in the Sudan where God no matter what name he is called in that tongue is supreme and the ancestors or saints work miracles and intercede on their behalf?" When no man could find an answer, he continued." I teach you these things because there are more truths than those you are readily taught. I teach you these things so you can understand your place in this world and your history. You know of The Fall and The Watchers because these things are taught to you by the scholars the clan patronizes. But you need to understand what I am telling you to understand who you are and what it truly means to be an Al Takruri or an Alfiere . The true name of your family has never been Al Takruri. Your ancestor is Sile Sadio, Solomon the first silatigi." Cazador's eyes widened with wonder, until his rational mind asserted himself. "Aye and my ancestor is Tyr the heathen war god of the northmen!" Sniggered Roland. Merfynn smiled, even his forefathers were said to be sired by Belli Mawr. Kings and princes, Cazador could accept. But the great sage himself? He had never know Idris to lie, or exaggerate and that alone gave him pause.

Idris grinned wolfishly at the Norman blooded Italian knight. "When the Watchers corrupted humans and mated among us many things occured. The children of Samyaza, or the Suudiibe and the Djinn and the servants of the Nameless one those races that survived the great flood were only granted dominion in the places that sheltered them. They have no power over humans unless we are in their domain, or it is granted to them. The Creator charged them as custodians and guardians of nature, and they carry a mastery over the elements. Despite their great power they can only influence our world from the shadows. Yet even from the shadows many humans were seduced into their worship. Their seed is spread far and they held great power until Christ. So, it's possible. But I've see you fight, so perhaps not." said the grizzled Almogovar with a crooked smile and everyone but Idris and Roland let forth a hearty laugh.

When the laughter died down Idris continued. "As son's and vassals of the Alfiere line it is your lineage and duty to stand against the darkness. Your ancestors have fought against more than the forces of men in this world since the time of Sile Sadio. No amount of jokes or disbelief will change this truth." The hard glare on the old man's face brooked no argument. "An attack on the Alfiere 's and the Du Maurmonts is never simple. For we strive not against flesh and blood, but against principalities, against powers, against the rulers of the darkness of this world, and against spiritual wickedness in high places." Idris quoted from Scripture. "The ancestors came to this land to beat back those forces and establish a bulwark against the storm to come. Your lineage comes with ancient responsibility to uphold righteousness in this world and there is power in your blood that other men would kill to possess."

Cazador absorbed this, and looked to his kinsman to ascertain their thoughts from their faces. As sons of the Alfiere and the other cadet houses they had always known they descended from a royal line, but this was something altogether different. "In some ways I'm confused but in other ways things make far more sense," muttered Jaime. "So this would mean the famed mines of Solomon lay not in Abysinnia or Nubia, but perhaps Bambouk or even Bono." Said the ever thoughtful Izan. Idris shrugged. "If I knew I wouldn't be here with you lot." Jaime snorted. "Bugger that. Now I know why there is never any end to the damn woodwose! I had always thought the Grimauds or other rivals bribed them into their constant attacks but now I know they hate us for ancestral reasons. Fucking aggravating that!" Pedro loosed a low whistle of agreement. All but the new men understood that the Du Maurmont communes were a favored target of the wildmen. Descended from the giants of old, woodwose or wildman were known servants of evil and hated Christ and the Prophet with equal measure but seemed to make war upon the Du

Maurmonts with religious fervor. Cazador felt his heart race. Suddenly the ghul taking a town frequented by La Compangnie and Knights of Saint Atillo took on a far more sinister aspect. As did his betrayal and banishment.

That night they slept on the boat with the animals. It was after all warded and Cazador felt particularly exposed. As the oathsworn lord of all present not a soul argued with him and he doubted they would anyway. Tomorrow they would sail on to somewhere they could sell the boat and travel the rest of the way to Bobastro overland. He had questions for his grandfather. So many his tired mind swirled with them making sleep elusive. When he was sure all the others were asleep he began to pray. The oaths of his kin and newfound friends say heavily upon him. The funny thing was rather than feeling as though they were a yoke about his shoulders, the oaths felt rather like a set a armor crafted with such love and beauty it would be a crime to mar. Caz was not only responsible for their lives but their fortunes. Now he felt as though they had been drawn into something nobody but his grandfather might fully understand. With a single conversation all of his goals and plans had been shaken. He needed more information, he needed guidance, and he needed strength. So with his face pressed to the wooden boards he prayed.

Chapter 9: Great Expectations

Oberon had spent the better part of an hour in stunned silence. Thousands of years of tradition turned on its head. From time immemorial each leader of a Samyazan Enclave was independent both militarily and politically, subject only to the high king in war and one in twenty in trade. With the high kings long dust, each enclave had become ever more autonomous. The only unifying force was the church who brokered borders, trade agreements, and marriages. Now with the advent of the First Middle Earth Crusade the private hosts of each enclave were disbanded. The rulers of each independent enclave would have their rights curtailed by a new governing body called The One Hundred. Formed of the one hundred poorest folk from each enclave to be replaced by a new one hundred each year. The One Hundred were empowered to veto the decisions of their ruler, backed by the full power of the Church of Inner Earth and the newly minted Host of the Seelie Court. Each enclave's One Hundred elected a Speaker who would reside at the Seelie Court as a member of the Symposium. Each ruler was to provide tribute every three moons.

These taxes were raised to support the war host and to support any widows, orphans, or any other collateral it created. It was to be an entirely mixed force. Elves, dwarves, Fae, Mouros, Encantados, and even the Djinn would serve side by side.

The fae, riders of moose, bear and dire wolves would form the heavy calvary units. The dwarves with their stocky frames and unparalleled swordcraft and heavy armor formed the shock infantry alongside the warwise Mouros. The

Encantado would serve at sea as sailors and marines at sea, and on land as light infantry with their nets, spears, and hatchets. The Djinn would serve as scouts, spies, and archers. This left the elves as the grunts of the army. The griffons their mightiest weapon of war were taken from them. Oberon swore it was the jealousy of the light elves that made it so. The Ljósálfar of the Seelie Court had surrendered their dragons long ago. Thus grounded this was likely their way seeking the same fate for their Ēlifi cousins. The Great Teacher had decreed in her wisdom that they were a weapon best kept hidden at home until an hour of great need. Thus the elves held the role of spear pushers, sword and board battlers, and crossbow shooters, mounted infantry the backbone of the army. Last were the paladins. They were brothers and sisters of the church skilled in the manipulation of mana and weapons serving as the officer corps.

The basic unit of the military was called an agema and was twenty four fighters strong, four from each of the six races centered around a paladin and his squire who served as the spiritual and military leaders of the unit. As an ordained royal and blooded veteran Oberon was anointed a paladinship and thus qualified to be an officer. Four agemas made a lochos of around a hundred fighters led by a paladin called a lochagos. Two lochos made a company. Five companies begat chiliarchy led by a paladin called a chilliarch. Chilliarchies were grouped into bunches of five called taxiarchiai and commanded by a taxiarch paladin. Taxiarchs answered to a strategos who commanded a total of five taxiarchiai. As a rule the royalty of the enclaves were only allowed to the rank of taxiarch as the ranks of the strategoi were reserved for the twenty five best living military commanders still capable of combat. They would serve under five polemarchs who were the the wisest and most successful military leaders of all the Samyazans.

The beauty of it was that Oberon's military expenditures would be negligible compared to what they had been. Instead expenses would be shared by every Samyazan enclave. Each would have the means to defend themselves independently and be able to rely of the full might Army of the Seelie Court for support in times if need. Hundreds upon hundreds of years of fueds, raids, battles, wars, and strife wiped away. Enclave and tribal lines banished. The dwarves of Atlas's Might would serve beside Ljósálfar of Hugënhall. The warriors of Penume's Reach would march beside the Fae of Gurio Lamanna in Italia. It was unnatural and Oberon thought that even if it could be glorious for a time, it would all come to tears in the end.

The Megalos Didáskalos had implored them to look the the example of the Iska, the mixed blood Samyazans. Reviled by their full-blooded parents they were found a way to carve out a life on the fringes of Samyazan society. The law stated that a full blood parent of an Iska child must rear it to the cusp of adulthood before initiation into the higher mysteries when they would be turned away as outlaws. With no others to turn to the Iska banded together and the communities of outcasts grew from bands of raiders to a tribe of warrior traders with enclaves all their own carved from the blood of servants of the Nameless and Samyazans alike. When the Ljósálfar waged their war of conquest the Iska had been the first to meet them and during the Harrowing they had fought well and were honored by Christ becoming the early backbone of the church and it's most ardent supporters. The Megalos Didáskalos believed that if the unwanted among could find strength in unity so could the rest of Samyazans.

It all sounded good but Oberon knew one didn't erase thousands of years of habits. With these thoughts and more swirling in his head he lead his taxiarchiai through the deep ways riding on horseback like a peasant. As a newly minted Taxiarch with an honor guard of a thousand elves from Penume's Reach to augment his command, Oberon's first mission was to make contact with the Cynocephali, the dog men. Their ilk was called the Daji, or the wild and like the free woodwose the Cynocephali were vassals to none and potential enemies of all. Bred before the flood from dogs and woodwose as a tool for a nephilim warlord to search and destroy the human armies of his foe's, they were savage, industrious and obedient to their chosen pack leader.

Some had followed Yeshua in the Harrowing and even now lived among the

Iska, but others lived in caves studding the mountainous area middle earth called the Carpathians and the Hindu Kush where they mated with wolves and reveled in barbarity creating kin wilder and more savage yet. Oberon however was being sent to engage them. In the past they often served Samayazan enclaves as mercenaries, in a formula that while ritualized, was still primal. A lord, lady or officer would make the traditional offering of cattle speak his intention and allow the pack leader to sniff his or her scent. One of the cattle would be butchered and the pack leader would be served the beasts heart and liver. If the pack leader accepted the offering the a deal was struck. If it was rejected sometimes the the pack leader's next meal would be the throat of the unfortunate server.

Oberon felt a familiar tension settle across his shoulders. He along with other noble Samyazan taxiarchs would be meeting with various Daji leaders carrying the words of the Megalos Didáskalos and the Seelie Court. The clans of the Daji would be full members of the Seelie Court with all the rights and responsibilities due Samyaza's children. The Cynocephali would be given easy access to the one thing the rest of the Samyazans had that they valued food.

The Seelie Court had seen Oberon taxiarchiai well provisioned for their months long journey. He did his best not to seethe over being grounded, and the beauty of the deep ways proved ample distraction. Cascading waterfalls plummeted from jeweled precipices to pummel ponds untouched by sunlight. Forests of limestone columns hung with cave nettle stretched to the abyss or valleys of cave grass that were actually tiny tubular fungi that nourished Samyazan livestock. From the ground he was getting to explore Inner Earth in a new way. With each passing mile Oberon gained a new appreciation of his homeland, struck by the thought of how sad it would make him to never return.

Hours of interminable speeches during the council had revealed one elemental truth. The forces of the Nameless were moving. Their agents were embedded in the kingdoms of man, manipulating human events and corrupting the faith. If allowed to continue unchecked the Nameless would weaponize the humans against them. The eons old balance was in danger meaning the Samyazans could no longer huddle against the night in their fastnesses. If the humans were overcome then the Samyazans too would face slavery or extinction. When Oberon had cast his vote it had been simple. The choice had been between fighting the coming war on middle earth or at the gates of Penume's Reach and he knew which option he vastly preferred. The return of a unified Seelie Court might have meant a minor reduction in power but it also meant stable trade, supply lines, and an end to the infighting. With their forces united the bulk of their power could be concentrated on holding the borders against the servants of the Nameless. Only the forces of one polemarch would march against humanity while the others while the others would form a wall of flesh, bone, and magic against the T'efa, the lost who served the Nameless. That's why Oberon and the other royal taxiarchs had become recruiters.

His second Fahreed, high lord of Bimmah's Gate rode beside him. Sensing the scrutiny of his commander he favored Oberon with a feline grin,his cat like eyes dancing with mirth. As the second most seasoned warrior in the command unit his place was unchallenged. "This is my first time traveling the deep ways. I had feared I would find it oppressive, but such beautiful humbles me. Your home is a wonderful place." Oberon beamed. "Surely the palaces of the djinn of Upper Earth are a wonder beyond wonders." Fahreed shrugged. Like all soldiers of Seelie Court he bore a cloth of silver tabard blazoned with falling stars in vert on the chest. Unlike Oberon or the others he bore no metal armor opting for a gambeson of many layers fine silk stiffened with dragonbone plates."No artisan djinn or otherwise could compete with El, my friend." he replied. A recurve bow of the dragonbone sat unstrung across his saddle. Arrows tipped with diamond chips filled no less than four quivers. After weeks of drill with his taxiarchiai Oberon had become well aquatinted with his second's horrifying skill. In his human form Fahreed looked much like any other man if one ignored his cats eyes and legs. He was graceful as a breeze and deadly as poison but he would be wasted as a front line soldier. Fahreed's talents lay in his how and capabilities as a scout, archer and spy. Unlike their associate Minerva.

The snort of the mighty war moose announced the presence of the fae cataphract. Her gossamer wings seemed at odds with the gleaming solidity of her orichalum lamellar hauberk glinting from under her tabard in the light of the shining lance she effortlessly held aloft. The fae tribes were wild, and passionate to the point of seeming fickle. Minerva seemed little different and always spoke her mind. "We've been marching for six stades lord taxiarch," she grunted in greeting. " It's been a good days tread, and I've had to stop Zeus here from eating the foot soldiers for the last six stadia." As if to illustrate his rider's point the fat war moose moved to nip Oberon's stallion. Minerva hauled on the reins savagely. "See what I mean." Oberon nodded. Six stades was over one hundred and eleven Roman miles. "Signal the halt he said spying a likely site to camp. A great gash high above leaked light from middle earth and water to form a rill of sweet smelling purplish grass that only thrived in areas such as this, called a venting. It was too good a camp to pass up and Oberon gave the order, eliciting a grunt of approval from war moose and rider.

Oberon watched the marching camp unfold. With the new treaties of the Seelie Court in place there was really no need for a ditch, palisade and pickets, but practice made perfect. Each agema with the exception of Oberon's command agema spread out forming a ring around the command group. Suddenly Oberon could feel the air around him take on a frenetic charge as the Samyazans of his taxiarchiai raised their channels and accessed their mana. Like each member of his command Oberon held the image of what they were creating in his mind and together they sang. Notes without words filled the air with the rumble of earth and roar of stone as the a ditch ate away at the ground in a perfect circle as cylindrical pillars of stone shot thirty feet in the sky. Behind the pillars a platform rose as though racing with the over two hundred long house style structures complete with lean to's for the animals of each agema. In the center of the camp an inner round rose providing a place of refuge in the event of the camp being overrun. Task complete the exhausted closing of channels made the air seem to pop. For what they had accomplished in moments, the drain on the collective manna seemed negligble t, but it still didn't make Oberon and the rest of the Samyazans any less tired.

Soon campstoves filled the air with a different sort of magic as the smells of charcoal and cooking food filled the enclosure. The agemas on first watch tossed good natured insults to their comrades as they took their places along the palisade or filed through the gates for patrol. Oberon hadn't been on a proper campaign since he'd been a squire for his father and bloodied his mace on Ljósálfar raiders that had spent generations haunting the deep border woods of Penume's Reach. Then, they'd been home in a fortnight Oberon would be lucky to reach his destination in that time. Over twenty thousand Roman miles from the Seelie Court to the completion of their journey. With his Taxiarchiai augmented by the dog men he would join in the first assault on middle earth.

With the camp complete Oberon gave a nod to his second. "My lord of Bimmah's Gate your have the camp." Next Oberon gave his squire a distant cousin from the west called Osric instructions to see to his mount and entered his long house. Oberon laid out his bedroll, suddenly exhausted by the enormity of his task.

* * *

She liked this body. The flesh of the young Nubian was young, strong and beautiful with skin the color of gold and clay that embraced the sun rather than cowered before it. The full thighs flaring hips and buttocks were a delight as were the heavy breasts on her chest. So unlike her original tall and willowy body bred on the shores of the Danube. She was being shipped to convent in France. An utter waste in Marcela's opinion. Her name had been Marwah and she was inquisitive and wide open in the way of the young. For all that she was in the full blush of womanhood she was sheltered, therefore in many ways still a girl. Her sharp mind and even sharper imagination had made it all to easy for Marcela to seduce her. In the end Marwah had required very little effort to take. She had been drawn to the reliquary holding Marcela's mortal remains almost from the moment her family had joined the caravan. It had started in the girl's dreams. Marcela visiting her night after night as she slept. It began simply, Marcela had asked questions, listened and learned. Marwah was from Jebel Adda and was determined to see the world and take pilgrimage before entering her holy orders. She filled the young woman's head with many ideas. Power, freedom and independence. Concepts the mortal little understood beyond the pursuit of her own desires. Where the girl had offered curiosity, Marcella had offered options. It had taken some time, but three weeks travel outside Cordoba Marcella made her move. Revealing herself as the spirit of the lady saint carried by the fat merchant in their caravan. She told Marwah that she had chosen her for great things in service to a higher power. Then she told her exactly what to do and say to receive the blessing of. The Lady of the Desert. *What girl wouldn't want to touch the sacred remains of a female saint?* That was precisely what girl had told the merchant and the guard, echoing Marcella's words perfectly. When the girl opened the reliquary Marcella was free from her prison for the first time in generations. One moment there were the finely powdered bones of a saint in a jewel studded reliquary, the next a sandstorm erupted swirling with such speed and violence that the curious young woman fell back in dismay and the two men guarding the tent fled in terror as Marcella forced her way inside the girl. Marwah's soul was a bright and vibrant thing. A thing Marcella subsumed as she possessed her body.

Glorying in the swaying stride of the ripe young body, tasting the air for the first time in centuries reminded Marcela how far she had come. Long ago in she had been simply the lady of villa built around an oasis in the hinterland of Mauretania Caesariensis. Marcela had watched the Roman world collapsed around her and did what any sensible initiate of the mysteries would. She set about making pacts with the lares of the land. Pacts that would give her the power to allow her to keep her people safe. Favor, so that what they had built would flourish. Marcela had learned how to commune with the spirits at her mother's knee and despite years among Christians she had not forgotten. The power she had gained was remarkable. Over the years children she had bounced on her lap became grandparents and withered elders, and but she'd remained ageless, blessed by the spirits of the land. The people whispered of her, but with tones of reverence. She was a part of them. A part of the land. They called her Protectress, The Mother of the Oasis. The Domina, Oracle of the Lares. Their love was shown with offerings and libations.

Marcela's original mortal form had been turned to dust a thousand years ago. But the beauty of working the mysteries was that death became a minor inconvenience. That is, if a soul made the proper deals. As time passed she had been revered, a desert mother, a goddess in her own right. Her mana work had sustained a vibrant community where only sand and scorpions should have thrived. Then had come the Lamentation. The Conqueror had cast down pantheons of beings greater than she, and as her lot had been cast with Nox, her star had fallen with the rest of her ilk. She had languished in obscurity, starved of the reverence and worship that fueled her mana. A harrowing time where Marcela had hovered dangerously close to dissolution. It was a pain like no other.

With a sigh and a shudder Marcela allowed herself to remember. Even being torn from her mortal frame had not hurt as much. She would never forget how the bastard raiders had drained her of manna, doused her in iron dust and slit her throat before throwing her body into the oasis wrapped in iron chains. Little did they know who Marcela was or that she had done the blood rites required to make the pact with Samael, the angel of death. She was killed but did not die. Marcela awoke as a revenant, abeing neither alive nor dead, a bestrider of the veil. She was no longer fully of the flesh, but a craver of it still. As she'd floated in the oasis that had sustained her and her people for so long, she knew instinctivly that manna could sustain her now, but no. She'd needed something more visceral. It had been a time of vengeance and she chose to be sustained by blood.

Once a supplicant of them, now Marcela was a lares in her own right, becoming one with the spirits of the place she called home. Like her they had been angry and they too cried for vengeance. *They too reached out for blood.* Marcella had subsumed them all and she could feel the spirits inside her like babes in the womb. She would be their instrument. Imbued with their strength she had shattered the chains, burning her hands on the iron the process. The pain has been exquisite, pushing her once mortal mind to the brink of insanity. It was just as well, insanity suited her purposes just fine. Free of the chains Marcella climbed from the water and stalked into the night. Like a lioness she hunted, devouring the men that had pillaged her home eating their livers, making a red ruin. First she used her bare hands to snap unsuspecting necks before tearing flesh and rend bones. With red stained hands she picked up a bronze hilted sword from among the fallen and embracing her fury she became a storm. Flush with victory and drunk on looted wine the attackers of her village slumbered or caroused oblivious to the terror that had come for vengeance. Marcela brought them blood and horror killing them and devoured their souls like rare and succulent fruit.

So it has been and so it would be again. Marcella thought as she walked into the night nestled in the body of the caravan girl. Even after so many years, even draped in the skin of a new body, the movements violence and bloodshed were as familiar to Marcella as breathing. The merchants guard poked his head back into the tent. The swarthy Arab dark brown eyes were wide and liquid below his turban. Marcela reached out and snatched his beard pulling his chin up as her stiffened fingers found his throat. The cartilage collapsed and the man fell gasping for air that would never come. Marcela stepped over the dying body pausing only to draw his sword from his sheath. When the portly merchant saw her, his face went through an entire range of emotions. First relief, then confusion, and finally fear. He stared at the naked sword in her hand and then the body of his guard. He tried to speak but what ever he said was lost when the blade in Marcela's hand flashed and sent his head leaping from his shoulders. His body fell and Marcela walked to the next fire blood dripping from her stolen blade. She butchered her way through the camp until the fools stopped fighting and started cowering before her. The last were caravan guards, a motley mongrel crew of Sudanese, Amazaigh, Arabs, and a few Feringee renegades. Nine in total, and to Marcela's endless delight, all were ghul or practicioners of the dark arts.

Marcella smiled at the memory. In the beautiful girls body she had led them in taking a small town by the river, eating or turning it's inhabitants and visitors, creating a small army of ghul. It had been working perfectly until they had admitted the party under the Thebeai banner, Marcella had come to know as Knights of Saint Atillo. They had butchered her ghul and burned her town.

Naham, her ghul captain wanted to pursue them but Marcella had stayed his hand. She had watched the battle unfold and saw the potency of their protection, and although the sight of her glorious new demense in ruins angered her, Marcela was loath to waste the resources she had left. Still, she felt drawn to these men and wondered what she might accomplish if she were to turn them to her cause. She set a familiar to follow them, if an opportunity for vengeance arose. She would take it.

Chapter 10: Road to Bobastro

I dris watched his newly sworn lord as they prepared for the days sailing. Cazador had the best of the Old Lion in him and with a certain fatalistic belligerence that came from his mother's folk. Only time would tell whether or not he would crack under the weight of his bloodline. Too many of the men of the Alfiere line were great warriors, and builders, as well as astute businessman, but they were not renowned for their leadership. Instead they preferred quieter lives. Cazador born in a far off land amongst a strange people had a star that shone brightly, in a firmament of strong sons. Idris had trained them all, as he had their fathers before them. Officially he had retired years ago, but now he had sworn a new oath binding himself once again to the heirs of Sile Sadio. Idris knew it wasn't his fate to die a farmer or tavern keep. Instead he would keep an eye on the Old Lion's investment.

As the only one with any real experience of boats, and thereby the pilot and skipper. Content to watch his young charges prepare the boat to leave, Idris thought about his route. Sailing the boat all the way to Nuevo Bobastro would be impossible, but he could get them as close as Badolatosa. From there it would only be a few days ride to their destination. Briefly Idris wondered what Cazador might do after seeing his grandfather. He had said precious little about going on Crusade in Outremer which was more that fine with Idris. He'd been on more than one crusade and saw the darkness that the pursuit of the Holy Land pulled from men's souls.

Outwardly Idris' hawkish glare swept the rich farm where they had camped.

Neat rows of barley waved in the morning breeze burnished gold by the rising sun. On the other bank fat melons bent the supports that held their vines. In his minds eye Idris saw starving men tearing horses apart to dine on raw flew. Bloated bodies launched from engines, and burning belfries disgorging panicked soldiers. Atrocity under the banner of God. Turning his gaze to the group of young men under his care, Idris grunted and spat into the Genil. Despite his youth Caz had seen much ugliness. From his first campaign in France to the sack of Constantinople, Idris couldn't blame him for being jaded. Somehow he managed to still hold some of the curious and intelligent boy that had run through Bobastro. There was a strength and faithfulness there that Caz couldn't even see in himself and Idris would be damned to see that snuffed out like it had been in his father before him.

Cazador would draw steel on any man who said i,t but he was achingly like Guillaume. Idris knew his mother saw it too, which is why she had been so hard on the boy. She had done her best to work the impurities from the iron and now that the boy was a man, the steel was good. Linda and Miryam had cornered him and told Idris in no uncertain terms that he would attached himself to Cazador's retinue and look after him and their nephews as well. Cazador had a legendary temper that had gotten him in trouble as a youth, Idris had been around long enough to know that his true work wasn't in keeping the young man safe. Lord knew there was no separating an Al Takruri from a fight no matter what name they called themselves by. No, his work would be in not letting bitterness ruin the temper, and maybe just maybe Caz could be forged into his destiny. Idris spat again resisting the urge to grin, now he was starting to sound like Hamza. He would talk to the Old Lion when they arrived at Nuevo Bobastro. Looking toward the river Idris began snapping off orders, instructing a bickering Pedro and Pablo on how to set the sail. Cazador and the others took their places at the oars and Idris took the tiller in hand. Life is like this river. The old Almogovar thought. The current is inexorable, but with the right adjustments you can get where you need to be. As long as your willing to work.

* * *

Izan sat pondering the events of the past few days. When they were young, their futures had seemed so set. War and glory. Fat manors to retire on with good hunting and bandits for diversion. Things had been so clear cut. Now, their future was muddy like the river that carried them. Izan was surprised he didn't mind. He was sworn to Caz now, and leadership suited his cousin even if he didn't see it. Like the Old Lion Caz was bold and possessed of a deep cunning. The combination could make for greatness but it could just as well leave a man paralyzed.

He looked across to where Cazador pulled his oar to the cadence Idris pounded with his spear. Catching his cousin's eye he grinned. "Having fun yet Caz?" His kinsman barked a laugh. The dark expression that had clouded his visage fading. "With you ugly sods there's naught but fun to be had." Izans broad mahogany features widened further as he laughed. "Hear that lads we should have stayed with La Compangnie, our leige finds us offensive to look upon!" Izan shouted voice laced with mock hurt.

Roland snorted. "I don't know about you lads but the maids tell me I'm as fine as baby's hair." He said preening. "Aye you mean smell like shit from a baby's ass surely..." Cazador said to a chorus of laughter. Roland flushed slightly but his blue eyes sparkled. "I see now why your elders were so keen to banish you." For a moment the only sound was the thump of Idris' spear and the churn of the oars. "Mayhaps your right sir Roland." Cazador said. His tone was light, yet dangerous in a way that sent a momentary shiver along the spine of everyone listening, except for perhaps Idris. "Yet it matters not because I'm better looking than you." The laughter returned as the river galley glided of the Genil.

* * *

Alberto was enjoying his time with Cazador and the others. The men of the du Maurmont clan were well educated, cultured, and fought like demons. They made for excellent company. They were curiously pious, yet irrepressibly irreverent. All in all they behaved in a way that made Alberto comfortable with choosing to swear to Cazador's service. He had served in the Holy Land and beyond as a the guardian of a missionary who's goal was to spread the faith in the east and he had been as far as the lands of Samarkand in the Khwarezmian Empire. Traveling je had seen and learned many things, meeting people from all walks of life and exposing himself to strange and foreign cultures. It had been humbling experience that shattered the view of the world his family's priest had taught him. Still filled with the fervor of faith, Alberto had signed up to fight in the Abesingian Crusade. It was there after the siege of Lavuar amid the screams of hundreds of burning Cathars that his faith had died. His choice to go on Camino and had been born from his desire to rediscover that faith. An experiment of sorts. If a journey east and fighting a crusade in the west had purged him of his faith, maybe a journey west and a Crusade in the east would reverse his affliction. To his mind it was simple enough. He had hoped to meet other knights or at least fighters along the way that might join him. After witnessing the events in the du Maurmont camp, his oath, and Cazador's words, he thought that maybe he had found fellow crusaders as trips to the Holy Land to kill Saracens seemed something of a family tradition. He was certain to see Outremer or at least Egypt again from how Cazador spoke.

He was less certain of his new lord's supposed ancestry. Idris ibn Idris didn't strike him as a man prone to fanciful tales, but descent from Solomon seemed to stretch Alberto's expanded imagination. If not for the glow and hum from the charms the Du Maurmonts wore as they fought the ghouls Alberto would have dismissed it all out of hand. He had seen all manner of charm and trinket from holy relics to humble clay tablets, and never saw any do that. It stirred the ashes of his dying faith and so, he'd given Cazador his oath, if for nothing else than the desire to know more.

They had docked in a town called Badolasta. A collection of cobbled streets and white washed buildings that seemed to glow in the morning sun. During the time of Cesar it was known as Vadus Latus, and the elder statesman of there merry band had piloted them with expert efficiency. From what Alberto could see the convivencia or coexistence was alive and well. In the market he could see belled Jews, haggling with olive skinned Christian merchants in iron crosses and burnt umber toned Moors from the Sudan. Tawny Saracens sipped tea outside of a tiny shop as they played chatrang. Berthed nearby was a smaller ship so laden with barrels and crates it had less than a handspan of freeboard.

Cazador manhandled the gangplank into place and strode to the jetty bearing a pack of fresh clothes. He knew that Badolatosa had a well run bathhouse and although they would be riding hard he wanted to be clean. "Come we smell like Feringees!" He said marching across towards the square. Merfynn and Roland groaned and Alberto sniggered. His ancestors had lived under Mohmedan rule and had also picked up the penchant for regular bathing. It was decidedly unchristian as not only was it sinful but bathing was said to open the pores and allow bad airs to invade the body.

Alberto's snigger turned to a full blown laugh. Alberto knew wounds were less likely to fester when clean clothes and clean bodies. Cazador turned, the metal plates stitched to his jazerant flashing in the sun. Although he was veiled the others could see the mirth dancing in his eyes. "You are all my men," Cazador said grandly. "I'll not have you dying of filth. Nor I from your smell! So consider this an order!" The Lord Captain of Order of Saint Moses said with a chuckle. Alcazar loomed over both men clapping his meaty hands on Roland and Merfynn's shoulders pushing them along. "Come come, I promise no harm will befall you. If Caz can lead us in battle, I'm quite sure you lot will survive a real bath."

An hour later they were all clean and dressed in fresh clothes. Cazador had purchased long sleeved knee length tunics of grey linen, loose indigo pantaloons, and tall riding boots for each of them. Over the kaftans they each wore black quilted sleeveless gambesons made from layers of silk a linen. Their heads were adorned in cotton backed maille coiffes covered with black wraps. Cazador was dressed similarly with only small shows of status to the well trained eye. The elaborate embroidery around the cuffs of his tunic, the jet and amethyst signet ring he bore on the pinky of his left hand, and sword belt of silver plaques cinching the fresh sleeveless gambeson decorated in the Sudanese style with fine stitch work matching the tunic around the collar and hems. Cazador swaggered on, one hand on the hilt of his wootz steel sword he wore at his waist instead of in a baldric like his forebears.

They returned to the jetty where the final items from the ship beside their own had finally unloaded by the exhausted looking workers and a wealthy looking man in fine silk robes embroidered with flowers. He spoke to another man with the bandy legged stance of a life long sailor. After retrieving their horses and pack animals from the ship, Cazador had a short conversation with Diallo who went promptly to the well dressed man.

Drawing himself up to his full height and pulling his most charming smile Diallo hailed the rich man. "Greetings," he said performing an elegant salaam. "I am Diallo, humble djali to the Faris Sayaad ibn Wilayam, ibn Hamza Al Takruri. My lord must journey overland for a time and fears our fine rivercraft would suite you far better than him. He would be persuaded to part with it for three hundred gold dinar." Merfynn frowned wondering what was going on. Diallo had spoken in flawless Arabic and while he had Latin, Spanish, French, and even Greek he had no ken of the tongue of the Mohmedans. He noticed Roland smiling appreciatively. "What'd did he say?" Roland leaned close, "A thousand pounds for the boat." He whispered. It was a goodly sum. It was a fine boat, and Merfynn was intrigued.

The merchant bowed "I am Suliman

Ibn Tariq Ibn Farheed. Humble merchant and seller of fine ceramics livestock, leather, and and tin. This is my kinsman and business partner Sharif ibn Zayid ibn Farheed." Both men returned Diallo's salaam. The family resemblance was striking. They bore the same dark eyes, prominent nose, curly hair, and beard. Sharif's sun darkened complexion and bowlegged stance gave him away as a the true sailor of the two. He gazed at their boat hungrily. "Indeed your craft is a fine specimen but were I to part with such a sum my kinsman and I would be beggars. I can do no more than two hundred dinars even for a craft as fine as this. "

Diallo looked crestfallen. "Ahh gentleman, it saddens me, I can only imagine what two boats to ply your trade along the rivers of Al Andalus would do for your profits. Two boats could soon become ten, and that ten, a score and soon the two of you would be merchant princes. But alas it's not to be. My lord Sayaad would feel slighted and might cast me out or kill me were I to part with this fine vessel that skims the river like a leaf yet, is steady like a mountain that could float in a puddle for less than two hundred and seventy dinars." He bowed low. "Good day gentlemen, it was a pleasure to make your acquaintance." Diallo turned to leave and the Ibn Farheed's bickered for a moment, Sharif gesturing to a tightly wrapped bundle at the aft. "Please wait!" Suliman shouted. Diallo froze and turned. "Yes?" Suliman cleared his throat and smoothed his colorful robes with jeweled fingers. He cast a baleful glare at Sharif before smiling at Diallo. "We can do two hundred and fifty gold dinars and we have some leather cuirasses from Morocco. Very fine. Thick and well baked, stiff yet supple enough to flex. I will part with sixty five of them and two maille shirts from Algiers." Suliman's tongue darted out to wet his lips as his eyes flitted from Diallo to Cazador and back.

Cazador sat his horse face veiled his eyes simultaneously conveying boredom and a calculating coldness. They were a party of armed men and well mounted. It would be all to easy to rob the man and ride off. With a slight nod Cazador acknowledged the deal. Suliman handed Diallo a heavy purse, and instructed his workers to transfer the goods. When the pack animals were loaded, Cazador led them from Badolatosa heading east with banter and good cheer.

* * *

They had ridden through the morning into the afternoon and took a break before taking a break to rest the horses. "You see the two hills in the distance there?" Cazador asked as he sat with Alberto and Merfynn. Following the line of his fingers west both men nodded. "Caesar fought and killed Pompey son of Pompey not far from there. We will cut south past those hills and pass it by less than two miles." Merfynn's eyes lit with wonder and Alberto looked thoughtful. "I wonder what it would have been like to fight in the legions of the Romans. When peons were supreme and foot soldiers conquered the world. If not for the twenty five year term of service I think I would have joined on." Cazador murmured. Alberto looked scandalized. "You wouldn't have wanted to ride among the equities?" Cazador shook his head. "I can ride, and maybe even kill on horseback, but I'm no cavalryman. Not truly. Not like Maurice, or Roland here. No for me there is nothing like the ground beneath my feet when steel and blood fill the air. Merfynn nodded emphatically. "Damn horse might pick a time to have a mind of its own at the wrong time." Merfynn agreed conspiratorially. "I hadn't thought about that part." Alberto said staring at the horse he'd been riding as if he was seeing it for the first time. "I don't trust the buggers either," Muttered Alcazar Al Thawr, his large frame rendering all but the largest horses, a steppe pony. "But you might wanna check your newfound mistrust before it's time to mount up." He slapped Alberto's shoulder with a meaty hand.

With a wary eye on the horizon Cazador thought about their route. "I wish I had men to scout ahead." he muttered. Alberto looked to his new liege. "You expecting trouble?" Caz favored him with a mild grin. "Perhaps trouble should expect me..." Idris snorted a laugh. "Lets hope it doesn't milord." Cazador shot Idris a sheepish smile and shrugged. He felt exposed and his instincts were screaming at him. Not to mention his gris-gris was cold to the touch despite the hot Andalusi sun. Cazador cursed himself for not asking the archers and almogovars from his command to join him. There hadn't been time. He'd been too angry and years of chidings for being too angry to think rang in his ears. "Armor up." Caz said quietly. Jaime groaned. "Its too damn hot for maille." But he removed his turban and slid a maille corselet from a saddle pack, unbelted his weapons, and wriggled into it before pulling a grey linen tunic over his armor. Alberto did the same. Cazador retrieved the new maille shirts from the pack mule and tossed them Merfynn and Roland before returning with two helmets captured in the caravan raid. Alcazar, Pedro, Pablo, and the others pulled on aketons made from layers of cotton reinforced with a lattice of rolled rawhide tubes, or maille haubergons which they covered with voluminous linen tunics like Jaime.

Diallo had wriggled his portly frame into a maille jack and helped his jatigi don the roaring lion pauldrons his aunt had given him. Once armored Cazador ordered the party to arm themselves before they set off. They rode, making for the path between the two long hills that sat like a wrinkle in the tablecloth of the land. As it hove into view Cazador turned their party south at a heavily trafficked portion of road. Idris grunted his approval. "Wise young lord. Any pursuit will think you went to Al-auriat or Osuna with your newfound wealth." Cazador nodded. "Lets ride."

They had traveled for maybe four miles making for the Alameda. Cazador had promised them a night in a real bed before pushing on to his grandfather's estate. They rode in a loose double column formation with the pack animals in the middle. The sun beat down mercilessly from a cloudless blue sky. Olive and cotton groves lined the road casting scant shade making Cazador long for the cooler paths of the mountains looming before them. The heat was like a living thing filled with a seemingly malevolent hatred making armor a punishment. Caz was just beginning to feel sheepish about baking his oathmen when he caught the glint of sun on steel in the still air. At the same time Idris whistled a jaunty tune, an old family signal for trouble. Cazador freed his spear from it's holder in his saddle and checked to ensure his sword was loose in his scabbard. By the time a score or more of the enemy swarmed the road, they were ready.

Two riders made for Cazador riding at the head of their hasty chevron formation. Rather than couch his lance, as Alberto had been taught Cazador threw it at the lead rider bearing down upon them. His lance took a flat arc towards the fastest of the enemy sinking into his brown shield tipping it precariously toward the earth. Cazador roared as the man was vaulted from his saddle when the spear's butt spike jammed into the ground. Spooked the riderless horse veered into the path of another. What happened next Alberto doubted he would ever see again. The enemy charge was thrown into a moment of chaos, yet two riders once again targeted his new lord. Cazador screamed a cry of wordless rage, his Wootz steel sword already in his hand as he spurred his horse forcing the rest of them to accelerate with him. The first lance, painted a gorgeous murray with gold stripes almost too pretty to waste as a weapon, came from his left. Cazador flicked it aside with his shield before angling his arm and bashing his attacker with the rim. At the same time his sword chopped down forcing his right hand attackers lance away, before riposting with a vicious thrust into the riders throat. Before either of them could hit the ground he parried another probing lance and riposted with a rising chop that tore into his opponents throat even as he was yanked from the saddle.

No cavalryman my ass, Alberto thought before instinct shut off his brain in lieu of his superb training. Raising his shield at an angle he sent an enemy lance skidding up and away. Rising in his stirrups Alberto spurred the superb du Maurmont destrier to more speed as he leaned into his thrust. His point took the man in his mailled chest threading the gap past the man's shield. Dropping the lance, Albert drew his Damascus steel bastard sword hooking his forefinger over the quillion to give him better control of his point. With a blood thirsty roar Alberto spurred his horse at his nearest foe.

Determined not to be totally outclassed he nudged away a strike and lanced his enemy's throat with the tip of his blade as he passed. Cazador's cousin Jaime beside Alberto parried a enemy's lance with his own before using it to lever the man from his saddle. The Welshman Merfynn used his axe in both hands hacking wildly at any foe who came close, battering maille and slashing horses. Alberto scanned for another kill, instead the mysterious enemy wheeled and charged. Alberto was ready for a fight preparing to spur his flagging horse when the enemy suddenly changed directions. Instead of the headlong crash he'd been expecting, they showed them their backs fleeing west. Alberto grit his teeth, his horse, like the mounts of the others was blown. Pursuit would be a fools errand and likely end with them all dead. Still he drew the beautiful bow he had been gifted on the steppes of Central Asia. The power in the recurve bow made from layers of sinew, wood, and bone lacquered to perfection for strength and protection. He fired, three arrows in and many heartbeats. He paused briefly to adjust his aim and began firing again clearing the saddles of the would be escapees.

The bodies of dead and dying men and horses littered the ground. One of the survivors lay groaning in pain and fear, his leg shattered by a blow from Izan's mace. Cazador slid from the saddle and pulled the man's helmet free. He was older, more salt than pepper in his close cropped hair and beard. His left cheek and lip held an old scar leaving a permanent sneer. His skin was tanned dark but he didn't seem to be a Moor or Arab. "Who sent you?" Cazador growled French. The wounded captive spat a wad of bloody plegm that Cazador ducked casually before kicking the man in his face in a single motion. "You can be a tough old cunt or you can live." Cazador said his voice cutting through the moans of the wounded men and animals like a blade. "Answer my questions and I can let you live, a good doctor will ensure you survive and maybe walk again. Make me angry and I let my horse step on your cock and I leave you to die." The man blanched his face going pale. "We were paid by an Occitanian." The wounded mercenary grunted. "Spoke like an Italian though. We were off to sell our swords to Aragon or Castile but he offered us nearly two years wages. Said our conroi would be enough. Didn't say nothing about no archer though. Nor that you were so well armed." The man grimaced his face hovering between pain and disgust. He spit again but this time into the dirt, and we'll away from Cazador. "Where were you supposed to meet him." Caz asked. "He told us a man from Monaco would us in Malaga where a boat and crew await to take us to Genoa." Cazador grinned. "Fucking Grimaldi's." Idris squatted next to Cazador. "Where did this man find you?" Idris asked behind his blood spattered maille veil. "Cordoba." The old almogovar met Cazador's eye. "I didn't think Richard had the balls. But it makes sense." He muttered softly.

Chapter 11: Nuevo Bobastro

When the bird from his eyes and ears in had arrived bearing news that a party matching the descriptions of his grandsons had landed by boat. After the news from Miryam he was concerned. Strife was nothing new among the families that made up the houses of du Maurmont clans. When not united against a common foe, they would fall into petty disagreements, but this, this was new. These were precarious times where the power of the emirs in Al Andalus was waning, and Christian armies marched against other Christians in France. It was precisely why his plans for the inheritance of his grandchildren had been kept secret. Hamza sighed and went to his desk. The sun warmed mahogany was for once not littered with scrolls and ledgers. Instead a map showing England France, Al Andalus, Italia, Ifríqiya and the Sudan. Trade routes outlined generations of careful marriage alliances, deeds done, and debts owed. Years of steel, fire, and blood had transformed his family from humble soldiers and farmers into scions of a small empire built on trade, pilgrimage, and military service. Each child of the family fostered, each marriage alliance, and every mercenary contract built the links of a chain that would be used to pull the Alfieres and the Du Maurmont clan into a glorious future. Sometimes Hamza dreamed of his time in the Sudan and Morrocco. As a boy he had driven cattle through Tassili n'Ajjer the ancient domain of his people who had ruled the lands north of the Sahel from the times of Kemet. The old folks said the the Hapulaaren, Wolof, Sereer, and even the Kel Tamsheq were all kin once, the rulers of the western deserts called the Badari. In the times of Rome, the light of Christ had been known througout the Maghreb and the Sudan, Now only the lands of Abysinnia, Makuria, Alodia, and Nobadia were Christian and they fought dearly to survive.

The soothsayers and seers were a buzz with rumors that the world was changing. Whispers of the Children of Samyaza and even agents of the Dark One rising to challenge for middle earth once more. If the rumors were true then all must be prepared. His instincts told him that England would be important. The Aos Si and their ilk among the Children of Samyaza once ruled the misty island and still held much sway amongst the people there. Great magics were said to bind part's of the deep forests to the realms of the elves and fae. The people of Woolpit in Suffolk even told the tale of the green children who had wandered into middle earth from such a place. Some many spaces on the board, for so few pieces he could trust in play.

His own dreams had been fraught with visions of battles in Egypt. In other he saw warriors under a strange in battles against a hoard of woodwose and ghouls and things worse still. The knights of Saint Atillo were his to command. But he needed forces he could move with impunity. There was his nephew Omar's force of mounted fighters armed with swords shields and javelins was one. He hoped Cazador would lead the other. The Company of Saint Moses consisted of eight mensies with knights and mounted infantry, men-at-arms, archers, squires, and almogovars. Leon had counted on his grandson being able to swell his ranks with the feudal might of Le Cannet Des Maures, but the bastard council had done for that. Now Cazador would be forced to recruit and pay his own men. If Omar's force was his javelin then Cazador's was to be his mace.

The Old Lion had put much thought into his plans for protecting Europa and the Western Sudan. With the king of England sending letters about knight service due to protect the Scottish borderlands it made sense to send Cazador who has been raised as a Christian and knew the country. He would send Omar east to the lands he held in Georgia. The hope was that his grandson would grow his force on his own. Perhaps the by the time he had fulfilled his service in England as Lord of Moorhouse, Leon would be able to scrape up some spear and crossbow men to fill his ranks. With the Reconquista ramping up once again the Old Lion was forced to dole out knights and men at arms among the many feudal loyalties owed by his clan. Both the emir of the Almohads and the kings of Aragon and England and even the Holy Roman Emperor were all owed service. Beyond that were the ever present demands of the knights of Saint Atillo to which three in ten of all Du Maurmont fighters were due. If the Samyazans and the Nox were truly rising then it was the oaths to his blood that mattered most.

As heirs of Sile Sadio the descendants of Saif Al Takruri came from an ancient royal house related to the other royal houses in the east. The Order of the Line was a secret society of kings, clergy, and warriors comprised soley of members of the heroic bloodlines and their closest vassals. As David stood against Goliath, so must the children of his blood stand against the forces of Nox and The Nameless they served. Even hidden it was a great legacy, and the burden of it had crushed many of the sons and daughters of their legendary line. Omar, Dreu, and Martis were the flower of their generation. Now The Old Lion looked to Cazador, Izan, Jaime and the others to be the flower of theirs. He prayed they were of finer steel than their fathers because the world needed them.

For a moment the old man allowed himself to dream. An empire to rival Rome, stretching from the Gulf of Aden across the Sahel, reclaiming the Holy Land, the lands of Almohads and the Ayyubids as the Fatamids once held. He dreamt of uniting the nations for the Sudan. Subject to the Negusa Negast humanity could fight the Nox and the Samyazans preventing the chaos that had preceded the flood. For generations it had been a fools dream but now it was a necessity, and as the highest ranking silatigi of the clan it was his responsibility to see if through.

As silatigi or master of the hunt Leon had faced the twelve clearings of Koumen. He could command manna, or the ability to draw energy from The Creator and marry it to intent and create channels from the planes of the powers to the mortal plane itself. Many saw the spells and encantations and thought magic was something complex, but to Hamza it was beautiful in its simplicity. To his mind casting manna was no different to drawing lines in the sand to funnel the tides. Fire magic was initiated by using manna to connect a channel between the wielder and a Chalkydri an angelic species that carry the sun's heat. Earth magic came from a channel to Arakiel. Nature magic was summoned with a manna channel to Zuriel, and so it went. He hadn't cast in a long time. After all being a Moor made him different enough, he couldn't afford a charge of witchcraft. With what lay ahead the time would come when the Pope himself would call for magi. The Old Lion knew that the Samyazans and the Nox craved manna like addicts of the poppy and it was plentiful on middle earth. If either was able to gain a foothold in the world of man the consequences would be dire.

* * *

They rode out of Antequrra after too much wine and good sleep. Even in the expensive tavern where they'd lodged Cazador still insisted on two hours watches with a man guarding the hall as the others slept. A few hours ride brought them to the Valle de Abdalajís before the land rose to the passes and foothills of the mountains where Cazador and his kin had grown to manhood. He felt himself relax knowing his name meant something in these lands and for the first time in a while he felt safe.

Late in the afternoon a series of birdcalls from Idris ibn Idris heralded their entry into his grandfather's lands. It was a message to his fellow almogovars watching from the forest that they were friends. Although he couldn't see them he knew they would be amonst the trees watching. Had Cazador's party been an enemy force, arrows and javelins would have harassed them until it was time to close with sword shield and spear. Any invader would bleed, and by the time the enemy force reached the ruins of the church and the original

Bobastro keep, they would die. Rugged, yet lush the his grandfather's estate in Al Andalus reminded him of the lands around Monts Des Maures and he loved it like a second home.

As a young man he had heard the tales of the of the Muslim turned Christian who led an uprising against the Emirate of Córdoba in response to their injustice, high taxes, and wanton cruelty, all the things that has made Cazador's ancestors turn from Islam to Christianity. The old man had visited the land and found it good and purchased it believing the history of the area and the spirits of the earth would fuel the gris-gris of his household.

Refusing to touch the ancient stones of the first Bobastro, the new keep was built on a escarpment a quarter mile east and above the site the ruined castle. The path to Nuevo Bobastro doglegged through the ruins forming a perfect ambush site for invaders attempting to force the path the the ribat above. The front of the edifice faced west with two crenellated square towers and a gate barbican. All were built in bands creamy tan and dark brown reinforced brick. Cazador sighed contentedly. He loved Bobastro and he never ceased to marvel at how the late afternoon sun made the masonry glow. Archers patrolled the crenellated walkways on the wall while armsman lounged watchfully from the gate barbican. The surrounding forest had been shorn to create an ample killing field before the gates that were only occluded by a large baked leather guard tent fronted by an ample awning standing to the right of the gate. It served as shelter from the sun and would provide cover from any unexpected cloud of arrows. Beneath it stood six men at arms with big kite shields on their arms, and takoubas or falchions at their belts. Inside there would be at least six more. On either side of the path they could smell the heads of bandits lining the wooden stakes placed especially for the purpose. The gates stood open in invitation as if in direct of opposition to the grisly warning of the heads.

Cazador rode through the gates with his company. The fortress was divided into inner and outer wards separated by a wall and pierced by a second barbican.

To the left of the gate built into the walls of the outer ward iteslf were arcades of Moorish arches that provided shaded alcoves for traders, and craftsfolk. Above them were rabs of six room apartments, and a funduq or an inn for travelers. To the immediate right of the gate composing an entire quarter of the outer ward was a large coraal and stables to house the castle's livestock. Built into the wall just to the right of the inner gate barbican lay a church and on the opposite side a small public library. In the center of the ward lay a garden ringed fountain. As beautiful as it was with it's ornate stone and brickwork the mosaic cobbled courtyard was still little more than a gorgeous killing field.

Alberto, Merfynn, and Roland gawped. The drab robes of priests and scholars contrasted with the brightly colored silks and patterned cottons of the traders who hawked wares from the the shade of the arcades and the men and women who perused their wares. "You grew up here?" Alberto asked eyes filled with wonder. The air was redolent with the scents. The smell of the fountain and dozens of different spices from traders stalls, competed with flowers and grove of orange trees surrounding the fountain to drown out the animal scent from the coraal and stables. Cazador and his cousins grinned and shrugged. *"We have rooms here and sometimes we get to stay here."* Jaime began emphatically. "But mostly we live in tents or rude huts guarding Alpine passes or escorting pilgrims." Izan finished for him. Cazador chucked. "Sometines we even get to live in a cramped castle, or tower in Provence." He added cheerfully." Alberto's intelligent hazel eyes scrunched in confusion. "But why?" He asked. "As pages, then squires, and then as knights we rotated between posts performing our duties as knights of Saint Attillo." Izan explained and Alberto nodded but Cazador could see more questions burning in his eyes.

Leading his party along the dirt track towards the corral and paddock dominating the right corner of the outer ward. "No horses are allowed past this point." Cazador explained dismounting. Stable boys approached with a half dozen slightly older lads close on their heels. "Porto?" Asked the eldest in Catalan indicating the bags. He was stocky about sixteen with a halo of curly dark hair and bronze skin. Cazador nodded. "Do you fight in the castle militia or are you content to be a porter?" He returned in the same tongue. The youth nodded vigorously. "How about to rest of your crew, do they fight as well?" Cazador questioned waving to the gang of a dozen or so other boys waiting to carry their baggage. The youth nodded seriously, introducing himself as Giorgio de Ardallah. " The others are like me, strays brought in by El Lleó Vell. It's our honor to fight for our home. We all hope to prove ourselves as capable in the militia and be offered a place as men at arms." Cazador smiled. "Thats good to hear."

Excusing himself Cazador made his way to see one of the few people he was desperate to see more than his grandfather. Antonio Bonifas a smith, poet, and sometimes mercenary. He had battled his demons, fighting an addiction that had seen him lose his kin and trade eventually landing Antonio in Spain. Cazador remembered the day he'd met the man. With his tattered robe, wild blond hair, and bright blue eyes they'd thought him a mendicant monk who he found to be both gregarious and dark tempered by turns. Instead they had found a very competent fighter and smith.

After the encounter with the ghul Cazador was in desperate need of his services. Tempest was a beautiful sword that had served him well. He had carried it against Byzantine Varangians and other heavily armored troops in the past and having to use it as a bludgeon would see it destroyed, and not to mention was a lot of work. Such a fate Cazador couldn't abide for his prized weapon. Where others had gone to maces and axes to deal with the armor he too wanted something durable to use against heavy armor. "Care if we join you?" Asked his djali Diallo who stood with Merfynn. With a nod, Cazador invited them to join him.

Antonio looked up from the falchion he'd been sharpening at the grinding wheel in his outdoor area of his workshop and smiled brightly as Cazador hailed him. He cleaned his hands and a nearby barrel and dried them before taking Cazador's arm in a warrior's grip before drawing him in a rigorous embrace. "What brings you my way? Have you come to drink all my wine and cost me another days work?" Cazador feigned shock. "Never! But I have come to put some silver in your purse if you're of a mind..." His grandfather employed a small army of smiths in the castle but Cazador wanted something specific that nobody would try to talk him out of. A mace. Knobbed, simple and deadly. He knew his friend Antonio wouldn't argue with him for it was the rare Italian that argued against good sense and hard silver.

After explaining what he wanted, Antonio brought him to the table of wares and like magic led Cazador to what he sought. The Italian handed him a mace with a wickedly knobbed head a little over two feet long. Beneath the head the shaft was wrapped with glued twine to protect it from sword blows, while the lower handle sported a simple leather grip and rawhide wrist cord. Taking a few experimental swings Cazador smiled in pleasure. This would suit his needs perfectly.

As he continued shopping, his mind turned to his company. As they rode to Bobastro Cazador had been struck by the sinking feeling that he would never hold the lordship of Le Cannet Des Maures. Although birthright mattered, no man or woman could be lord or lady without the elders approval. Something Cazador was sure he had lost. He still had Moorhouse Manor in England, and The Company of Saint Moses. Sixty four men wasn't an army but it made for a very respectable the host for a small manor. Eight lances just large enough to turn a profit as a company but small enough not to be a factor major in war. Unless he followed the path of his cousins. Omar, Dreu, Marfin, and Ilyas. His older cousins had been much the same and now their names rang as being among the greatest knights in the clan and each a captain of a free company with manors unimportant enough to the family commerce to be left to stewards. Nothing that would distract them from their efforts in the field. Unlike the household troops and family knights of the du Maurmonts the free captains had lands gifted to them from church possessions and were therefore free from feudal obligations to the crown of Aragon their status as noble mercenaries gave the family and clan the ability deny any involvement in their actions while secretly reaping the benefits. They had grown their hosts to nearly princely sizes with chapters in Outremer, Europa and even the Sudan. If he grew his force he could retake Le Cannet Des Maures by force if need be. But it saddened him knowing he could probably never go home without walking over a pile of bodies first.

Seeking distraction Cazador made his way to a the castles tea shop reserved mostly for visiting scholars and merchants. For the first time since she handed it to him Cazador checked the scrip his Aunt Miryam had given him. Unrolling a tight cloth revealed over a two hundred dinar which explained the immense weight of it. "Holy Christ!" Cazador muttered. *"I'm...rich!"* Combined with the money from the sale of the boat he had real coin. Reviewing the documents for The Company of Saint Moses. Named for Moses the Black, Cazador's favorite saint. The tightly rolled cloth proved to be a banner depicting a beautifully stitched icon of Saint Moses wearing a black cloak and green scarf. Gooseflesh ran along Cazador's arms. This would be the flag men would fight and die under under his command. He felt the weight of it settle somewhere in his chest. Long ago Cazador realized war and violence were his trade as wood and saw were to a carpenter. Fighting was what he did and he enjoyed it. It was easy. Leading men into battle was not.

Rifling through the rest of his script he found two pennons and collection of woven patches. The first he recognized from the charter as the arms of the Company of Saint Moses a sable field with a argent escutcheon showing eight swords in vert The other pennant and patches were unfamiliar to him. A field divided per quarters argent and azure, depicting in sable a lions head sable in the first quarter and a gauntlet clenched in the fourth. Digging deeper he found a billet of documents. With a sinking feeling Caz scanned them, and struggling to swallow past the lump in his throat he realized the unfamiliar arms were his own, as the arms of the Lord of Le Cannet Des Maures were no longer his to bear. He had fought under the argent and purpure his entire life and as gorgeous as the new arms were, they brought with them a deep sadness.

Suddenly Cazador felt the need to pray. His feet led him to the chapel of Nuevo Bobastro's outer ward. Beyond it's heavy cedar doors the walls were adorned with mosaics depicting scenes from the Bible. To Cazador's left on the north wall lay the birth of Christ, the magi, Mary, Joseph, and of course the infant Christ were picked out in painstaking detail. Stained glass windows cleverly worked into the mosaic made the halos around their heads glow as the light filtered through. The altar lay on east wall, backed by the a scene of Christ feeding the multitude, and to the right lay portraits of saints. Saint George, Saint Maurice, Saint Atillo, Saint Moses of Egypt, and others stretched to the darkened recesses of the vaulted ceilings. His grandfathers architects has done well fusing Mozarbic, and Byzantine influences with architecture native to the Sahel. Eyes lingering on the image of Saint Moses Cazador knelt and prayed.

He thanked God for the blessings he had received, and the strength and wisdom to meet his challenges. As Cazador prayed his mind swirled around the image of the patron saint of his new company. He knew the story well. Before he became a saint, Moses had been a bandit chieftain famed for his bravery and sword skill. After being thwarted several times in a robbery he was forced to take refuge in a monastery, where he gave his life to God. Whilst praying in a desert cell he had been set upon by bandits who he refused to kill and in sparing them they turned to the service of the Lord. When raiders came to attack the monastery his brother monks wanted to stay and fight but Moses relented saying those who live by the sword were destined to die by it. Sending his brother monks to safety Moses and the former bandits stayed behind to fight the raiders becoming martyred in the process.

Cazador chuckled into the stillness of the empty chapel. *Everything is a lesson.* It was a line he had heard from the mouths of the Old Lion and Idris both. It was something he and his cousins had repeated as well with varying degrees of scorn. But here it was, a lesson, a reminder. Hidden in plain sight. Saint Moses was often said to be frustrated by his lack of Christian perfection, and was told that nothing happened overnight. It was a lesson Cazador promised himself he'd remember.

Chapter 12: Way of the Ancestors

After completing his series of purchases around the castle market, Cazador retired to the keep. His rooms in the at Bobastro were paradise after months of tents and sleeping rough. Tapestries depicting scenes from the Chanson of Roland adorned the walls. The Battle of Bremule, The Battle of Gisors, Marganice and his fifty thousand. The images had fired Cazador's young warlike imagination and he wondered one day what poets would say of Cazador Alfiere. The tapestries were also reminders of their history and heritage. His windows sat positioned to provide an ample cross breeze keeping it cool on summer nights like this and afforded views of the mountains beyond. The baths were a short well remembered walk to the basement where cisterns of clean water was heated and pumped to the castle and bath house. After was clean Cazador brushed his halo of dark tightly curled hair till it shone and dressed in a blue tunic decorated with silver thread belted under a simple black gambeson of silk and black linen with Sudanese pantaloons tucked into a newly brought pair of calf length riding boots. Belting Tempest at his waist he set off to find his friends but was intercepted by one of grandfather's stewards. "Greetings Sir Cazador, your grandsire requests your attendance at the gates." Suppressing a groan he nodded. He was tired and road weary but a request from The Old Lion was as good as an order and Cazador had been drilled to obey.

***

121

Cazador rode in companionable silence with his grandfather as the elder knight led them up a hunting track toward the lake at the mountains summit. They passed what looked like a cave but Cazador noticed a cleverly hewn window in the raw stone. Beside it a rough door below a cross intricately carved in the living rock. The Old Lion dismounted with the grace of a man many years younger. "Come, let us lay homage to the Almighty and those that have gone before us to His glory." the old man said in quiet tones that seemed suited to the reverant nature of the mountain side chapel.

Cazador nodded and dismounted following his grandfather inside. The Old Lion used flint and his belt knife to ignight a trench of oil that chased away the gloom. The shadows retreated to the recesses of the vaulted ceiling illuminating a cruciform nave. The gallery they walked through was dominated by detailed murals of Moorish knights in maille with spatha's held across almond shaped Byzantine kite shields bearing the Chi-Ro. In the center a six pointed star punctuated by stone sarcophagi. In the center of the star were stone pews and an altar in front of which sat a single alabaster box.

Cazador marveled at the artwork, the age of the place filling his soul with reverence. "Long ago, the Maghreb and the lands north of the Sudan were the heartland of Christianity and a bastion of Romanitas." His grandfather intoned quietly. "Then came the Vandals, almost blotting out the old glow of Rome until Belisarius came. We fought the Romans and when John Troglita sued for terms our ancestors became foederati of Rome." the old man said leading him deeper into the chapel. His grandfather was dressed like the old Provençal rogue he was. The yellow silk hose tucked into ankle high boots of soft leather, matched the ornate stitching in his red tunic. Rubies flashed in his sword belt off setting the plain wooden grip of his sword Rooxaan Abuure or Ghost Maker. The Old Lion had gotten it in his youth from a Kanemi trader who had gotten it from smiths from the lands far to the south of the Sudan. It was called a Boa, and had a thin aerated ricasso that flared into a weighty enlongated leaf shape blade ending in a very fine point that Cazador had witnessed pierce maille with ease. As a youth Cazador had lusted after the heavy cut and thrust blade.

He began to wonder why they had come. In Cazador's experience prayers didn't come with history lessons but the Old Lion was as chaotic as he was meticulous, one never knew what to expect so Caz waited patiently.

Leon Alfiere , looked upon his grandson with genuine affection. He did his best not to play favorites, but since he was a small boy Cazador had listened when he spoke. He looked at his grandson waiting patiently for him to continue and suppressed a smile. "It was during this time that the heirs of Sile Sadio or Solomon and other heroes were joined for the first time in many many generations. The bloodlines of Aksum and the lines of the Maghreb and Sahel came together all serving under the great Byzantine Empire. A pact was made, and an early version of what we would call a knightly order was formed The Order of Saint Elesbaan. It was decided that the Order of Saint Elesbaan would serve as soldiers for the empire because it was agreed that the eastern Romans was the best chance for the peace and unity needed to stand against the darkness. The best machine to stand against the foedus finis. The end of the great pact between God the father and the children of Samyaza and the Nameless. They fought against the invasion of Ifriquya standing with the Byzantine forces under the great queen Dhiya. When Roman control was wiped out in Ifriquya was ended a new plan was formed. A network of blades, whispers, and money, always money. Blending with governments, swaying rulers, guiding and leading armies. Anything to fight the foedus finis." The Old Lion met his grandson's eyes with strange intensity.

Cazador didn't understand. "Grandfather what is the foedus finis?" He understood the Latin. It meant pact's end. But what pact?The Old Lion's eyes glittered in the flamelit chamber. "You know of the flood and it's remnants?" Cazador nodded. Monsters like woodwose, dragons, and ghul were said to have hidden away in high places or in sealed chambers during the flood. "I do read the Codex of Saint Atillo, grandfather." The old man cackled. "Well that's good but it's only part of the truth.

There are beings darker than ghul and more terrible than dragons that survived the flood. The Suudiibe or the Samyazans and their enemies that reside in Inner Earth are more beautiful and terrible than you could imagine boy. That's why there only basic shit in the books and scrolls." Leon Alfiere offered his grandson a crooked grin.

Slapping him on the shoulder he said, "After the flood, God made his pact with Noah and his descendants. But he also made a pact with the Suudiibe. They would be allowed to live as long as they kept to their places of refuge. Giving unto man the world of Middle Earth where we reside for a span of time. That span is now expiring. Mankind's sole dominion of middle earth is ended and our very freedom and existence is in peril. Beings who's kin were worshipped as gods and saints will strive against us." Cazador fidgeted with his sword and tugged at his short beard. Suddenly things made sense, but the vastness of it all gave him a sense of vertigo.

The Old Lion watched Cazador grapple with the information. The weight of their family legacy has crushed many but Leon knew his grandson were made of finer steel than their fathers and Cazador had risen as to lead them. He wasn't the biggest or the strongest but he was a gifted fighter and possessed a powerful intellect. A natural leader from the time he could talk. Cazador like his kinsman had been raised to fight, run estates, and further the interest of his family. The world was about to change around them and the life and future he had planned for himself would be vastly different than the reality he would face. Leon felt a moment of solemn pity mixed with deep pride for his grandson. He has always done what his family had asked of him and now The Old Lion would ask for more.

He placed a gnarled hand on Caz's shoulder. "I know that Le Cannet Des Maures has been taken from you by the council, but it was never your destiny to be a country lord content with killing bandits, hunting, and crusades. You are a true heir of Saif Al Takruri. A warrior and leader of men. You are meant for a greater path." Cazador felt stung understanding his grandfather would not force his claim to his birthright the seat that had been his father's and should

have passed to him. "Rember well the Parable of the Talents, grandson...
" The Old Lion chided. To squirrel you away in La Marche, would be akin
to burying your talent Caz. We don't need a strong lord in Le Cannet Des
Maures. We need a free captain a kèlè -koun with a mounted kélé-bolo" The
Old Lion said firmly using the Sonninke words for war head and an infantry
unit known as a war arm. "This is why The Company of Saint Moses was
formed." The Old Lion went to box in the center of the chapel. These six men
that lay here are you ancestors. The last to fight against Islam in Ifriquya. The
first anointed knights of the Order of Saint Elesbaan. I had this entire chamber
disassembled and brought here from the ruins of old Mauretania." Eyes wide
with deference Cazador scanned the intricately carved sarcophagi searching
for his own features in graven faces of his forebears.

Cazador wandered the knave. Stopping at each sarcophagus brushing the stone
swords held in repose across his ancestors chests. The details of the carving
were so lifelike he half expected the stone knights to stir at his touch. The
gris-gris around his neck hummed softly as if in attunement and Cazador felt
the calming presence of his ancestors. Wondering if they found him worthy
he turned to his grandfather. Leon smiled knowing well his grandson's love
of history. Knowing he would feel the power of the place.

"Cazador Alfiere, called Sayaad Al Takruri called Silatigi Sadio called Obom-
mofo Salomo. Kneel before the altar." The Old Lion roared into the stillness
invoking all four of Cazador's given names in his battlefield voice. Moving
swiftly to obey Cazador knelt. His grandfather stood before him. "Do you
swear to accept the anointing of your blood, and become an avowed enemy of
darkness, spite, and hatred wherever it may rise. To protect those who cannot
protect themselves?" Cazador felt the temperature in the room drop, and his
breath mist before him. He didn't need the emanations of his gris-gris to
tell him his ancestors hovered close. "I do." Cazador said firmly. "Like our
Savior we stem from the line of David. Do you vow to seek the face of The Most
High, ever to stand with the downtrodden and against injustice?" Cazador
smiled, "I do." The Old Lion met his eye. "Despite the darkness all mortal

men hold in their soul, will you fight for the light?" Without breaking his grandfather's gaze Cazador said, "With all my heart." The old man nodded fondly. "Do you swear to forsake wine, wealth, and women?" He asked wryly. Cazador blanched his copper toned face fading to a paler shade of brown. "I,—" Cazador stammered and Leon Alfiere roared with laughter."That fortunately is not part of the oath son."

Still chuckling at his grandson,the Alfiere patriarch opened the alabaster cask and retrieved a arming sword with a cruciform hilt and round pommel similar to those of the Sudan. "This is L'Auxifar. The Crush. The swords and sword hands of each of your venerated ancestors were used to make the steel of this blade. This blade was forged by Saif himself in case this chapel was ever lost. Today I gift it to you and welcome you to The Order of Saint Elesbaan ." Cazador took the heavy hand and a half sword in his hand it's juju or magic was strong. It sweep to sink with his gris gris immediately. Cazador stepped away to take a few experimental swings noting the suppleness of the vibrating steel as it sang through the air of the chapel. Cazador struck a guard smiling with a joy his grandfather found infectious. "Its not a rich estate but this is your birthright nonetheless. May you ever shine brightly grandson."

* * *

As they rode back from the mountainside chapel he had told the Old Lion of the river town and the ghul, now he sat in his grandfather's war room. It was the first time in his life he had been invited into the room to do more than pour wine and learn. Maps of Europa, Ifriquya, and the Sudan covered the table, Cazador listened intently as he outline the movements of Aragon and the other Christisn forces. "The Caliph requested forces. I sent two hundred almogovars under Dreu, and Omar's host. To Aragon I sent Marfin with his host of five hundred spearman, two hundred almogovars, and twenty knights." Cazador nodded. Knights and men at arms were expensive but almogovars were a Du

Maurmont specialty. When the Umayadd Caliphate and later the Almoravids conquered, they did so using many men from the Sudan. Where the Berber and Arabs fought mounted, Sudanese troops had formed the backbone of the infantry. Due to the extreme heat of their homeland these men specialized in light infantry tactics that had become the hallmark of almogovar combat style. They were cheap to equip with sword, spear, javelins and gambeson. Cazador could see from the maps that resources were being stretched to meet to many demands. With the Holy Land drawing knights, men at arms, and sergeants aways from Europa to Outremer as Knights of Saint Atillo and feudal obligations to the king of Aragon for their lands in Provence along with the Caliph of Al Andalus. Then there were the curious units he had watched his grandfather shuffle to England with a pensive look.

Unable to contain his curiosity he looked to his grandfather and asked. "What of England? I see you plan to send troops there as well." The Old Lion smiled and nodded. "Yes long ago my father won land in England free of duty and taxation for long years until now. I've got your old friend Sir Gregory there training the locals and acting as steward, but Moor House needs a lord of the manor and that is you. The king is ramping up for his war in Wales and wants bodies he can trust ready to defend the Scottish marches." The Old Lion met his grandson's eye. The very impassiveness of his face was more than enough to let him guess Cazador's mind. All Cazador could think of was rusted maille and saddle sores chasing hairy assed Scots bandits through rainy Northern England. "The Aos Si once held sway there and there's many who hold to the old ways if given the freedom to do so." Cazador nodded, "Grandfather I have less than one hundred men. What could I do with that against the Suudiibe with that?" Leon Alfiere smiled like the big cat he has been nicknamed for. " You seemed to do well enough against the ghul. Recruit men, swell your ranks and lead the charge against them. The Bishops will drum up support quickly enough." Cazador nodded feeling less than sure.

Fighting bandits, cattle reavers, and typically any other human was one thing but the *Suudiibe* or the Hidden Ones divided into the Nox or Samyazans was something else entirely. In Monts Des Maures even Al Andalus the prospect would have been far less daunting, but on an island cut off from family support surrounded by strangers filled him with fear, and maybe... maybe some excitement. The Old Lion was giving him an opportunity to make a name for himself as one of the great knights of Christendom, but there would be nobody to catch him if he fell. Suddenly the question popped into his head, "Grandfather...who is supposed to pay for all this?" The old man laughed. "You sound like your grandmother." He grunted. But Cazador noticed he didn't answer the question.

* * *

Alberto woke to the wolf light of Matins, years of traveling with monks had ingrained the habit. though he had lost his faith, The Divine Office still dictated the ebb and flow his routine. With a sigh he heaved himself from his bed. Quietly leaving his room in the inner funduq, Alberto marveled at the beautiful simplicity of Bobastro. Built like a caravanserai within a caravansarai within a caravansarai, the beautiful galleries of Moorish arches set in creamy stone were embellished with rich blue scrollwork surrounding mosaics depicting scenes from the Bible, hunts, or battles. Refusing to be outdone the garden below held a walled fountain surrounded by a square portico. Beyond it stone walkways lined with cycas bushes divided the courtyard garden into four sections, one dedicated to a small grove of orange trees and grape arbors, a second of alternating rows of sorghum, herbs, and vegetables, a third held a low stable and a yard with a small herd of goats, cattle, and sheep. The final was a simple field of grass empty but for a few adobe outbuildings and another long squat building that had the look of a barracks the world over. Alberto could see archery butts at the far end and in the opposite corner a collection of worn dummies mounted on stakes were under assault by a pair of familiar figures. Alberto hurried back to his room to retrieve his weapons.

By the time he made it to the garden it was full dawn and the muezzin was calling the Mohomedans to prayer. Cazador was there with his kinsmen Izan and Jaime, each lost in their own world attacking the cane stuffed targets with abandon. Alberto paused and watch the Moorish knights work. Each of the dummies was equipped with a spear, maille, helmet, and shield at various angles and positions of attack. Cazador fought with his kite shield strapped to his forearm and gripped the short spear Alberto had learned was called a tagheda a short double ended spear with a slim head. In his right hand he bore his Wootz steel sword. Using his shield he swatted aside his targets spear, even as he stabbed high at his targets face with his tagheda. Instinct, Alberto knew would draw any trained fighter's shield up. Quick as thought Cazadors sword came whistling in an upwards stike that struck under the maille and between between the target's legs, right where the left thigh joined the hip at the groin in an explosion of ochre powder. Alberto winced, but Cazador was already attacking the next dummy. Pivoting he ducked low, stabbing high with his spear before firing a thrust into the next dummy's groin. Turning to a third he blocked the low spear, thrust at his target's inner thigh with his short spear and twisted his wrist turning his blades point horizontal as Cazador flicked a thrust into the visor of the target's pot helm for his third plume of dust that Alberto assumed signalled a kill. Leaving his blade imbedded in the target he reached for a new weapon, an arming sword he didn't have on the journey here .

Cazador turned to a fourth dummy armed with a dane axe and with a war cry thrust his shield rim into the haft and used the sword for a mezzano strike to the maille covered throat of the target. "Fuck a nun..." Alberto muttered barely audible above his new friend's battle cry. He held a hand to his cheek where a rivet from the maille cut him as it escaped the oblivion of the target which pitched sideways in a new explosion of reddish dust. Jaime and Izan spun at their cousin's sudden roar as the sand and cane dummy cartwheeled into Izan's, and It was only then that Cazador saw Alberto and smiled broadly. "Fuck a nun indeed my friend!"

Seeing Alberto and his weapons, Cazador's smile grew. "Come to train with us sir knight?" Alberto grinned back and nodded, eager to vent his swirling thoughts with steel and sweat. He joined his Moorish friends in attacking the dummies, losing himself in the rhythm of practice. By the time morning prayers were complete the adjacent yard was filling with men who entered the small buildings and returned with kit. Swords, large hide shields, bows, arrows and quivers of javelins, as well as the larger version of the tagheda called an allargh differentiated not only by their size but the wide spatulate head on the oppostite side shaped like a single frond of a water clover. The large spears were propped up on a rack before they shook out into a loose formation. Some drew bows, others hefted javelins and the throwing steels Alberto had seen Cazador and his kin use against the ghuls. As one they took aim at the forest of archery butts and unleashed a hail of projectiles. With the first salvo unleashed the force trotted forward, the archers on the flanks pouring a continuous rain of fire at their stuffed foes. When the force closed to within twenty paces the center unleashed a barrage of javelins and throwing knives, then with the beat of a drum and a chilling war cry they charged at the targets, the center colliding with the imaginary enemy center and as the wings of the formation wrapped around the flanks.

Alberto who had seen fighters from all over the world asked the question that had tugged at his mind from the start. "You fight with the spear but don't issue pikes to your peons, why?" Cazador smiled and laughed. As Knights of Saint Attillo we escort pilgrims, Crusade, and guard the passes through the Massifs Des Maures and the Southern Alps. Dense woods and steep slopes make horses and long spears less useful. Even when we are escorting pilgrims " He explained. "Besides we don't fight as the Franks do at least not always and especially not our foot soldiers. In Europa infantry are used to spear fencing from a distance. Our ancestors came from the Sahara and the Sudan, lucky for us there brought their way of fighting with them. On foot instead of waving spears at horsemen we shoot at them or hurl darts, kill their horses. For infantry we soften their lines with ranged attacks and then we close." Cazador finished smacking his left fist into his right palm. Alberto understood. He had seen such things amongst the horse tribes of the vast steppe lands to the east .

Alberto nodded. "So your tactics are similar to that of the Almogovars and Almocaden?" Cazador thought for a moment. "Yes, but Almogovars raid, loot and slave, and we don't do any of that." He said to a round of laughter. "But all japes aside, Mon Amie," Cazador said, "Our weapons and armor are chosen to help us fight this way. When you get close to your enemy, a long weapon is a hinderance more than a help. In an attack, horsemen or the fleetest of foot occupy the flanks and the heaviest armored go to the center. Before my grandfather's father returned to Europa he lived in the Sudan. Esteve, known among the English as Steven the Moor served as a Kele-Koun or noble captain of infantry in Mali and after distinguishing himself in battle earned a place at their court. He brought the skills he refined fighting in the Sudan blended them with the ways of the Kel Tamsheq and Sanhaja and brought them back to Europa. Those skills continue to be instilled in his descendants today. We add our ways to those of the Franks." Alberto listened fascinated. Although he had traveled the breadth of Europa, Outremer, and Asia to the lands where Alexander tread, Alberto had yet to see fighters quite like the men from Monts Des Maures.

Cazador continued. "The fourteen primary strikes we use come from Al Matrag. It teaches us to strike at the head thighs, gut, groin, and inner thigh." Cazador stood with his sword side foot forward and snapped through the series of cuts he had drilled since he was four years old. He melted into a series of guards before switching to the sword and buckler style favored by the Germans. The motions somewhat awkward with the large heater but still effective for certain plays. Alberto watched attention rapt as Cazador explained.

"Add that to guesting every other year for a for a few months at a time we would live and train in the households of other family's allies adding those skills to the way our kin has taught us to make war." Izan chimed. "By thirteen years old most of us had killed our first man. Turks and Andalusi, Germans, Italians, and every brigand in France thought they can make a living as a bandit on our lands. Make no doubt about it the Old Lion, our grandfather made us into weapons just as much as scholars and gentlemen. Even our women train to fight and learn to read and write." Alberto let loose a low whistle. "Come," Cazador said let us find some food and wash. Then we can go to the market, we meet the Company of Saint Moses for their first official muster tomorrow!"

Chapter 13: First Contract

Cazador rode down the winding trail away from Nuevo Bobastro with Diallo, Merfynn, Alcazar, and Izan for company. Idris was playing Chess with the Old Lion, and Maurice had disappeared, likely off to see his favorite widow that lived not far from the castle. Cazador smiled warmly. Alberto had lost himself in the library. Jaime, Roland, Pedro and Pablo had found dice games and wrestling matches amongst Bobastro's guards and were busy gambling. Leon was off somewhere wooing unsuspecting servant girls with Rodrigo. "Where are we headed?" Merfynn asked cheeks ruddy in the dying sun of the late evening. Cazador had insisted they all dress in the newly purchased uniform of The Company of Saint Moses. Black jazerants covered by green silk surcoats and matching pantaloons. The green boots matched the hoods secured with black headscarves that tied the ensemble together.

Cazador looked to the Welshman and smiled. "To a tavern dear Merfynn when we shall combine drink and work!" Diallo who had been strumming idly at kora as they rode look up. "Ahh we go to the Taverna del Leon." Alcazar clapped his hand against his thigh. "Bless you Caz!" He said heartily. Izan moved closer to his cousin. "What work is there for mercenaries at a tavern?" Cazador slapped his maille covered shoulder. "The easiest part of the job. Recruiting!"

Before long the well worn path wound down and the taverna came into view. The rambling three story adobe structure had accommodations for travelers on the top two floors and a sprawling common area filled with tables and chairs, a bar and even a stage. Rumor had it that the Old Lion had founded it himself. Cazador and his party dismounted near the stable and he tossed coins to the boys who appeared to take their horses. Diallo retrieved a portable desk from his saddle and together they made for the taverna. The sturdy wooden door looked as though it had been built to withstand a siege and maybe it had. Once beyond it they were greeted by a wall of sound, heat and an melange of smells. Simmering lamb, and baking flatbread warred with the fug of overwarm bodies. Cazador meandered to an open table. A long bar occupied the far corner next to doors leading to the kitchen. Cazador waved to a pretty serving girl with mellow light brown skin and light eyes that made his heart flutter just a bit. He ordered three bottles of wine and instructed her to bring cups as well and with a saucy smile and a curtsy she made for the bar. When she returned he tipped her well enough to keep her eye for the rest of the night. The patrons had marked their presence in the way all armed strangers were. Cazador felt their eyes and welcomed them. The crowd was a good mix of travelers, castle folk and the people that lived nearby. Several farms and small villages dotted the area and it was a few of these he hoped to attract to his banner.

Cazador had settled into his second cup of wine when Diallo leaned over, "Are you ready milord?" Cazador nodded. In a blink Diallo leapt upon the table with a nimbleness belying his size and soft bulk. "Ladies and gentleman!" He roared in a rich voice priests and bishops would kill for. "May I present to you my lord Sayaad ibn Wilayam, Ibn Hamza Al Takruri and he is looking for fighters for his retinue! Fair and regular wages!" Diallo said it three times, in Arabic, French, and Occitanian. Conversations hushed and heads turned, several men approached.

The first was a burly young man in a simple workman's shirt and hose. He was of obvious Mozarbic ancestry. He had skin the color of copper, dark eyes and his long wavy beard was oiled and glorious. "How much does it pay?" He asked meeting the eye of the man he would swear to. "Pay is there and a half shillings a week with bonuses for good service." Diallo said grandly. The man nodded, "I am Amastan ibn Iithan. I will sign."

Another man stepped forward. He was balding with more salt than pepper in his beard and a respectable paunch. "Are your men responsible for their own equipment?" This time Cazador answered, "No, I will provide arms, armor, and clothing and whoever marches with me eats from my larder." There were murmers and soon men and boys were signing with Diallo.

When the serving girl returned, Cazador turned with a smile. "Three more bottles of wine if you please," Her fierce eyes met his own, "I'll take your order lord, but I've some business to attend to first. Me and the ladies here would like to sign on." Cazador could see the challenge dancing in her emerald gaze. Alcazar choked on his wine and Diallo's salesman's smile faltered. Merfynn, cheeks flush from the wine murmured, "but women don't fight..." Before he could say more Cazador cut in, "I'll have you know that my own mother is a belted knight and indeed a woman." The heat that had come to the serving girls cheeks calmed at his words. "Please if it is your wish to enlist lady..." The serving girl raised her chin, "I am Asmā bint Alghar my great grandmother's, grandmother rode against El Cid she said her pride clear." With a bow Cazador said, "Welcome granddaughter of heros. My ancestors too rode with Yusef Ibn Tashfin." His eyes didn't leave hers and he felt a tension build. Cazador studied her face, high cheekbones and full be stung lips with a straight nose. Her eyes were the color of forest and he felt himself look away. "Thats enough of that!" Alcazar boomed "We are here to recruit soldiers eh! You can order her for private inspection once she signed and paid..."

Cazador's elbow shot back smoothly catching Alcazar in his mailled ribs. "Ow! Dammit all, that hurt even through the maille you bastard" Flushing slightly in embarrassment Cazador gave Alcazar a gimlet eye. "What?" His giant friend asked clueless as Asmā signed. With a smile and curtsey she moved on. He surprised to see she was just the first of many women who had wandered into light along with the farm boys, wood cutters and apprentices.

He took their names and stories, committing faces to memory. When the line had ended they had added forty new souls to the sixty odd already on the company roster. "Muster is the day after tomorrow after midday prayers!" Diallo announced to the new recruits and called each forward to distribute the small purses Cazador had prepared as a signing bonus. It was just three pence but it was still about the same value as a day's work and the new recruits were pleased with the promise of more to come. True to her word Asmā returned with wine and a steaming platter of lamb and flatbread. Merfynn clapped in delight and Cazador felt his own stomach rumbling with too much wine and too little food. There was a moment of civility as a bowl of water was passed so each man could wash his hands and then like wolves they tucked in.

As they rode back to Bobastro Merfynn asked the question Cazador knew would come eventually. "You truly plan to let the women fight?" Cazador nodded in the moonlight. "I do. We are a small outfit and at this point I can't afford to be picky and they make up half our numbers. I have sisters and a mother, they're fiercer than most men I know. Woman can fight as well as they can do just about anything else. The way I see it a careful man can live his life to old age before he looks death in the eye and fuck all he likes. But women, they know death comes knocking just from the simple act of spreading their legs, or because they don't. That breeds a different kind of tough and I'll take it and respect it. As your lord I expect you will too." Merfynn nodded. "Aunt Miryam would be proud of you." Izan said. "I think it's brilliant." Alcazar said from where he rode. "How so?" Asked Merfynn unable to help himself. "Well..." Alcazar began drawing himself up into the posture made famous by Idris ibn Idris. "Anything to distract or disrupt the enemy should be used to your advantage-" he gruffed, mimicking the grizzled almogovar turned armsmaster. " and the way I see it tits are a distraction." he finished tone philosophical before bursting into a fit of laughter. Cazador shook his head. "This could be very good, or very bad for morale." Izan said conspiratorially. "But Big Al does have a point." Diallo strummed his kola and sang *Oh the Amazons of Cazador*. "It will be memorable, I give you that lord. Such things make for good songs and good songs mean coin, and coin is always good for morale." Cazador found he couldn't argue with that logic at all.

* * *

Izan waited patintly for things to begin. Like the other knights of his cousin's mensie he wore the black boots with the green tunic and gamboised chausses over black hose. His cousin had spared no expense with maille coif and matching bar nasal, helmets torsed with the black, white, and green. He felt downright dashing. Cazador had chosen the militia training ground to hold the first muster. Tables with the armory of the company lay spread out at one end of the field next to a few wagons and a temporary coral of riding mules and pack animals. Crossbows, axes, maces, and, long knives graced the board Next to them were racks of spears, rows of januwiyya shields with hardwood rims, thick rawhide faces, and iron bosses, painted with the company arms. Two strange contraptions resembling tripods with ropes and pulleys cast awkward shade. Cazador had been quite coy about what his plans and with addition recruits and Izan was quite curious. Especially about the pulley tripods. At the far end of the field a thicket of cane and straw dummies were staked in formation like waiting foeman.

The initial roll for The Company of Saint Moses was compromised of eight, eight man conrois consisting of a knight, a squire, two man at arms, two almogovars, and two archers totalling sixty four fighters. Some were faces he recognized, like the final addition to his mensie, Rodrigo of Marseilles, who's father was a wealthy lawyer and merchant that had grown rich in service to La Compangnie. So wealthy in fact that he had purchased estates and sent his son to the Old Lion as a page. Cazador greeted him warmly, "Rodrigo you scoundrel it's good to see you. Cazador strode over to embrace his old friend remembering their childish antics as they distracted each other from their duties around the castle. Men at arms like Bekou of Bono, Abdul Al Daza, warriors from the Sudan who came to serve under the Du Maurmont banners.

Behind them were squires young men Cazador has seen as pages to knights of Saint Atillo, La Compangnie, or du Maurmont retainers. Familiar faces all. The almogovars and archers like the other unit were a mix of fresh faces and seasoned veterans.

Cazador organized the lances taking Alcazar, and the formidable Abdul Al Daza as his men at arms, and his young kinsman Marco Alfiere as his squire to replace his nephew Leon, now a knight in his own right. Marco was already bigger than Cazador himself and would be a fearsome addition to his warband. He grinned, eyes bright under his mop of braids, his mahogany skin flush with excitement. He had grown much since Cazador had seen him last and he hadn't recognized him until young Marco called him out. "You ready?" Cazador asked him with a sly smile. "We can spar any day big cousin and you won't find me afraid or wanting!" Cazador nodded pleased seeing that the son held his father's steel and good nature. "You'll do." Caz said.

For his almogovars he selected another old companion Idris ibn Idris ibn Idris, youngest son of the Old Lion's near legendary companion. "Little Idris!" Cazador called. Little Idris was the image of his father except for the fact that he had hair. Where the elder Idris was bald as an egg, the son wore his hair in a halo of ear length box braids and sported a short goatee. Grinning boldly Little Idris swaggered over to where Cazador's personal retinue was clumped. To join him Cazador selected Duku an Akan warrior who had come north to sell his sword rather than emigrate south with his people. The archers he chose with care selecting Constantine of Axum come into Du Maurmont service through their close ties with the kingdoms of the eastern Sudan. Nubian archer had a tradition stretching back to ancient Egypt and Greece. His hardwood self bow was easily six feet tall and could drive a bodkin arrow easily through maille. To round out his retinue he chose N'faly of Gao. The Old Lion had brought him a few years ago while visiting the Morocco finding him on a auction block in Marrakesh.

When the Old Lion had asked him why he was sold as a slave, N'faly had told him a depraved tale that involved elephant ivory, and the wife of a powerful merchant that had led to N'faly allegedly almost fighting his way free with his short bow. When asked how he was captured N'faly told him he had run out of arrows and been forced to throw his knife. After a test of his skills N'Faly was given his freedom and brought to work as an archer for La Compangnie. Unlike Constantine he favored a short Turkish recurve bow that had less range and power than the long bows of the Nubians and the English but was faster and just and accurate at intermediate ranges. "Sir Alberto, Sir Merfynn, and Sir Roland, as knights of my mensie I would be honored if you'd join my personal conroi." The three ferhingees had been looking on, expression ranging from boredom to abandonment. Cazador beamed at them, "You didn't think I had forgotten you did you?" Relieved they walked their horses over to his clump of riders.

Cazador, Jaime, Izan, Pedro, Pablo, Leon, Maurice, Leon, and Rodrigo sat at the head of their respective conrois. As soon as they had shaken out Cazador blew a small horn and another group marched to the center of the field. They were all he had managed to pilfer from the castle and the surrounding area. They were a motley collection of porters, drovers, shepards, weavers, dyers, stablehands, a few scholars, Abbysininan and even Sudanese pilgrims. Then there were apprentices from trades ranging from carpenter, mason, tanner, and smith to priest and potter.

No matter the background they thought they would escape their current lives and try their hand as soldiers. Cazador grinned broadly. A few hours in a taverna a half hours walk down the hill from Nuevo Bobastro had yielded forty souls, which included a group of twenty women escaping fathers, or husbands who Cazador accepted without comment or question. He had been able to recruit forty more fighters scouring the castle and nearby town. Looking at the assembly he was proud of what he had been able to do. Each has been given the green surcoats with the black boots and aketons. Those who Cazador pegged as spearman were given heavy black canvas chausses, those he had set as crossbowman had chausses in a barry of black and green. Torsed leather helmets over maille coiffes completed the armor. They turned out smartly standing under the icon of the saint and arms showing the black border, green field, white shield and eight green swords.

Among the group he spotted his first additions. Sixteen men that Cazador hoped would give his small unit an edge, and their pants were black with a green stripe. Among them was Bayan ibn Abdul Al Bagdadi. A scholar and architect who specialized in mathematics but was fascinated by battles and weapons and had studied much of the Roman siege works. Cazador had met him days earlier during a trip to the library looking for more information on geometry. They had got to talking and he had introduced Cazador to Nabil a fellow scholar from Tunis and Cazador had convinced the two men to sign on as engineers. The rest were miners and carpenters and masons apprentices lumped with a few local men. They would be his sapper corps.

Cazador had worked alongside the two scholars, a journeyman carpenter named Bashir, and a Sudanese smith named Jahid. Together they had cut the lengths of wood and worked the fittings to Bayan's specifications. To create two field engines. The machines were called an al-manjanīq or mangonel and could be adjusted with pins along the main shaft to fire projectiles at varying ranges. While each could be loaded and fired by one man Cazador had tasked teams of three to each. One man to load, one to fire and the engineer to aim. The others would be tasked with preparing ammunition, defenses or protecting the machines and their operators.

Cazador looked to his djali, signalling Diallo to begin. With a nod and a swelling of his lungs he began. "Black pants, form a line and being selecting a shield and spear and side arm. Black and green barry select a crossbow and side arm. Green stripe select a shield and side arm and muster by the mangonel." Diallo's words rang across the field, lines formed and the men and women armed themselves.

When everyone was armed and the sappers, spearman and the crossbowmen and women were in three distinct groups, Cazador set aside two spearman and crossbowomen who he sent to the sappers as guards, and set about separating the rest into three groups of twenty. 'Today we will teach you the basics of attack and defense. How to march and how to form a line, and how to get into formation." He bawled with a large grin. "Lets get to work."

Cazador ordered his fellow knights and the squires and men at arms to fan out and begin teaching small groups. They were walked through the basic attacks and defenses of Al Matreg just as Cazador and his kin had been taught long ago. After several hours of drill when arms were aching and swings growing wild Cazador ordered for line and marching drill. Groans of relief turned to moans of horror as Cazador and the knights marched then back and forth across the field moving from marching column to the shield wall, to the fighting circle, and back again. When exhaustion set in Cazador called a rest. "Not a bad days work so far." Grunted Izan. Cazador swished water from a skin and spat it from his mouth before taking a long swig. "I'm pleased. These are border folk used to fighting off raiders and bandits and with occupations that leave them no strangers to hard work." There was a round of nods from the knights and after food had been distributed and eaten Cazador ordered practice weapons distributed and soon everyone was back to work.

The second session involved more drill work with spears, crossbows. As spearman learned to hold the kneeling position as the ranged troops in the ranks behind them fired quarrels tipped with wads of cloth. Cazador was pleased to see Asmā set herself apart as one of the early adepts. He took turns with the other mounted men charging formations of spearman, cheering when squires and men at arms were unhorsed, cursing and booing when the infantry lines were broken. His enthusiasm was infectious and soon the vintenaries or groups of twenty were vying for the most praise from their captain.

As the knights, archers, and infantry drilled the sappers had been training on the mangonels or with the pole slings that in combat would be used to launch vessels of naptha or heavy stones. The first display of the mangonels power came when Bayan sounded his horn and the man powered engines hurled a hail of fist sized rocks that flattened straw targets in a spectacular display moving almost as quickly as a longbowman firing shafts. "Where did you find these Caz?" Jaime asked voice hovering between shock and excitement. "The library!" Cazador said grinning. "Best part is, they're light. I can mount them on the back of mules! I'm thinking of having two more built. They wont tear down a castle but they will break gates, shatter charges and punch holes in lines if used properly." He finished. Idris the younger eyed the machines like one might a fine horse. "The ambushes we could plan. Hell, fill it with some heavy caltrops..." his voice trailed into low whistling. "You have a deviant and dangerous mind, lord Cazador." He tutted sadly, seconds later he brightened. "It's like we're brothers." He muttered with a grin. "Idris the elder kinda did raise us all." Izan pointed out to a well earned bout of laughter.

By the time the sun began it's descent in the sky the company was led to the camp Cazador had picked on a relatively flat hilltop near the arroyo. By the time night fell the Company of Saint Elesbaan was eating goat and lentil soup with flat bread and hummus. The meal was mostly silent. All but the seasoned soldiers among them too tired to chew. They were far from professionals, but they were game and they worked hard. That was more than any commander could ask for. Cazador made his way from fire to fire getting to know his company handing out small purses for their hard work and sashes to the vitenars or leaders of twenty. Eventually his rounds brought him to the lovely Asmā. "You proved you deserved to be here today," he said. Then more loudly he continued, "All of you ladies have done exemplary and will make fine soldiers." He could see the pride shine in Asmā's eyes and felt a pang of warmness in his heart. Already men were calling them the Amazons of Saint Moses or Cazador's Amazons after showing themselves the fastest and most accurate twenty among the crossbow shooters. Her smile seemed to make his steps lighter as he made his way back to his tent. He wanted to be ready for tomorrow's training.

* * *

Leon Alfiere and his old friend Idris the Elder had spied on Cazador's Company of Saint Moses for the last three days. The Old Lion smiled hearing Idris' signature: keep your shield up or I'll spit in your eye and break your fucking nose! Snarled by a half dozen throats. "Guess the little fuckers did listen eh!" He said clapping the Old Lion on the back. "Only a couple weeks huh?" The Old Lion grunted. "Mmm, first I wanted to see what his plans were with the women. They are the best of the lot honestly. But by the time I started bringing you down here they all look sort of like professionals." The Old Lion looked nonplussed. "Well he is my grandson." Idris snorted. "Him and a few dozen other bastards running around these mountains, *and* Monts Des Maures, *and* maybe *Outremer* as well." Idris said ticking off his fingers. Leon had the good grace to flush even though he shot a stiff arm at the chuckling Idris from his saddle. With the ease of a much younger man the almogovar slipped to the side of his saddle as if dodging arrows before popping back up.

"Now who's the smug bastard." The Alfiere patriarch gruffed. Idris laughed harder. "What do you think of the company Idris?" The veteran shrugged. "They are going to be a terror. The Scots will learn to shit themselves at the sight of that banner when Cazador takes to the border." Leon looked pensive, "I was thinking of putting him to use a little sooner. Replenish some of the coin the boy spent." Idris spat and looked thoughtful, "You unleashing him on the Almohads or Castile?" The Old Lion shook his head. "Neither. Some merchants have paid well for an escort out of the path of the crusade. With Castile, Navarre, and Aragon coming the requests for protection have been thick as fleas. I figured I'd have Cazador shepard them back here and fill his war chest a bit before sending him to England. Besides it will give me time to have ships prepared." Idris couldn't fault his old friends logic. "What do you say we offer your grandson a contract then?" Together the two old warriors broke concealment from the rocky outcrop above the militia grounds.

"Idris," Leon called as their horses picked their way down the slope. "I know your retired, but will you ride with the boy, just this last time? I ask not as you liege but as your friend." Idris knew Leon Alfiere , the Old Lion better than he knew his own son's. He knew he was concerned about this job for reasons he wasn't talking about. "Of course Leo, I'll make sure he doesn't get distracted. But what aren't you telling me?" The Old Lion shrugged and sighed. "The merchants have been camped with Al Nāsir's army, and the Reconquista is blocking John Lackland's shipment from the Sudan." Idris' eyebrows climbed under his turban. That raised the stakes. "It will be a good first test of his company." Idris said quietly and he and his old friend went to offer the contract.

Chapter 14: Old Ways

Gladr checked his axe, it's brass blade as hard as some of the human steel. His silver plated bronze maille glittered like jewels in the sunlight covering his pearl toned skin. Eyes the color of glacier swepts over his warband. The Ljósálfar were the greatest of all elves, once rulers of Inner Earth and worshipped as gods on middle earth. They were the elves the first men of Lucifer, marked with his light in their very skin that all might know their glory. The foremost of the Nox mightiest of Bezaliel who his enemies feared his name. Slayers and slavers of giants breeders of dragons. Until Yeshua came harrowing hell breaking their power and restoring dominion of Inner Earth to the God kneelers. Their shame had been great and their penance for failure long. But now mankind's unchallenged dominion of Middle Earth was at an end.

Idolon heralds of high king Bezaliel had come from the imprisoned throne to bring news to all lords of the Unseelie Court. Make war upon man. Build kingdoms upon Earth, bring terror and rule in my name. The pronouncement had been like music to Gladr's ears. No longer would they be bound to overcrowed enclaves and endless skirmishes with the cursed Samyazans. No longer chained to summoning circles, star alignments, and the feeble trickle of manna available.

Gladr had ruled his home of Lítla Dímun on the Faroe Islands as his forebears had for generations. His ancestors, kin of the Aesir who had fought the Tuatha De Dannan for mastery of the enclave on dragon back from Glittetind. The last of his family's dragons had perished fighting the Elves of Cnoc nan Uamh a century ago when Gladr was a babe in arms. So he found himself forced to lead his warband on foot. Behind him a line of warriors a thousand strong, pure bred Ljósálfar born and raised in the honeycombed recesses of Lítla Dímun which stretched far beneath the ocean. Using the last of his manna reserve he willed the earth to stretch and a bridge formed from the living rock stretching to the nearest inhabited island. The humans of the surrounding islands once worshipped his ancestors and Gladr decided he would swell their forces with their numbers, but first a show of force would be required. While the other lords of the Unseelie Court fought each other for power or struck uselessly at the Samyazans, Gladr would make himself a god like his ancestor Odin.

Even with the massive drain on his reserves he could feel the ambient manna rise from the humans of Sandvik who witnessed shining warriors emerge from the earth and the birth of the bridge. He sucked at it greedily like water in a sponge. Glorying in it, Gladr ran his hirdmen pounding on the stone behind him. The terrified humans had summoned up warriors a hasty shield wall forming on the rapidly approaching beach. Gladr could taste their fear... their reverence. The salt spray and soaked his beard and the wind whipped his platinum blonde braid into a sodden rope beneath his gilded bronze and whalebone helmet. His two handed axe felt feather light in his hands and Gladr twirled it glorying of the power thrumming through the weapon's shaft as it head cut the air. "For Odin!" He roared leaping the final five paces into the midst of the defenders. A wall of cloud followed him obscuring the sun protecting the gentle skin of the light elves from middle earths hateful Sun. The first human died beneath his boots as the first slash of his axe shattered a middle aged human warrior through his maille in and explosion of blood. His second attack took off another humans leg at the knee and Gladr flattened his throat with brass butt cap of his axe. A third human charged Gladr with his shield seeking to deny his weapon's range. Gladr kicked out connecting with his opponents lead leg with an audible crack before crushing the man's maille coiffed head as he screamed.

Two more men died to a vicious disemboweling sweep that tore out their unarmored abdomens. Everything was pandemonium. Gladr was screaming, the humans were screaming, and blood filled the air like morning fog. His hirdmen had already gained the beach and most of the defenders were dead, dying or had thrown their arms down in surrender. Others fled, although to where Gladr did not know. All these lands would soon belong to him. "Humans hear me! I am Gladr, blood of Odin who your ancestors worshipped as a god. Kneel before me and you shall be spared. Serve me and you shall be lifted!" For a moment silence reigned, until a human warrior bearing the sign of the Christian God, roared a challenge. "Die you devil!" Gladr could feel the malevolence of the steel spearhead as it flew toward his chest. Shifting his hips he swatted the spear away and almost didn't catch the sword that the charging warrior thrust at his face. He felt the heat of it sear his skin as he jerked his head away using the haft of his axe to thrust away the impertinent human aiming a kick at his knee that popped the joint like old wood. His axe rose and fell again ending the man's screams. "I will make the blood eagle of any man woman or child who does not obey me! I am the blood of the All Father bow before me for it is the only salvation you shall see in this world! All hail Gladr!" He roared pumping his bloodied axe in the air. His hirdmen took up the the chant and soon the humans roared it too.

With adulation ringing in his ears Gladr marched to the church of Sandvik. Flush with manna he opened a channel to the Chalkydri angelic beings of the suns heat to the palm of his hand. Taking the briefest moment Gladr focused his will, igniting the air before his outstretched hand until the building was naught but ash. His newfound followers cheered and Gladr looked out at faces ranging from those of the terrified to those on the verge of religious ecstacy. Grey beards stripped to the waist baring swirling tattoos of wolf, bear and raven a generation old. Men tore crosses from their necks

He could feel the manna as thick in the air as follower after follower was swayed to become a fanatical convert to his new faith. Christians who refused to bow were brutally sacrificed in the streets. Looking to the sky through the thick smoke he noted the sun had barely moved and people were already his. There were boats in Sandvik but not enough for what he required. Tasking sailors to prepare the first of his invasion fleet from the ships he had siezed, they sailed out an hour later heading for Hvalba, a larger settlement a short trip away.

The only route of the deep ways led south to Scotland into the teeth of an enemy enclave. This meant that Gladr had to capture as many ships as he could in the Faroe Islands, then he would strike south for Scotland and east to Norway, where he would rally more humans to his banner. With iron wielding humans under his thrall he would easily be able to take or force fealty upon the smaller Box enclaves until he was able to assert his dominance as a great lord of the Unseelie Court. Hvalba fell on a wave of blood and worship. It was as easy. Mankind had destroyed many of their manna workers and wise ones. The church called it witchcraft and condemned it, the faintest accusations would lead to torture and death. This meant that mankind was weak and unprepared for the storm that Gladr would bring against them. No longer were the Nox and Samyazans cast out like simple spirits. No longer would they be forced to act through human puppets. Freedom. Something Gladr's ancestors hadn't tasted in many generations. Even in the time before Christ they had been shackled but now the children of the fallen ones would stride the world as kings as they had before flood. Gladr Odinsblood would be the father of a new pantheon and today was only the beginning. The old ways would become new once again. Gladr kissed his bloody blade and swore it.

* * *

Leaving Genovova to look after his interest amongst her family Richard rode for the nearest port. He had already sent birds to Le Cannet Des Maures ordering his feudal host to assemble and meet him at La Londe Des Maures. With any luck he would arrive at the same time as his army. The elders of the family had supported his descision to fight for Aragon. The Al Takruri wing of the family had already sent troops to Al Nāsir and now the Du Maurmont wing would do the same thus maintaining appearances. It also gave Richard the power to act. Cazador was dangerous and The Old Lion was worse. Richard refused to go anywhere near Malaga with anything *less* than an army at his back.

His gambit with Du Grimaud has failed spectacularly in all aspects but one. He had finally wrested a seat out of this miserly family. He had no idea how long the spell that had given him sway over the elders would work, but he knew that with an army and the favor of the King of Aragon it would be too late to change their mind.

When Geoffroy IV lord of Thouars sired a bastard on a Mooress that was a handmaid to the lady Aenor de Lusignan, the woman had been set up with a small house in Caen and a purse. There Richard had been born and while his family held vast estates in France and Outremer, he had been content with small room and his toys. His mother Saracena, had filled their home with love and life. Until she fell ill. For months Richard had watched his mother wither into a shell of herself until she eventually died.

Her body was barely cold when he had been turned out of the house and young Richard had been forced to live in the gutters for six months. Six months of fights and mud with too little to eat and not enough to keep warm. The only thing that kept him going was the fact that he was descended from great nobility, that God knew this and that one day what he deserved would come to him. Richard's fortunes had begun to change when he'd been taken on as a page by a passing de Lusignan knight.

Life as a street urchin had taught him that he had a talent for violence and an hatred of poverty. Two years later he had become a squire, and a year after that a knight. Because of his looks he was often sent as a spy amongst the Saracens. Years of blood, filth and toil amounting to nothing until he met the Du Maurmonts. He'd left the Holy land with La Compangnie and never looked back. Working for Miryam and the Old Lion had led to the offer of marriage to Genovova. Richard had jumped at it, seeing a path to wealth and land. True enough he had coin, but the small estates Genevova had inherited were nothing like what he had promised himself on those cold nights in Caen.

Richard had seen much in this world. The mundane, and the magical and it was to the magical he turned. Years of spending money on spells and cantrips had finally put him where he wanted to be. A castle, land and the possibility for more. If he played this right he could become one of the great knights of Christendom. It would just require some things that would be highly un–Christian.

Making camp for the night Richard hobbled his horses not even bothering to pitch his tent. This wasn't about sleep. He meticulously cleared an are, keeping his breathing even preparing his mind for the task ahead. Taking out candles and a large bag of salt Richard made the appropriate inscriptions. It was said that the great shamans and those with natural affinities could shape manna with wands, song, or even thought alone. Like the elves, fae, or the old ones. To ease the path mankind used images and rituals. He had studied for a long time and now when his need was greatest Richard was prepared to summon a familiar.

* * *

Marcella could feel the portal open and the mortals feeble attempts at summoning. His will was weak, his aura clouded with greed. She had broken off the pursuit of the Moors who had burned her town to follow this one. Through his unguarded dreams she had learned of his fear and loathing of the man called Cazador, the same warrior that had caused her so much trouble. Unlike the other Moors she had been following, this one was not loaded down with charms and ancestral protection. He dabbled in things he barely understood, dangling his soul like ripe fruit for the plucking.

He would be no prize like her original target who seemed to shine in the spirit world, but he would do. She sensed this man, this Richard was resourceful, brutal, and loyal only to himself. Qualities Marcella could exploit. She allowed herself to materialize slowly into the mortals summoning circle. The skin of the young mortal woman she now wore suited her perfectly, and so she chose to appear draped in it. It was a weapon against men such as this. Long legs flaring to shapely thighs and hips. Her stomach was soft and her breasts pert and pendulous on her chest. The cinnamon colored skin and dark eyes of her host body screamed beauty and whispered mystery. She was a goddess, and not only was this mortal unworthy, he was unprepared.

Richard looked at the apparition before him, mouth suddenly drier than it had ever been in the desert. "I am Richard lord of Cannet Des Maures and I have summoned you as my familiar spirit. Serve me or be banished!" He tried to say the words forcefully as the tomes and tutors had taught. Rather than authoritative he felt as though his voice had come out in a whine. There wasn't a single horn, scale, nor cloven hoof. Instead before him was a creature that defined beauty clad in white silk so gauzy it might have been made of thoughts alone. Fear and desire rampaged like lions in his gut.

Marcella laughed a high tinkling sound, and watched as it sent shivers down the mortal's spine. She had touched his dreams and knew that he was no more the Lord of Le Cannet Des Maures than his horses were. For all his ambition, pride and intelligence, his fears and lusts made him small. Small enough that he might fit in her purse. His eyes blazed defiantly but she could feel his fear, taste it like sugar on her lips.

Richard screwed up his courage, but deep down he knew this creature was beyond him. He had gone too far. *Grasped for too much too soon!* Richard wracked his brain for a way to stop this but his mind was blank. "You did not summon me mortal and you do not and will not ever command me!" The apparition spat her voice sharp like lances breaking at the tilt and Richard quaked with a small animal feeling he had never known. "Kneel!" She thundered and Richard dropped as though his tendons had been cut.

Marcella smiled down at the mortal.He was no Lion, but he was a wolf. She could see hatred and fury fighting fear in his face and rigid posture. His was steel that she would hammer to her will. All she had to do was plant the seed and he would howl and bite for her. "You have great dreams Richard. Dreams of respect, glory, security, empire..." Richard shuddered. "I see it around your head like crowning glory. It's why they hate you." Richard looked up into the eyes of the being that has invaded his summoning circle and tried to rise. Instead he froze like vole in a raptor's gaze. The weight of age, pathos as madness that radiated from the creatures stare seemed to pull at the bindings of his soul. The night faded around him, his existence narrowed to the single points of the woman's glare. He could see his own reflection in those eyes standing proud in gold chased maille with a crown fused to his helmet. A dream, he'd never dared dream. A greatness he felt he always deserved. Richard had begun this night looking for a servant, but he knew now that for the reward promised in those ancient eyes he would serve.

* * *

Linda was enjoying their journey to Bobastro. It had been many years since she rode the trail with the Al Takruri, and she was anxious to see her son. She knew that losing Le Cannet Des Maures had hurt him, and she feared what that anger might bring. Miryam had given the boy a company and an obscene amount of money. She hoped she would see him before he sailed for England.

Linda's dark brown eyes swept the landscape. The rugged hills and mountains of Al Andalus reminded her of her childhood, traveling through the countryside with her grandparents. He grandfather had been a soldier who inherited land to the north outside Zaragoza. The relentless pressure of the Reconquista had forced her family south even after converting.

As they camped for the evening her grandfather taught her the blade with the last of the sun. But by day the lady Martha would tell her tales from their blended ancestry. Faro and Pemba from her Mande roots and the exploits of Sadio Sile from her Pullaren ones. She had taught Linda of manna and it's two forms nyama, and wanzo. Nyama was everywhere and in everything djali, artisans, and blacksmiths, leather workers and wood workers used it in their craft, used it to heal. If not wielded by Nyamakalaw or those with the ability to shape nyama it would run out of control and cause chaos. Wanzo is negative energy that the old ones say bled into the world by Muso Kuroni's dark influence.

The ability to work nyama was inbred into her blood. Before being drafted into the armies of the caliphs her ancestors had been blacksmiths who were revered for their ability to work nyama. Their caste has a special language and rite of passage. Her sons ath As members of the Du Maurmont clan all scions of the Alfiere house were educated not just in the arts and sciences but in the ancient traditions of their ancestors. It was expected of each male child to learn a bit of the numu of their ancestors but lacked full immersion in the trade. As nobility their occupations were set to war and chieftaincy with secret societies all their own. But only Nyamakalaw could safely work nyama. She was sure by now that Cazador's grandfather had inducted him into The Order and he she wondered how he took it. And where it would take him. Would he cave like his father and uncles, or would he rise to the greatness in his blood. Linda believed in Cazador. He was educated, pious, and a battle tested veteran and she was proud of him. But she feared for him, now mother than ever. The family priests had dreamed dreams and seen visions. There was trouble on the wind.

Miryam looked over at her elder sister, who rode next to her, but from the look in her eyes she was miles away. Sunlight glinted from the thread of her ankle length jazerant of purple embellished with gold flowers. Linda's sword slung in a baldric at her shoulder proclaiming her status as a warrior. Her modesty was further protectected by black pantaloons tucked into riding boots complete with gold spurs. Her posture perfect as she rode, amatch any man in the column. "A penny for your thoughts sister." Linda looked over and smiled but it failed to dispel the worry in her eyes. "Just hoping to spend some time with my son." Miryam sighed sadly. It's a shame I was looking forward to wintering at La Marche and watching my nephew grow into being a lord." Linda's hands tightened on the reins hard enough to make the horse snort and the leather creak. "Blast the eyes of the elders, blind fools that they are! I swear to you that Richard is a witch! It makes no sense at all otherwise." Miryam met Linda's eye again seeing the steely conviction there ramping itself up for a fight and simply nodded. Instead she said "Its sad that these are not the old days where we had the luxury of time, and folly. Where our menfolk could play at war and dabble in trade. But when the storm comes this generation will be ready to face them, if not there will be nothing to worry for because we will all be dead."

* * *

Magnus Haraldsson looked into the cold blue eyes of Gladr Odinsblood and knelt. His maille gleamed like sunlight on waves. His mighty axe glinted with malevolence as it's ornately runed haft rested across his knees. "I am Magnus Haraldsson bastard brother to the jarls of Orkney and I will serve you. I renounce Christianity and take the faith of my ancestors! Hail Gladr, blood of Odin!" Like thousand of others Magnus had come to answer the call of gold and glory. A return to the old gods and a time where the paddle strokes of their ancestors struck terror in the hearts of men. He felt the eyes of the godling on him, weighing him. Measuring as one would a horse or a sword.

Gladr looked at the newest recruit who had come to swear fealty. He had many drengr kneel before him but what he needed was a jarl. He had cast the divinations expending mana to pluck at the strings of wyrd for emanations of things to come. He had forseen a human captain that would catapult him from war leader to worshipped. The dark eyes of the young man before him spoke of a deep cunning and ruthlessness. His weapons were tools instead of toys and his manner screamed killer. Gladr smiled and took his oath.

The road up to this point had been pleasurable. Sailing from the Faroe Islands he sailed to Norway he used his mana to heat the surface of the Whale Road so that a fog dense as cloud blanketed his fleet as they pushed toward the Trondheim Fjord aiming for the city of Nidaros. Gladr had come to send a message. His ships full of the first generation of Viking in two hundred years, sea wolves all, veterans of the Birkibeinar faction markamenn drawn from the marches. Generations of fighting the church backed Bagli made them ideal recruits.

Expending an enormous amount of mana he once again pulled a bridge of earth to his ships. With a howl of merciless glee Gladr's drengr had clambered over the rails charging into Nidaros from the mist like wraiths of madness, hungry steel flashing as they cut their enemies down. The command was simple. Bow to the new god of the North, Gladr, and return to the ways of their forebears or die. The Cathedral of Nidaros had been the first target. As priests were blood eagled in Gladr's name, knights from the castle stormed to their rescue only to add their screams to those of the so called holy men as Gladr's warriors Ljósálfar and human both turned them into corpses. After the battle Gladr had marched his army a few miles east to Ranhiem where he had erected the hall behind him now.

The humans of this age were weak. Cut off from the spiritual power of their ancestors and ignorant if mana. The Church of Rome had strangled spirituality into a force of temporal power wrapped in holy cloth. The faith of The Prophet was little better. The true holy men, the mystics never rose to power. The lands far to the south and east were different, but this was an altogether softer target. The faith had never rested easily in the lands where his ancestors Odin, Tyr, and Thor held sway. Now he looked upon his human champion. Magnus Haraldsson who had greatness and war fame dancing about his head like a crown if stars.

There was a roar of acclimation from the crowd and Magnus was welcomed into Gladr's Hall. Built in the old style it had a central hearth before a raised dais where what could only be called a throne sat Lord Gladr would hold court. On each side of the hearth was an aisle that branched off like a herring bone into rows of stone benches and tables. Bearded growlers sat drinking ale and mead feasting on animals slaughtered after the raid on Nidaros. The walls were adorned with carvings of the Aesir and the the conquests of Lord Gladr. Arm hair standing on end and warmth spreading through his chest Magnus felt a queer sensation. He was Magnus the bastard. Magnus the unwanted. Magnus the bandit. In all his young life he had never felt a feeling like it. Magnus felt as though he had come home. When his brothers next saw him he would seek blood rather than kinship for now he had all he needed.

Chapter 15: Despeñaperros

Diallo sat by the fire with Cazador, Jamie, Izan, and Leon. The training of the new company was progressing well and the Old Lion had offered them their first contract. They were to head towards Despeñaperros Pass in the morning. Like all djali of the du Maurmont clan he was born to his trade. While caste was not as strictly enforced in Provence as it was in the Sudan, tradition was hard to break. Diallo had grown up studying the cosmologies of the Mande, Pullaren, the Bible and part of the Quran. It was his job not just to record Cazador's deeds and be a keeper of history, but to work nyama. The first true test of his talents had been during the fight amongst the ghul. He had sang in the tongue of his cast countering the wanzo of the undead fiends and lending strength to his lord and allies. "Is all well my friend?" Cazador asked. While their lives had been on very different tracks they had spent time serving the church and in the training yards together forming a sort of friendship and rivalry that even after a long time apart had survived into adulthood. "Just thinking about what song I'll sing the company out to. Marching songs are quite important you know." Cazador laughed. "I ought to dock your pay for lying. " Diallo smiled. "Maybe it was your grandfather's insights that startled me." Cazador nodded & the two old friends fell into companionable silence. He could remember feeling distinctly discomforted by the tactical situation too.

After the Old Lion and Idris the elder had come to offer them their first contract, they'd lingered on sharing the fire with Cazador's mensie. Diallo had sang mystifying the camp with song, make the evening something out of a troubadors tale. The mission was simple enough, march out retrieve the merchants and their goods and march them back to Bobastro. It wasn't much different to what Cazador and the others had done for much of their fighting careers. The job would pay two hundred English pounds with fifty pounds up front, which would pay the company more than well. He also gave Cazador patents granting safe travel, one set in Latin and French for Christian authorities and another set in Arabic for Al Nāsir and his vassals. They had all thought this would be easy money.

Then the Old Lion said he had news with a look and tone that had troubled them all. Richard as Lord of Le Cannet Des Maures had raised his host and was bringing them to Al Andalus to fight for Aragon. Cazador had fought to master his rage until his grandfather curbed it with his next revelation. There had been reports of dark blood rights among the slaughtered Jews and Moors, compounded by sightings of ghul, Idolon, and even a shetani following the fight for the Fortress of Rabah. Suddenly an easy mission was looking like trouble, but if they pulled it off they would sail to England with a bold reputation. Jaime looked to his cousin across the fire. "I know that face Caz," Izan and Leon chuckled. "What are you planning?" they asked in unison. Cazador smiled.

The following morning they rode out. Banners waving armor shining, to the lively beat of Diallo's drum and the cheers of the castle folk. With the infantry walking Cazador wasn't counting on making more than eight to ten miles, but it was a beautiful day and the sun was shining. Diallo's voice rang off the tree lined mountain path. "Grimgundison was Dane, threw slanderous deeds on Cazador's name. To perpetuate a lie, a deciet, a game. So a duel was called to clear the stain. Grimgundison came, long of axe and large of frame. Sir Cazador was unafraid. He blocked the axe and smote the Dane! Cleaving the villains throat in twain! Innocent, the priests did proclaim! If he's your lord than shout his name, let's hear it roar! Give three shouts for Caz-a-dor!" Diallo looked at his lord and grinned at his embarrassment. Morale was high and the company sang along. It was on the backs of such songs that reputations for companies formed and Diallo worked nyama, imbuing the newly formed company with confidence in their leader. Despite himself Cazador felt a sense of accomplishment and warmth spread through his chest.

The van consisted of Cazador's conroi with Duku and Idris the younger a mile ahead on foot scouting. His archers Constantine and N'faly rode to either side of the path as Cazador, Alcazar, and Adbul. Behind them rode Merfynn, Alberto, and Roland. Marco the younger rode behind them holding a lance with the company banner flying proudly. Behind the banner were Izan, Jaime, Leon, and Pedro's conrois followed the first vintenary of spearman carrying hide heaters with tamba spears and falchions or straight swords at their hips made by Mande smiths in the Old Lion's employ. Behind them Cazador's Amazons. The green and black barry pattern of their hose, as much as the weapons propped against their shoulders marking them out as crossbow troops. Rodrigo and Pablo's lances held the middle of the column with the second and third vintenaries of spear and Maurice held the rearguard with the sappers and the baggage. Cazador had hired a score of the lads working at the castle as porters as pages and horseboys. Their column wound their way south and east from the Old Lion's mountain fastness.

They forded river Guadolahorce and Cazador sent Pedro and his conroi ahead to the ancient town of Abdajalis. Late evening as the sun was disappearing behind the mountains, Cazador and the van were trotting into the area staked for a camp site. From the pack mules came thirty five octagonal umbrella pavilions big enough to sleep four and their war gear. Per the rules of the company every hale member participated in building the camp defenses. Bundles of wooden slats secured tough rope were hammered into the earth as four foot ditches were dug as the last tent was erected, a line of horses was led from Abdajalis and Cazador smiled. From this point forward the company would be mounted and they'd make better time.

The following evening they paid a farmer north of Estepa to camp in a fallow field having made around thirty miles. For fear of abusing the farmers hospitality the order went out that the company need only to pound the stakes. After camp was set up Cazador walked the camp forgoing the fancy Byzantine curiass he wore on the march for his gambeson and hood. As fortune would have it the first fire he came across was that of Amastan the first man to enlist. "Good evening Captain." he said rising with his comrades. "Sit sit." Cazador murmured and scooted into the empty space beside Amastan. "How do you find the march vintenar?" Amastan grinned his teeth flashing white from his beard. "Nothing but a lovely stroll in the countryside sir!" Amastan said grinning. "Speak for yourself, I don't know whats more sore my ass or my feet!" Cazador laughed with the rest of the spearman. They were a mixed crowd. Native Spaniards, a handful of Sudanese, Moors, and Amazaigh. The vast majority were some mixture of all, like Amastan whose intellect, brawn, and controlled aggression made him ventenar of the the first ventenary of spears. Most of them were Christian although Cazador had spotted a few men on the rolls as Muslims. All were welcome and Cazador broke bread sharing a meal lentils and dried goat that had been simmered long enough to be chewable.

After sharing jokes and small talk Cazador made his goodbyes and picked another fire at random. "Hail the Amazons of The Company of Saint Elsebaan!" He said grandly, smiling brightly at his all female vintenary. Cazador had planned a jape, but when his jovial gaze swept Asmā's green eyes the words dried on his tongue. Christ say something, you can't be the captain and look like an idiot. He chided himself. "Good evening captain, what brings you to our fire?" she said saving Cazador from himself. He shrugged expansively. "I plan to place a bet that this vintenary would have the highest kill count and came to scout my future investment." Cazador said recovering a taste of his normally silver tongue. "Oh really?" Asked Fatima, the daughter of a wealthy local farmer who had joined the company than to suffer being married off her unwanted suitor. Cazador nodded. He'd actually planned no such thing but now that the idea was our in the air it began to sound like a decent idea. "Of course, those bolts you shoot have bodkin tips and could rip through maille at a hundred and fifty paces! You'll reap an enemy like wheat! Paint your bolts yellow so we can identify your victims." Cazador said with a wolfish grin.

Cazador spent a while with the women, listening to their stories and learning about their lives before the company. Asmā stood across the flames from Cazador, animatedly relaying a tale of a childhood fall from a large tree. Every so often their eyes would lock and Cazador felt his pulse quicken. His eyes lingered on the curve of her lips and the way she filled out her undertunic, and hose. There were several beauties among the company's Amazons but Asmā radiated something that despite himself Cazador found irresistible. Making his goodbyes Cazador walked to his tent, Asmā's parting smile seared into his imagination.

* * *

Two days ride brought them to the outskirts Baílen where Scipio fought the Carthaginians for control over of Iberia. As they had passed Espeluy Cazador had hired three barges, and purchased as much fodder as he could find. With the army of Al Nāsir so close, there wasn't much, but he needed every scrap. As they made the Al Nāsir's camp Cazador laid out his plan. Pointing at the well worn map, he began "When we arrive, Maurice, Rodrigo, and the Amazon's will march immediately for Espeluy, and board the barges with the merchants. I've instructed the captains to sail twenty five miles west to the fortress of our granduncle Ibrahim. The barges will continue on to Cordoba but we will be riding south to Malaga. This way we should throw off any pursuit."

Cazador's knights looked thoughtful. "Most people hear merchant and think ships, if I were a brigand, I'd follow the boats." Jaime said. "Why not just take the ships to begin with?" Asked Maurice. "Barges into Cordoba, hire out some galleys and sail round to Malaga. Ships are easy to defend and with the crossbows, archers, and your sappers we'd make short work of any pirates." Cazador took a moment to roll that notion around his mind. "Too slow, and I'd rather be at the mercy of the roads than the mercy of the sea whilst taking the shortest route." Maurice nodded and then shrugged as though he didn't care either way. The Old Lion had leveled with them all about the risks of the mission. Fear of failure loomed larger than fear of the unknown.

They approached the camp slowly flying the Al Takruri banner, and were met by riders bearing familiar colors and arms painted on their shields. A black field with a curved sword in the first quarter and the crescent in the fourth in dark blue marked the riders as belonging to the mensie of his cousin Omar. "State your name, master and purpose!" The lead rider barked in Maghrebi Arabic. Cazador performed a perfect salaam before tilting his head imperiously "I am Sayeed Ibn Wilayam, Ibn Hamza Al Takruri. Rayiys of murtaziq employed by the Caliph Al Nāsir's my Allah bless him to escort merchants from the camp. You will escort me to the Caliph or my charges, that choice is yours." The horseman's eyes flicked to the banners carried by Pablo, and back to Cazador. "Welcome sir Cazador," said the soldier with a slight bow in flawless Provençal. The soldier whose name was Arsuf was a liuetentant to Omar and leader of a hundred horseman. He first led Cazador and the company to a suitable placement on the edges of the Almohad encampment instructing them to take their leisure and promising to return with refreshments. He soon returned with water for washing and for the horses and barrels of fruit juice for the men in addition to a string of goats for the cook pot.

After erecting his tent with his squire Cazador washed and dressed in a black linen shirt and pants pulling on a clean blue gambeson before belting Tempest and L'Auxifar at his waist. Threw his maille coiffe on and with a fresh torse and joined his Izan, Jaime, Leon, Pedro and his other nights as they remounted and followed Arsuf through the camp towards the heart where the caliph's luxurious tent took pride of place. They were met by the caliphs guard who asked them to wait. Rather than some officious functionary a familiar smiling face emerged from the ornate tent. To join them. "Cousin!" Omar roared embracing Cazador. "When grandfather said he'd send an escort for the merchants I had no idea he would send me a hero!" Cazador rolled his eyes. Since his return from the east and the battle with Grimaud Cazador had been the subject of good natured teasing from his older kinsman for his short lived battle fame.

Omar led him through the camp where the attitude seemed lax. "These Almohads had little fear of the Ferhingees eh?" Cazador questioned his cousin. Omar shrugged and screwed up his face in disgust. "Its not bravado, just a lack of interest. They haven't been paid in months and have refused to practice arms or drill." Cazador looked at the Almohad army. Faces in shades of brown seemed pinched and the mood was sour as though the men would have preferred to be elsewhere. The typical camp smells of humanity, cooking food, excrement, and woodsmoke filled his nose. "I feel down right overdressed." Izan said dryly. A casual glance revealing maybe one in every five men appeared to be armed at all. It was clear why the merchants didn't feel safe here. "Lack of pay is no good reason to get killed." Cazador muttered shaking his head. Omar grinned ruefully and brought his mount closer. "At least the mercenaries like me are paid." The mad sparkle in his eyes showing the truth of his words.

A short while later Cazador and his mensie were led into a well laid section of camp reminiscent of a caravansarai. A long wide tent occupied the center space with tables displaying wares that any soldier would need. Gloves, boots, knives, axes, maces, spears , and even a few swords. Another section had armor including an array of helmets, maille haubergons, and shields of all varieties. When the merchants saw his party they visibly shook off their boredom with hopeful looks at the Cazador and his knights. "Cousin, meet your charges." Omar said brightly as he reigned in before a tall thin Sudani man who introduced himself as Muhammad ibn Bilal Al Fezani, first among equals for a group of traders managing a network representing interests that ranged far as Kano in the south and Kanembu in the east. There were a dozen merchants in all, four were women with eyes harder than anvils in rich silks. The seven other men were a mixed group. Two were Kel Tamsheq with skin as dark as Cazador's where it peeked through their indigo tagelmusts. Another bore the ritual scars of the Mande, beside a clean shaven Akan in a garish gold and red kente standing in the shade of a cotton umbrella. One by one he was introduced, not bothering to learn their names. He was to escort and defend them. There would be plenty of time to get to know his charges later. For now he had to get them moving. "I am Cazador lord of the manor of Moor House and captain of the Company of Saint Moses. It is a pleasure to meet you all. You may refer to me as captain, or Sir Cazador. Indeed I am young however I have fought in France, Provence, Byzantium, Al Andalus, and Morea. I am a knight and warrior, I have sworn an oath to protect and escort you. You have two hours to pack your belongings and prepare for departure. Al Fezani goggled "Surely captain you don't mean to leave today?" Cazador lifted his chin imperiously. "Indeed I am. I am now responsible for your safety and that of your cargo. Although we are not aboard a ship, I am the captain and this caravan is now officially my vessel, and every captain must pilot their vessel with absolute authority. Anyone who challenges that authority, challenges me and I answer all challenges with steel." While polite Cazador's tone brooked no argument and although daggers were stared at him he smiled.

The merchants were marched to the company's camp, where their wagons had been unloaded and reloaded onto pack mules and horses. The merchants looked perplexed and once again their spokesman Al Fezani stepped forward. "Sir Cazador, my colleagues are curious as to the meaning of all this..." he began. Cazador smiled and stepped close to the gaggle of merchants. "We are in a camp of thousands of unpaid men, and we all know the lands of the Almohads are as rife with spies and intrigue as it is stones and sand. Anyone watching will see the company bringing it's charges into our camp. Then they will see a party ride away to seek and lodging for the morrow. When the bulk of the company will march out defending those..." Cazador pointed to the now empty wagons. "People will see what they expect to see, and I can say no more. You never know who is listening." Cazador winked and spun on his heel calling for his squire to kit the new recruits.

Marco came running with company surcoats passing one to each of the merchants. "Vintenar Asmā!" Cazador bawled and the leader of his Amazons jogged over. "Captain," she "Please escort these ladies to the Amazon's quarters that they might change in in dignity." Asmā nodded and invited the women to follow her. As they passed one of the female merchants Sa 'da bint Hassan stopped him, "Sir Cazador, you employ women amongst your company?" Cazador nodded, "I do my lady and in fact Asma is an officer of the company." more that one set of appraising eyes as the female merchants passed him by on the way to the women's tents.

Two hours later the caravan was winding its way out of the caliph's camp. "That was well done little cousin." Omar said. Cazador shrugged. "They can't fault me for doing what they hired me to do. But they could argue, so being of the warrior class has its privileges." Omar chuckled and slapped Cazador's shoulder. "Your not the stripling you were when I saw you last." He said grinning slyly. "The Via Miryam has that effect." Cazador said drily." Why are you out here as one of the Old Lion's claws. I thought you would be settling in to Le Cannet Des Maures by now..." Omar noticed Cazador's open countenance close with sudden anger. "Uh oh, I sense a tale." Cazador snorted. "A tale most twisted indeed." He met Omar's eyes. "Better one of grandfather's claws than shackled to the elders." Cazador spat. They watched the caravan wind itself ever further away from the camp of Al Nāsir, the banner of the Takruri family flying proudly. Once he had thought his future lay in Le Cannet Des Maures, but apparently The Lord had other plans for him. Rather than the land he had come of age loving and defending his future lay at the edge of the world in a place he had never seen and a company that had never seen battle.

* * *

Leaving Maurice and Rodrigo to their work Cazador and retired to the camp site with promises from Omar to return. Cazador felt anxious and irritated but dismissed it as nerves about sending less than forty fighters to escort his charges to the first checkpoint. It's a good plan. He told himself. To any outsiders it would seem as if a party of the company rode ahead to secure lodging for the main force. Tomorrow morning the bulk of the company would depart with unladen wagons as decoys. It was a stratagem worthy of the Old Lion himself whose guile was legendary. However Cazador just couldn't shake the the sense of unease that seemed settled in his bones.

Making his way to his tent he found a large covered pot next to his camp stool. It was still warm and filled with steaming hunks of roast meat flavored with garlic and onions. Filling a bowl, he sat in the shade of his tent and tucked in using a piece of flatbread as an edible spoon. Moments later Alcazar arrived with an expectant look on his face. "My compliments." Cazador said prompting a good natured grin and humble thanks from the gruff man at arms. "Had to save you some before the rest of these savages devoured it all." Cazador smiled at his friend. Alcazar might be a lover of battle but he was a lover of good food first. They had been like brothers from the day they met and like brothers they competed, bickered, and fought but their genuine respect and mutual fondness was as strong as steel. His talent for cooking had come as something of a surprise and he guarded his supply of spices as other men would a hoard of gold. Cazador had tried to promote Alcazar to the rank of knight many times, but for whatever reason it was an honor Alcazar refused. His excuse was he was too poor to be a knight and as a sworn man he got to keep more of his coins. Looking to his old friend Cazador said, "I feel like we should break camp, put some distance between us and the Almohads. I would feel better if we put ourselves that much closer to Bobastro." Alcazar looked thoughtful. "By the time we break camp again it will be damn near dark. But the men haven't been drinking, so it may work."

Ribald laughter sounded from outside Cazador's tent. Before he or Alcazar could rise to see the cause of the commotion the wooly head of his squire popped through the flap, "Cousin Omar has returned bearing gifts." Marco said beaming as he tossed Cazador a stoppered skin. Popping it open he squirted the liquid into his mouth and was pleasantly surprised to fund wine instead of juice or water. Marco came inside followed by Omar himself. "I thought your men could use a little real refreshment after a long ride." Cazador smiled at his cousin's gracious gesture but inwardly his stomach roiled with anxiety as his plans to depart today slipped away. As the wine continued to flow and Omar plied him for his tale he began to relax, but like a pebble in his boot Cazador couldn't shake the feeling that when man plan God laughed.

* * *

As time passed Caz's worry eased and he fell into the familiar company of his kin. Omar was among his favorite cousins and although the time was fraught with dangers he had enjoyed his years as his squire. He'd marched beside Cazador in his first campaign teaching him the ways of war and command in the field. From his earliest days Omar had imparted knowledge, investing in Cazador, imparting wisdom and beaming like a loon at Cazador's right of passage ceremony.

Surrounded by family his Omar had removed the veil from his face revealing a square jaw and full lips that were quick to smile but were now flattened in a harsh frown. "I can't believe those old fools disinherited you. I'm pleased that the Old Lion has sent me to Al Nāsir, now I might meet that cur Richard on the field." While Idris the Elder has taught Cazador how to fight and kill it had been Omar who taught him to be a lord of battle. "Where are you due after this?" He asked his sharp dark brown eyes focused on Cazador's own. " Moor House in England," Cazador grunted. Omar frowned, "Ahh so a hedge knight indeed then. No matter you will make your fortune with your sword and not your land. The life of a routier is not so bad and with your skills you'll never want for coin." He said with a wink. Cazador nodded cooly. "So when do we take back the Alfiere ancestral seat?" Cazador couldn't stop the harsh laugh, shaking his head as though there weren't nights he lulled himself to sleep with thoughts of the same. "The Old Lion assures me my destiny lies elsewhere." Cazador said soberly despite the wine. His grandfather had never lied to him. Cazador clung to that fact. "I might take it myself and give it back to you." Omar said airly. "Its not right!" There were growls of agreement. The mood in the tent turning grim.

Omar watched his younger cousin, the incredible temper that the had managed to hone into a formidable battle fury during Cazador's youth spark. "Richard best hope he never comes any where near me for I will challenge him to a duel and kill him. Sure we could march on Le Cannet Des Maures, to what end to kill kin and men so loyal to our line that it makes no distinction? To make war on our own?" Caz pounded his chest. "I am a Alfiere , a Sile of Takruri! Nothing can take or change that. What is mine by right of birth and effort will always be mine and Richard will always be a pretender. But let us not get distracted.

We've merchants to escort and money to make first, and when we are rich as lords we can talk about taking castles! " Izan clapped his hands and shouted "Here here!" Omar nodded his assent, pleased by his kinsman's words. He had watched Cazador grow from a brash angry youth gifted with intellect and a warriors spirit into an honorable and competent young man. The injustice of his circumstances rankled, but didn't control him.

Talk flowed freely as the wine although Omar noted Caz drank sparingly, his eyes pensive. "Did I tell you the story of my sword?" He asked. The chatter in the tent died out as everyone present sensed a tale. Cazadors eyes locked on to the black grip peeking from his cousin's waist. Drawing the weapon Omar revealed a Jile short sword with a handle and blade as black as a starless night. "The Old Lion sent me a contract that carried me far past Egypt, Alodia, and Makuria into the land of Punt. We had taken to riding at night with to spare us the depredations of the sun as we traveled from Adal to Mogadishu. The job was a simple one. Retrieve the shipment and bring it overland back to Makuria. One night my camel God curse them for the obstinate beasts they are took lame as I rode at the head of our column. The beast had been in the rudest health but a quarter glass before when we had stopped to rest so his laming was odd.

No sooner did I dismount when my gris-gris began to vibrate against my chest. I drew my sword, a Feringee arming sword not dissimilar to the new one Cazdor carries at his hip, and took my target in my fist. Moments later a keening rang through the darkness loud enough to shake the stars from the firmament. All around me my men put arrows to their bows or drew steel." Omar eyed his audience letting the tension build, even Cazador was rapt as he continued. "There we stood, eyes straining against the darkness, ears fit to burst from the racket, on legs like jelly, even my lamed camel looked fit to bolt.

My djali began to sing and beat his drum working nyama and the first spear ripped from the darkness to take his life away. We could see nothing but cold darkness leering back at us. Night vision be damned I ordered my rear ranks to strike torches and hurl naptha. Flames lit the darkness and the screams began. Later men would say they heard the voices of their wives, sisters, or children screaming back at them in pain and terror. For myself I heard my own mother screaming at me but my eyes beheld horror. Shetani, three score of them or I'm a goat raced towards our lines. They had once been men of that much was obvious, but their bodies had been mutilated into assymetry. Single eyes lit with unholy fire, single arms gripping weapons while the other was hewn off and weeping foul corruption. Yet others had but a single leg and shambled along on grossly elongated arms. Horrified my men fired, for none of the Nox can withstand iron and nothing in all this world prepared us for what came next."

Omar paused to take a slug from his wine skin. "The monsters, those not immediately stricken ducked or leapt, sending precious arrows skittering into the night." Omar met the eyes of each man in the tent. "I swear to you in that moment I wanted to run. To flee to the nearest consecrated ground and lock myself in for the rest of my days. But my blood, our blood does not flee the darkness, so instead I charged, the gris-gris around my chest glowing like a lantern and lay about me. I was so afraid it was all I could do. My men came on behind me. We were two hundred against three score. They were without maille and the least of my men at least bore a maille vest. My terror turned to confidence The shetani roared with delight and met us. I lost forty men in half as many heartbeats and the demons unnatural agility and strength burst links and shattered helmets. I wet my blade with their foul blood parrying and reposting, ducking and slashing like I too were a man possessed. Never had my skill been brighter." Cazador thought back to the fight with the ghul and remembered his fear melting into some sort of unstoppable fury.

Omar's eyes had gone far away, his cheek twitching as he relieved the fight in his minds eye. "Eventually I marked out the captain among them. A firey circlet sat upon his brow and he bore this in his single hand." Omar said holding up the black jile. "He cut at my head and and I met his monstrous blow crossing my sword arm and buckler. I stepped aside and struck his head from his shoulders. With their leader gone the shetani broke along with my Frankish sword. Less than four score of my men survived the fight. When I bent to retrieve the sword the decapitated head of the shetani lord spoke. You hold Al Aswad, forged from a fallen star, brother to the stone of the Kabba, mortal. It's power is great." The fiend could say no more. I was afraid I split the rogue's skull. It was like cutting soft cheese with a hot axe." Omar said reverently sliding the weapon home.

Some time after his story was done. Omar took his leave of his kinsmen riding back to his camp. After his tale, Cazador had seemed to return to himself a little, the strain and worry easing from his visage. With no children of his own Cazador was as a son to him and Omar had made provision for him in his will in secret. Like Omar himself Cazador had become a free captain and had proven himself a warrior and leader of men. He would make his way in this world not as a pampered lord of the Monts Des Maures or as a faceless Knight of Saint Attillo bound to the whims of the church and the elders. A harder life perhaps, but one he was built for.

Chapter 16: Las Navas de Tolosa

Richard watched as the herdsman was escorted through the camp. He couldn't stop the toothy grin from spreading on his face. The lady Marcella had been correct, and the prospect had thrilled Richard like no other. He had acquired his troops and pushed them hard to meet up with the crusade, finding them on the road from Toledo in time to join the assault on Malagón. While many of his fellow Christians looked upon the mostly Morisco retinue with disdain but with thirty thousand men deserting due to Alfonso's humane policy, they were in no position to turn away men willing to fight. After proving his worth to King Pedro he and his men were given pride of place for the assault on Calatrava.

Richard had gone to his lady Marcella for advice and she had ordered him to sacrifice a horse to her. Volunteering for patrol he used the time away from camp to perform the ritual away from prying eyes. Pleased with his obedience Lady Marcella taught Richard the making of a potion using the sacrificial blood. "Paint this upon your shields or armor and know my favor." Richard had done as instructed and he led his men in an escalade of Calatrava to great success. Arrows, stones, and spears missed them. Sword and axe strokes fouled. The slaughter had been glorious. Pedro of Aragon had gifted Richard with a purse from his own hand showering him with praise. Ignoring the jealous murmuring of the Knights of Santiago and Order of Calatrava he had basked in royal favor.

Since that victory they had found themselves frustrated. Miramollin had blocked the known passes through the mountains and the foreign knights unused to the heat grumbled loudly. Richard had begun to despair of his opportunities for further advancement when his goddess came to him with a prophecy of a simple shepard leading the army to a hidden pass in the coming days, instructing Richard to take heart and speak encouragement to all. He had prattled like a fishwife to all who would listen that a solution would come if they just kept the faith. Following Marcella's mandate had borne fruit. His perceived faithfulness brought him into the confidence of the Arch Bishop of Toledo, His Eminence Rodrigo Jiménez de Rada.

Dining with such a powerful personage of the faith had terrified Richard to no end. Anxiety consumed him making his stomach fragile and his nerves fray. His had fears proved unfounded as he learned the Arch Bishop an extremely educated man who has not only read the Quran but planned to have it translated to Latin. His greatest surprise was that the goddess, his goddess was known to the bishop as one of the Desert Mothers. That very night he appointed Richard de Le Cannet Des Maures with a new title, Lord Commander of the Knights of Our Lady of the Desert. Now not only had he the eye of Pedro of Aragon, but the Arch Bishop of Toledo as well. Even after the failed attempt to force a pass Richard's confidence was unshaken. He stood grinning like a loon as Martin Alhaja was brought before the leaders of the Crusade where he told the most powerful men in Spain that he knew a path to the valley of Las Navas de Tolosa.

* * *

The gris-gris around his neck seemed to dance on his chest waking Cazador from a troubled sleep. Meeting Omar had been a pleasant surprise. It had been an enjoyable evening, but now he had woken with a feeling of dread. Something was wrong. Missing. It felt the same way it felt when he'd missed drill, or muster for patrol after a night of drinking, only worse. Moving to the flap of his tent Cazador peered around the camp. Mist slid from its birthplace in the mountains to the blanket the camp lending an ethereal quality to the semi darkness that ruled the sky before before wolf light. With a pounding heart he scanned his surroundings for any sign of trouble. Ducking back in his tent Cazador roused young Marco who helped him arm in his lamellar curiass which he covered with his green surcoat bearing a badge of the company arms prominently displayed with a patch over the left breast. Pulling hi torsed helmet over his head and belting on his tassets that protected his hips and upper thighs and finally his weapons, Cazador felt like he could breathe. Looking to his squire who had already donned his aketon, maille shirt, and helmet, was belting on his own sword with practiced efficiency. Taking up spears and shields Cazador and Marco strode from the tent.

A sense of wrongness rode the fog. The rest of his mensie was emerging as well with similar looks of trepidation darkening their visages. All of them were armed, grim spectres of the men who had smiled and feasted the night before. "I dreamt of boots. The Crusade comes." Diallo spat uncharacteristically grim. Gone were his instruments of music and in their place were instruments of war. In his hands he bore his falchion and shield. Omar appeared, his black jazerant swathed in indigo robes, and his face veiled in maille and cloth mounted on his black horse. "Ride with me cousin." Cazador nodded jumping on his horse. "Diallo, rouse the camp!"

Cazador tore the the camp on Omar's heels, passing unchecked until they reached the caliph's Sudanese guard. "Rayiys Omar wha-," the captain began, "Wake your master, the Christians come!" Omar spat in Arabic, but there was no need. Al Nāsir strode from his tent fronted by a rich tapestry, fully armed in shining gold chased maille with plates at the shoulders and protecting his ribs. He stepped aside to reveal Idris the elder who grinned at Cazador and winked. " Ahh Al Takruris, I have been apprised of the situation. Rayiys Omar I give you command of the right flank of Maghrebi calvary. Rayiys Sayeed," The caliph fixed Cazador with the a steady gaze. "I do not know you, as I do your cousin. When the merchants said they had hired Christian knights as an escort, you were not what I expected. I had heard that the Old Lion had infidel kin in Provençal but never thought to meet one. I see an unfamiliar man before me, but the steel I see in your gaze is known to me. This old rogue" He said gesturing to Idris the Elder, "Has done nothing but sing your praises. I have fought beside your grandfather, and now I ask will you support my center, take command if need be all I ask is that you fight for me. Buy me time to save Al Andalus." Before Cazador could speak Al Nāsir guestured and a servant brought forward a bag of gold dinars. "Buy me the time to get the innocents away from this place," Al Nāsir said with a weathered smile. "and I will give you this and your horses weight in silver…if we all survive this mess." Cazador nodded. "I would be honored lord caliph." Cazador said with a bow unsure if he could refuse even if he wanted to. There was only one right answer. His kinsman were serving in the caliphs lines and if he refused there was no guarantee he would leave the caliph's camp alive. The merchants should be well on their way to safety, and somewhere in the crusader host would be Richard according to Omar. Cazador could slay him and no man could gain say him for it. "Excellent! Consider this our verbal contract. I want you to position your men behind the jihadi and the rest of my regulars will form around you. Now go, let us see what we can save from this disaster." Omar and Cazador turned and raced away.

Dawn was still a suggestion when The Company of Saint Moses stood with thousands of the caliph's Almohad infantry who were drawn from the breadth of the caliphate including many men from the Maghreb and Sudan. The front lines of Al Nāsir's forces we made up of Andalusi fighters and behind them jihadi. To the flanks were the Dukkala, the Banu Magir, the Hazmira, the Ragraga, and the Haḥa of the Masmuda confederation of the Magreb, and Arab mercenaries. Cazador couldn't have picked a better battlefield. The crusaders would have to fight up hill through woods, steep gorges and ground cut up by streams. "I could hold this place against the hordes of hell with a thousand men." He muttered to Alcazar beside him. Alcazar snorted shrugging his mailled shoulders. "Maybe if you had a thousand men under your direct command. Let's just kill the fuckers and be done." Cazador growled his assent.

Arrayed against them were the banners of Alfonso of Castile, the Archbishop of Toledo, and the Lord of Biscay in the center. The left was led by Cazador's nominal liege lord Pedro of Aragon while the the right was led by Sancho of Navarre. For a moment Cazador felt a pang of jealousy as the flower of Christian chivalry unfolded before them. He would win no fame in this contest. Even a victory here would leave his and the company's name reviled in Christian circles. Therefore the holy icon of Saint Elesbaan would remain unfurled. The company sat at the center of the Almohads infantry just behind the jihadi. He busted up the mensies and formed his front rank of the his knights and men at arms, behind each knight was his squire flanked by spearman. The almogovars were set at the flanks and a few paces behind was the second vintenary of spearman protecting the archers and sappers who would sling as many stones and arrows as they could before they reinforced Cazador's second line of spearman. They had wasted too much time and the enemy would be on the before the ranged attacks could bear any real fruit.

The crusader charged surged up the hillside like a tide. Cazador was unsure of what to do so he drew L'Auxifar and plucked up the short hunting spear in his shield hand, and roared his defiance as the forces under the Lord of Biscay and his banner of two running wolves rolled over the Andalusi. The jihadi howled and threw themselves forward even as the Maghrebis tore into the flanks of Navarre and Aragon. "Fuck this!" Cazador growled. "Fire at will!" Arrows and stones whipped into the crusader lines as they battered aside the jihadi formation. "I will not die here! Takruri! Takruri!" Cazador bellowed and charged dragging the wedge forward towards the stunned and disorganized Christian force. With Alcazar to his left and Abdul Al Daza to his right and Merfynn, Roland, Alberto, and Marco behind him, they barreled toward the enemy line. Cazador swept L'Auxifar from where he'd chambered the blade behind his back in a vicious cut that tore away the unarmored leg of a Castilian man at arms. When the man behind him tripped Cazador stepped forward behind his shield and plunged L'Auxifar into his eye. The third came on behind his shield blazoned with the wolves of Lopez de Haro. He fired a blistering swipe with his axe, catching the strike on his shield, Caz pushed the blow offline before stabbing at his opponent's face. The De Haro man at arms got his shield up to block but could do little as Cazador pinned his shield and thrust up and under the skirt of his maille gelding him.

Beside Cazador, Abdul Al Daza parried a cut with his sword and riposted with a swift cut to his opponent's arm, and finished him with a thrust to the throat. Alcazar met his foe shield to shield using his bulk and immense strength to throw the man down, caving his maille covered chest with a blow from his falchion. Blocking another attack Alcazar batted aside his opponent's shield and shattered his collarbone. Throwing his shield up, Cazador blocked a thrust, then using the lugs of his hunting spear he hooked his newest opponent's shield out of position and struck a fendente that landed in the sweet spot below the jawline and he fell as if poleaxed. Cazador heard Marco grunt behind him and his squires spear shot out from over Cazador's right shoulder to plant itself in a crusader's maille clad chest. For a glorious collection of moments the enemy were pushed back. They reeled away in blood and dismay terror clear in the eyes of many.

The Company of Saint Moses stood firm, blunting the Castilians and stiffening the Almohad regulars. The press thickened as their forward momentum slowed. Cazador sheathed L'Auxifar and drew the shorter and lighter Tempest, throwing his shield up to stop a sword cut from a mounted Knight of Calatrava that struck with the force of a horse's kick. Arm stinging with pins and needles Cazador lashed out, the knight with a cut of his own. Driven by fear and surprise the blow was strong taking the knight across his mailled shoulder spilling the stunned man from his saddle. Something about the blow felt odd as his sword's grip vibrated in his palm. Returning to guard, something hard bounced off Cazador's boot and looked on on shock staring dumbly at his blade's pommel on the bloody earth beside his foot. Tempest, his faithful battle companion fell apart, the blade slipping from the wooden core of it's grip to reveal a shattered tang. Fear, disgust, and dismay bordering on horror galloped through his mind. In a fit of rage he leapt upon the stunned knight and bashed at his skull with the base of his shield. "Broke! My! Fucking! Sword! You big bastard!" He roared punctuating each strike. Seething Cazador mastered himself. They had broken another crusader assault but he could see the bloodied Castilian forces steeling themselves for another thrust.

Scooping up the valuable Damascus steel blade and slipping it in it's scabbard he freed the mace. It was the opposite of Tempest in every way. It was inelegant instead of graceful, more brutal than beautiful, made of cheap steel where Tempest was made of the finest in the world. But it would serve. Sliding back into formation Cazador clashed the new weapon against his shield rim and hurled abuse at the enemy who surged once more. "Come and die Feringee dogs!" A clump of knights in the tabard of the Order of Santiago spurred at them supported by footman. Arrows and throwing knives arced over head thinning the crowd but doing nothing to stop the richly clad knight aiming his lance at Cazador's head. Using his shield Caz punched the lance off line and used the mace to bash into the horses forelimb even as he thrust his spear into the side of the Santiagan knight unhorsing him and setting the muscles in Cazador's shoulder screaming. Spitting bloody froth the knight rose wading forward gingerly. Feinting with his head and shoulders Cazador faked right and struck a vicious blow from a high guard to the knights left. The knob of his weapon caved in the crown of the knights helmet with a musical crunch. Wootz steel it was not, but Cazador had never struck such a telling blow with Tempest. He had barely lifted the weapon free before he was forced to parry another knight of Santiago, hacking into the knight's attack sending the sword spinning away before chopping into his maille covered arm bursting rings and bone even drawing blood. The knights horse carried him away and Cazador roared exhorting his erstwhile Almohad allies to press the attack.

The center was fully engaged as were the calvary on the flanks who swarmed like angry dust clouds of iron and blood as the horseman fought hand to hand. Cazador could see the banners of Castile down the slope and for the first time thought they the caliph's forces might pull a victory from disaster. Alfonso of Castile looked beaten, a churchman harangued him, gesticulating wildly toward the carnage upslope. Another wave of Crusaders threw themselves forward bringing Cazador back to the task at hand. Fouling an axe blow on his shield from a mounted knight bearing a lance with the banner of the Order of Calatrava in his left hand. Cazador took a moment to marvel at his foe's horsemanship before he struck with his spear using the lugs to catch on his harness pulling him from the saddle. Punching out Caz put his mace's flat top into his enemy's throat, crushing his windpipe. Whipping the weapon around he collapsed the dying standard bearer's face. The knights of Calatrava hated the Knights of Saint Attillo much like Templars hated Hospitallars and vice versa. *Oh how the Old Lion will crow when he hears this!* Cazador started to raise his arm and roar to redouble their attack when a flash of color down slope caught his eye.

Roland watched Cazador cut down the standard bearer and roared. Another attack had been blunted and bulwark of bodies equine and human formed a tideline of violence. With every stroke of his sword Roland muttered a Pater Noster, wondering what old Father Benedito would have said to see him now. He forced it all down under the relentless pressure of the necessity to survive. Chances were if he didn't kill them standing with his lord and captain, they'd be trying to kill him as they ran. So kill them he did. The mad Welshman Merfynn blocked a lance with his shield before he buried his axe in the chest of a knight of Calatrava hurling him from his horse. He was obviously having fewer issues killing fellow Christians than Roland. Alberto dueled with a mounted knight deftly wounding his hand before slashing the horse's throat trapping the rider beneath his dying mount. He looked to Cazador again and saw his eyes scanning the field. He had expected Cazador to renew the assault but instead he heard Diallo blow his horn sounding the command to open ranks. Eager Almohads surged through the company lines. Diallo blew his horn again this time sounding the command to withdraw. Shield locked with Merfynn and Cazador's kinsman Izan, Roland wondered what caused the shift in tactics until he noticed his captain's gaze trained on the banners of Castile. Alfonso's calvary was riding hard for the gap between the cavalry skirmish on their left flank and the center making straight for the Caliph. "Al Bagdadi get some fire on those horseman! Archers left flank skirmish line left flank!" Cazador snarled and men scrambled to obey. Arrows and stones whipped out at the Castilian charge clearing saddles but far too few. Screaming Cazador raged impotently as the Castilian charge tore past. Diallo was sounding the call for mounts and the pages that had been guarding the horses raced towards the company leading strings of read mounts. The Almohads fought on gamely, completely unaware of the disaster unfolding to their rear.

By the time the company was mounted Alfonso's conroi was a mere sixty paces from the camp. "Whats the plan?" Shouted Jaime casting a gimlet eye at the Almohads upon whom realization was beginning to dawn. Cazador swigged water from a flask and spat. "Its time to go. We were paid to stiffen the center and buy Al Nāsir time. We've done that, and look..." Cazador pointed to where a band of Moorish horseman were speeding away from the camp. Al Nasir was riding away from the battle as if devils chased him. "Its time we do the same. I won't shed blood for a running man." With that Cazador led the company away from the battle riding fast enough to tax the less adept riders among the spearman and sappers.

Looking over his shoulder Cazador could see the crusader center stiffened by the Order of Santiago roll over the remnants of the Almohad infantry. Those who didn't peel away when the company had disengaged were being bloodily routed. Looking to his right Cazador gasped in horror. His cousin Omar, robes and jibbah slashed in a dozen places to show gleaming maille fought gamely against knights bearing purple and argent. With an anguished roar Cazador sawed at his reins. "Company of Saint Moses on me!" Tearing L'Auxifar from it's sheath Cazador aimed for the group of circling horseman. "Al Takruri! Takruri for aah!" Cazador screamed leaning forward in his stirrups to skewer a Le Cannet Des Maures man-at-arms in the the throat. The bodies weight pulled it from his sword and Cazador cut up disemboweling an enemy mount even as his own crashed into it chest to flank. The rider disappeared under the bulk of his mount and was trampled. Sword red with the blood of his countrymen Cazador parried a slashing sword and riposted before his enemy could raise his shield. L'Auxifar slammed into his attacker's helmet with arm numbing force spilling the man from the saddle.

Eyes scanning furiously, Cazador sought Richard. "De Caen you scum! Come fight me!" Cazador blocked a knight's lance contemptuously with his shield, leaning across his saddle to strike with such force that although the enemy knight managed to get his shield up, he fell from his mount to die under a comrades hooves. N'faly of Gao was shooting from the saddle clearing enemies from his lord's path as their column tore into the Aragonese. The Company of Saint Moses wheeled for another charge. "Amastan take the spearman and sappers and ride for the rally point!" Cazador barked and with a frustrated growl and his vintenar obeyed. Omar had managed to extract his men from the melee and noticed Alfonso's mad charge. Drawing a horn from his saddle he sounded the retreat. Cursing Cazador followed in his kinsman's wake.

Disgusted Cazador led his six conrois in search of their spearman. The Caliph's mad dash from the camp had doomed the battle. They arrived just in time to see Alfonso and his knights leap the tightly packed formation of Al Nāsir's famed Black Guard. It clawed at his soul to abandon them but when he saw the women, children and other non combatants from the nearby town fleeing as best they could from the impending violence, he could buy them some time although that meant there would be no time to catch their infantry and sappers. Cazador led six conrois deeper into the valley, spying a place where they could at least slow the enemy horseman by blocking the road. Cazador spat knowing he had a choice to make. Ride on to safety or protect the civilians. Be the mercenary, or be the knight. Conscience made the choice for him and Cazador pulled off to the side of the track bloody sword still in his grip.

Jaime looked on aghast as Cazador went to the side of the road and stopped. His horse didn't appear lame or overly lathered. "Whats going on Caz?" Izan asked voicing the mutual confusion of the conroi. Cazador pointed to the fleeing folk down valley. "I would give them a chance at life." Alberto seeing his captain's plan pulled his mount beside Cazador's. "Caz be serious, we will die and the peasants will die too. It's a waste!" Jaime pleaded fury and sorry warring in his eyes. Cazador shook his head. "I will order no man to stand with me. I will stand here alone if I must. Honor demands it." Jaime issued an impressive stream of curses that would whiten a sailors hair but he walked his horse over to his cousin all the same. Aunt Linda will kill me for returning without you, so I might as well die here beside you. Your Satan's own turd Cazador." Merfynn sighed. "In for a penny, in for a pound." Lilted the Welshman. One by one the knights of The Company of Saint Moses moved to block the road with their captain and sworn lord.

Cazador ordered the icon of the saint furled and the company stood to arms blocking the road. The force of Castilians that rumbled toward them was large and Jaime didn't know whether to honor his cousin for his courage or spit on him for his foolish pride. They had fought an entire battle without losing a man and now the core of the company would die. It seemed unfair, and Jaime promised he would punish his foes for such an ignominious fate. "Halt in the name of God the Father and Christ our Lord and Savior! We are a Christian force!" Cazador shouted. Either they could not hear him or did not care to for they came on. As soon as the enemy hit range the fourteen archers in their party including Diallo and Alberto fired a cloud of projectiles. One hundred and fourteen arrows were in the air in sixty heartbeats. Jaime watched as the charge faltered in a welter of churned earth, arrow stuck men at arms, and wounded horses.

They came on again, dismounted this time. When the enemy thought their raised shields would save them, Cazador ordered them to sling their tamba and throwing knives low aiming for feet and legs. Castilians fell, but gamely they came on. Jaime watched with grim satisfaction as they bled the enemy for every inch of ground. So the enemy was a wounded beast rather than a ravening lion when the lines met.

Jaime feinted low the high, plunging his spear into an enemy man at arm's unarmored sternum. Feeling the spearhead grate against bone, Jaime gave the weapons savage twist to free it he felt the point snap off in the bone. Snarling Jaime dropped the spear and drew his Mande sword. Blocking an axe strike on his shield Jaime danced forward lashing high drawing his foeman's shield high, rolling his wrist and slashing up and under the man's maille. Beside him Cazador had traded L'Auxifar for the mace he had begun calling El Martello the hammer. With his still blood spattered spear in his shield hand he thrust forward still covered by his kite shield using the lugs to hook a Castilian's shield pulling it hard enough to unbalanced him and smashed El Martello's knobbed head against a Castilian's helmet with enough force to send blood jetting from his foe's nose across Cazador's shield. Jerking his weapon free from the dented steel Caz ducked under his shield shoving away an enemy spear, and riposting with his own punching through his attacker's teeth. Opposite Cazador the mad Welshman Merfynn lay about him with his axe splitting shields and helmets making himself a threat to everyone within his reach. So, the Company of Saint Moses was holding their own. The broken terrain surrounding the stretch of road they defend would force the enemy to send flankers on foot. With the full company they could have defeated the Castilians outright instead the best the could hope.for was a fighting withdrawal.

A bulwark of bodies marked the toll extracted by Cazador's men but it was only a matter of time before they would find themselves surrounded. Being better armored than the gambeson clad Castilian fighters Cazador hoped to make the butcher's bill high enough for the attack to end. The enemy fell back leaving more bodies to litter the dusty earth. Sheathing El Martello, Cazador drew L'Auxifar and raised it high. "For God and Saint Moses!" He roared and leapt toward the Castilian lines. An axe wielding man at arms jumped to meet him. Taking the axeman's strike on his shield Cazador punched his spear at his face and when his enemy's shield rose Cazador stabbed L'Auxifar into his groin. The man fell screaming in horror. Scything his blade low and to his right Cazador took another mans leg at the ankle and returned his sword to guard. Jaime, Alberto, and Izan hit the enemy shortly after bowing the Castilian center. Hope bright and hot sparked in Cazador's chest until he heard the telltale twang of bowstrings, and the shouts of the squires acting as rearguard.

"Stop! STOP THIS AT ONCE!" A loud voice boomed. Immediately the Castilian troops backs away several paces and Cazador gave his men the order to stand down. A priest with the bearing of a soldier shambled onto the battlefield. "These men fight under the Icon of a Christian saint. They should at least be allowed to surrender."

* * *

The Castilian's stripped them of their gear. The choice had been to sacrifice the non-combatants or capture. Cazador was forced to stand in cold fury as no less than three men armed with crossbows aimed at his head as Cazador was stripped of his fine armor. "I am Cazador Alfiere of Monts Des Maures, lord of Moor House, Captain of The Company of Saint Moses and a Christian and knight of Saint Atillo! Open the patent amongst my pilfered possessions and you shall know the truth." He spat as the Thebeai symbol that hung with the cross around his neck seemed to burn in sync with his fury. They could hear the vanquished and routed Almohad army was being butchered or enslaved. The scent of blood and offal was heavy in the air as piteous prayers to Allah intermixed with the moans of the dying and the cheers of the triumphant Christian force. As a Christian he knew that he should cheer the victory of his faith over that of Mohammed but it was more complicated than that. Too many of those being killed or enslaved looked too much like him and his captors wouldn't know of care for the difference between him and any other Moor if he recited a Pater Noster in a bucket of holy water. The Europeans adapted their style of music, dress and even their ways of fighting from the Moors. They had no problem studying translations from Moorish scholars or adopting their astrology or medicine either. It seemed to be only the Moors themselves they hated so. The very fact that his company under their Christian banners had been attacked was proof. Slowly Cazador drew out the chain all Du Maurmont clansfolk wore. He let the heavy silver cross and amber Thebei sigil dangle and counted on the avarice of the Castilians to do its work.

One of the Castilians saw the symbol and whispered something to his commander a gaudy knight in yellow and green. The man paled slightly, Cazador caught El Lleó Vell, in his captors hushed conversation and smiled. He looked to his kin where they were forced to kneel guarded by crossbows with spears aimed for their unarmored backs. Jaime's bald head glinted in the sun his, beard quivering with silent laughter. "The Old Lion is our grandfather you stupid fucks! What do you think his letters to your king and his dear friend the Cardinal might say when he learns you have captured his grandsons? " He said falling over in a fit of laughter. Cazador eyed the Spaniards with a wolfish grin. "I demand trial by combat for the lives of my men." The knight's face paled, but it was one of his sergeants who spoke. "I say the Moor is a liar and a bandit. Any thief with a gift for tongues could weave this tale! Let me fight him lord. We captured this unit and these Moorish bandits are rich and we could all do with the booty from this fight." He gave Cazador a look of cold fury, "besides he killed my brother." There was a roar of agreement from the knight's retinue as they had taken heavy losses from Cazador's company.

The knight sighed. "No Pascal, my father would never forgive me if I returned without both the sons of his oldest friend. I will fight him. Give him his weapons." The sergeant Pascal stepped away to retrieve Cazador's gear. Cazador now stripped to his sweat stained gambeson and the pants he wore tucked into his riding boots scooped up his bar nasal blew the dust from the twisted black and green torse and popped it on his head. Next he picked up his belt strapped it on before hefting his buckler and drawing El Martello. "I am fidalgo Julio El Lobo de Salamanca and if you yield or die, the lives of your men and your possessions are forfeit." The Castilian knight growled as he dismounted drawing a bastard sword from the scabbard on his saddle. Cazador watched his opponent. The man wore a short sleeved hauberk of good maille with a canvas coif under a bar nasal. "I am Cazador Alfiere , I have killed bandits in the mountains of Occitania, Varangians on the walls of Constantinople, and noble French knights at Mirebeau. I have watered the thirsty soil of Al Andalus with the blood of many Castilians this day and when your joins theirs, my men and I shall ride free with all our possessions." The Castilian knight growled his assent and launched himself forward with a vicious overhand slash, both hands on the blade. Cazador stepped offline and punched the strike aside with a rising block. Using the spikes of his mace Cazador pulled the weapon away to his left and punched the fidalgo in the face with his bucklers rim before using the space to snap a blow across Julio's forearms. Bone shattered, the bastard sword fell from neveless fingers as a scream of shock and pain erupted from his mouth shortly before Cazador slammed his mace into it.

"Moorish bastard!" With barely enough time to move Cazador threw his buckler up to catch a blow from the roof guard launched by an enraged Pascal. Using his mace he pushed his opponents blade away. With a roar Cazador stepped in to wrap his buckler around Pascal's arm and levered him forward landing a vicious blow to his aventail covered neck. With his opponent's throat crushed the Cazador allowed him to fall into a gasping heap. Springing forward roaring like a madman he aimed for the cluster of men who stood between Cazador and his kin and their horses and weapons. Ducking low he swung at unarmored thighs and legs clearing space. Within moments Jaime, Izan, Alberto, and the others were armed and attacking the surprised Castilian's. Angered not only by the death of their lord but the loss of the valuable war loot, many threw themselves at their former captives. Reaching the rest of his gear Cazador sheathed Martello and snatched up L'Auxifar and threw wild cuts at the axe and falchion wielding peons, sending up sheets of blood. There was a halfhearted attempt to rally but Cazador and the others had armed themselves and had already made their way to their horses. Mounting up Cazador watched as his men rode past casting a jaundiced eye on the kit they were forced to abandon before spurring his horse back towards Bobastro.

* * *

Chapter 17: Only Family Can Stab You

Richard stalked the battlefield and scoured the lines of Moorish captives for sign of Cazador or Omar, or any of the other claws of the that decrepit old beast in Bobastro. During the main battle he had stayed well away from the center close to the forces of Pedro of Aragon, contenting himself for smashing Omar. It had been going well until Cazador's blasted company had charged him, killing his knights and men at arms forcing him break off and reform giving them the time to withdraw. Like Miramollín the Takruris among the Almohad force had absconded.

Richard knew he had squandered an opportunity to secure himself in his rule but it mattered not. He had found a Castilian fidalgo that also served Lady Marcella and had sent him to tail them whether he found success or not Richard had opportunities. He had the eye of Pedro of Aragon and ingratiated himself with clergy not tied to the Knights of Saint Atillo and therefore not in the Old Lion's pocket. With the Almohad force broken the soft underbelly of Al Andalus had been exposed and land was up for grabs. Including Malaga.

Breaking off his search Richard made for the wilderness with only a bag of salt, a captured goat, and his weapons for company. An hour outside camp he found a level space and cleared it for a summoning circle. Leading the goat to it's appointed place Richard drew his hand and a half blade and severed the beast's head in a mighty two handed stroke. As the blood gushed forth upon the earth Richard intoned the words taught to him by his new deity. "Domina nostra irae. Domina nostram deserti fons. Domina nostra aeternae illusionis, mater deserta, domina bellica, fidelium servulorum protector firma. Audi me ut serviam et glorificem." Our Mistress of rage. Our Mistress of the Desert spring. Our lady of eternal defiance, desert mother, warlike mistress, steadfast protector of faithful servants. Hear me that I might serve and glorify. He intoned with an uncommon reverence. He had never felt this way in a church for all he was a belted knight of a Christian order. God was always an abstract, but his lady was tangible.

As Richard knelt in his circle he felt water lap at his knees soaking his hose and lapping across the toes of his boots. *She has come.* Since swearing to The Lady Marcella Richard had learned the nature of her presence. She was a water goddess. A human sorceress who had ascended to godhead to protect those loyal to her. To a true believer, one of her chosen the sensation of water symbolized her presence and favor. In the pool of spectral water surrounding him Richard saw his Lady's plan for him. Of all the crusaders Richard alone could ride into south into the province of Malaga unchecked.

Richard returned to the crusader camp making for the gules and yellow barry tent of his liege lord. Pedro or Peter of Aragon called 'The Catholic' was also the author of the crusade against the Cathars who had refused to accept his rule. As the first king of Aragon crowned by the Pope he was also a ferverent supportor of the newly minted Knights of Our Lady of the Desert. Leaving his weapons with the guards that ringed his liege's tent he was admitted into Pedro's presence. Still dressed for the battle in fine Byzantine lamellar of dark lames laced with red leather and banded with red silk. Below his golden crown his lustrous light brown hair cut a to curl along the jawline was at odds with his pale pinched features and coal dark eyes. The planes of his face seemed born to scowl, as if he regarded all he saw with varying degrees of disdain. Knees sinking into a luxuriously thick carpet Richard knelt and bowed his head, "Your majesty..." Pedro regarded Richard for a moment before saying "Rise Lord Richard, hammer of Almohads and our friend! You fought brilliantly today!" Rising and nodding to the praise, "His majesty is too kind."

The king of Aragon snapped his fingers and a page boy hurried forward to press a goblet of chilled wine into Richards hands. "To victory!" Pedro shouted and the tent full of clergy and attendants seconded the cheer. Richard drained his goblet basking in the glow of success. Emotions in the Crusader camp were high. Although the Caliph had escaped, his army had not. The mood was such that Richard thought they could march across the waves to Morocco itself on nothing but optimism alone. Buoyed by the mood he issued his gambit. "Your Majesty, I seek a boon." Richard said feeling the soothing waters of his Lady's approval flowing through him soothing his mounting nerves. For the first time in Richard's life he had the recognition he'd always felt his skill merited but royal favor was tenuous and easily squandered. Pedro regarded him, his eyes beady and unfathomable as a bird's regarded him. "Speak." The monarch said with a smile that didn't reach his eyes. "Your majesty, I seek your blessing for a raid against the Saracens. I ask only for the men of my order and my household troops." Face softening imperceptibly Pedro said "Go with my blessing." Richard smiled and made his excuses to leave. One step closer to a dream he'd never dare dream.

* * *

The gates of their kinsman's castle loomed after nearly fifty miles of hard riding. Cazador's banner flew from the castle's single tower alerting him that all had gone according to plan. Letting loose a long pent breath, he sighed in relief fighting not to sag in his saddle. Their headlong flight from the Almohad rout had been aided greatly by the horses Omar had managed to liberate from the Almohad herd. Each man had a mount and at least one spare giving wings to their travel and Cazador thanked God and all his ancestors they had made it before night fell.

While the castle itself was built by their ancestors the town had existed since the the Romans. Nestled in a bend in the Guadalquavir, and close to the ancient via Augusta, it was prosperous with trade and boasted inns and restaurants. His kinsman Ibrahim Al Takruri had ruled here collecting taxes and tolls on river trade making him the equal of the Old Lion in wealth if not power. Qaleat Bawaabat Alnaafura, of the Castle of the Fountain Gate was not large but within the main courtyard lay a lush garden of date palms and citrus trees and namesake fountain that spoke of opulence. Cazador was pleased to see fighters from the Company of Saint Elesbaan walking circuits on the castle walls along with the retainers of his kinsman. Tasking his other knights and with finding lodging for his people, Cazador and Omar made directly for the keep.

Welcomed by a steward wearing Al Takruri purple. They were ushered into a gallery where they were greeted by Maurice, Rodrigo and the merchants who sat with a tall older man dressed in a purple cotton darra'a. It could be none other than Ibrahim, whose almond shaped eyes and high cheekbones were familiar to Cazador from his own reflection just cast narrower with a nose that would do a an ancient Roman patrician proud. His pointed beard braided in gold wire was shot through with strands of iron and his head was covered with a alasho in the Ahenya style. He regarded his Christian kinsman thoughtfully before smiling brightly. "Young cousins welcome to my home." Lord Ibrahim intoned warmly. Cazador feeling shabby, bowed graciously in his blood spattered aketon. "We Thank you for your hospitality lord, it is good to be amongst kin. I am Sayeed Ibn Wilayam Ibn Hamza Al Takruri of House Alfiere . Captain of the Company of Saint Moses and Lord of Moorhouse. " He said humbly, desperately wishing he had his fine Wootz steel blade, armor, and pride intact. As Omar introduced himself Cazador envied the fact that he at least was in maille.

It would have been nice to show himself as a display of the pride and wealth of his line. Instead he was stained in sweat and blood lamenting the loss of his kit, every inch the bedraggled mercenary. The Du Maurmont elders would have shamed him for appearing thus. But rather that disdain Lord Ibrahim looked sad. "I see you, young Cazador el Martello de Grimaud. I can also see you come with fell news hanging from your shoulders like a cloak." Cazador nodded and Diallo stepped forward and sang his lord's tale and when he was done Lord Ibrahim nodded in appreciation and slapped his knee. "You have a fine Djali and deeds worthy of him Captain Cazador but alas I have grim tidings to add to your news." Heart dropping Cazador nodded slowly meeting Ibrahim eye to eye. He wanted nothing more than to bathe and sleep, but something in his kinsman's eyes told him he would be robbed of sleep. "Not four turns of the glass before your arrival my half brother Aziz came with a warning. He would storm the this castle with a band of crusaders if I did not cede lordship to him. I have until midnight." Exhausted Cazador looked to his kinsman for the story.

Lord Ibrahim wove a sordid tale of harem politics and betrayal. His brother had led Ibrahim's forces to join the Caliph leaving him with a skeleton force of three hundred to hold the castle and town. After promptly getting most of Ibrahim's forces butchered earlier in the day he had took those loyal to himself to the Christian's to turn his coat. Numbers swelled by the stragglers of the Almohad force Aziz had over a thousand men to fight for him. Compounding matters Aziz controlled the river to the east with two galleys to crewed by another party of allied adventures, seeking to intercept the barges holding the wealthy merchants and their remaining goods. Scouts had reported rest of his small army blocked Cazador's path south occupying the verges of the forest all the way to the old Roman bridge. They were in effect trapped. Looking to the embattled lord Ibrahim, Cazador made his decision. With the crusade coming from the north Cazador knew that it was only a matter of time before they were over taken by a much larger force. "Diallo, rouse the company." Cazador said wearily all thoughts of bed and bathing vanished. A plan was already forming in his mind.

A smiling Rodrigo approached him. "A fight it is then milord." he said clapping Cazadors unarmored shoulder. "You missed a fair scrap back with the Almohads but it's likely you'll wet your sword tonight." Cazador grunted, grumpily. His mind was on the battle ahead. "My captain might need this then..." Rodrigo walked to the corner and heaved a bag up on his shoulded and walked over to Cazador. " grinning wider than ever. Inside was his spare kit, the black jibbah with it's steel plates, and his green company surcoat and maille shirt. Cazador met his friend and sworn man's grin. "I don't have anything to replace Tempest, but I do have the rest of your kit. Maurice and I thought it would be funny to set the squires in fit, as a bit of a prank but all is well that ends well I suppose." Cazador embraced him. "Oh so you rogues just happened to let me present myself before my kinsman like an impoverished hedge knight! I shall return the favor when next we spar!" Maurice laughed. "Agh! Save a man from poverty and see how he treats you for it!" Cazador pulled a face and Maurice laughed all the harder. "At least we looked good!" Maurice said with a shrug. "And your humility made you appear all the more noble." Rodrigo chimed almost managing to keep a straight face.

Heartened by the good cheer of his friends Cazador washed and changed into a fresh shirt and hose before donning a new aketon made of cotton and linen. Over his aketon went the maille and green silk surcoat. Rodrigo had loaned him a belt done in ebony chased in silver from which he used frogs to belt on L'Auxifar, and El Martello to his left hip. He placed his torsed bar nasal on his head pausing to settle the rings of his cloth backed maille coif over his shoulders. Armored once more Cazador was feeling confident. While the Company of Saint Mostes had escaped without casualties, Omar's force of seven hundred had been whittled down to only two hundred fighters, their lighter horses being no match for the heavy destriers in close quarters, his kinsman's company had paid a heavy price. Together with Ibrahim's remaining forces they were not so badly out numbered and Cazador had a plan.

He made his way back to the gallery. Ibrahim had also dressed for war in shining maille with a purple wrapped turban helmet on his head and a Turkish sword with a well worn handle belted on his waist. A map and table had been brought in by the few servants who hadn't fled. Joining his kinsman by the map Cazador studied the positions marked by Ibrahim's scouts. The low curtain walls surrounding the city were too expansive to be held. The enemy was camped in three separate places blocking the passes through the rugged hills ringing the city, the Roman bridge and a force holding the river. "My lord Ibrahim, what is your plan to resist your brother?" Cazador asked. The older man looked at the walls of his castle and let forth a wistful sigh. Aziz will storm from three places. Even with the addition of your men we cannot hold the town but we can hold the keep against Iblis himself. The lines of Saif unified in battle once more!" Pride shone in the old man's eyes. Cazador however had other ideas. "Why let him bottle us up when we have a couple hundred fine horse archers among our force in Omar's company?" The Lord of the Castle of the Fountain Gate looked intrigued. "What did you have in mind?" Cazador smiled a wolf's smile. "Mayhem and havoc milord. Mayhem and havoc."

* * *

Bayan Al Bagdadi chief engineer of the Company of Saint Moses rode with his party of sappers, the crossbow wielding Amazons and both vintenaries of spearmen. Before this morning he had never killed a man, never seen battle outside of the mock combats planned by his father's weapons masters. Now he was about to participate in his second in a day. His calculations had torn souls screaming into the embrace of death and he wasn't quite sure how to feel about it. All he knew is that he must do it again, or risk dying here in an Andalusi field far from home. There destination was some poorly defined point on the main road leaving them somewhere in the no man's land between the town and the usurper Aziz's central pickets and the wall. Ahead of then Sir Cazador and his lances were preparing to strike the centermost of the enemy positions. Somewhere behind them would be Sir Omar and Lord Ibrahim. *How did I get here? Disowned by father, and no longer able to support my scholars lifestyle you become a soldier.* He told himself. Riding across a field three hours before midnight, arse sore and voice raw from screaming orders huffing like the pack mule carrying his precious shot, Bayan found he was enjoying himself more than he ever had at university. Judging his position to be about midway between the town and the enemy he called the halt. As he ordered them assembled, Bayan could still hear the creak and snap of the traction trebuchets that had devastated the crusaders earlier in the day and hoped they would prove and equally nasty surprise tonight.

Cazador had grabbed a shield and an ascona muntera from the company supply and walked his horse with his eight conrois along with forty horse archers borrowed from Omar. Most were from the Nubia where the sons of Meroe still practiced the art of the bow from horseback. Some were Turks born to the saddle recruited from the ranks of the Turcopoles in the Holy Land. Others were Mandeleku lancers from the western Sudan or Du Maurmont clansmen. When combined with the sixteen archers from his own company the would have the ranged support for what he had planned. The enemy pickets consisted of teams of spearman and crossbwmen stationed every twenty yards supported by a staggered picket of horseman. They seemed alert and ready, Cazador smiled. He was ready as well.

They crept into bow range blessing the torches that ruined the enemy's night vision. Positioning themselves in a wedge forty eight fighters and one djali strong. It was by no means enough men to carry the encampment, but it was more than enough to start a fight. Which is what

he intended to do. Once everyone was mounted Cazador plucked a throwing knife from its baldric. "For God and Al Takruri, Saint Moses and Alfiere !" Beside him Diallo sounded his horn and arrows shot over their heads hissing and flapping like a flock of birds taking sudden flight. When the first sounds of pain and terror reached them Cazador led the charge. The gap between the line of torches and the shadowed forms of his foeman closed quickly and Caz hurled his throwing steel at a maille clad rider trying to spur his mount to counter charge. The heavy knife spun end over end to bury itself in his mailled chest. The struck rider, stunned and wheezing slid from the saddle but Cazador didn't see. Hurling his second knife he struck a crossbowman in the face as he shouldered his weapon sending the deadly bolt zipping into the side of spearman's head.

Cazador flew past the dead footman and tore L'Auxifar from it's sheath. Scanning for a new target Cazador spied a knight rallying nearby troops, his desperate Spanish harangue clear even over the sounds of battle. With a joyous roar he spurred for the Spanish knight who lowered his lance and bellowed defiance. Turning his mount before the spear could reach him, Cazador dropped his sword low and slapped the lance aside high and wide. He had just enough time to see the Spanish knights eyes widen with horror as he backhanded L'Auxifar into the side of his pothelm with thunderous force knocking the light from them forever. The crowd of footman torn between fight and flight died. Cazador's horse made the first disappear under a flurry of hooves as he thrust his sword into the face of another impaling his head. Using his knees he turned his mount to free his blade and covered his left leg and horse with his kite shield. Blocking a blow from and eager brute with an axe, Cazador leaned across his saddle and drove his sword's edge into his attacker's neck. The maille held but the man fell. Reversing his blow Cazador cut away the hands of a footman reaching for his bridle. Turning his mount right then left he trampled two more foes and punched his sword through the teeth of another. He had just enough time to wonder where the rest of his wedge had gone when Alcazar, Marco, and Abdul erupted through the remaining crowd of footmen.

At the sound of Diallo's horn they disengaged, laying low over their saddles as a flight of arrows arced overhead. The knights men at arms and almogovars passed through a gap in the archers lines as the ranged troops proceeded to pour four more flights into any pursuit. Two hundred twenty four arrows in half as many heartbeats completely blunted the enemy counter charge. Horses and men screamed the snap of bone and wood was loud in the night air. When Cazador heard screams to reform and press the attack, belted in a half dozen languages from the enemy lines, he smiled.

* * *

Amastan watched as the captain and his riders returned. His ass was still sore from the long ride here and he was glad to be out of the saddle even if he had to stick a few fuckers for the privilege. The archers took their place with the sappers in the middle of the hollow square formation while the knights, squires and others took their places on the southern and eastern faces. He locked eyes with his captain meeting him with a feral growl as they clashed their helmets together. "You ready Mas?" Cazador gruffed using the nicknamed he had acquired during their short training. For all his wealth education and titles Cazador treated Amastan like a friend and after the mornings battle they were brothers in arms. The captain's lance slid in among his vintenary and he found himself beside Cazador with the hulking Alcazar Al Thawr to his left and the Fezani man at arms Abdul to his right.

Sir Cazador sheathed his longsword and drew his mace. Amastan hefted his own monstrous falchion to his shoulder, then he counted his half dozen tamba in the earth by his shield for the dozenth time. Beside him the captain and his picked men were calm almost bored as though they hadn't just ridden in a wild moon lit charge and riled a large enemy force.

As the thunder of hooves began again the field engines manned by the sappers creaked and snapped to life. Stones and pots of expensive naptha and saltpeter and water whistled malevolently toward the enemy. When the renewed charge was struck, it was like something out a nightmare. Men and horses exploded in flames and bright light to expose pulped and smashed bodies. Human pyres danced like demons sprung from hell and beside him the captain cheered. Hooves, this time from the east were met with the same fate and swatted with the same firey god's hand that had just laid their comrades low. Flights of arrows like the ripping of scores of sheets tore into the night trading steel, wood, and sinew for blood, pain, and death.

Amastan had seen this all in practice. He had seen a taste of it this morning. He had listened to Captain Cazador explain the plan. None of it had prepared him for the reality of what was unfolding around him. He looked at his captain who was laughing with a mad gleam in his eye. Fighting on foot was a bit like a tavern brawl with a bit more organization and a fuck ton more pointy things. *That* he enjoyed throughly, but this was different. Cazador's organized murder felt altogether more nefarious than he was used to. He found himself grinning back at the captain. He was having fun and that scared him. He hadn't even stabbed anyone yet.

* * *

By the time the enemy infantry pushed through artillery and arrow range, Asmā had begun to feel particularly cheated. Shouldering her weapon she screamed the order to fire and a wave of bolts snapped forward. She whooped when she saw her own bury itself in the throat of a bearded almogovar in a faded aketon. She was already hooking the weapon over her foot to reload before his body hit the ground. The Amazons as they were called by their comrades were mounted and using the extra height to shoot over their forward ranks into the enemy. With a grunt her weapon was charged and a bolt dropped into the slot. Taking a moment to check for leaders among the enemy she exhaled and fired sending her next bolt into the chest of a roaring man at arms. Asmā's third bolt scored a lucky hit deflecting from a helmet to slide into another mans visor.

She reloaded her weapon for a fourth shot but the enemy front ranks were engaging with the company's own. "Pick your shots and switch to tambas and throwing steels!" She bellowed before standing in the stirrups to fire her final shot. The third ranker died with a quarrel in his throat and Asmā shoved her crossbow in her bag and pulled a tamba from the bucket attached to her saddle. With a grunt she threw it high to arc into the packed mass of the enemy rear ranks. Pausing to select a second javelin she saw her fellow vintenar Amastan standing with the captain and the arrogant giant Alcazar each were working feverishly to out compete each other in murder.

The captain slammed the rim of his shield forward, bashing into an enemy footman's before yanking it down with the lug of the short hunting spear and slamming a monstrous blow into he enemies maille coiffed head killing the man instantly. Beside him Amastan feinted high drawing his enemy's shield up and cut low taking him in the leg at the knee with his falchion and bashing him away. Alcazar with speed belying his great size blocked an enemy spear with his shield and shot forward using his long arm to propel his shields edge into his enemy's face with enough force to toss the man back to his comrade with his face a ruin of blood and stark white bone.

With a shout of feral glee Asmā tossed her second spear taking an enemy in the chest before he could get his shield up. It was a divine throw. Seconds after it landed Sir Cazador plunged his spear into the throat of a wild eyed axeman. Forced to drop his spear and duck a slashing sword the captain rose from his crouch as he chopped his other weapon into his attacker's ankle, and punched him away with his shield rim. The captain's enemy fell away jaw hanging, teeth shattered, and his left ankle a mangled ruin, just as Asmā's kill fell to Cazador's feet presenting the tamba like a gift. The captain plucked the weapon free and turned as though not surrounded by men trying to kill him and saluted her with the lopsided grin that made her feel warm and anxious at the same time. "Alfiere and Saint Atillo!" She shouted and the captain roared turning back to the slaughter.

* * *

Cazador pressed his lips into a grim line as blood splashed his face. He could feel Asmā's eyes on him sending a strange thrill through his bones and pushing him to fight harder. El Martello was a short weapon requiring him to close to kill or down opponents meaning he used his shield for offence as much as defense as he flicked aside attacks and battered foes. Using the sagittate leaf shaped head to catch on enemy shields and armor to pull men into El Martello's range, Cazador wrought red ruin. The creak and snap of the torsion engines which had fallen silent shuddered to life once more. Soon the sound of shattering ceramic and the juddering impacts of shot striking the earth came from his right. The third part of Aziz's forces had come. N'faly of Gao barked orders like a man possessed directing the arrow fire west toward the closing threat.

Cazador sensed the weakness of the opposing line. Illuminated by the still burning flesh of their comrades he could see fear in their postures and the rolling whites of their terrified eyes. They had come for plunder. To raid and pillage. Instead they had found fire and death. They menaced and made desultory lunges with their spears across the corpses of their fallen, but Cazador could feel the truth. The Company of Saint Moses had reaped them like wheat. "Diallo, the signal if you please." Cazador said calmly and the djali thrust his bloodied sword into the earth and drew his horn to blow four loud notes. The signal to Omar and Lord Ibrahim clear.

* * *

Ibrahim had been lord of the Castle of the Fountain Gate for forty years and had had fought in over a hundred battles and skirmishes but never in the shadow of his forefathers castle. When he heard the signal he needed no speech or stirring words, there was simply a wordless cry of rage as his expensive Norman destrier sprang towards the enemy. His lance felt light and balanced in his hand, his shield cut the wind as he raced towards the enemy. He could see them clearly marked by fire as Cazador had promised.

The young mercenary captain had provided the perfect anvil on which to break the enemy. Already what looked like half his brothers host lay broken like so much floatsam on the beach of Cazador's company's steel. Ibrahim felt a feral grin tug at his lips. "Takruri!" He bellowed standing in his stirrups and plunging his lance into one of Aziz's loyalists taking him in the throat and plucking him from the saddle. Allowing the body to fall from his point he hurled the weapon to impale the horse of another. Drawing his Turkish sword he cut left and right chopping and wounding any man in the path of his wild charge. Throwing his shield up to block an enemy lance he used his knees to turn his mount into his cut catching the side of his helmet with a vicious dent. The stunned enemy man at arms was helpless to stop the follow up cut that crushed his windpipe and tumbled him from the saddle. Hunting his errant brother, Ibrahim Al Takruri screamed a battle cry into the night. He could hear his ancestors singing in the war din and they compelled him filling him with vigor.

* * *

Aziz watched in horror as his force disintegrated around him. He saw his elder brother born to their father's first wife tear through the last of his reinforcements cutting the Venetian boatmen to pieces. Another mounted force was currently circling like a desert storm, decimating his forces with arrows and javelins. By some miracle he had gotten spearmen between his rear and the approaching calvary and was now watching helplessly as his brother's allies shot them to pieces. The singular cloud of horseman had split and now formed two revolving circles that spat arrows, javelins and the cursed Zanj throwing knives. Men dropped like flies as knives and javelins cleaved legs and groins while arrows fell seeking necks and chests.

To his front Aziz faced implacable opposition. The same mounted force who had raided his camp now faced him dismounted and had meted out fierce casualties breaking the spirit of his force. He had sent wave after wave only to have them pulped by artillery, flayed by arrows, or butchered by hungry blades. What was supposed to be his moment of glory had turned to disaster. With a horrified groan his rear guard imploded and the once ranged horseman poured into the gap led by a rider with a sword so dark it seemed an absence of light. "To me!" He roared but his last few fighters seemed paralyzed by the horror of the new reality as the warrior in the green surcoat screamed for a charge.

* * *

Cazador pulled the front two ranks with him in his wild charge. Rather than a fight it was slaughter as the enemy were caught between running and fighting, they did neither and died. Shoving with his shield he smothered an axeman before chopping into his unarmored thigh and slamming El Martello into his face to finish him. Shoving the corpse back he got his shield up in time to stop a falchion and punched the tamba into the man's eye before he could recover. Suddenly there was space in front of him. A nobleman on a fine white warhorse, his pale features washed by moonlight spied him and leveled his unbloodied lance at Cazador spurring his horse in a charge. The lance closed the space between them in an eye blink, and only a wild parry born of instinct and terror saved him. Cazador back cut savagely tearing open the horse's flank with the maces sharpened knobs even as he drove his spear at the rider. The steel spearhead met his enemy's torso squarely but the links of the expensive maille held and instead the rider was pitched over the high back of his saddle instead.

Man and horse hit the ground at the same time and Cazador slammed El Martello's flange against the riders camailed neck crushing his windpipe. The nobles legs scrabbled frantically and his back arched as he fought to breath. Moments later a screaming blood spattered lord Ibrahim exploded from the night plunging his lance with bone splintering force into the dying man's chest. With a mighty sob Ibrahim tore his lance free, tears cutting tracks across his blood spattered face. "Aziz!" He screamed voice raw with anguish. "I bounced you on my knee! The little brother I had always wanted! How could you let greed bring us to this! You took everything from me!" Lord Ibrahim screamed at his brothers corpse. Cazador hung his head. Unable to face raw emotion in his kinsman's voice. Even the wounded and the dying seemed to hush themselves before he force of such pain. They had won this battle, but Lord Ibrahim had suffered and unspeakable loss.

Chapter 18: Fangs of Betrayal

Oberon led his force from the deep ways into the dazzling sunshine of middle earth. The high valley was forested with oak, lime, fir, and hornbeam. They gave way to an beech forest that was old when his ancestors were young. There were no trails, simply game paths. This area was home to wolves, wildcats, deer and cynocephali who unlike men elves and dwarves needed no road to travel upon. "At least the ground cover is thin." Minerva said from atop her war moose. "But I will see what I can do to get us a road or else driving the gift herd through the forest will likely be the death of us all. Muroni stalk these woods." Oberon lifted a hand, "Belay that, we are guests here and I would be loath to upset our potential allies or the spirits of this place." Minerva nodded giving Oberon the sense that he had passed some sort of test.

Establishing the channel to Zuriel was as easy as drawing breath. The spirits of the trees and land were old and deep, the manna here as plentiful as water runoff from a glacier. Oberon didn't want to destroy a single branch, he simply requested space for his column to traverse the depths of the ancient wood. A crackling filled the air as though some great beast lumbered through the trees. Branches swayed as though tossed by a storm and inexorably the game trail began to widen. Roots thicker than a man's thigh slithered through the cold damp earth and trunks immobile for countless years moved. A voice high sweet and clear rang out as Minerva added her song's magic to Oberon's channeling.

Unlike humans, Nox, or other Samyazans the fae folk sang and danced their magic, manipulating manna with tone and movement. Minerva's song seemed to intertwine synergistically with Oberon's channeling. He could feel rather than see the sacred geometry that they created together as he was struck by a sense of attunement. It was beautiful and Oberon felt no shame in the tears that rolled down his cheeks. Fae and elves had been enemies or ignored each other. Such had been the way for so long but Oberon couldn't understand why. *What wonders might we have wrought together.* He thought as the trail had widened enough for three of the great fae war moose to walk abreast without their antlers touching.

With a peaceful heart and a sense of satisfaction Oberon led his agema to into the forest beyond. His eyes met Minerva's and something passed between them. Something that Oberon could not shake. She was the epitome of fae beauty. Pouty lips below a button nose,and almond shaped eyes that blazed above her high cheekbones. Her sun toned skin was like diamond shot gold and she smelled of mint and jasmine. She was both muscular and plump in ways that intrigued Oberon far more than they should. It was the last type of distraction he could afford but when Minerva suddenly smiled at him, it was hard to care.

Even with the widening of the path the branches of the trees interlaced far above their heads diffusing the sunlight to dapple the path around them. The smell of life was everywhere both similar and different from forests in Inner-Earth. Many of the plants of his homeland required manna, these bled manna replenishing his reserves to make his expenditure earlier negligible. "This land is wasted on the Cynocephali." Fahreed muttered. "All this manna and no access to it, it's like living in the ocean and being unable to eat fish. Oberon shrugged. "None have had the strength to take it. from them." Farheed smiled wickedly. "Simply because no djinn have come to these lands." Oberon smiled wanly at his second. "Shouldn't you be off scouting?" Oberon asked his second.

"I've just returned." Farheed said shrugging. "There was a curious absence of tracks that makes between my shoulders itch. A game trail should have tracks. Boar, deer, even the Cynocephali themselves. Yet there is nothing. It's as though someone wiped the forest for clean of all passage. Where there are no hunters there should be prey. It is the law of nature. Even with your working. *Especially* with your working to make the trail there should be many signs of panicked beasts escaping our line of march." Though far from a woodsman Oberon understood the way of things and recognized the threat.

Alert now, the cathedral of trees seemed more like an ambush waiting to happen than a thing of beauty. Even with his elven senses far keener that those of man, mauros, dwarf, or fae he kept the scouts of his agema well forward and to the flanks of the main column. Nobody had told Oberon where to go. They had pointed to a map and said that this area was the territory of the Dinte Rosu. He didn't want to stumble into a camp of village and be seen as hostile. He also didn't want to be caught strung out like drying fish. The ancient trees loomed like silent sentinels in the dappled gloom. It was easy to imagine they hadn't left the deep ways. The massive karst and deep caves had woods every bit as ancient and significantly less foreboding.

A horn sounded moments before a fleet footed djinn scout raced towards Oberon's agema. No sooner than the horns echo perished in the trees came a chorus of howls and yips that set Oberon's shorthairs to standing. "Greetings King Oberon, my lord of Bimmah's Gate sends his compliments and asks that the herd be brought forward with all due haste." The breathless djinn uttered. He had a horses legs and large dark eyes under a cloth of silver turban. Oberon nodded and turned to Minerva, "The herd milady if you please." Signalling to a fellow fae heavy calvary Minerva fell back to where the drovers led the cattle.

She returned moments later, leading a massive bull by a tether. The rest of the short horned cattle were moving at a brisk trot behind her moose and the bull. Minerva winked at Oberon as she handed him the tether and took her place beside him. Not bothering to call up his bodyguard Oberon drew himself up and spurred his mount following the scout down the path.

The Cynocephali were not what he expected. Thirty or so of the tall beings stood in baked leather armor covering human like torsos on dog like legs. Their leather helmets were shaped in the likeness of dogs and they carried seven foot spears with bronze tips and large hide shields. From their necks hung a pendant bearing the symbol of their pack. The leader among them was obvious for he bore a corselet of bronze scales and his open faced helmet revealed a coal grey furred face with a wolf like snout and amber eyes that blazed like small suns in the half light of the woods. Stepping forward the creature spoke in Latin better than Oberon's own. "I am Fier, Huntmaster of the Dinte Rosu." The beast man's voice was somewhere between a growl and an oddly nasal whine. "I am Oberon, King of Penume's Reach and taxiarch of the Army of the Seelie Court. I come seeking friends of allies and bring an offering of fatted cattle." Oberon dismounted and walked forward all but dragging the bull, freezing as Feir sniffed him. When the cynocephali chieftain completed his circuit he favored Oberon with a small bow. "You are well met King Taxiarch Oberon." Feir said solemnly.

The King of Penume's Reach drew his mace Sebarī and brained the beast beside him and a single fluid motion, the bull loosed a confused grunt and fell over dead. With skill born of a lifetime of hunting Oberon had the beasts heart and liver out and on his shield which he offered to the lanky cynocephali. Fier eyed Oberon and his offering imperiously down the length of his iron colored snout. He met the dog man's eyes. Oberon didn't fear this creature nor any force of arms he could summon. He has six thousand well drilled fighters yet to be blooded as a unit and Oberon would welcome a test. He pushed all these thoughts into his gaze. Fier's lips pulled back in an expression Oberon guessed was a grin before scooping the meat from the shield and into his mouth with alarming grace.

With the meat devoured Fier let forth a loud howl. When the last echoes of his utterance rang through the trees Fier looked to Oberon, "Follow us, we will seal our agreement with food and drink!" Oberon nodded offering a shakey smile and loosed a breath he didn't know he'd kept pent up. He thought back to the words of his commanding strategos, Illyargen. *The Daji will be the key to this war, for good or ill.* It was why he of all the Taxiarch Paladins had been sent on this mission. His home, Penume's Reach was an old and respected Kingdom. It's rulers had been intergral to the fabric of Samyazan history. Sending Oberon had been a calculated move to show the Cynocephali that the full weight of the Samyazan aristocracy was behind the invitation.

With an honor guard of Cynocephali warriors they set off. After an hours march they came to a massive clearing. In the distance Oberon could see a timber wall studded with adobe towers and a large gate fronted by a wide ditch. "Your force may camp in the meeting meadow." Fier growled pointing to well drained field studded with chamomile and lavender. "We will give your people time to settle in and will join you at sundown to discuss terms and settle in for a welcome feast. Fier said grinning toothily. Oberon nodded. "Thank you Lord Fier, this valley is beautiful and will make a fine camp. Your hospitality is appreciated." Oberon knew from his study of the Cynocephali that the dog folk rarely if ever allowed outsiders into the pack den. Instead they would camp side by side with allies and share hospitality. Oberon barked a stream of orders for his taxiarhai to encamp, his stomach already rumbling at the thought of roasting beef.

Oberon was clean and dressed as diplomat. The dust of the long march has been scrubbed away returning the glow to his amber skin. Bare headed barring his circlet of rank he wore loose silk pantaloons and short silk tunic under a fresh Seelie Court army surcoat. He belted it with loops for his mace on his left hip and a short sword on the other. Oberon was checking himself over when the runner from the man gate was admitted by his guards. "Lord King a messenger from the Cynocephali has come." Shouted an elvish soldier, his features hidden by the cheek guards of his helmet. Oberon followed the trooper to the gate of his camp where he could see the tall form of the cynocephali messenger. The dog man's features were more human than canine with sandy blonde hair slightly lighter than it's tawny fur. Rather that a true snout as

Fier sported, the messenger instead bore an overlarge nose and enlongated mouth. When Oberon came into view the cynocephali smiled, showing off a mouth full of teeth little different to Oberon's own. "Greetings King Taxiarch Oberon, I am Priscus." The creature said with a bow causing his pack pendant to dangle from his neck. His voice carrying none of the yowling tones of his lord Fier's. "Before the festivities begin, the elders ask that you come and present your proposal to the people formally." Oberon smiled, "Of course allow me a moment to set my affairs in order here and you may escort me." Priscus bowed a courtiers bow. "Of course!" He said with just a hint of mockery as he shot Oberon a toothy grin.

When Oberon set out with Priscus it was with a modest retinue. With him were Farhad, Minerva, a pair of heavy infantry one a dwarven woman called Ayatope and a Mouros called Arskan. Where the dwaven folk were short and stout, the Mauros were of medium height and well formed. Both races were famed for their craftsmanship and their bronze armor ornate under their Seelie Court coats. The twins Marco, and Leopoldo the Encantando light infantrymen of his Agema swaggered along like the bravos they were, their longing for the sea was a distant storm in their eyes. Last was Guion his guardian since they were five year old boys in the high keep of Penume's Reach. Together they represented the core races of the Seelie Court and he prayed the symbolism wouldn't be lost on the Cynocephali. They were offering more than alliance at this point, they were offering community.

As they strode through the well made main gate Oberon was astonished. He wasn't quite sure what he expected. The streets were paved with smooth stones and lined with trees and statues of armored cynocephali. The symbol of the Dinte Rosu, a set of fangs dripping blood in blue on a yellow field was everywhere. The buildings reminded Oberon of overturned ships, most were three stories tall and lay on either side of the paved road that spiraled inward as they walked. Everything was painted in vivid blues and yellows matching the clothing of many of the Cynocephali. Men women and children, young and old had turned out to watch the procession. They stared on with curious eyes and Oberon noted a few snarls of disdain. For long centuries the Cynocephali and other Daji had lingered on the outskirts of Samyazan society as outcasts, bastard siblings. Oberon hoped that he was equal to the task of closing a gulf millenia wide.

Priscus led them into a market consisting of a warren of orderly stalls and pens. Vendors and their patrons alike stood bearing mute witness as Oberon and his party marched toward a large structure painted a vivid blue with a domed roof of yellow gold leaf. At the door guarded by two cynocephali warriors wearing bronze plate armor from the featureless helmets guarding their heads to their toes, bearing long swords. "Who approaches the den of the elders?" One of the guards yowled in the near musical tones of the Cynocephali. Oberon stepped forward drawing himself up to his full height. "I am Oberon, King of Penume's Reach and Taxiarch Paladin of the Seelie Court." The cynocephali guard's amber eyes seemed to pierce his soul and weigh his worth. It was only a heartbeat it was interminable before he nodded and Priscus led them inside.

The interior was dim lit by a single fire surrounded by Cynocephali. Hanging above their heads was their pack banner of dripping fangs. Their great age was clear from the grey along their snouts and eyes that screamed antiquity like the great trees of the forest. As they approached one of the elders rose. Judging by the way the tunic pressed against its withered frame Oberon guessed it to be a woman. 'Why do you come before the elders of the Dinte Rosu Oberon King." Oberon bowed using the movement to gather his thoughts. He knew that to fail in this would doom his cause. While his offering had been accepted, no deal had been struck. Oberon knew his next words had to be careful. "I have come to right an ancient and egregious wrong." He began, tamping down on his anxiety like a rider curbing a skittish horse. "The Seelie Court has been reformed and it is the will of the people that all Samyazan's have equal right and representation. Your people have long served as brave and loyal mercenary forces, however we seek allies not just in war but in peace as well. I have come before you to ask that the Cynocephali join us." As Oberon's voice faded into silence he felt the tension in the room rise. The scrutiny of the elders lay upon him, their gaze like millstones on his shoulders. Oberon felt his heart sink. The journey had been a waste of time, the chill wafting from the Dinte Rosu elders was answer enough.

"We smell no deciet and can sense the purity of your cause. We applaud you for making the journey here and for your attempt to right an ancient wrong. The history of Penume's Reach and it's leaders are known to us even here in this far flung backwater. Tonight we feast and celebrate the future of the Dinte Rosu and the Seelie Court." The lead elder's words came just as Oberon was about to turn away. It took all his willpower and noble upbringing not to sag in relief like a popped bladder. Taking a breath Oberon bowed to the elders. "I give you my thanks." He said almost giddy with relief.

***

Even as a king, Oberon had never seen a board so laden with game. Roe deer, fallow deer, Mouflon, chamois, mountain goat, and boar joined a variety of fowl and fish. The Cynocephali had set up camp a short distance from Oberon's taxiarchy and pitched enormous tents and large tables between the two. Mead and wine flowed like water and Oberon was sure the few Agema he had left on guard were just as drunk as the rest of them were. It mattered little Fier had been an immaculate host toasting, joking, and riddling. The entire evening bore the air of a midsummer's idyll.

Oberon turned to Minerva who sat at his left hand where they were placed at the center of the table. Her dainty appearance belied the fact that she could quite possibly eat more than he and her war moose combined. She had attacked the venison steaks with the same abandon that she seemed to do everything else. She grinned at him over her pitcher of wine. Her cheeks were flushed her eyes sparkled and Oberon simply wanted to bite her for reasons that he both could and could not understand. "Dance with me." She demanded. Oberon rose and allowed her to lead him to where Seelie Court soldiers and Cynocephali cavorted to the haunting and rousing music of their hosts.

Oberon did his best to mirror Minerva's steps and they shook, twisted, and gyrated to the drum and lyre based music that the Cynocephali wove with their oddly beautiful singing. "You dance well for an elf." Minerva said unable to hide her grin. Oberon smiled back afraid to speak and show his delight at her praise. He was her officer and he knew that what welled inside him was at best impropriety. He tried to fight it but the press of her unsubtle curves against him swept away his resistance, and from the glint in her eyes the fae noblewoman knew it. Their people had been allies and enemies for a thousand,thousand years and such history paled in comparison to the overwhelming curiosity driving him to need to know what her lips tasted like.

Oberon was saved by Fier who roared for a toast. With a rueful grin he joined their host by the board and was immediately handed an absurdly large jug of wine. "To the end of injustice!" Fier roared. Oberon raised his drink with a loud roar and a smile. He quaffed the wine like it was water noting the sweet floral notes different than the wine he'd been drinking earlier. It went to his head so fast Oberon found a chair and sat before he could fall and embarrass himself. Casting around for a sight of Minerva he sighed. It was only a matter of time before he would be forced to seek his bed. The feast was petering out. Many of the Cynocephali had long since sought their beds so that only Fier and what appeared to be his kinsman or maybe hearth troops remained hosting Oberon's people.

It wasn't long before even the redoubtable Fier had buried his snout to his chest issuing rumbling snores. Most of the Seelie Court soldiers had retired to their camp and only he and a few dozen others remained under the open sided feasting tents. Minerva lay face down in a puddle of drool not far away. Oberon couldn't take his eyes from her. *She's beautiful.* He thought drowsily, his mind both pleased and regretful about how the night ended.

***

Oberon woke with a start. He'd been having the most delightful dream involving he and Minerva. He had been nibbling a long her inner thigh and caught in the throes of her excitement she had splashed him with a delightful surprise. *Maybe I made it back to my tent after all*. Oberon thought, until his eyes unglued themselves and his ears made sense of the din. He opened his eyes to see a djinn soldier slumped over the table across from him, head tilted at an obscene angle from the red smile sprouting from his neck. Oberon shook his head trying to make sense of what was unfolding around him. His camp was on fire people were running, screaming, fighting and dying. Wiping blood from his face he saw him. Three feet away lay Guion cold and lifeless body rent by dozens of wounds.

Frantic Oberon searched for Minerva finding her still sleeping before noted that the slumbering form of Fier was gone. Heart pounding he reached for his mace finding it still on his hip and pulled it free. Minerva rose and nodded at him lifting her hammer from its tube like sheath between her wings. They were a bubble of calm in a sea of chaos as once friendly Dinte Rosu Cynocephali turned into implacable foes. By some silent accord Oberon and Minerva burst into action simultaneously.

Oberon swung his mace Sebari into the leg of a Dinte Rosu warrior attacking a soldier of his taxiarchy, the leg crumpled with a satisfying snap and Oberon reversed his blow to crush the beasts head, leather helmet and all. Minerva lay about her with her hammer. Such was her ferocity that the enemy fell back in dismay. With a beat of her gossamer wings she leapt towards the tents roof before propelling herself down to smash a surprised foe into a puddle of shattered bone and flesh. Putting her fingers to her lips Minvera whistled a long shrill sound that gave the dog men pause.

Seconds later an enraged war moose charged the pavilion throwing the

Cynocephali into disarray. As the survivors of the Oberon's agema scattered about the tent coalesced, Oberon jumped the table and stood shoulder to shoulder with the gore spattered Minerva. Beating aside a Dinte Rosu spear and bashing aside the shield he punched his mace in the dog man's face leaving his snout a gnarled mess of blood and broken teeth. He feinted low at another and struck high colliding with the leather helmet with enough force that the beasts eyes popped free from the visor slits. "

"Good kill." Minerva grunted through a manic smile as she flicked he hammer under a cynocephali's shield tearing her foe's leg away the hammer barely slowing at the impact before she brought her weapon in an arc over his shield to crush his throat.

Oberon's Agema and the other surviving Samyazans nearby began to fall in around Oberon and Minerva. When a blood spattered dwarf bumped into his left hip, Oberon belated remembered his short sword and drew it. Swatting away a spear blade, the King of Penume's Reach stepped forward and buried the leaf shaped blade in his enemy's fur covered throat. Roaring he charged into the enemy, refusing to be outdone by a fae. Even if she was the most graceful and beautiful force of devastation he had ever seen. Parrying a spear, Oberon responded with an inline riposte that carved a bloody path along his opponent's snout before plunging into his eye to grate along its skull. The Cynocephali fell away and Oberon followed the corpse into the gap pulling the rest of his tiny force into his wake.

The Cynocephali for their part were just as drunk and bleary eyed as Oberon's force. Their spear thrusts and footwork were sloppy and for that reason alone the disaster that currently unfolded was less than it might have been. The cynocephali fought in small phalanx type units of eight allowing each to function as an island should the need arise, but that required coordination. In their current state they were as much a threat to each other as they were Oberon's taxiarchy. They tangled their shafts and pinked the shoulders and necks of their own, For the Samyazans drunken brawling might we'll have been a national sport.

Oberon's mob burst free from the thin cordon of Dinte Rosu attackers. He thanked El that the dwarves never seemed to go anywhere or do anything without armor and for the Mouros inability to be without their jeweled swords and shields. As they reached the camp Oberon witnessed the agemas of his taxiarchy fighting gamely along a well established perimeter. As he aimed his force at a knot of attacking Dinte Rosu he felt a moment of relief. Until he saw the bodies. Elves, dwarves, fae and Mauros wearing the colors of the Seelie Court and the stylus of Penume lay in puddles of congealing blood at the entrances to their tents or in the lanes between. He spied Atrabetian a Dwarf who served as as chiliarch of the 3rd flat on his back throat torn away with a wineskin still in his hand. Proof that the violence had begun suddenly and without warning. Conducted under the guise of friendship.

Anger sliced through the remaining haze that had clouded Oberon's mind. In the distance he could see Farheed organizing the defenses under Oberon's personal banner bearing the stylus of Penume. "For El and the Seelie Court!" Oberon screamed aiming to break through to his main body of fighters. He felt naked without a shield or armor so he covered himself in rage and reached for the manna. The channel to the Chalkydri, angelic beings who gifted the heat of the mighty sun burst open like a river in flood and in breaths a whip of fire exploded across the Cynocephali ranks. Dog men bodies burned like pyres of the damned vividly illuminating the battlefield. In the distance Oberon could see shielded ranks of shielded warriors bearing maces and short swords covered from head to foot in pale scale armor with doglike faces showing through their open faced helms. Oberon fought to choke back a sob striking anything with fur that moved within range of his sword and mace as they passed over a tideline of of dead elves from his personal guard.

He made to call out a warning when the other dogmen began to attack the Dinte Rosu. The collision was savage sending Dinte Rosu warriors several feet into the air before the terrible swords and clubs descended on their enemies. His fire spell has created the perfect diversion to cover their attack and the Dinte Rosu died. They tried to flee but the agemas of Oberon's Taxiarchy formed the anvil for the strangers hammer. Spells, stone, and bronze sang and the Dinte Rosu went from predators to prey breaking in full rout.

Their new allies howled in bloodlust as the agemas of his taxiarchy shook out into their lochos led by their hundred leaders and charged after the fleeing dog men. Oberon focused his manna, splitting the energy into two channels as his father had taught him long ago. He set his eyes of the gates and opened himself to Baraquiel to channel lightning and Arakiel to channel earth. The gates that had so impressed him earlier exploded as the ground punched up and lightning stabbed down. Fleeing Dinte Rosu simply ceased to exist.

* * *

The day dawned red and bloody and for Oberon it fit. The morning sky would have been a flawless sheet if not for the smoke that smudged the cloudless red orange vault. Oberon's taxiarchy stood blood spattered and triumphant in neat columns on the main road of the Dinte Rosu settlement. Not that it could still be called that. As Oberon surveyed the devastation. Not a single living Dinte Rosu remained within the walls. To call it a battle was an overstatement. The wages of treachery are death, his strategos would understand. Every time shame at his own savagery crept in he stared at his boots still wet with the blood of his countrymen. He could still see Guion's broken body. Over six hundred souls would never march under his banner again, but for all that the mission had been a success.

Emerging from the ruined gate Oberon was met by Fier. It was Fier who had crept away from the massacre and brought the warband of his native pack to Oberon's aid. The Os armored themselves in bone scales and had been enemies of the Dinte Rosu since before the flood. Grinning his wolfin smile Fier marched towards Oberon and knelt baring his throat. Behind him thousands of bone clad Cynocephali followed suit. "

My wife was a treacherous bitch. She dishonored herself, her clan, and me with her actions. Such betrayal is not the way of the Cynocephali. We the Osu accept your contract, not as mercenaries but as vassals of the Seelie Court. Your wars are our wars, your enemies are our enemies as long as my pack shall hunt." Fier said speaking the ancient words of alliance. Oberon walked to the kneeling chieftain and raised him up. Smiling he said,

"Welcome to the army of the Seelie Court." Oberon led his combined force away from the ruins, Fier's long strides easily keeping pace with mount. "Agents of the Nox were but a few days ahead of you." Fier confided. "Many of Daji clans have sided with the children of the Nameless. The Idolon, and Ljósálfar have been busy. Here and in the east. Word has been that a warlord has risen to the north. Gladr Odinsblood Lord of Lítla Dímun on the Faroe Islands. He's captured Sandvik, Hvalba, Nidaros, and Ranhiem." Oberon's eyebrows climbed under his helmet. This was news. Oberon had been traveling, and thus out of the loop, but he knew that the strategoi were torn on what the objectives of the invasion of Middle Earth would be. Leadership was counting on the Nox's propensity for infighting to give them time to formulate a coherent strategy while they consolidated the military might of the Seelie Court. He halted the column, causing Fier to look on in confusion. They were several miles from the smoke and wreckage of the Dinte Rosu settlement. Turning to Farheed he gave the order to strike camp. He needed to prepare.

An hour later Oberon sat in the command tent with his Agema and Fier. All but the Cynocephali leader was feeding manna and lending their power to their taxiarch as he opened a channel to Zagagel. Communication magic was tricky requiring great amounts of energy and focus. Half a world away it should have been impossible but the members of the taxiarchy's first Agema were uncommonly strong and Oberon was confident. Probably more confident than he should be, but this message was too important not to warrant a little arrogance.

With the power of his comrades augmenting his own working manna was different, not unlike adding rowers to a boat changed the rhythm of the stroke and the pressure needed to guide the tiller. It was a dance of power and tempo.

Oberon pictured his commander and held the idea of Illyargen his mind. When both were set firmly, he cast his sending. *"My mission is successful, but I have news. Gladr Odinsblood of the Nox waxes in the north. He conquering cities and raising a host. What are your orders."*

There was a single beam of orange light that blew through the tent flaps and shot across the sky. Sweat beaded on his skin and his body trembled as he pushed the message to it's recipient. When the sending was cast he sagged in exhaustion, bones aching as if he had physically wrestled with the forces he had directed. Fier located wine and served it to Oberon and the others as long minutes passed before they were recovered. "Did it work?" Minerva asked her beautiful face looking as drawn as Oberon felt. He was about to answer when it felt as though he had been kicked in the head by a particularly angry and large booted foot. Oberon cried in pain and alarm. *"Make all haste north to Oddmire in Albion. Fortify it and aid the local Samyazans. Do everything you must to stop him. Help will come soon."* Came Illyargen's voice as though the ancient elven warlord had spoken loudly in his ear. Bleary eyed Oberon looked to his compatriots. "We go to Albion."

Chapter 19: Phantasms of Strife

Richard's smile seemed irrepressible as he basked in his lady's favor. The newly sewn banner of his order snapped in the wind filling him with rare delight. The white fountain on a gold wavy cross against a argent field was crisp in the bright morning sunshine. The banners matched the tabards every man of his newly minted military order. The Order of Our Lady of the Desert was three thousand strong even after his grievous losses fighting Miramollin's force. He had begun with four hundred and ten men. Ten were knights, one hundred men at arms, one hundred spearman, another hundred archers and almogovars. After routing the Moorish forces he'd lost just about half of his Le Cannet Des Maures men. All his his knights, half of the men at arms and half the spearman. His almogovars had been mauled as well losing a quarter of their number. His infantry had been in the center where Cazador's Company of Saint Moses had wrought havoc and paid for it dearly as the clever bastard's field artillery took it's toll. They had stiffened the Almohad center like a wall for a time, until they broke off to cover Miramollin's retreat and rescued Omar's force. With a start he realized that he would have to fight his wife's cousin again at some point. He contented himself with the fact that he now had a much stronger force.

His Order waited for him in the camp outside Ùbeda. Ten, ten man conrois of knights and five hundred men at arms formed his mounted force and the cream of his order. He also had thousand spearman, seven hundred Castilian almogovars, and seven hundred crossbowman. Many of his host were abandoned when their knights quit the crusade. Mostly Frenchman,

Castillians, and Navarrese. He had taken only a fraction of the force for his current task. One hundred of his Castilian almogovars, and sixty of his French crossbowmen all mounted rode in neat blocks of twenty behind two of his conrois of knights of the order. They would be more than enough for what he had in mind.

His first target, after breaking away from the main crusade was El Acebuche. A little known La Compagnie property producing olives, olive oil and horses. It also served as a repository for La Compagnie wealth, the sleepy estate making a perfect hiding spot with both the benefit of being remote tucked away in the foot hills of the mountains yet not far from the river. His force was already hardened and bloodthirsty after the sack of Baeza and Úbeda, they had captured their share of a hundred thousand slaves and were hungry for more loot. El Acebuche would simply be a delightful little morsel to his army. A mere twenty miles from the camp it was too good to pass up.

They skirted the little towns between Úbeda and their target to come riding out of the hills just as the late afternoon slid into evening. They had furled the banners of Le Cannet Des Maures and Richard allowed himself a satisfied smile as the postern gate in the simple mudbrick wall was opened without question. Guardsmen in du Maurmont clan livery met them led by a bored looking greybeard. "Sir Richard, we've had no bird to expect–" Richard drew his sword and cut the old captain down before he could finish his sentence. Spurring his horse he rode down two other guardsmen and cleared space for his knights to ride in behind him. He could feel the faint sensation of water flowing over his skin denoting the Lady's favor and with a cry he spurred his horse at the stream of men coming from the small barracks.

When they saw him coming the knot of men in purple and gold froze forming a small shield wall. He could feel the power of his Lady flowing through him making and knew they would not stop him. The du Maurmont men knew their work and held firm expecting the rider to sheer away. Richard's horse ran at the men like a thing possessed. Spears bounced off his horses barding and skated from his maille. Richard laughed for the pure joy of battle and the favor of his Lady as he punched his sword through faces and hacked it's keen edge against necks and collarbones. Circling his mount he turned the knot of spearman into piles of broken flesh and trampled bone. Looking around he could see that his men overwhelming the rest of the small garrison.

The crossbowman swept the walls while the almogovars penned the Du Maurmont clansmen on the catwalk. Some of his knights ranged the courtyard killing anything that moved not wearing the colors of the order. Others had traded swords for axes and hacked at the doors to the manor. There was a sort of order to the chaos. Less a wild raid and more like an orderly robbery with a bit of organized murder. Richard gave a sharp whistle, catching the attention of half a conroi of knights. "Clear these barracks." He ordered. The five men saluted and grinned like devils. Within moments they were dismounted and hefting their shields for a charge.

Richard didn't stay to watch them work. Instead he rode the short distance across the blood spattered yard. Dismounting and ascending the steps just as two burly Gascon knights sheered through the door and the bar beyond. Stepping through the wreckage of the portal Richard faced down the resident knight Yaya ibn Mustafa Al Takruri who looked every bit the Almohad warrior if one ignored the cross around his neck. They were of an age and had served together in the Holy Land, once they called each other friend. Richard had hoped the man would've been elsewhere, but it wasn't to be. The look of shock and betrayal on his face was hard to bear. "Richard what is the meaning of this!" He asked from behind his shield, battle axe raised to strike. Despite the Lady's blessing coursing through him Richard felt a moment of shame so deep it bordered on anguish. His expression was bleak when he raised his eyes to meet those of his former comrade. "Betrayal." he said his voice almost a whisper. His sword flicked out, the rising cut turning into a thrust faster than the veteran fighter could block. Richard couldn't stop the wince as his sword slid in his old friend's eyesocket and to the brain beyond. With a roar the his men at arms rushed the remaining Du Maurmont retainers.

Ten minutes later when the killing was done Richard followed the gentle pull of his Lady to the cleverly hidden trap door. He had been drawn to the kitchens where he had found the door behind a wall hanging. On the other side of it lay a veritable dragons hoard. Gold dinars, silver shillings, and pfennigs sat stacked in the small closet. He quickly detailed a handful of Le Cannet men to help him shift it to their pack animals unwilling to trust the almogovars and crossbowmen, the lesser men with the task. All told it took more time to move the coin than it took to take the estate.

As the horses and pack mules from the estate were rounded up and loaded with the coin and other look Richard began to understand for. the first time the great wealth of La Compagnie and the Du Maurmont clan. El Acebuche wasn't a large holding or even a large depository and it has still required almost forty mules to carry just the coin. As much as it fired his greed it gave his pause. The Du Maurmont clan could likely challenge kings, yet they did not. It was something to ponder as he rode back to his camp.

* * *

Sabri Aznar had been proud to be a man at arms for the Alfiere s and had been excited to go on campaign. Such pride and excitement had long since faded. Richard de Caen or simply Don Ricardo to most of the men was not precisely a bad lord, but he wasn't a Alfiere , and he wasn't exactly a good lord either. He campaigned well enough and had kept them fed and watered. He had even kept most of them alive until they had clashed with Miramollin's Almohads. Oh don Ricardo had led them ably enough but the men of Le Cannet Des Maures had paid a heavy price leaving half their number on the field. It was almost as if he had deliberately led them against Don Omar. Even Sabri knew that attacking a fellow clan member would draw the ire of Sir Cazador whose wild charge had killed almost all of the Le Cannet Des Maures knights and took out a number of men at arms. Sabri spat. All men knew that Ser Cazador was supposed to be the Don of Le Cannet Des Maures and taking up arms against him had left Sabri and the other survivors feeling dirty and wrong even if the Company of Saint Moses had been retained by the enemy. It had all seemed downhill from there. Men had been willing to ignore Don Ricardo leaving the camp with a goat and returning alone covered in blood. They had overlooked his general lack of piety and his strange fervor for the mysterious Our Lady of the Desert. But the taking of slaves and the sacking of a clan estate had been steps too far. Since paying them their share of the loot their lord has barely spoken to them. It was just as well especially since the men were now given to discontented grumblings.

Since becoming Lord Commander of The Knights of Our Lady of the Desert Richard had treated his feudal host as an after thought. He instead kept to the company of knight brethren and even lavished attention on the foreign almogovars leaving his household warriors simmering in discontent. Indeed the illustrious Lord Commander had only come to speak to them now that it was time to fight again. He has simply rode into their section of the camp and ordered them to be ready to march in full kit at first light. Their destination, Bengíjar was a small but wealthy town flanked by vast olive groves to the south of the town centered around an old Gothic castle that had been renovated by the Mohomedans. As men of the Du Maurmont clan they bore no love for the Almohads and Sabri like the others looked forward to being able to vent their frustrations.

Idly Sabri wondered why Don Ricardo had bothered with allowing them to lead the attack today. Leaning over in his saddle he wispereed to Issac, the only friend he had left among the men at arms. "Looks like Don Ricardo finally remembered who fought for him before he was Lord Commander." Issac chuckled behind his maille face mask. "We will show these pretty Frenchman and preening Gascons how the men of the Monts Des Maures fight." Issac growled in return just as the clop of hooves announced the arrival of Don Ricardo who took his place at the head of the column.

Sabri was in the second rank of men at arms behind the don's color party. He could pick out the arms of the Al Takruri family and the banner of La Compagnie with its green Alphynargent field. His confusion mounted and he longed for someone to ask what was going on. Don Ricardo turned in his saddle. "When I blow my horn kill them all." He grunted before spurring his horse to a trot. Confused, Sabri and the other Le Cannet Des Maures men barreled after their lord.

Upon spying the banners the gates of opened. *Maybe this isn't an attack at all. Maybe it's just a show of force.* Sabri thought as they cleared the gate. They were met by an officious looking Mozarb in a green turban and robes flanked by guards. "Don Ricardo!" The man said beaming in genuine warmth. In flawless Nicard Occitanian. "Has La Compagnie come to grace our market?" Sabri felt himself relax. Don Ricardo looked at the Mozarb, "Indeed I've come to enrich myself Lord mayor. Perhaps however not in the way you might be used to." Sabri felt something cold settle in his gut as his earlier sense of relaxation burnt away like mist in the morning sun. Smiling jovially Don Ricardo leaned forward in his saddle as if to take the man's hand in the warrior grip with his right hand. Still smiling Don Ricardo plunged the spear in his left into his unsuspecting target.

Sabri's mouth fell open at the same time as the stricken mayor's. There was a moment of shocked silence where no one moved or spoke. Every eye seemed to be glued to the fountain of blood that the man coughed into the bright morning sun. The Don Ricardo put his horn to his lips and blew. Sabri drew his sword, knowledge of his orders warring with the shock and suddeness of his don's cold murder. Somewhere far away he could hear the command to attack. Someone screaming for the archers to clear the walls. He felt his body moving but was somehow detached from it all. Sabri batted aside a spear and cut down at the Moorish man at arms feeling more puppet than man. The almogovars were already among the enemy falchions and spears flashing. Still horrified, Sabri spurred his horse at another foeman. Before he could even strike his horse struck for him and the man disappeared with a vicious bite and a flurry of hooves.

Madness. It can be the only answer for there is no honor in this. Sabri thought as he killed again, slowly absorbing the horror. It wasn't battle it was slaughter. They had ridden through open gates under a banner of friendship. Now they were killing people who expected nothing more dangerous from them than a bit of drunkenness and a tavern brawl. Wheeling his mount Sabri took in a scene that could have sprung from hell itself. Dismembered limbs, gut ropes, and bodies of the dead or dying were everywhere. The wailing of innocents filled the air like the dirge of hell. Don Ricardo was far beyond him now leading the charge incarcerated in the blood of innocents as his blade rose and fell on any man, woman, or child that crossed his path.

* * *

Three days later Ossigi was a repeat of Bengíjar. The only difference was they had refused to open their gates. He had stood in his place with the rest of the men at arms just out of arrow range. The fleet footed almogovars pushed a good boiled leather mantlet ahead of their ladder bearing comrades. He might not enjoy serving Don Richard but the man spared no expense on equipment.

Within moments the ladder had gone up and he had followed the cursing almogovars to the battlements where Sabri had used his shield and armored bulk to bash defenders from the wall. In moments they had carried the tower and he had locked his shields with other men at arms to defend the almogavars who opened the gate for the rest of Don Ricardo's force. By the time the footman of the order had charged through the gate it was all over but the screaming.

That night the camp carried a festive atmosphere. The drums, pipes, and horns of the military band filled the night air like the smoke and smells from the cookfires. The Order Our Lady of the Desert celebrated yet another victory.

Another fat town that yielded mounds of loot and trails of slaves. Men rejoiced. The men from Le Cannet Des Maures did not. Like his comrades Sabri felt stained by it all but it didn't stop him from taking the extra wine rations. It was the best he could manage to fight against the hollow feeling that has sat in his chest since Bengíjar. Like all the others not on duty Sabri loitered in the parade square. Don Ricardo insisted the open space be exist in every camp. Torches blazed brightly driving back the night and illuminating the now drunken knights and armsmen of the order. Long tables had been fetched from Ossigi and fairly bent under the weight of the food it held. It had become Don Ricardo's habit to hold court beneath the awning of his pavilion each night as his men gorged themselves.

The gates to the camp remained open. Small clumps of men wandered back and forth from the camp to where the slaves were kept penned a short distance away. Sabri paid it little mind. Until what sounded like the jangle of maille drew his attention to the main thoroughfare. A woman in cloth of gold raiment seemed to glide between two ranks of men in dark pothelms and long maille byrnies. As they approached he saw that the woman was the most beautiful person Sabri had ever seen. Skin like gold kissed bronze and dark liquid eyes like wells set in a perfect face. The way he robes flowed showed that every curve was ripe as fresh fruit. The closer she drifted the more he could feel the personal force of this woman, who had not yet uttered a word yet had captivated an entire war camp by sheer force of personality.

Sabri felt the strangest urge to kneel, it was almost inexorable as his knees weakened. He saw that many men had. Almost every man bearing the black and gold tabard of the order was on bended knee. Including Don Ricardo. Sabri watched as the strange procession made its way to the center of the cleared ground before Don Ricardo's pavilion. "My lady…" the don said breathlessly. As he stumbled toward her face slack with admiration. Indeed the woman favored the painted icons of The Lady of the Desert.

The raw admiration of the Knights of the Order disturbed Sabri in ways he couldn't understand. He just knew it unsettled him. The guards of the lady were no better. The eye slits of their pothelms were naught but pits to the abyss. Their blackened maille hung from their bodies like funerary armor complete with the slight stench of corpse. "From the banners above this camp I see you are all devotees of my lady." Said the woman, her voice high and clear like water flowing over smooth stones. She locked her gaze on Don Ricardo and he knelt at her feet as though transfixed. "Indeed, we are the Knights of Our Lady of the Desert and we honor her." The woman smiled and Sabri felt a happiness so complete he throught he might burst. "I am Marwah. Our Lady of the Desert appeared to me in a dream. and from that day I have spoken with her voice." Don Ricardo's mouth dropped open in astonished wonder. "A prophetess..." Don Ricardo said his voice barely above a whisper. "She tells me that you shall all find glory and conquest. In Our Lady's Name." Marwah said with a smile that went from radiant to transcendent. Her pronouncement elicited a cheer from the men of the order that was loud enough to strike with a physical force that snapped Sabri from his reverie. As he looked around noting with disgust the ecstatic faces of his comrades and felt a shiver down his spine. *Madness madness indeed.*

* * *

As late evening began to fade Cazador rode at the van of his column. He had been pushing hard. He was as eager to distance himself from the dark cloud that hung over his kinsman's lands as he was to get away from The Crusaders. They made the ancient stone bridge well before sundown and set up a camp. Twenty miles was a good push for the first day and everyone needed rest. The campsite the scouts chose was just on the other side of the river. Something about it struck him as odd, for it seemed a prime place of a town or settlement and for there to be none there was off. The sirens song even though the safety of Bobastro's walls called to him. He felt it in his bones he needed to return with all due haste but the recent fighting has left him feeling worn and his young bones old. They would camp tonight and push on to Malaga tomorrow.

The haggard expressions on those who had fought at the disaster of Las Navas de Tolosa told it's own tale as they circled the wagons and dug the ditch and set the stakes. They eschewed tents for the night, opting instead to sleep under the stars. As was his habit Cazador roused himself to take the first watch. He found most of his conroi slept with the exception of Diallo. It was piss poor discipline but after all the fighting and riding Cazador had not the heart to wake them. Together Cazador and the djali made their way to the edge of camp to stand guard at the ancient stone bridge. The night was still and the vault of the sky was bright and seemed close enough to touch. The sound of the water running beneath the bridge was pleasant in their ears. Soon enough Cazador's apprehension about their campsite faded as he and his Djali kept the vigil.

"Do you ever think of the Romans Lord?" Diallo asked as their boots trod on the ancient stones. Cazador beamed at his djali, "Only every day. Sometimes I ponder how different things would have been if Lucius Quietus had lived to ascend the purple. The entire world would be different." Diallo's eyes went far away for a moment. "Roman roads along the coast and Roman cities along the Niger. Tekrur as the Byzantium of the south." The djali murmured. Cazador nodded. "What Marcus Aurelius did for Libiya, Quietus would have done for Mauretania Tingitana. A push south to the gold fields would have meant no splitting of the empire. No invasion of the Vandals and the reverence of the prophet would likely be limited to Arabia. No generations of war for the Holy Land. No Baqt in Nubia. We would be free to die in pointless wars without the need to lie on God to cover the avarice of men." He said quietly.

It was Diallo's turn to nod, something inside him stirred by the conviction in his jatigi's words. The Alfieres and their direct kin were the most recent of the Du Maurmont clan houses having only been in Provence for a hundred years but the Takruri line they sprang from was ancient and noble. "You speak of the empire as if you would see it rise again." He said and Cazador laughed. "My ancestors once fought under the eagles and *I helped sack Byzantium. I am a destroyer of Rome.* In deed ,if not intent. To even think such makes me feel either a mercenary at best and a hypocrite at worst. No, Rome is dead. I would not see the dead rise. I would see something better in it's place. If I could I would carve out a fiefdom and rule as my grandfather rules as Bobastro. A place where all can be accepted and happy and build lives and wealth. That I would fight to build and die to protect." Diallo could see the light of glory shining in Cazador's eyes and taste a hint of destiny in his words.

As the two men talked a mist rose. It was of little notice at first, but soon it so thick that the when Cazador looked towards the camp he could barely see it. All sense of earlier wellbeing vanished as a wind cut through his maille to chill his bones but left the river mist undisturbed. Suddenly the sense of wrongness he'd felt washed over him again. His heart pounded with so much force that he barley felt his gris-gris dancing on his chest. The sound of his pulse roaring in his ears almost drowning out the sussurus of whispers that seemed to rise from the ground itself. Instinct alone had him drawing L'auxifar. The blade of his ancestors glowed with a blue tinge and Cazador felt dread inch up his spine with icy fingers.

Diallo had strung and knocked an arrow to his bow. Cazador cursed himself for not waking the others. The mist had thickened and the far end of the bridge dissappeared in it shroud. "Stand aside little pigs. I hunger and I fear not your little tusks." Hissed the night and Diallo loosed three arrows in as many heart beats trying to pinpoint the source of the sound. Terror ravened in his gut but Cazador shouted,

"There are no meals here! I will not yield."

The voice in the night laughed a horrifying sound filled with malice and cold mirth. Shadows moved in the fog shot darkness. The sound of foot steps and heavy treads surrounded them in the darkness. Something seemed to caper just on the fringes of his vision, taunting his sight and teasing his nerves. Tightening his grip on L'auxifar Cazador pulled his buckler free from the hook on his belt and slid into a high guard without conscious thought. "I will not be eaten. Nor will my command." He hissed to Diallo without taking his eyes off the darkness. "We hold this damn bridge." Diallo stamped his foot. "For Saint Moses and Saint Atillo!" The djali growled and continued to stomp sliding his feet with a melodic rasp on the ancient surface of the bridge. As he began beating a counter beat with arrow in his fingers against the stave of his bow. As the rhythm took shape Diallo began to sing.

Cazador couldn't understand a word. He knew that in times of need djali's would sing in the tongue of their societies, a secret to all outsiders. He could feel his arm hairs stand on end and his heavy bastard sword was suddenly very light in his hand. A predators grin tugged at Cazador's lips until his teeth were bared in the feeble moonlight. His body felt fresh. The fighting and hard riding fell away from his muscles and it felt as if he had spent a month resting. *And this is why we pay djalis.* Cazador thought thanking the ancestors that Diallo was with him.

Shadows still danced at the limits of his periphery but ignored them. Instead he focused on the indistinct form coalescing in the dense fog at the end of the bridge. Guts churning to a froth with terror Cazador took three paces forward. "Come then you raven starving shadow of a worthless bastard!" Cazador screamed turning fear into fury and conviction. "If you so tire of this vicious little half life you call an existence then face me now, or slither back to the devil's arse crack from whence you came!" There was a strangled roar and the shadows solidified further. "This is my bridge little pig. The souls of all those who cross it are mine." Came the sibilant hiss that reminded Cazador of bloodied bodies being dragged across wet cobbles. Terror scratched at his mind with frantic claws, but the more fear he felt the angrier he became. "Why do you think you can try me shadow of nothing?" Cazador asked genuinely curious. Trouble seemed to be finding him and he was frankly getting tired of it. Was a quiet watch too much to ask for? His frustration grew as the beasts sibilant growl tore through the night. "Enough! Let the stars bear witness and the night watch as you attend me shadow!" Cazador screamed as the air filled with the smell of mouldering corpses and the sound of boots thudding along the bridge. The shadows that stormed Cazador and Diallo were yellow eyed and their wispy forms were like coils of black steam braided into the shape of men, holding wicked looking barbs of deeper darkness in shapeless hands. They screeched in furious unison and charged.

The djali's rhythm ceased, but his voice never faltered. The twang of his bow sent an arrow leaping past Cazador to bury a glowing blue head between the shadow beasts yellow eyes. Cazador barely registered the pop and flash of the creature dissipating as he got his shield between him and a barbed spear of darkness and scything L'auxifar from high to low severing the shadow man's legs. Cazador back cut and with an eerie cry blue light burned his foe away to nothing. Diallo's bow twanged again as Cazador blocked and overhand blow that sent shivers of pain and cold shooting down his arm. Gritting his teeth with a growl building in the back of his throat he thrust L'auxifar into his attackers featureless face. Thrusting at another shadow Cazador growled as it flowed away from his blade like water and parried knocking his blade down and to his right. Blocking the creature's riposte he rode the momentum and twisted his hips bringing his blade around for and overhand chop that cleaved the shadow from left shoulder to right hip.

Looking up Cazador spied a lone spear and shield armed figure at the end of the bridge mounted on a ethereal black horse. Where the others were hazy and indistinct Cazador could see skeletal remains of a face under a visigothic helm and the impression of maille under a tattered cloak of shadows. The rider charged and Diallo sent an arrow to meet it. The shadow revenant blocked with it's shield and hurled its spear at Cazador who barely got his buckler up in time. The spear spun away with a thud and Diallo's voice went silent. The revenant wasted little time fluidly drawing it's sword and bearing down on Cazador who threw up his shield as he stepped off line to his left bringing L'auxifar around in a vicious arc across the back of the ghost horse's neck. With a grunt Cazador fought for leverage to keep the revnant from bringing it's blade to bear even as he twisted his wrist for a stab. The monster was impossibly strong and knew it. A dry chuckle rasped from its dessicated throat.

"Time to die little pig!" The monster crowed as it clouted Cazador across the head with it's shield sending him to the ground senseless.

* * *

Asmā had woken from a nightmare of the camp being under attack. Since she was a girl she had learned that such dreams were not to be ignored. Heart pounding she knew what she must do. Asmā wasted valuable time trying and failing to wake her tentmates. Her efforts did little bit make her feel frantic. With a mounting sense of dread she quickly pulled her maille shirt over her aketon and belted it with her falchion and quiver. Snatching up her crossbow Asmā emerged from her tent to find the camp blanketed in mist so thick it lay like dark snow. Not a soul stirred, it was as if she awoke to a camp of the dead. *Something is terribly wrong.* Heart thumping like a bad thing trying to escape the cage of her ribs, she picked her way through the camp. Clinging to the solidity of the smooth wood of her crossbow's cheekrest against her face Asmā fought for each step against the part of herself that called her to flee. She could hear disembodied voices in the night, strange singing in the distance that set her small hairs on end.

When her foot touched something too soft and too yielding Asmā was nearly undone. Amastan's burly form loomed like a miniature hill in the mist. "You big bastard I nearly shot you!" She hissed as she knelt to check his pulse as the wise woman had taught her long ago. Though his body was cold like her tentmates, he slumbered in a sloppy heap awkwardly curled around the shaft of his spear. He looked for all the world like a poleaxed bear and the thought made her giggle. Then it occurred to her how mad it was to laugh at a time like this and that made her giggle all the more. She was still chuckling to herself as she cursed and stumbled towards the sound of the singing and the now unmistakable voice of her captain shouting. It drew her on until she reached the ancient stone bridge.

As she neared it the first thing that struck her was the immense unnatural cold that made breathing hurt. Asmā's vision danced with stars as her throat and lungs constricted around the frigid air. Despair threatened to engulf her but the strange song grew loud in her ears and she pressed on towards the sound of pounding of hooves, the twang of a bowstring and a clash of steel. The portly Djali Diallo stood by Cazador bas they faced down a charge from a black clad rider. There was a blur of darkness and her sense of dread increased as the singing abruptly stopped when Cazador flinched wildly and the djali fell. Heart racing, kit jangling Asmā ran towards them through the dark fog. As her feet pounded the planks of bridge she saw the black clad rider on a dead horse attacking Cazador. The captain with his sword a blade of blue light blocked with his buckler and cut at the horse's neck felling the beast in a single stroke. But before he could get his shining blade around to attack, the rider struck with shield so dark it ate light. It came around and smote Cazador on the head, Asmā heard the steel of the helmet crack and saw the blood spray as the captain reeled back. "NO!" She screamed as her heart filled her throat She fired, not even bothering to look. In her next breath Asmā's foot was in the stirrup and she was hauling back on the cord for all she was worth. Her second bolt came a mere heartbeat after the first was swatted aside and buried itself in the throat of the black clad warrior. Eyes redder than hot coals locked with Asmā's own. Fear and terror plunged it's claws deep in her soul. "You would save the little pig, mouse?" The voice came from everywhere and nowhere at the same time but Asmā knew it was the black rider. "Flee now mouse his life is not worth your bravery." The rider croaked raising his blade. With shaking hands and fingers cramped by cold Asmā hauled back on there cord, and dropped a bolt in the slot. She remembered Cazador's easy smile the night she had met him. The way he beamed with pride when he named her vintenar. The sound of his laughter as he joked with his mensie. "He is my captain and you shall not have him!" She shouted shouldering her loaded crossbow and fired again. The bolt lanced the creatures sword hand sending the black sword tumbling from damaged fingers. "You will die mouse! Your soul will languish with that of your precious captain!" Shadows and mist swirled as the creature launched itself at Asmā, but she was already hauling back on the cord again.

"For God and Saint Moses!" She screamed pouring prayer and frustration in equal measure into the shot. As she pulled the trigger the iron head of her bolt glowed a bright sky blue as Cazador's sword had. The monster snarled and raised it's shield too late. The glowing bolt slammed itself home between the monsters eyes and the monster screamed as it's shadow wreathed body evaporated in a flash of blue smoke.

Warmth returned with the moonlight as the arcane fog faded. Asmā noticed none of it as she ran across the bridge toward her two stricken comrades. The djali's helmet was knocked askew but he sat up groggily. Cazador was an entirely different matter. Blood sheeted the right hand side of his face his helmet gashed open revealing a cut to the captain's head. His breathing was deep and even and Asmā set aside her shock and dismay behind a mask of professionalism. Wound care was familiar ground. What had just happened was not. She removed the broken remnants of the helmet and gently cleaned away the blood. The moon, bright now that the fog had faded shone down and she used it's light to check to if his skull was broken.

Satisfied that the captain's thought box was whole Asmā breathed a sigh of relief. She cupped his face gently and she cradled Cazador's head on her lap. He would scar but it wouldn't be so bad. Cazador's eyes fluttered open with a wheeze. First panic then something altogether softer registered in his eyes. "The revenant...the camp." Asmā shook her head. "Gone and fine." she said with a triumphant smile. Cazador's face took on an odd expression, a half smile tugged at his full lips and something indescribable danced in his dark brown eyes that made her suddenly and urgently aware that a man lay between her legs. Cazador sat up slightly, bringing his face inches from hers, so close she could feel his breath on her lips. So close she thought he might kiss her. "Thank you for saving me lady Asmā. Thank you for saving the company." Cazador said softly. "I have gazed upon gardens, oceans, and mountains. I've walked the fabled streets of Constantinople, and I know looking at you now, that my eyes have never seen a true wonder until the day I met you. I owe you my life, my lady." She might have laughed if not for the earnestness in his eyes. Instead Asmā's cheeks heated and she felt herself wondering what his bottom lip would taste like and why despite the iron tang of blood he smelled so good.

The space between them slowly evaporated until the jangling of kit announced they were no longer alone. " What happened here?" Izan demanded his bald head gleaming in the moonlight. Cazador looked up at his cousin and then to his vitenar. "Asmā is a hero."

* * *

Marcela raged, using all the strength in her stolen body to pound the earth as she screamed into the night. She could feel the human guards outside her tent flinch and she fed on their fear. If anyone questioned her presence with de Caen's detachment Marcela was unaware.

In her mortal skin they called her Lady Prophetess, or Lady Marwah, head of the newly formed sister order, The Daughters of Our Lady. The men of Richard's growing Order of Our Lady of the Desert *worshipped* her. She had appeared with Naham and her the remainder of her ghul as guards to Richard's force after their sack of the ancient town of Ossigi. Since then she had played her role as benevolent nun. They had taken two more towns since her arrival, and with each wound she healed or charge she led she bound them closer. None as close as Richard who was like having a savage wolf as a faithful puppy. He was a nearly a perfect tool. The one thing holding him back was fear.

She had seen in his dreams that he feared the one called Cazador. To Marcela's endless intrigue it was the same man that had sacked her town of ghouls. He was an interesting human, a knight with great spiritual power. She had tried to invade his dreams but had been frustrated by his protections, and what Marcela could not control, she would destroy. She has slowly been building a coalition of those children of the Nameless who would swear fealty to her.

232

Ghul, revenants, fellow Idolon spirits, and even clans of Woodwose. It was from this growing number of servants and allies that she has selected Athalgild of the Visigoths in his grave for over five hundred years as her agent. He had had been a sorcerer and war leader in life and a puissant revenant in his death. Like Marcela he too sought worship and reverence and the manna that came with it. He was strong and ambitious with his own retinue of revnant thralls. She had ordered him to assasinate this Cazador, instead she felt his death scream in the spirit realm. His loss would weaken her. Marcela had promised Richard the death of his nemesis as a reward for service but now she would have to make excuses. Marcela stamped an exquisite foot against the carpet clad earth as though she were grinding the troublesome mortal's bones into dust. Goddesses didn't make excuses.

Chapter 20: Bone and Blood

The road wove through winding hills dotted with groves of citrus and olive. The late afternoon sun beat down on man and beast with sullen heat. Even though they had put over thirty miles between themselves and the ancient bridge Cazador still felt as though they were being hunted. A feeling he did not like at all. They had forded the river just north of Benamexir and still he was unable to relax. Since the clash with revenants on the bridge he had felt as though the hourglass had been turned. The sands flowed and time worked against him and he longed to bring his charges to safety. Another day of hard pushing and they would reach his grandfather's sphere of influence and relative safety, but if Cazador had learned anything in life it was that safety was an illusion. He rested his hand on L'auxifar drawing comfort from his ancestral blade.

With the rays of the setting sun still touching the land they made camp. Cazador had ordered the ground to be blessed by Diallo before a single shovel hit the dirt. After the camp was secure Cazador roamed the pickets with a roving patrol. Although he was confident that his company was alert and secure, he unable to expunge the nervous energy that had filled him since he had awoken to Asmā standing over him. Even through his anxiety Cazador felt a smile tugging his full lips into a smile. As if summoned by his thoughts she hailed him from the head of her own small column. "How goes the watch Captain?" There was something about the way her green eyes blazed in the setting sun that left him kinda breathless. Then she smiled and something Cazador didn't even know was knotted within him came undone.

Were she any other woman he would have said the watch was beautiful if only because he was able to see her. If she was any other woman he would have said that her eyes in the sunset were more breathtaking than the stars at midnight. He would have slipped to a knee and took her hand and kissed it, but she was not any woman. She was Asmā Shade-Killer his vintenar of crossbows and such a thing didn't strike Cazador as proper. He was her captain and paymaster. For her, to refuse him might be seen as risking her position and Cazador would never be that type of man. So instead he said, "Much quieter than last night, Lady Vitenar." Cazador's eyes met Asmā's and he bowed to the woman that had saved him. Sound faded and the world seemed to pause as the gold flecked green orbs snared something in his soul. "I've never seen a more perfect hero." He said, lips running away with words not meant to leave his mind. Cazador bit his lower lip to stop himself.

Cheeks burning he thanked God for the night and his brown skin that hid his fluster. Asmā's expression danced with mirth and something more nefarious that tightened Cazador's chest and groin simultaneously. *High treason! Traitors the lot of you!* Cazador screamed at himself from the safety of his thoughts. "I thank you again for your bravery. All slept but you, and without your aid I would surely be dead." He said trying to salvage himself from looking the lecher. The bowel clenching fear of the fight returned, the cold certainty of death that had stalked that night cooling his ardor. He could feel the eyes of his conroi on him. He could almost hear them judging him and the jesting that would come.

"Actually milady I would speak with you." Asmā gave orders to her unit and nodded her assent. Cazador motioned and they walked together for a while, winding their way through the camp until they arrived at the fire of the knights. Cazador used the time to best formulate his question. "How did you come by the bridge last night?" He finally asked quietly. Asmā stopped waking and Cazador stopped with her. Turning to face him she pinned Cazador with her emerald gaze and shrugged. "I woke from a dream of the camp being under attack and I went to find you. When I saw you laid low I did what I must. I could not stand idly by and see you laid low by a devil. You are my captain." Something in how she said the words and the intensity of her gaze left him feeling giddy. He wanted to kiss her but instead he said, "Kneel please lady Asmā." Asmā went to one knee as Izan, Jaime, Rodrigo, Maurice and the others gathered around as though summoned by his intent. Cazador drew L'auxifar, " They say that a woman cannot be a knight but I know this to be rubbish." Cazador said eying his sword. " Any knight can make a knight as all here know. This is the blade of my ancestors forged from the blades of seven great warriors of my house there is greatness in this blade, as there is greatness in you." Cazador said to Asmā's kneeling form. "Now I ask you brave lady, will you be without fear? Will you be brave and upright that God may love you and speak the truth always, protect the helpless, and do no wrong?" Asmā nodded and in a clear voice said, "I do." She said. Cazador tapped her with the flat of his sword on each shoulder and then steeling himself struck Asmā a mighty blow on the shoulder that nearly sent her sideways into the dust. "Let that be the last blow you ever receive without returning in kind and rise as Cavalleresca Asmā of the Company of Saint Moses." The surrounding knights cheered as Asmā rose grinning wildly her eyes shining like pools of verdant flame. It was highly irregular but Cazador had rarely felt so proud of himself.

* * *

Richard knelt as the Prophetess Marwah blessed the blood spattered Knights of Our Lady of the Desert and the men of Le Cannet Des Maures. The words were foreign and unfamiliar but he felt the telltale sensation of water flowing over his body indicated the blessing of The Lady. The Siege of Carcabuey had taken three days. The Moors had contested every inch of the town and then held the castle like men possessed. The blessing of the lady had kept casualties low, but the one thing it could not change was time. The fight has taken three days and might have taken longer had lady Marwah not entered the fray, storming the walls with her guard, in the escalade that finally won them the castle.

Richard felt bones in his spine click and soreness in his muscles fade as his bone deep weariness seemed to fade. "And you shall mount up on wings like eagles. You will walk and not be weary. In Our Lady's Name let it be so." Marwah intoned. Minor wounds that had nagged him faded into nothing and Richard felt refreshed as he had never been before. All around him men began to rise their features fresh under the dirt and grime of battle. As her prayer ended the haggardness that had plagued both man and beast had vanished.

Men murmured their wonder at the the gift of their patroness and her Prophetess Marwah. She stood backlit by the burning ruins of Carcabuey like a goddess come to life. Richard felt an overwhelming sense of adoration and joined his men in bowing his head into his cupped hands as many had taken to doing instead of crossing themselves.

"There is an enemy ahead of us." Marwah said, silencing the crowd of warriors. "They race ahead of us to our target and this we must not allow, for though we outnumber our foe, if they reach the narrow places before us our numbers matter little. Therefore we will march without rest until we catch our foe. We will catch them in the open plains and crush them! Are you men ready to march?" Richard screamed his assent with the others. They set out every third man bearing a torch into the starshot night.

Dawn came and went and midday was fast approaching. Richard felt as if he had spent two days abed rather than a long night and morning in the saddle. His horse too seemed ready to run as if walking and cantering for the past eighteen hours was merely a warm up. With his entire force mounted on captured horse flesh the miles had fallen away. Their usually twelve miles had doubled in the span of eight hours marching. The had left the steep hilly paths behind for rolling plains as they crossed the Genil. Richard called a halt at the river and sent his almogovars out mounted to spy the lay of the land and any potential threats. As of yet none had returned.

* * *

237

The following morning, it was a heartened company that rode out from their camp. Asmā's promotion had done wonders for morale as every man and woman learned that good service was rewarded in kind. The creased nature of the land meant that the almogovars of from the lances were out a quarter mile ahead and to the flanks of the main column. The merchants and mule train were in the center of the column with the spearman on the extreme flanks. His paranoia had not faded but he felt confident. The morning sun was bright on their left shoulders sparkling from helmets maille and fittings.

A flash from the east caught his eye and Cazador turned to see Duku and Idris the younger riding hard for the column. As they drew closer he could see that there was blood spattering men and mounts. Idris's horse threw clods of dirt as he reined in before his captain. "We have company. We crossed the Genil and spotted an army marching under the banners of Le Cannet Des Maures and some strange banner with a cross and fountain. I counted a little over three thousand of them. Knights, spearman, crossbowman, and almogovars." Idris the younger said in the same clipped professional tones as his father. It was as though the news of a hostile force outnumbering their own ten to one was of no more consequence than needing to sharpen his sword. "We ambushed their scouts, so they don't yet know where were are, but they are moving faster than a force that size should. They are stopped by the river likely waiting for a report. We found their scouts on the old Roman road, meaning once they move we have an hour at best before they're on top of us." Cazador fought the urge to curse and panic rose to choke him. Instead he projected as much confidence as he could muster he said, "Its time to kick Richard in the teeth then!" Inside his guts were churning with anxiety.

Turning in his saddle Cazador surveyed the landscape. His knights and command had drawn close including Omar. Cazador could feel his mentors silent scrutiny. The rugged hills were gone replaced by olive and citrus groves and thick stands of Tamarisk dotting gently rolling hills. "Caz we must away from here." Maurice hissed, but Cazador shook his head. "To run is to die. We must bloody them drive them into disarray. We must make the lion fear the mouse. Better that than be caught strung out." There were grim nods all around and Omar gave him a firm pat of approval. Cazador's eyes however never left the dense trees in orderly rows lining the road as if one of them would hand him a way to salvage this situation. "Ladies and gentlemen it's time for an ambush!" Cazador said savagely. "Rodrigo, I want you to take your conroi and the pages. Mount them and make sure they draw armor, throwing knives, shields, spears and maces. Once the boys are kitted I need you to keep going with the merchants and baggage. Leave nothing but the siege engines, and ammunition. We will buy you time and you should be relatively safe because it's me Richard wants. " Cazador said grimly, the beginnings of a plan forming in his mind. Rodrigo slammed his fist to his chest like a legionnaire of old. "I understand and shall obey." He said with no trace of his usual humor. Cazador could sense his annoyance at being forced to play the nursemaid to merchants and baggage once again.

Pushing those thoughts aside Cazador said, "We will backtrack and meet them near Belda." Turning to Idris the younger Cazador said, "You, Constantine, and Bayan, and I will find a good hill." Idris nodded, next Cazador turned to the stocky Dúkú you will lead sir Omar and half his force to spy on the enemy and slow them down. Contest their crossing. Kill as many of their horses as you can I want their knights and men at arms crippled and their almogovars nervous." Both men nodded, and Cazador met Omar's eye feeling the strangeness of giving orders to a man who had taught him he finer points of being a knight and warleader. Omar didn't say a word he simply smiled and gave Cazador a proud wink before riding back down the column to his men.

A quarter of an hour later Cazador stood atop a hill near Belda. He could clearly see the enemy across the river. The road across the crown of the hill was occupied by the sappers and the onagers loaded with the best approximation of Roman plumbatae that Nuevo Bobastro's smiths could give him.

The edge of the hill itself was embedded by the arbalestiers and the company archers with fifty of Omar's dismounted horse archers. Cazador and the other knights would ride to their positions but would likely fight dismounted beside the almogovars as would the squires and men at arms. They would man the hasty barricade across the road that wove between the olive trees where the hill rose sharply across to where the hillside dropped away into a steep rocky gully.

Three thousand men. Cazador thought as watched as fourteen fifty man blocks of crossbowman and another fourteen similarly sized blocks of almogovars move towards the river. Behind them knights in conrois of ten and ten blocks of fifty men at arms waited impatiently ahead of twenty blocks of spearman. In the distance Cazador spied the men of his patrimony holding the rearguard. They were hemmed in by a swamp on their right and behind them olive groves stretched to the hills beyond.

The trail led from the ford and ran alongside the hill before doglegging toward the summit. Allowing his eyes to scan beyond the banks of the river he saw Omar and Dúkú strike. They exploded from the enemy's left like a summer storm. With a series of snaps Cazador could hear from where he stood, a cloud of arrows fell on the enemy crossbowman and almogovars like rain. The composite bows propelled the shafts with titanic force and by the third volley hundreds of the lightly armored enemy were down. The well drilled horse archers wheeled their mounts turning in their saddle to launch another three volleys devastating the once orderly blocks of the unsuspecting enemy. The white and gold clad knights and men at arms charged towards Omar's riders, but within moments they were thundering back down the road from whence they emerged.

Using their lighter faster mounts Omar's horse archers outpaced Richards riders. Cazador watched as his cousin led his force in another tight wheel pouring arrows at the knights and men at arms. Omar's horseman revolved like a wheel of death flaying horse and rider alike with deadly bow fire. Cazador marvelled at his kinsman's skill, but also at the way the enemy seemed to refuse to flag, the large war horses still game after chasing Omar's company for a quarter mile.

After clearing scores of saddles and felling at least a hundred horses Omar's cavalry exploded back towards the ford, laying down a line of strafing fire as they whipped past the enemy less than two spear lengths away. Cazador could see Richard, shield bristling with arrows haranguing his men to get their mounts turned, his own mount already racing toward the fleeing enemy.

The company cheered their comrades and Cazador allowed himself a grim smile. The enemy infantry stood in a disorganized clump seemingly torn between crossing the river or waiting for their cavalry. Omar's force hit them in a wedge, presaged only by the hiss of arrows as four hundred fell on the disorganized rabble. Without missing a beat bows were stowed and swords, axes and maces were drawn and they hammered into the enemy. They had been turned east and Omar had come from the north. Not a single spear had turned in time to stop their thunderous charge. Within moments a hundred men had killed or injured five times their number as they tore through the enemy and across the ford.

When the last of Omar's riders had cleared the river Diallo began to sing a war song. Cazador looked to Asmā, "Commence fire lady knight." Asmā beamed and gave the order to fire. The archers and crossbows sent a wave of shafts that descended upon the enemy like a flock of angry birds. Eighty six arrows and bolts flew and each hit their mark leaving causalities where foeman once stood. The disorganization and panic in the enemy ranks was a delightful thing to watch as another wave of arrows and bolts struck. The third flight was descending just as Richard and the knights returned.

Cazador smiled with malicious glee as horses were struck and riders cartwheeled through the air like an angry child's toys. All around the illbegotten Lord of Le Cannet Des Maures men met death as they rode into chaos. Richard himself though seemed blessed by God as not a single shaft touched him. Sheltering behind his shield, cloth of gold caps streaming behind him, Richard rallied his men and charged across the ford as arrows fell like iron tipped hail. Within minutes the returning men were adding their own shafts to the barrage.

A blood spattered and grinning Omar approached Cazador who took his arm in the warrior grip. "That was a fine bit of organized murder dear cousin." Cazador said. Omar shrugged. "Its like the Holy Land eh, just in reverse." Both men laughed the sound odd amongst the unfolding violence. Even under the withering fire Richard and his men were forcing the crossing. Omar held up the empty canvas bag that had once been filled with caltrops. "This should be fun." He murmured mischievously. "I think I've taught you too well little cousin. Dropping these across the ford was downright evil but a nice touch." Omar said as they turned to watch the mayhem unfold. Cazador laughed maniacally as the screams rose to echo off the hillside as wicked steel points found the feet of man and beast. What had begun as a grand charge ground to a halt and all of Richard's lead elements bunched together. The archers and arbalestiers fired at will now picking targets and aiming for horses and unarmored flesh.

Cazador looked to Bayan and nodded. The scholarly Arab waved his mace like a baton and the grunt of the sappers preceded the creak and snap of the traction engines. The strange woosh of the plumbatae filled the air as they took flight. Bayan had spent the nights traveling to Miramollin's camp tinkering with a skein of pulleys and a stone counter-weight that wieghed as much as a well fed child. It would allow a single team to launch a twenty pound projectile four hundred feet. That meant that sixty of iron and lead darts in each of the hinged buckets. One hundred and eighty of the darts descended on the men trying to cross the ford like a curse from on high. Arrows and bolts continued to fly as the second barrage of plumbata hit. "Thank God for the *Strategicon*." Cazador grunted as he saw the dusty words of the long dead Emperor Maurice brought violently to life.

Cazador mounted his horse and drew L'auxifar. "All right you laggards mount up and get to your positions!" He shouted at the knights, almogovars, squires, and men at arms. As he wove through the olive trees back toward the road. The barricade was formed of the wooden slats that were used to protect the camp at night. Together with the ditch they provided a seven foot wall of protected. Hammered into the earth as they were, the five foot piles only stood three and a half feet high. By no means were they the walls of Constantinople but combined with the men behind it, they would stop a charging horse or warrior and that was enough for Cazador.

Taking his place in the rough center of the barricade Cazador, contented himself with the fact that he had chosen the best battlefield he could. They would hold Richard off as long as they could and escape but first there was killing to do. Cazador had strapped a small buckler to his left arm and took up a short spear in his left hand as his knights and men at arms fell in around him. They formed the first of five rough ranks that would hold the barricade against the enemy. Cazador longed to know what was happening at the ford but he pushed it from his mind.

When a handful of the archers and arbalestiers began taking their positions on the hillside above Cazador knew that enough of enemy had crossed the river. The rest would come when it was time to close the trap. Such were the orders he'd given Asmā. From the ford to where they stood was less than a quarter mile and sure enough Cazador could hear the hoofbeats. Jamming his sword and spear into the ground before him. He reached for his brace of the Sudanese throwing knives and stuck several in the wood of the pile before him keeping one at the ready as the sunlight glittered from their wicked points. It was something to do to distract him from the growing nerves from the impending fight. Cazador could feel the battle fury waiting for him close but it sat tantalizingly just out of reach. Instead he had cold fear sitting in his guts. Not of death, but of a maiming crippling injury that would be the end of his career before it even started. Sure his aunt would find a place for him, but it wouldn't be the place he wanted, and that was only if he could stop Richard. Suddenly the fury found him. Cazador could find no other reason for Richard to be here, so far from the main crusade. The social climbing scumbag should be sucking farts from a kings ass rather than here, yet here he was and Cazador would do his level best to ensure he went no further.

The pounding of hooves grew ever closer and Cazador prepared to hurl his throwing knife. The road doglegged sharply, forming a blind corner. As the first of the enemy cavalry rounded it, Cazador didn't bother giving an order. He simply announced his intent by hurling the knife he clutched in his right hand. No sooner than it had left his fingertips, he reached for another and unleashed it before his first knife struck. His first target a large black horse with white socks and a white blaze across it's nose took his knife to the chest. The steel sank deep to send the beast crashing forward throwing his rider over the horn of his saddle. His second knife took a knight in the arm. His lance dropped and catapulted him clear to the base of the barricade. Izan leaned forward dispassionately and caved the man's helmet in with a mighty blow from his axe.

All told two score of the enemy riders died in the initial charge. A wall of dead men an horses lay forty feet from the company's barricade. Sadly Richard had not been among them. There was much shouting and whinnying back around the bend and Cazador wished he knew what was afoot. Moments later a wave of crossbow bolts sent them all scrambling behind their shields. Figures appeared as the enemy began to drag away bodies. Cazador hurled another knife, but the second rank of crossbowmen were already firing. Cazador missed the solidity of his lamellar armor as the bolts whizzed past him. Diallo's rich tenor rang off the hillside to drown out the screams of the wounded and dying and Cazador hunkered behind his shield crouched behind the barricade.

His instinct was to leap the barricade and order a charge but he knew it wasn't the right call. Throwing knives and javelins came from the rear ranks saving him from his own rashness. One moment the crossbowmen were firing from neat files where there was always one man shooting while others reloaded. The next they were dying a score going down in the first barrage. Using the disarray Cazador rose with a roar throwing the last of his knives as fast as he could. The crossbowmen pulled back but the damage was done. The bulwark of bodies had been cleared. Throwing knives and tambas were passed forward as the Company of Saint Moses prepared for another charge.

A great shout reached them, "Desperta Ferro! Per la dama! Per la Dama!" The battle cry announced the charge of Richard's almogovars. They came in a a wall of black leather shields painted with the wavy cross and fountain. Spears and throwing knives leapt to meet them as the enemy almogovars threw spears of their own. The enemy's shields soaked up the worst of the damage but here and there a man fell, their black surcoated bodies transfixed by spears and knives. Men died or took wounds and others stumbled but the enemy rolled forward undaunted roaring like lions. Cazador slung his next knife low and watched it scythe into unarmored legs and men fell. Cazador roared his own defiance plucking his spear and sword from the earth.

The first of the bearded Castilians reached the barricade and Cazador struck like lightening. He batted aside the almogovar's spear with his own and riposted, slamming his spear through his enemy's black surcoat and gambeson to deep into the man's gut. With a savage twist Cazador freed his spear. He heard his squire Marco grunt behind him and his throwing knife took a charging almogovar in the skull, the point finding a gap in the almogovar's vented helmet. Too busy to congratulate his squire Cazador blocked an enemy's falchion with L'auxifar from the high guard and back cut for his opponent's head. The lithe almogavar got his shield around but Cazador punched his short spear into his groin leaving the man to whimper and die. As soon as had the spear gelded man fell another replaced him. Cazador's new foe was all dark beard with narrow hazel eyes tinged with fury. He hammered his falchion at Cazador who blocked his first two strikes and riposted with his spear on the third flicking it at the almogavar's face. As the shield came up to block, Cazador cut high to low to take the Castilian's leg at the knee. He fell back with a strangled yell exposing the man behind him who stopped the spear thrust, but took L'auxifar to the throat.

All along the barricade the enemy almogovars battled the men of the Company of Saint Moses. With their superior numbers negated by the narrow front the heavier armor showed it's worth in the tight press. The rearward ranks still threw projectiles into the heaving mass of enemies and men died as they forgot to keep their shields overhead. Cazador blocked a wild slash with his shield and stabbed at his new attackers head the man ducked tucking into his shield. The streaks of grey in his tangled beard proving he hadn't gotten old without being a canny fighter. Cazador wasn't without tricks of his own as he slammed his spearshaft on the almogovar's shield rim and used the hooks on the back of the spear head to pull the shield down with a mighty heave as he sent L'auxifar flying in a lightning thrust that found his opponents throat and tore it open. Cazador twisted his sword, feeling it grate on the skull bones as he recovered his blade.

From the corner of his eye Cazador could see Izan's mace stove in an almogovar's helmet his foes blood bright as it sprayed from a broken pate. Maurice was beside him, and parried a flashing falchion. Twisting his pommel over his opponents wrist, he cut and laid open the enemy almogovar's throat. Maurice's sword flashed faster than the enemy could block, and tore away the man's throat along with his life. The enemy broke off leaving the dead and dying behind. All along the barricade bodies lay five or six deep in a blood oozing pile. The once hard packed dirt of the track now a slick morass of mud and viscera. Cazador sucked in lungfuls of air as he surveyed the grim testament to his company's skill. Richard had taken grievous losses. Hundreds of spearman, crossbowmen, and almogovars had went down in Omar's attack, hundreds more had died assaulting the barricade. The problems was Richard still had plenty of men to throw at him and he'd yet to deploy his spearman against them.

As if summoned by his thoughts Cazador saw shielded men bearing long spears round the corner at an orderly trot. Rasing L'auxifar high he screamed, "For God and Saint Moses, we will not yield!" All around him his companions roared and projectiles leapt to meet them. The rear ranks lobbed their weapons high and when shields went up the front rank cast low. Cazador looked on dissapointed. The attack was no where near as effective as it had been. Equipped with the large kite shields the enemy was better able to protect themselves from the barrage. Cazador once again took up sword and spear to meet their charge.

The enemy spearman rolled forward in one cohesive mass only to stop twenty yards from the barricade. Cazador was confused. *Why are they stopping.* Confusion gave way to bowel watering terror as crossbowmen were revealed positioned behind the shielded spearmen raised their weapons to fire. "Shields! Take cover!" Cazador bellowed as he sheltered behind his defenses. The sound of booted feet warned him of the impending charge. Stabbing his spear into the ground he freed his left hand and pulled the horn from his satchel.

* * *

Asmā watched as the path flooded with spearmen, and crossbowmen, behind them the remaining knights and men at arms stood in a neat column flanked by the remaining almogovars. As one the enemy rolled forward until the suddenly stopped and the front threw ranks of spearman knelt. Crossbowmen stepped forward, fired and stepped away to reload as their comrades fired. Bolts punished Sir Cazador's position in successive waves. The efficiency of it made the recently knighted vintenar of crossbows sneer with professional jealousy. Asmā contented herself with the fact that they had forced the usurpers men to pay a bitter butchers bill to cross the river. She had always had a head for figures and had calculated that no less than forty men a minute had died or been injured for a quarter hour. It had been glorious.

Now she watched in fury as her comrades suffered a similar fate. *Blow the horn you stubborn man! If you die down there I will kill you!* She fumed no longer allowing herself to be surprised by the depth of the emotion she felt for Cazador. After standing down a shade on his behalf Asmā couldn't deny that she wasn't just a tad bit fond of *her* captain. He reminded her of a storm. Beautiful, loud, and powerful. Utterly dangerous. A thing to be sheltered from even though the wind and rain of his presence called to be danced in. *Blow the horn!* She fumed and suddenly, as if he could read her mind, she heard the horn. As one Asmā and the other ranged troops rose and fired.

The effect was immediate and Asmā smiled as she hauled back on her cord. Arrows and bolts punched into the lightly armored crossbowmen sending scores to the earth in shock and surprise. Asmā fired again as they doubled their hits before using her flint and steel to light the two naptha pots Cazador had given her to mark targets for the sappers.

The first she hurled into the middle of the enemy front. The clay orb shattered on a helmet splashing to turn two men into human pyres and setting the surcoats of two others aflame. The other she carried to where the enemy knights and men at arms sheltered behind their shields. Asmā hurled the naptha and watched as it struck a shield rim and set the paint and leather alight sending a wave of fire down a maille clad arm sending the man and his horse into a frenzy of terrified screams. Asmā hustled back to where her tent party was directly covering the barricade. She had barely shouldered her weapon to fire when the artillery struck. The weighted darts tore holes in the enemy formation sowing panic and shock as men tried to reconcile the sudden death that descended from the sky like judgement.

The unit at the barricade resumed hurling projectiles adding their own spice to the cauldron of chaos. Asmā fired, reloaded and fired again savage glee rising in her heart. The enemy formation writhed and heaved like a giant beast. A knight in a gold cape was forcing his way to the front. She could hear him screaming but his words were lost to the din of battle.

Sighting carefully she took aim the late afternoon sun glinted from the wicked point of her needle bodkin bolt. She fired, feeling a thrill as the stock vibrated with the force of the shot. The bolt flew straight and true cutting an inevitable path between Asmā and her target. It could not miss, yet somehow, it did. "Son of a puss riddled whore!" She swore impressively. The knight she'd missed carried on, never knowing how close he came to death.

* * *

Diallo sang and Cazador steeled himself as the spearmen charged their position. Richard the usurper had pushed his way to the front lines. He screamed and rallied his men as death rained from above. They had been in total disarray ready to break, but Richard pulled them back together like a man lacing a boot. Within moments his spearman had a house of shields interlocked and they were moving forward. Heart pounding Cazador readied himself to enter the storm of steel. The wall shields grew inexorably closer, the steady tramp of booted feet pushing the wicked spear points closer and closer.

Cazador felt fear and anxiety churn. Protected by the shield house the rain of projectiles was futile. They would close and use the reach of their weapons to snipe at Cazador's men until they were able to roll over them. Fear turned to defiance and fury and Cazador roared at the wall of shields as though his anger alone would fell his enemy. When the field engines hit them it was like a gift from God. A mix of heavy stones twice the size of a man's fist and the plumbata swatted a hole in the center of the enemy line. The next two strikes came mere heartbeats after the first. A solid wall of shields was reduced to a mass of panicked men, splintered wood and bone and blood.

He had hoped they would break but instead they came on bravely. They desperately tried to reform their shield house but the archer and crossbow women on the hill above wasted no time in creating more gaps. Richard snarled, barking orders at the men around him. He looked across to where Cazador stood. They locked eyes for a moment and Cazador could feel his hate like warmth from a fire. Richard pointed at him with his spear and Cazador simply smiled. With about two score men rallied to him Richard charged the barricade.

Using his own shorter spear to sweep aside the enemy's, Cazador riposted aiming a low strike at his opponents inner thigh. As soon as his opponent's shield dropped he slammed L'auxifar into his gullet. He had barely withdrawn his blade before Richard was on him. Whatever guardian angel or ancestor, who was guiding his arm had his thanks as his buckler came around by nothing but instinct alone saving his life.

Snarling Cazador flicked his spear at Richard's face like it was an axe. The usurper of Le Cannet Des Maures threw himself backwards narrowly avoiding death. "Why are you here Richard? Why are you fucking chasing me?" Cazador snarled already thrusting low. Forcing Richard to skip away again. "Because fuck the decrepit old man, that bitch and her company! I will take it all and be king in my Lady's name!" Richard spat eyes wild with zeal and Cazador resisted the urge to leap the barricade. Instead he punched his blade at Richard's head before jamming his spear at his opponent's gut. Whipping his blade around he cut from high to low clipping his enemy's leg with a thrill of triumph thumping in his heart as the usurper's lifeblood joined that of his minions in the slurry before the barricade. Richard went down hard helmet bouncing free, eyes glazing as his half severed leg flopped spurting great gouts kf his vitality in the mud. "This is why nobody ever liked you little Dick. Always wanting more. Greedy little gutter rat worse than a mad dog biting the hand that feeds him." Cazador spat disdainfully as he reversed his blow intent on crushing Richard's unarmored head like a melon.

Richard's look of horror turned to turned to one of triumph. Cazador's blade felt as though it met stone, the angry hiss of water filling his ears. Richard scrambled away laughing. "Glorious in my Lady's name." Richard burbled as he stood his leg healing before Cazador's eyes. "I am the champion of Our Lady of the Desert Fountain. We are the knights of her order. We will be victorious in *her* name. I will take Bobastro and carve a path from Malaga to the Monts Des Maures.

Cazador goggled at the impossibility of it. He had seen the leg flopping by the gristle. He didn't need the gris gris vibrating against his chest to tell him something was very very wrong. "This is annoying. Somebody tell me *how* he's fucking standing!" Alcazar bellowed unable to hide his fear and confusion as his voice shifted octaves. Richard's laugh rang high and clear as even his own men gaped at him in shock. Ignoring his enemy's rant he let fury take him. "Are you the devil's turd now Little Dicky?" Cazador spat refusing to be cowed.

Richard's face shifted from laughter to anger so fast it turned Cazador's stomach with its inhumanity. "You can die now cur!" Richard snarled lashing out so fast the air seemed to shiver. Cazador could do naught but catch the blow on L'auxifar rolling his wrist to shed the force like rain from an angled roof. Stepping offline he flicked his wrist again as he twisted his hips. L'auxifar came around behind Richard's wild slash. Cazador's blade bit hard catching the usurper across the wrist sending his sword and hand flying over the barricade. The Company of Saint Moses cheered and it was Cazador's turn to laugh. "Regrow a hand in your lady's name,*Champion*!" Cazador sneered as he punched his spear into Richard's midsection. The links of the usurpers maille held but he could feel the snap of his enemy's ribs vibrate through his weapon. He brought his sword down to finish him but met only air as Richard's retainers dragged him away. He wanted to be be angry to rage and chase down his prey. Instead he watched them retreat with a baleful glare. It was over. He had won, a great victory but Cazador couldn't help but feel like they had narrowly escaped by the skin of their teeth.

Chapter 21: Dawn of Darkness

Marwah who was Marcela was too exhausted to be angry. Today had been a close thing. The sheer amount of manna required to *bless* the Order had taxed her to the extreme. It was all she could do to make sure that more hadn't died. As it was her champion had lost half his army to a mere handful of mercenaries. Over a thousand of her most ardent worshippers gone in a single day. The nascent goddess felt depleted. The enemy had possessed staggeringly potent magical protection. While they had lacked a true magi, the enemy did have powerful charms, nyama infused weapons, and a puissant djali. The songs he wove had battled her blessing at every turn sapping her strength. She could see now that Richard's fear of Cazador was not unfounded. He was a killer and a tactician worthy of respect and caution.

If not for the wave of reverence and devotion she'd received after she'd healed Richard's leg she'd be finished. It was only a matter of time until her maimed champion came begging for succor. The bastards had taken the hand as a trophy, meaning healing him would be difficult. She could feel the ebb in belief. Her worshippers had been butchered and those that remained knew doubt and defeat. Her power over them teeterd on a precarious edge. It was time for something drastic. She needed her champion and his order if she was to make the full leap from spirit to goddess. Richard's war on his kin would give her Malaga itself and all the power of the ley line that ran through the port city. It would be the seat of her kingdom and her bid at godhead would be all but unstoppable. But that was only if she could salvage things now. Eschewing her golden maille armor she donned the black and gold surcoat over her cloth of gold gown. Taking up a bag of salt she hobbled from her pavilion.

Naham and he Sleepless Guard fell in behind her without a word and only a whispering of maille and the tramp of boots to announce their presence. As she walked through the camp the men of the order still awake nodded to her in respect. She saw one man a spearman with intense grey eyes and mousy brown hair, cradling a broken wrist. She walked to the man, taking his injured arm and kissed it, hearing the bones knit and click back into place before she withdrew her full lips. The soldier gasped and fell to his knees. "Hail to Our Lady, blessed be she always!" He sobbed overwhelmed. Marcella who lived in Marwah's skin smiled. "Blessed be the soldiers of Our Lady." She said before moving on. The drain the healing put on her manna was as nothing compared to the boost from the raw adoration that welled from the onlookers. *I am your lady still.*

They came to here then. The luckiest of the walking wounded. Those who couldn't move fast enough had been abandoned in their headlong flight to the hill north of Belda. She healed their cuts, sprains, and bruises, feeding off their abject devotion. With each man she healed a piece of her came back until it felt as though she was bursting with power compared to how she had felt after the battle. She allowed her manna to play across her skin, delighting in the soft ethereal glow. The purity of the adulation she received left her feeling giddy and euphoric, but she needed more.

Marcella as Marwah circuited weaving among the soldiers of the order until once again she reached the center of the camp. The once deserted communal space soon filled with expectant faces. The survivors of the battle each among them bearing some type of wound. Even Richard, with his shattered ribs and single hand stumbled from his tent. When he saw Marwah's glowing form the Lord Commander of the Knights of Our Lady of the Desert Fountain fell to his knees before her. Face awash in her golden glow he sobbed." Oh holy prophetess! Forgive me for I have failed Our Lady!" He wailed looking utterly broken. Marcela looked upon Richard through Marwah's eyes and laid a matronly hand up on his head. " Fear not brave Richard. The Lady is with you still. This day the Order had suffered it's first defeat. But under the moon and stars the Lady shall bring victory!" She shouted voice ringing in the night as if reflected from the stars above. She sent out a pulse of manna, a wash of healing energy that sent a ripple of movement through every man present. Aches faded and bleeding slowed as cuts closed. "If you still believe, then follow me and I will show you her power. The power even to defeat death!" Marcela led her faithful from their camp, all the while she sang, a seductive call coaxing forth her allies. She had tasted defeat, but tonight she would gather her power, the faithful would truly learn who they served. It was a risk but the time for coy measures had passed.

The battlefield lay a mile and a half to the south and Marcela as Marwah marched towards it. Behind her a procession of soldiers stretched into the night. Her hymn danced on the wind. As they approached the ford the alarm could be heard from Belda. *Good let them come, let them stand and watch what I do here. Let them bear witness to the glory of the Lady!* Marcela thought as she led her party to where the first attack had begun. Never had over a thousand men been so quiet. The corpses of comrades and horses littered the ground around them. Marcela could feel their shame and guilt as she used the salt to scribe sigils that interlocked with pentacles and keys of Solomon. The expenditure of manna was oppressive, but every drop was necessary. Tonight Marcela would rise from mere sainthood to godhead or she would flame from existence in an explosion of manna. Either way her song would truly begin or end here.

The people of Belda lined it's walls to watch the glowing woman as she traipsed among the corpses. They watched intently as she crossed the ford leading the warriors behind her up the blood soaked trail. She paused the procession to continue her work Marcela could feel townsfolk's fear like a cold wind and feasted upon it. The barricade was gone but the tideline of bodies remained. She continued inscribing until the entire battlefield was connected in a great sigil that thrummed with latent power. It called to the shades and lesser spirits of the land pulling them to her.

Pushing manna beneath her feet Marcela as Marwah relishing the gasps as rose in the air. She did so slowly until she floated above the highest tower in the nearby town. She hovered there glowing in the sky like a low slung star. Closing her eyes she shut out everything and opened a channel to Sammael the angel of death and sent forth manna, reveling the necromantic energy.

All of the men that had fallen were consecrated to her, and had fallen in her name. Their souls were hers to command. Glowing ropes of manna floated from her to the great sigil tying themselves around her outstretched palms until she floated like a spider in the center of a vast web of pulsing energy. "Witness the power of the Lady of the Desert Fountain! The Lares of Lares. The Great Lamia, The goddess of the Well! She walks this world through me! I am her incarnate and through me those who have fallen in my name will rise again!" She roared in a loud enough to be heard miles. As one corpses began to rise as if they had only been asleep rather than dead. Gossamer forms of silver smoke rose like fog from the earth. "Even the shades and Woodwose heed my call!" She thundered to be answered by a a mighty howling from the hills as the wild men driven by their shamans drawn by her song arrived in this hundreds.

In moments over a thousand glowing dead eyes starred back at her as dead men rose. Marcela could feel the hunger of her newly risen ghul, eclipsed only by the shock and fear of the spectator's . The living men of the Order and even the savage Woodwose fell to their knees. "Those who worship me with a true heart shall never fear death, but become it!" She thundered and throats of her faithful both human and otherwise cheered their adulation. It was rapture and Marcela basked in it.

Allowing herself to gently float back to the ground Marcela landed before her champion. "Lord Commander your army has been restored." Richard prostrated himself in the bloody mud before her. "I will serve forever my goddess!" Marcela smiled at Richard fondly. The expenditure of manna had been extreme. Raising the ghul and summoning the spirits and Woodwose had been twice as taxing as the battle, but it was well worth the cost. Looking to her adoring champion she whispered, "Build for me an altar of non believer's bones. Convert them or make me an offering of blood!"

* * *

Sabri and the other men of Le Cannet Des Maures had been forced to guard the lady Marwah during the battle and were thus kept far away from the danger. Normally this would gall and shame them but Sabri wasn't the only man who was relieved not to have been at the slaughter. The group of warriors from Provence had slowly grown more and more dissatisfied. Last night had been the final straw. The sack of Belda had been a bloody orgy of violence and forced conversions, but it had paled in comparison to the sick horror of watching dead men rise. Necromany on such a scale was unforgivable. Then came the Woodwose from the mountains. The hairy beastmen who had long been an enemy of the men of the Monts Des Maures and the reason the Knights of Saint Attillo were founded. It was too much. While the men of the order had been busy pillaging, raping or sacrificing the men of Le Cannet Des Maures had voted amongst themselves to leave unanimously. It was one thing to serve a bad lord. It was an entirely different thing to serve evil. When Don Ricardo had ordered them to blockade the road south between Belda and Alameda, they had simply kept riding. Let the don think what he liked.

Before the wolf light of dawn colored the sky they had pushed on moving as fast as the infantry could manage on their stolen horses. Somewhere out there was Don Cazador, a true son of the Alfiere house. Their natural lord. They had decided to seek him and offer their blades to his service. Nobody wanted to talk about what would happen if he refused them. As masterless oathbreakers their options were few. Given their options, it was worth the try.

* * *

Richard and his order waited outside of Belda. The first conquest of the Order in Malaga. Before they could continue there was the small matter of a miracle to attend to. He watched intently as the silver hand was removed from its wooden casket carried by a knight of the order. Marwah, avatar of his goddess lifted it free and held the cold lifeless appendage to the stump that had once held Richard's living hand. He'd lost count of the number of times he'd forgotten he'd lost it in the last three days. He would reach for thing with it only to curse his own stupidity and he had yet to master the art of pissing with his left hand. Worst of all the damned thing itched constantly and at times he could swear he felt his fingers twitching. A lot of trouble for a limb that likely no longer existed. It drove him to the ends of his sanity, but now his lady, his goddess would make him whole again.

Richard gasped in wonder as he felt the magic at work. He gasped again in pain as the tingle turned into a maddening itching that set him to clenching his teeth to hold back a scream. It hurt, but not as much as losing to that wretch Cazador. Richard had done everything right and still lost in the face of unfavorable terrain and his wife's cousin's legendary ferocity. Taking Belda had helped him sooth his injured pride but he would not stop until he had Cazador's head on a silver plate before him.

Closing his eyes he focused on the chanting of his goddess pushing the pain far away as though it was happening in another place to someone else and in time the pain faded. He cracked his eyes open marveling at the play of sunlight onthe silver hand he could feel it's warmth and his heart raced with excitement. Delight filled him as his body felt complete once again. His goddess incarnate reached out and took his new appendage. Richard smiled with joy as he could feel the soft skin of her hand against his. Just like that he was no longer maimed. "Glory to the goddess!" He bellowed in abject wonder.

Turning to the crowd Richard flexed his hand and touched each finger to his thumb. The crowd looked on in shock at the second miracle they had witnessed. Most fell to their knees bowing their heads into their cupped hands to show their devotion. Belda was now a town of the goddess The Lady Marcela. All those who had refused to worship her had been sacrificed leaving behind only the faithful. For now it was only a few hundred people but as tale of what happened here spread, her worshipers soon would number in the thousands.

The goal had changed, he now had thousands of Woodwose and ghul at his command. He would send them ahead to harry Cazador. Bobastro and the rest of Malaga with it would fall and in it's place Terra Marcela would be born with Richard at its leader. He would instead focus on capturing land, not just raiding. The more converts his goddess received the greater his rewards. Head filled with the goodness of his goddess and thoughts of future glory he led the order towards their next conquest.

* * *

A man could walk for three miles and not get wet. Such was the size of Gladr's fleet of *drakkar* ships. Thousands of human warriors had come to his banner bearing axe and spear hungry for plunder and battle. He offered a taste of the old days of their ancestors a way back to the times of conquest and glory. His fleet sat at anchor filling the Trondhiem fjord all the way to Røra. The towns of men knelt under his banner of the Odinsblood rune from Trondhiem to Tjøtta and Gladr had found his champion. Hakon the Frenzied. The so called King of Norway Inge Bårdson was weak and died during the invasion of Nidaros but Haakon was different. While Inge had created a fragile peace Haakon would make war on the Christ kneeling Bagler scum. They longed to be unleashed. Gladr knew that by giving him victory over the Baglers they would follow him anywhere.

But the army would have to wait. It was no accident that he had chosen Ranhiem to build his hall. This place called to him. He was the heir Woden, the *Draugadróttinn* the lord of the undead, the *Gondlir* the wand waver. Magic was his heritage and birthright and ignorance was his enemy. Books and scrolls of the old lore were rare and jealously guarded. Much had been lost since the son of El harrowed hell and broke the power of the Samyazan's and the Nox. Much of the knowledge of his ancestors had been destroyed or buried. Gladr knew that in order to reach his goals he had to be more than a ruler and warrior, but a seeker of knowledge as well.

Gladr rose from what had become known as the War Hewn Throne. Made from the broken spears and axes of his enemies and draped with their banners and surcoats as a cushion it was a symbol of his growing power. Power that he desperately needed to grow. As he strode to the door of his hall his hird of champions fell in beside him. Half elves from his home, half human one hundred strong. Haakon the Crazy and Magnus Haraldsson led the humans while Hrafn Ulfson served as captain of the elves. They glittered like a wyrm of silver and gold as the bright morning sun sparkled from the silvery iron maille of the men and shimmered from bronze scales of the elves. For weeks he had sat in the north like a spider in a web of power, ensaring men like flies growing fat with manna. It was odd to the point of being unseemly that Gladr hadn't seen a single rival step forward from the Nox. Subsumation was a time honored tradition among the warlike Nox. You were either a predator or prey and existence was defined by the tension between the two. The fact nobody had come for him made Tegri feel almost slighted. Compounding matters, the newly risen Seelie Court had also been slow to respond. He'd expected djinn assassins and Encantando fouling his ships. He'd expected war clamor from dwarven shield walls and javelins from elvish griffon riders. Instead there had been nothing but troop movements to the south. The nearby Samyazans seemed content preparing for sieges rather than meeting him in the field. How surprised they would be when he struck for manna rich Albion. *Let them cower in their strong places! When they face me I will be the father of a new pantheon too powerful to stop.* He thought as he led his hirdmen into the forest.

Trees that were old in the time of his grandfather towered above him. The air was full of a rich bouquet of scents that were still foreign to Gladr's nose. The trail was well worn by generations of human feet and seidr was thick in the air. He led his hird almost two miles to a large hill that had sang to him from the time his boots had touched the shores of Norway. Gladr froze feeling as though he stood before a precipice. *Here.*

The steep hill seemed wrong, the grade out of place for the landscape. *This is no hill.* Gladr thought as his thin lips pulled into a delighted smile. He could almost feel the presence of the ancestors. "Lord Gladr is there an problem?" Hrafn asked confused at his lord's sudden halt. Gladr turned to his hirdsman. "Everything is perfect drengr." Turning back to the hill that was not a hill Gladr reached for his manna, and opened the channel to Arakiel aspecting and attuning his working to earth. Waves of manna vibrated the air as it shot from Gladr's hands to flay the surface of the hill like a man peeling an apple.

Dirt, rocks, and turf sloughed away to reveal a sharply steepled roof standing no less than forty feet from the ground. The eaves and gables were richly decorated with runes and images of the Aesir. Windows with similarly decorated frames stood out from the pale wood. The main pillars of the structure stood out in a vibrant red the etched runes picked out in gold that winked in the dappled sunlight of the forest. "Behold, the god-house of my forebears!" Gladr shouted as the building was finally freed from its earthen prison. After all these years the building should have rotted away to nothing but instead here it was bleeding manna aspected by *galdrar* that protected it from the ravages of time and nature.

Stepping forward reverently he put his hands on the buttery smooth oak of the doors and marvelled at the power he felt emanating from the rune etched temple. Turning to his hirdmen he said, "Stand guard let none disturb me."

Pushing open the doors he stepped from the world of men into the presence of his ancestors. His elven eyes needed no time to adjust to the dimness of the god-house and the graven images of Odin, Thor, Freya, and Freyr staring down upon him from their alcoves along the wall. The scent of blood hundreds of years old was still sharp and coppery in his nose as it wafted from stained altars before the Aesir. The same pale wood that graced the outside dominated the inside of the god-house. It gleamed like the striated bones of a giant in the watery sunshine that leaked from the high windows. Every inch of it was etched with the tales of the old gods by the hands of a master. The tiny figures seeming to caper in his minds eye like players on a tiny stage.

The energy of the place thrummed through the entire structure like the ocean against the hull of the ship. Gladr felt like he could jump and float away such was the power of the place An inner sanctum sat at the center of the chamber and inexorably he was drawn to it eyes glued to the image of his ancestor Odin as he hung from the world tree. Every line was carved in such lifelike detail that Gladr could almost hear the creak of the great tree under the all fathers weight.

Gladr found his hand on the door without ever remembering placing it there. *"Gladr, son of Biflindi, son of Báleygr, son of Bǫlverkr, son of Darraðr, son of Eylúðr son of Höðr. I see you."* Gladr froze skin prickling as the voice of the *Fimbultýr* the mighty god Odin himself spoke. *"Open the door and enter my presence."* Heart pounding with fear and exhilaration Gladr entered the inner sanctum. On either side of the room was lined with shelves of the same pale wood bearing neat rows of rune carved stone tablets.

Scanning the first tablet to his left he read the elder Futhark of the first line. *The Nine Songs of Bolthorsson.* His mouth fell open. Walking to another tablet, he scanned the title. *The Eighteen Charms of Odin.* Gladr was so engrossed that he almost failed to notice the Allfather sitting in a throne like chair. Gladr fumbled the tablet in his hand nearly dropping it making the god laugh. His form was ethereal yet distinct hooded and grim his long iron colored beard hung like a swordblade from his lupine face. One eye as blue as sky stared forth from the hooded, the other a baleful hole that gaped like a portal to the void. For all the world the face he looked upon was the same as the reflection he saw in his axe blade, just infinitely older. "Relax boy. It's not every day that one meets a god. Even the shade of a god."

Gladr fell to one knee, "Hail Odin!" he shouted fighting the growing terror that maybe he'd been hasty in feeling slighted. *If the old one wants to subsume me he will find me no easy prey.* Odin was god of tricks after all and the gallows god's cunning was deep.

He thought as he pulled his manna to him. *"Rise boy, rise!"* The god revenant laughed. *"By Ullr you are strong, a credit to my blood in your veins! It's as if I spit you out. Mimir told no lies when he whispered of you in my ear. If I walk middle earth again it won't be in your skin boy it will be in my own! You are family not food, little Brúni."* Gladr felt himself relax. The similarities were remarkable the bond of kin strong between them. Gladr rose feeling as though he stood before a heloved grandfather. *"An axe man. Hmmph. Not what I would prefer but you will serve."* Odin grunted eying the great axe laying crosswise on Gladr's back. "It has fed many ravens and drank greedily the blood of the foeman, ancestor." Gladr spat feeling strangely defensive. Odin smiled a lopsidedly. "Axemen are always emotional, and that fire will serve you well if you are to lead the New Aesir." At his ancestor's words Gladr swelled standing straighter, a broad smile touching his lips. But when he met his ancestors single eye it faded. "I took a spear to my side, lost an eye,

and hung from the world tree for nine days. What will you give for knowledge I wonder?" Odin said eying Gladr like a wolf. "Pass me your axe." the Allfather commanded. Dutifully Gladr freed it from his back and passed it to the ancient. "Indeed this is a worthy weapon. Dwarven made." He said as he studied the runes. Odin's one eye glittered malignantly. Flicking his wrist Odin made Gladr's sang slashing his face from chin to brow. Blood misted Gladr's vision and before he could move again stars exploded and he knew nothing but darkness. Somewhere very far away the Allfather laughed.

Gladr awoke to pain. Cracking open his single working eye he stared up at a mountain, it's face verticle, gnarled and groved spanning so far into the heavens Gladr's mind spun with the impossibly. Looking down he saw the broken shaft of a spear jutting from his gut but no blood. Terror churned at his mind. *Fool fool fool!* He screamed in his own mind as he clawed at the spear futilely. before peeking past his dangling feet he could make out stone lined a pool. *"It is not your wyrd to die here if you are worthy."* Gladr heard three women say at once, even as his ancestors words returned. *"What will you give for knowledge I wonder?"*

Looking skyward again Gladr realized the its was wrong. He could see no sun nor moon but a dappling of light like a canopy on a but massive scale. Suddenly he knew where he was, and what he must do. Grasping the shattered spearshaft of what could only be Gungir, Gladr roared as he pulled at it. He could feel the cold metal slither from the ancient wood of the world tree wincing as it slipped free from his guts in a welter of blood. Gladr smiled as he stood upon a root of the great Yggdrasil. Below him was Mimir's well and he would drink deep.

* * *

As the weeks had passed he mastered many things. First was the sjel rune and necessary spells to trap a soul and feed from it. The ancient ones had been able to ensnare souls for hundreds if not thousands of years to use as a source of power. A capable practitioner could fashion illusions to entertain the souls they trapped, it was the key to godhead. Now Gladr could gift any who died dedicated in his service the illusion of Valhalla they craved. Such a promise was as an addiction to the humans.

He was wise enough to know that such thing worked both ways. In order to sustain his status he needed manna from human belief. Worship was to him what poppy was to an addict of the flower. The true ambrosia. As base as they were humans were like a flock of extremely useful sheep or maybe horses. Gladr knew he had to grow and protect his herd if he was to remain successful,

263

to *remain* a god. *Power always comes with a price.* A lesson Gladr's father had taught him and Gladr was mindful of it now. Especially since he drank from the well, the prayers of his faithful buzzed in his ears like flies in a bog. Luck, protection, wealth, war fame. They all wanted something from him. They leached almost more power than they gave but the rush was indescribable. As far as he knew he was the first of the Nox to stride middle earth as a god in over a thousand years.

* * *

Make haste north to Oddmire in Albion. The old elf had made it sound simple. Oh he had done what he could, but it was still taking entirely too long. He'd led his taxiarchy and Cynocephali allies north and west from the Carpathians through the deep ways into the lands of Ashkenaz called Alemania or Germania by the Romans. Since delivering the intelligence Oberon hadn't been keyed in on many of the command communiques. His last set of orders had instructed him to lead his force to refit at High Shield in Ashkenaz before continuing to Albion. That and little else. But the other briefings he had received pointed towards a defensive posturing. The high command of the Seelie Court filled with wily old strategists as it was, seemed loath to take any initiative. Eyes seemed to be focused elsewhere. The Woodwose and Nox allied Cynocephali were raiding. The northern Ljósálfar were gathering spears. In east where the Mongol horse lords fought and besieged the Jin dynasty. The elves of Xiaoxhai had long been the enemy of the Jurchen rulers of the Jin since the time of their slaving ancestors the Mohe, who were human allies of the Nox. Nobody knew whether the Mongols would be friend or foe so the Seelie Court prepared to fight both. To the south a powerful Nox Idolon was making a play in the lands now called Al Andalus. Ghul and Vrykolakas were reaping bloody harvests in Morea and Ionia. This meant entire taxiarchy's were being moved around like pieces on a board, none seeing direct action but being positioned to disadvantage enemy movements. Oberon read the underlying message. *Don't expect any help.* He contented himself with the fact that he would learn more when he stopped at the semi subterranean city of the High Shield.

The final leg of the march was gorgeous at it followed a gorge cut by the rapids of an ancient turquoise river. The trail wound above the river passing through the occasional cave other times offering tantalizing passages through the middle earth sun. On the opposite bank lay the bulging stone wall of the gorge. In some places there were shops cut into the living rock or terraces of wood, suspended from hemp cords as thick as three men.

Having never been to these lands before Oberon tried and failed not to gape like a bumpkin. Penume's Reach was beautiful, but this melding of inner and middle earth was something altogether different. As beautiful as the gorge was, Oberon's keen military mind still picked out the cleverly disguised choke points and redoubts were any incursions could be stopped by a handful of defenders. The gorge ran for about eleven stades before a side passage led them back to the deep ways.

The mountain peak that housed High Shield was flanked by glaciers on three sides and could only be approached from the south. What made it unique is the fact that part of the settlement was on middle earth itself. The main settlement lay inside the peak known by men as Zugspitz, but long ago it's population had spilled out into middle earth. Oberon and his taxiarchy left the deep ways through a crack in the mountainside and they found themselves on a rough mountain trail but less than a stade away stood a wall pierced by a gate barbican made entirely of ice and snow. In all his travels he had never seen the like. Soldiers of the Seelie Court opened the gates admitting their comrades and their oath sworn allies. Oberon had no sooner cleared the shadow of the gate before he was greeted by a smiling Illyargen.

The old elf looked tired but happy behind the cheek plates of his helmet his fair skin bore no fear of the sun, lacking as it did the glow of the Ljósálfar curse. The Strategos led Oberon deeper into the settlement. Lining the bowl of the mountain top were stately halls three stories tall, taverns, and temples all made from pale stone and living ice that shone like opalescent in the afternoon sun. The elder elf bore white bronze scale armor beneath his surcoat and despite his hundreds of years of life he stood unstooped by age. Even his stride was energetic. If not for the deep iron grey of his hair locked in thumb thick coils on his head, and the wrinkles on his face he could have been less than five decades old, instead of closer to a thousand. Closer now Oberon could see the faintest of greenish tints to his tone that marked him as a descendant of the line of Seth and Methuselah. He needed no manna to sustain his longevity, for the folk of the golden age routinely lived eight or nine centuries. Oberon's own ancestors had been born of the people silver age and could only hope for three of four centuries of life with luck and manna.

Despite the cold traffic was brisk as Samyazan's of all types went about their daily routines. Between the rows of halls and long houses there were arcades markets in circular towers ten stories high. It was a grand place. A place of beauty where manna lay as thick as the ice. He would have never imagined a city of the Iska to be so inclined to beauty. It made his own home almost humble and he felt ashamed that the he had shunned a people that brought such beauty. Maybe the Great Teacher has a point after all. He thought.

As they walked Oberon began to wonder why they had been ordered to stop at High Shield. As if sensing his thoughts Illyagren turned to Oberon, his lapis flecked golden eyes danced with what could only be described as mirth. His thin lips quirked into a smile as crooked as his oft broken nose. "I know you wanna know why your here rather than meeting a supply column somewhere on the march." He said. Oberon knew better than to lie to the old war master who had been a guest friend of his forefathers and a hero to elven knights for generations. "I had pondered it." He affirmed with a shrug. "Albion is a long way away." Illyagren chuckled a light and musical sound that seemed out of place coming from the lanky scarred veteran. "Anxious to get stuck in are ya? First to the fight eh Oberon? Did you know you were the first to carry the Seelie Court colors into battle?" The king of Penume's Reach stumbled. "What?

How?" He sputtered unsure as to how it was true. Illyagren raised an eyebrow. "You didn't know?" Oberon shook his head emphatically. Illyagren chuckled again. "Your fight with the Dinte Rosu was the first of the Risen Court. The first test of the army. The fact that you and your people fought your way out of that ambush was impressive enough, but to destroy the settlement with bronze and magic like that was a stroke of pure brilliance." The strategos slapped Oberon on the shoulder. "Your up for commendation and a promotion. Halt your column lord king and have your squire fetch you a camp stool!" Oberon smiled but it faded when he thought of poor dead Guion who had more often then not filled the role of Oberon's military squire. He started to tell Illyagren he no longer had a squire but he was saved as Farheed brought him his camp stool. Oberon found a lump in his throat he couldn't quite understand.

Seating himself on the proffered stool, feeling foolish sitting at the head of his column. Oberon watched as Illyagren removed a cloth of gold sash emblazoned with the green stars of the Seelie Court. The old hero settled it across his shoulders with all the care of an old soldier handling beloved colors. "Oberon king. Undisputed lord of Penume's Reach. By the powers vested in me, I hearby appoint you as Legatus of the Seelie Court. Rise and be acclaimed as a warleader of the empire!" Oberon felt his shorthairs stand on end as the roar rang from the nearby buildings and the aretes of the mountains. Both the citizens and warriors alike screamed their acclaim and Oberon felt his manna swell until a golden glow emanated from his skin. Oberon's doubts about a mixed force from all over inner earth binding together evaporated. Chants of his name left him feeling equal parts giddy and The men and women he had led from bloody ambush to abject victory over a hated foe roared their approval.

After his promotion Illyagren led them deeper into High Shield until the road which had run straight as a blade, showed two forks. Each path curled away from the main road like quillions into tunnels bored into the mountains. Illyagren led them to the right and guided them through a tunnel that must have taken a generation of artists and stone cutters to achieve. Bass reliefs showing the history of the Samyazans from the Commingling to the founding of the city and the deeds of the Iska. They emerged in the shadow of the peak on a great plateau. A great screeching and rustling reached Oberon's ears at what looked to be a massive drill and training yard complete with barracks soaring severals stories high. Thousands of Ruhk, the giant eagles found in the east, tethered to hundreds of large beautifully painted triremes with canvas wings at midship and with a smaller set at the stern.

Oberon who had grown up with griffins had never in his wildest dreams imagined such a sight. Illyagren grinned. "Impressive isn't it. A little concept I've been working on for rapid deployment. Six Ruhk per ship. Each retrofitted to carry two agemas of fighters and their mounts." Illyagren said unable to keep the pride from his voice. "Get you to Albion faster than you ever believed possible."

* * *

Flight was nothing new to Oberon. He was he had been a griffin knight, a lord of the sky, long before he became a king. Something about being whisked through the sky on a flying boat was something altogether different. The Ruhk were magnificent, five times the size of their smaller twin cousins the crowned eagles that hunted south of the great Sahel. The smallest of them were capable of snatching away elephants and still flying faster than a galloping horse. With six pulling the winged boats through the sky, the effect was equal parts exhilarating and terrifying. Beside him Farheed smiled with childlike glee a stark contrast to Minerva who had wretched thrice now and looked pale and miserable. "Nothing should ever move this fast." She muttered panic clear in the tightness of her eyes. Oberon tried and failed to hide a smile as Farheed sniggered. Minerva glared at them both. She muttered something under her breath that even elven ears could not catch as she fluttered her wings as if reassuring herself they were still there.

There were twelve berths on the foredeck and twelve on the quarter deck at the stern. The two were connected by a catwalk that held storage compartments. The lower decks that would usually hold the oarsmen had been converted into stalls for mounts. For all the world it was designed exactly like a seagoing ship. If one ignored the high sides that protected passengers from the worst of the wind and of course the Ruhk. By the time the sun sank below the horizon they were over the ocean that separated Europa from Albion.

It was an hour before midnight when they landed on the hills surrounding the Oddmire. Two large drum towers of worked stone flanked the crescent shaped shakehole that sat in the side of a hill. It was named for the fact that it was part of an interconnected set of of Fae settlements in northwestern Albion. He was greeted by the gate by swarthy dwarf his face clean except for a single braid hanging from his chin bearing the neck torque of a Taxiarch. "Greetings Legatus." He said offering a deep bow. "I am Prince Druad of Mongo ma Ndemi, twelfth Taxeis. The ninth and thirty seventh are also camped nearby we are ready for your commands." The dwarf said in the resonant musical accent of his home enclave. Oberon smiled. "Excellent! Any reports on the movements of Gladr Odinsblood?" Druad nodded. "Norse and Shetland raiders bearing the Odinrune banner have been raiding mostly focused on the humans. No word recent word on the elf himself. Our spies sent word that he has mastered the ancient arts of his ancestors after disappearing for a time inside a god-house in the forests outside Ranhiem. Since we got the reports we've felt his manna like heat from a forge."Oberon's smile faded as he nodded in understanding. He could feel the enemy sensing his general direction like a blind man finding the sun by the warmth on his face.

Druad met the eyes of his new commander and shared a knowing look. Oberon didn't need words to understand. Nobody wanted to be the target of an enemy that strong. Oberon tried and failed to remember who the ruler was here and instead asked, "How stand the defenses?" Druad immediately seemed more comfortable."In addition to the three taxiarchies here there is also the host of Oddmire ably led by Lord Aeryr, Prince of the Oddmire Fae." He said saving Oberon the embarrassment of having to ask. Druad smiled slightly and continued. "The Oddmire itself is a tough nut to crack even with its four entrances. Magical defenses that will flood or bolder choke any entryway. Cavalry galleries for ambushes and charges. The cost in manna and lives would be staggering. We could hold it for two hundred years before we had to even tighten our belts." Oberon nodded the Oddmire would be an ideal fallback location but hunkering down was not part of his plans not yet.

Druad led Oberon and his Agema into the Oddmire. Unlike High Shields stately beauty, Oddmire was a riot of color like a flock of tropical birds. The homes and buildings were mudbrick whitewashed and then glazed with crushed gemstones. The result were ten thousand hues and no two the same. The road was paved with semi precious stones no matter how narrow or haphazard the street seemed to be. The beat of Fae wings filled the air as the people of Oddmire went about their business flitting to and fro as they visited shops, traders or taverns, some hundreds of feet from the ground below. Looming above it all was the citidel formed from a stalagmite of glowing white stone. It reminded Oberon of a stack of candles that had been melted together. It dominated the center of the great fae city. The door guards fae knights in full bronze lamellar nodded respectfully as they admitted Oberon and Druad through doors of solid gold etched with the eagle of Oddmire's ruling fae clan.

Inside the citidel the riot of color was replaced by a vibrant green marble. The smell of sweet incense spewed from golden censors suspended from the vaulted ceiling high above. Candles larger than tall men and polished gold mirrors illuminated the space making the high throne at the far end of the circle seem to glow. As soon as he set his eyes upon him Oberon recognized Lord Aeryr. Tall for a fae with the luminous skin that hinted at his ancestry being mixed with Ljósálfar like many Samyazan noble houses. His high cheekboned face, hawk like nose and square jaw could have been formed of stone for all the expression they held. But his voice was warm when he greeted Oberon. "King Oberon, Legatus of the Seelie Court welcome to my home and hall!" He boomed in a voice larger and more sonorous than the slight frame in cloth of gold robes would indicate. "Illyagren said he would send a fighter to Albion and I see he did not lie. Your reputation precedes you." The fae lord said smiling now. Oberon returned the smile. Aeryr leapt from his throne arresting his fall with powerful golden wings. When he landed Oberon could see his eyes were alight with intelligence, and maybe a little madness. "Come honored Legatus let's take a meal in my study, we have much to discuss!"

Chapter 22: Interwoven

Leon Alfiere watched his grandson and nephew ride through the gates. Cazador's force more or less appeared intact while the men bearing the dark blue of his brother's son Omar were far fewer in number than they should be. Clan had fought clan when the caliph and crusaders clashed. The elders had arrived two days earlier, the same who had so brazenly supported Richard over Cazador had been forced to suffer a chain of reports that had hurt their credibility. La Compagnie properties sacked and towns raided after opening their gates for La Compagnie banners under *their* man, their *chosen* lord of Le Cannet Des Maures. Reports of Richard at the head of a mighty host of Feringees flying foreign banner and evidence of his betrayal of clan and La Compagnie. He could explain to the fool that they had been ensorcelled. But he would not. *stubborn old fools would never admit to it.* He thought. Such was the pride of the Du Maurmonts. They'd done nothing but eat his food, drink his wine and complain. The crusade against the Almohads had spoiled the trade of La Compagnie for the season and everyone was grouchy to the point of intransigence. The fact that they had backed a traitor kept made them look like fools at best and fellow traitors at worst. They might be light silver and surly but the truth of the matter kept them in line and that was enough. For now.

The one who they had shamed and cast down from his birthright was riding through the gates with the future of the clan's fortunes. The merchant group Cazador escorted were the key to securing their Sudanese supply lines in the event of an Almohad collapse and presented a way to circumvent Nasrid interference. With the Samyazan's and the Children of the Nameless once again striding middle earth priorities had changed. Iron from Benin, cattle from Fezzan, leather from Gobir, hardwoods and ivory from Mogadishu, the new group of merchants would be the source of wealth in the days of war to come. Cazador managed to bring not only the people, but their goods safely out of a war zone to the castle and with them thousands of gold dinars in revenue. Leon Alfiere had made sure his fellow elders knew this. He gave his grandson no more than four days of having his ass kissed before he all but fled to England.

Sighing the Old Lion set aside the thoughts of clan and family and settled himself in his protection circle. A deep sense of foreboding had filled him. Dreams and visions of blood and war, conflict and betrayal. His contacts in the kingdoms of Simien, Alodia, Makuria and Medri Bahri had been unresponsive. For generations the Al Takruri family of the northern arm of had been charged with holding open the door for the Negusa Negast and the might of a new Aksumite Empire. Because of this the magi of the Order of Saint Atillo kept tight communication with one another by messenger bird and magical means and it wasn't uncommon to conference daily via astral projection. However for the last six days there had been an ominous silence.

Packing his pipe with dried lotus flowers, Leon used a nearby candle to light it and took a long pull. As the smoke filled his lungs he chanted the words to his spell focusing his manna for the task at hand. As the flower took effect the Old Lion stood, and looked down at his physical shell. As always he was surprised at the signs of time's passage. His once raven hued tresses were iron grey, his features long beloved by the fairer sex marred by laugh lines and crows feet, his brow creased like a mountain range.

Ha! Old as the stones and still better looking than most. He congratulated himself. While not as impressive as it once was, his frame was still packed with slabs of muscle that he refused to let turn to fat. Turning away from himself he looked to the window and floated towards it. Although he had left his body behind he could still feel the smooth stone of the arrow loop as he pulled his incorporeal form through. For a moment he perched there like a gargoyle fixing his location and heading before launching himself like an arrow.

His castle and towns fell away beneath him hurtling past as small as a childs toys to a giant. In mere moments he was passing over Malaga and out over the cerulean jeweled surface of the sea. He kept his course only turning to position himself over the gleaming emerald band that marked the Nile that bisected the Egyptian desert. Zipping like the bolt of a god he made his way to the city of Roha where king Lalibella ruled.

Right away things were not as they should have been. The Biete Maryam was silent. No clergy walked the church grounds and for the first time Leon Alfiere saw no warriors come and go for blessings at the mighty rock hewn cross that was the Church of Saint George. Built as a new bastion for Christianity after the fall of Jerusalem Lalibella a mighty and blessed magus had summon angelic aid with hid manna to carve the rock itself to form the many churches that had made Roha famous. The brilliantly painted houses of worship were usually packed with pilgrims, they would normally throng the streets that now stood nearly deserted. It was a place of magic and majesty blessed by God and to see it such pained him. Gripped by fear the Old Lion moved on. The markets bore bored looking traders who bartered desultorily with the few listless customers. In the throne hall he sought his friend the king. Lalibella however was nowhere to be found. Instead his nephew Na'akueto La'ab sat up on his throne and the shadow sat with him With a heavy heart Leon Alfiere fled back to his mortal frame.

Part of longed to stay and investigate but he prayed there would be time for that later. The Negusa Negast had been dethroned. Without Lalibella there was no new Axumite empire. The long goal had always centered around getting the al Ifranj to ally themselves with the mythical kingdom of Preyster John. It had always been a long shot, but with the Negusa Negast deposed the dream was dead. Leon came back to himself with a great heave of breath as his soul reknit itself to his flesh. His eyes focused on the bust of his ancestor Lusius Quietus who rose from the Fezzan to nearly become emperor of Rome. A wild thought entered Leon's head as though his forebears had placed it there.

Rome once ruled all these lands, is it possible a new Rome could do it again? There was something beautiful about the order and splendor of Rome that he greatly admired. The Old Lion mused allowing himself to imagine an black on silver over the ancient red with the golden eagle of Rome. Legions of well drilled infantry and cavalry, corps of engineers, a courier system. *Meritocracy.* It could be done. It wouldn't be easy, or cheap but it was within the realm of possibility. He could see it unfolding. The forges of Bobastro and the Monts Des Maures working day and night making maille, spears, swords, shields and axes. Troops lured from the Sudan, a march to restore the ancient *Regnum Maurorum et Romanorum* the Kingdom of Moors and Romans and from it a Mauro Roman Empire could be born.

Mind racing with the possibilities the Old Lion rose, wincing as his knees and back cracked like boots through frozen snow. He had to see Cazador and the merchants before the elders realized they had arrived and tried to sink their claws in them. While Cazador was likely to butcher them as soon as greet them, the same couldn't be said of the merchants. His grandmother's words came back to him. Hab'b'ere buri ginawol, she would croon in Fulfide. Actions should be judged by intentions. He certainly hoped his would be. The time had come for bold action.

* * *

Cazador arrived in his rooms to find new clothes grey cotton trousers and grey dan ciki embroidered with swords and stars around the collar and at the cuffs of the elbow length sleeves. He completed his outfit with a new sleeveless damask tunic in argent, blue, and black, the colors of his arms with the sable lion and gauntlet embroidered over his right shoulder. lined with cotton and fine maille and matching blue suede ankle length boots. He belted on Il Martello, the short weapon being far more useful indoors than the longer L'auxifar which belted on his left hip, over it he hooked his black buckler. With the clan elders haunting Nuevo Bobastro he felt the need to appear every inch the warrior prince, even if he was a simple mercenary captain.

He made his way through the keep until he stood before the open doors of the great hypostyle hall of Bobastro. Cazador felt his anxiety spike. As much as he had longed to reach Bobastro's safety he felt decidedly vexed. *Oh hello grandfather, I've completed the mission you gave me while also bringing an army down on our heads. Oh how the elders will point their fingers and heap me with scorn.* He took a steadying breath. He was so lost in his thoughts he had barely noticed Omar along with Diallo, Izan, Jaime, and the other knights of his mensie loitering in the hall that led to kitchens. "Ho there captain!" Izan shouted radiating a bluff good cheer Cazador wished he could summon. "You didn't think we would let you hog all the glory to yourself, did you?" His cousin quizzed smiling. "Ah yes so glorious leading an enemy force to his doorstep." Cazador muttered miserably. Omar clapped a hand to his armored shoulder. "Fret not cousin. The beauty of being a mercenary over a sworn knight is not having to deal with the consequences. You did your job, you did it well. You turned and gave them a beating, then finished the job. The old man will not complain. Such is the way of things." Omar finished with an extravagant shrug. His indigo robes shone in the sunlit atrium, so new you could still smell the dye pounded into the fabric. Steeling himself Cazador returned the polite nods as walked past the door wards into the great hall of Bobastro

Massive sandstone pillars supported the vaulted roof. Each inscribed with scenes from the Bible, Sudanese legends, and the history of their family. One bore the images of Saif Al Takruri landing with Yusef Ibn Tashfin and the battle of Sagrajas. Yet another showed the efforts of Esteve Alfiere , called Steven the Moor fighting at Lincoln and at the siege of Ascalon. High windows fed in sunlight while a trio of fountains in the shape of roaring lions burbled cooling the air. Between the pillars captured banners hung from the bannisters of the mezzanines. At the far end was the seat from which the Old Lion held court. The simple camp chair was hewn from pure blackwood and cushioned with cloth of silver. He was swathed in a purple, black, and silver darra'a, it's wide sleeves pulled back over his shoulders. To his left sat the elders in a colorful yet disgruntled clump and to his right on colorful cushions Cazador's mother and aunt Miryam sat with his grandfather's other advisors and warriors of his mensie. He smiled broadly when he looked away from his conversation with Idris Ibn Idris to see Cazador. His eyes glittered with mischief.

"Welcome back grandsons and nephew. Your mission was successful and your deeds please the ancestors." The Old Lion boomed. Cazador clapped his right fist over his heart and sketched a bow. "I have also learned of the perfidy of the of Richard of Caen and how he leads an army toward us, an army which you blooded and slowed down. You have brought honor to the house of Alfiere and the Du Maurmont clan." The Old Lion continued. Cazador felt as though the foot of a giant was lifted from his chest. To say he was relieved was to call the ocean a puddle. *Of course his grandfather already knew.* He chided himself feeling foolish remembering Idris Ibn Idris at the caliph's tent. He bowed again. It was all he could do to not grin like a small boy given a sweet.

Having made a show of praising Cazador before the elders, his grandfather turned his attention to Omar. "Nephew, I have also had news of the battle between the caliph and the crusaders. Your company suffered greatly but your valor and skill are beyond reproach. The caliph survived the battle in large part thanks to your men." Omar shot the elders a feral grin before he bowed. "A pleasure to serve as always uncle Leon," Omar began pitching his voice like an orator making sure he didn't simply address the Old Lion, but the elders as well. "Though it was the Company of Saint Moses that held the center. It was Cazador's people bloodying the Knights of Calatrava and the Knights of Santiago blunting their assault. Then they broke off and hit their flank before helping us screen Miramollin's retreat. If not for him me and my company would likely be done for at the hands of the elected lord of Le Cannet des Maures, the traitor Richard."

Cazador felt his cheeks heat as his grandfather beamed, his mother looked triumphant eyes shining with a pride he had rarely seen. His aunt kept her features neutral yet conveyed her approval with a nod worthy of a queen. Even among the elders, especially those who knew him best, there were smiles. Cazador felt a sense of calm steal over him. Here was something that couldn't readily be stripped away. *Deeds.* He thought. Honor could be stained, respect could be lost, reputations tarnished, but it was hard to make success into failure. That's why men say glory is forever.

After the audience the Old Lion led them through the door to the right of the dais into the hall that separated the Old Lions study from the war room. Dreu, Marfin and Ilyas were already there standing before the great map table. Servants brought in chairs and they were all seated. The Old Lion smiled at Cazador. "I heard you broke a wootz steel sword boy." Cazador grimaced. The tang fractured at the weld to the pommel. The memory still stung and he had yet to mourn his favorite sword. "In addition to L'auxifar I've been fighting with this grandfather," he said pulling the macd he'd nicknamed Il Martello from its sheath. The Old Lion scowled thoughtfully at the weapon. "I can't have my grandson fighting with that. I've no doubt it's an effective weapon, but against ghul, woodwose, and armored men at arms I would prefer you had a bit more reach." His eyes rested on L'auxifar. "Its a good thing you bear a hero's blade that will not fail you." Cazador nodded, "I am honored to carry it grandfather." The Old Lion nodded. "But swords make for poor bludgeons." He said walking over to where he displayed some of his more prominent weapons. He lifted free a axe with a spiked poll, long enough for two handed use but comfortable enough for one. "Sometimes a warrior needs to *cut* and smash things to break his foes." He handed the axe to Cazador. "This is Alkasaara, The Breaker, may it shatter your enemies as it has mine." Cazador nodded his thanks. He could see the pride in his grandfather's eyes and it made him stand taller, warmth spreading through his chest.

The Old Lion clapped his hands and rubbed them together like a man planning. "Gentleman things have changed." He said moving to the map table. Cazador noted that the little bronze figurines that indicated troops were missing from Abyssinia and Nubia. "The Negusa Negast has been dethroned and a shadow bent king sits in his place. I've had no contact with the entire Aksumite wing of the Order of Saint Elesbaan . We must more forward as though we are alone." He said without preamble. "The goal however remains the same. We must create a stable, well supplied war machine to fight the Sudiibe. Initially we were to hold open the doors for the might of Nubia and our western Sudanese allies. Now we must form an empire of our own. We will revive the Kingdom of Maurs and Romans when we call our banners we will be the Mauro Roman Empire!" Leon Alfiere stared at his so called claws with such intensity they stood frozen like voles before the hawk.

His grandfather's tone was so rational it took a moment for the sheer audacity of his words to sink in. *Sure we have money, knights, and castles but an empire?* Marfin was the first to speak. The short, lean, egg bald war captain sported a blacksmiths arms and a short goatee. "I will fight and die for the glory of God and clan but this is a damn sight different than providing footholds. This is conquest." He said incredulity coloring his tone. Like Omar he was one of the greatest horsemen Cazador had ever seen. The Old Lion smiled looking more like a wolf than his namesake. Before he could respond , the tall muscular Dreu leaned forward on the map table, his red copper brown skin flushedwith excitement. "The firanji will never pull themselves together in time to do anything but die in a doomed stand. They couldn't even get six months into the crusade against Miramollin before falling apart. Uncle Leon is right, we strike for empire and strike hard." Omar was nodding and Cazador was too. *Maybe I won't be shipped off to England after all.* "The stakes are too high to do less. Gladr Odinsblood makes himself the idol of the north and has by all reports set his sights on England. His boldness will entice more of the Nox to build kingdoms on middle earth. Already the traitor is in league with Idolon who masqueraded as a saint to gain worship. However the lady of the fountain is no saint. She now calls ghul and Woodwose to her banner and Richard leads them here. We must crush them and set our sights on strengthening our alliances in Europa and seizing territory and securing supply lines." There were nods all around the table.

Cazador felt excitement welling in his chest. " The Company of Saint Moses stands ready. To defend Bobastro grandfather. When the traitor is finished I think we should sail south in two fleets. First capture Susa and then strike south of and make a base at Cyrene, then we can strike alliances with the Kanem. Another fleet should sail south and west to-" Cazador said leaning over the map table and The Old Lion clapped a gnarled hand to Cazador's shoulder halting him. "I know Caz, your blades would be of great value in what's to come. But your place is in England." Cazador felt his heart sink, but fought to keep the disappointment from his face. His grandfather's eyes burned like embers as he spoke. "You will be our spear in England and to that effect the Company of Saint Moses can be no more." Cazador couldn't stop his jaw from dropping open in shock as he struggled to form words. "Your arms were seen fighting for Al Nasir against the Christian coalition. You've already been granted new arms and a new name. Henceforth the Company of Saint Moses will be known as the Company of the Leopard." He handed Cazador a document ink still drying, bearing the shield divided per angled bend sinister or and sable. In the first quarter a leopard in sable marked the company's namesake. Cazador nodded. "You shall lead your company to England and fulfill your fuedal obligation, bring iron and fire to the Nox, *form bonds*. In order for the empire to have a chance Britain must not fall to Gladr Odinsblood. He must be humbled in the field before he can unite the North against the world. Can you bring us victory or barring victory at least time grandson?" The Old Lion's eyes bored into Cazador's own. He felt the weight of that stare like a child in a man's maille but he nodded. "I will not fail my lord."

Leon Alfiere squeezed his grandson's shoulder. "I know you won't. Rest and take your ease, you sail in four days...just enough time for you to help us plan." He said waggling his eyebrows with a roguish grin. Cazador smiled back. "Now tell me what you were saying about taking the Libyan Pentapolis." He said gesturing to the map. Off balance Cazador stammered, staring at his elder cousins for help as he tried to reorient his thoughts. "Well um erm, that is four forces and three fleets grandfather. One fleet to Libya, as I said to capture as much of the old Pentapolis as possible. The other fleet on a trading mission down the Nile to Nubia and Abyssinia and another west for Takrur. The western wing should take Podor, Awil, Oulata, Chinguetti, Oudane, Taghaza, Idjil, and Aoudaghost. If we can conquer the towns we should be able to raise the Sonninke and Serer to our banner. I think that if we arm and raise the slaves of the Almohads we can have old Mauritania by this time next year." Cazador finished, eyes shining with inspiration.

His kin seemed thoughtful. "What of the Sanhaji would you have us fight them across the desert while you sit in Misty England?" Marfin asked. Cazador raised an eyebrow, "Water cousin. From our coastal holding we distill as much salt water as the good Lord allows us. Seal the barrels in wax and float them in nets behind the ships. Hire miners to dig canals and irrigation systems. Instead of silos of grain, we build great casks of water filled by a steady supply from our distilleries. To people who have fought each other over water for a thousand years we can turn paupers into kings and kings into vassals. Wherever we go we make the desert bloom and become alchemists turning water into gold." The war room was utterly silent as the implications of Cazador's bold gambit set in. A broad grin split Omar's face. " Water for gold! Hah! I told you all Cazador was a genius." The Old Lion chuckled with the others but his face was still grave. "What of the fourth force Cazador?" Grinning Cazador looked around at his kin. "The fourth force takes Malaga, Gibraltar, Medina Antaquira, Cadiz, Cordoba and Seville. Old Roman towns all, and if we don't the crusaders will. With the ksars holding the southern trade routes, and the meat of Al Andalus in our teeth, we can turn to Canne, Nice, Toulon, Marseille, San Tropez, and Arles. We could even push as far as Toulouse and Carcassonne. With chunks of the North African provinces and a swathe of the old Gallic Empire the kings of Aragon, Castile, France and England not to mention the Pope will take us seriously." His grandfather kissed his teeth and smiled. "Well gentles, it looks like the youngest of the claws has planned our campaign for us." Dreu slapped him on his shoulder. "My grandmother always said you were bright." Cazador smiled although it felt as though he had been barged by a horse. His grandfather went to a cabinet in the corner and fetched a bottle of wine and a stack of simple silver cups. Popping open the bottle he poured a libation to God and the ancestors before filling the cups with wine and serving them out by his own hand. "To the empire!" He began. "And the souls who would make its dream a reality!" The Old Lion finished his toast and together with his claws, he drank.

* * *

Asmā was enjoying her new rank. Cazador had secured the company accomodations in the warriors funduq that lined the eastern corner of walls of the inner keep of Bobastro. As a knight Asmā had a private room, free from the snores, mess and smells of the nineteen other woman who she had previously bivouacked with. Each floor had its own hammam split for use by both genders complete with hot and cold rooms and a room for changing. For the first time since they had left for their mission she felt gloriously clean. She had slipped into a new black linen kirtle over which she pulled on a blue silk dress with tight sleeves in the new style. Over it a black silk cyclas embroidered with silver flowers at the neck line that hung to her ankles kept from the floor by black calfskin boots. From her belt of silver plaques matched the fillet that held her veil in place. It was the heavy bastard sword that hung from her shapely waist that gave her a thrill of pride. *Asmā Al Faris.*

She left the funduq and into the afternoon sun. While she had lived most of her life in Bobastro's shadow she had never seen the inner keep. Her family owned a couple small farms and worked as masons and carpenters doing brisk trade. They weren't abid or serfs, but they weren't considered noble by any stretch. Like many around Bobastro her family had been blended from the people who had lived here since Roman times and waves of settlers. Like other Christians they paid the jiyza. Asmā loved her family and the land she had grown up exploring but the thing about large families is for every smile there were a thousand tears. When Cazador had begun recruiting for his company in the taverna it was too good an opportunity to pass up. Her whole life had been about others, it was the first decision she made that was strictly for her. Now she was Lalla or Lady Asmā, chevaleresse. Any guilt she felt was tempered by her achievement.

She circuited the inner keep, strolling past the inner gate barbican where there was a small funduq, wikala, and a pair of bazaars that catered to the tastes of the wealthy that lived in or guested in Bobastro's inner keep. She passed the madrasa watching as robed students came and went. She smiled remembering her own time at madrasa in Malaga. There she had discovered a love of fine art and a mastery of arithmetic and calligraphy. Her fingers almost itched for want of a brush and the remembered smell of pigments and canvas made her nose twitch. A couple season as a mercenary and she would be able to finance her own education in comfort. A thought that thrilled her.

Asmā had dreamed many things but never this. Knighthood brought her opportunities she had never dreamt of. Unable to resist their lure any longer she drifted toward the bazaar. "A good day to you Lady Chevalerese," called the voice of an older woman. Asmā turned to see Sa 'da bint Hassan one of the female merchants they had escorted from Miramollin's camp. "Peace be upon you Lalla Sa' ada!" Asmā called warmly. The statuesque tradeswoman was swathed in a blindingly white silk robe and tunic embellished with roses and kufic script that matched her cloth of gold headscarf, she sat resplendent as a queen in her stall which held spices, perfumes, jewelry, and rich cloth.

The older woman beamed her teeth white in her sandstone colored skin. "And peace be upon you although peace may be a curse to one who makes their living in war." Asmā shrugged. "Being paid not to fight works just as well." Sa' ada laughed, eyes dancing in their kohl frame. "Ah but you are a delight. It makes me proud to see a woman in your position. Join me serve as my guard and I will triple what Sir Cazador pays you." Be my chevalerese and I promise you this and a black stallion of noble breed that you may ride to war and won't leave you barefoot and pregnant. Asmā's eyes widened even as she flushed with equal parts pride and embarrassment. Before she could speak Sa' ada said "Peace lady knight while my offer is real, I tease because I envy you and I've noted your and the captain's mutual admiration. That and the fact that to the women I represent a female knight could go far. You could be a queen, respected in a world of women who support each other and coin flows, rather than a soldier in the world of men. Adventure would still await you. Life as my guard would not be without its perils and I travel more of the year than I sit in my estate, but it's a life of silk and steel rather than simply steel and blood." Sa' ada's tone was light but her eyes were sharp as a barbers fleam. Asmā grappled with her shock and intrigue. She thought of what it might be like a guardian to a merchant queen. But then she thought of her Amazons, the women who she had come to lead and the bond of sisterhood that had begun to form. Then there was sir Cazador. The thought of not seeing him again made Asmā ache in a way she couldn't understand. She remembered standing over his stricken form facing down a nightmare to defend him. She felt drawn to the captain. Sa' ada smiled the smile older women only smile at young women. "Perhaps when your contract is complete?" Asmā nodded. "Perhaps, I'm flattered truly but, I made a commitment to the women I lead." She murmured feeling guilty and ungrateful.

"The spirits whispered to me that the two of you are linked. Your destinies intertwine like the strands of a rope. I knew tempting you away was a long shot, but I had to try." Lady Sa' ada said with a wistful smile. "I can see that they speak to you as well." She said with a matter of factness that brooked no dissembling. " I will leave you to to your afternoon lady knight but remember heed your dreams for they come from God through the ancestors."

Thoughts and emotions swirling Asmā took her leave. She had planned to do more shopping when she spotted Cazador at the head of his mensie leaving the main keep carrying an axe over his shoulder. She watched as visited various stalls including the sweetmeats vendor. He turned at something uttered by the giant Alcazar, and smiled the expression making Asmā warm as though she stood beside a hearth. When his eyes alighted on her his smile deepened and Asmā's knees momentarily forgot their function as something inside her melted. "We had planned to ride for town. I came to ask you to join us but your dress is far too fine to mar upon a saddle."Cazador's eyes sparkled as he bowed. "I had not known that I knighted a goddess." he said softly, his dark brown eyes sparkling they roamed her body taking in her new dress. Cazador looked spell bound and Asmā sealed her lips behind a smile. The fey temptation to tell him that he could remove it if he wished was dancing on the tip of her tongue. Since the fight with the revnant Asmā felt close to her captain. Their friendship feeling new and timeless all at once. It was as if he had always been part of her life or always should have been. Like her sword Asmā felt the need to keep him near. She had courted in Malaga, but more often than not she had kept suitors at bay and her maidenhead intact.

The captain was everything her mother and aunts warned her about. Too smooth by half, and a flirt by nature. He was bold, arrogant and violent. He was the captain, a man of war. But Cazador had a way with people that he didn't even know he possessed. Even though his lazy grin and hooded eyes hid mind sharper than any blade. When you put it all together he was like fire. Dangerous, but you could help but want to touch, to bask in its glow. Unwrapping his prize from the vendor, Cazador offered her a piece of mazapán made from almonds and honey Asmā thanked him and took a bite. As the sweet creamy flavor permeated across her tongue she was struck by a sense of de ja vu so strong it almost made her stagger. She had never been inside Bobastro. Asmā had never eaten mazapán given to her by anyone but her aunts. But... *I've dreamt this moment before.*

Goosebumps riddled her flesh as Lalla Sa'ada's words rang in her ears. Asmā met the brown tourmaline pools of Cazador's eyes, they seemed to draw her in until she found herself fighting the urge to touch him. Cazador stared back at her, he tucked his bottom lip between his teeth and sighed "But for my heroine, I will hire a carriage and buy a bottle of wine for the trip." He bowed slightly eyes never leaving hers. *Damn you Cazador Alfiere what are you trying to do to me.* Somewhat breathless, she agreed.

* * *

They arrived at Ard Allam by mid afternoon. It's well planned streets and whitewashed buildings seemed to flow away from the great ridge holding the castle like a floe of lava. True to his word Cazador had hired a carriage and supplied her with a carafe of exquisite wine. It was so exquisite she could not stop drinking it. It was a problem. It was not *the* problem. The problem was the captain. He had done nothing wrong, but if charm was a weapon then he left her dead and bleeding somewhere halfway between Bobastro and Ard Allam. For the first time since she was a much younger woman she wanted a man and that man was her captain.

Asmā had known that signing on to be a mercenary had meant stepping into a man's world. She knew it meant placing certain barriers between her and male counterparts. It was strange that to exist among men and gain their respect, was to swear off men. At first it had been easy enough. She had long since decided men were more trouble than they were worth and entirely unreliable to boot. She had been betrothed once. He had made a fool of her, and therefore made a castle of her heart. She had thought herself safe. Then came Cazador with his rouguish smile, bedroom eyes, and towering intellect. Then there were his lips, arms, and shoulders. Asmā found herself suppressing a sigh. She had known he was trouble from the moment he walked into the taverna. Trouble she could handle, this was something else. Her castle had been under siege since the fight with the revenant, but this was was an escalade and her defenses were somehow very weak. It angered her, almost as much as it sent a thrill down her spine.

She watched the captain dismount, wondering if grey pants of the nature her wore were even legal. *Indecent.* A corner of her mind roared as Cazador helped her down from her carriage. He shot her a smile so inviting she didn't know whether to kiss or slap him. *You know what your doing you clever bastard. Tempting good Christian girls with your devilishness.* Perhaps both a kiss and a slap were in order. *Virgin I may be, but blushing maid I am not. It's time for me to go on the offensive.* Asmā knew Ard Allam well having spent time here since she was a girl. Coming from a large family as she did he had cousins scattered around the aqālīm or district especially here in Ard Allam. Looping her arm in the captain's she shot her comrades a grin of her own. "I know the perfect place to celebrate the success of our mission." Cazador looked as if he was about to speak when Merfyn asked, "Will there be food...*and ale?*" Asmā fought the urge to laugh, "Oh yes, that and more." Merfyn smiled beautifically. "Lead the way Lady Asmā." He said to a cheer from the rest of their party. Now that she was a titled lady, it was time to act a bit unladylike.

It didn't take long for Asmā to lead them to their destination in the dhimmi quarter of the town. The funduq was as nondescript as it's name was grand. The sign named it's Ishtar's Palace, named for a pagan goddess from the east. Inside the establishment the plainness of the exterior was banished for a world of brightly colored silk and plush carpet. On the far wall across a sea of low side tables paired with chaises, divans, and soft cushions. The generous stage was flanked by a long bar. Women wearing gauzy dresses that left only enough to the imagination to inflame it adorned the room like living art. Some worked the room, serving patrons or dancing seductively. A few were even *servicing* patrons in the more secluded alcoves on the sides of the pillared room. Asmā watched the captain, while to others he might have appeared inscrutable she could see his discomfiture. Ever the tactician she watched his restless eyes as they sought assess the situation. Little did the hunter know he had become prey. He bit his bottom lip in thought and Asmā wondered what it would taste l like between her own. *Patience is a virtue*, she chided herself. Their party was met by a hostess whose dark brown skin seemed to glow through her sheer linen chemise, her body swaying like a willow in a storm as she led them to an empty table.

When they were seated and served with wine or ale in hand Merfyn let lose a low whistle. "Lady Asmā I do believe you have excellent taste in establishments." Izan raised a glass. "To the Chevalerese Asmā your spurs are well earned!" Asmā blushed with pride. She raised her own glass," and to the Company of Saint Moses!" She said meeting Cazador's eyes with a grin. The captain only shook his head. "The company of Saint Moses has been disbanded at the behest of my grandfather. We will now be called the Company of the Leopard, and our colors sable on or. Our arms are a field divided per bend sinister angled or and sable with a leopard in sable in the first quarter." Asmā cocked an eyebrow, "I think I'd look good in black and gold." Cazador favored her with a saucy grin. "Milady would look good in anything or nothing at all." Roland wrapped an arm around Cazador shoulder. "You don't say sweet things like that to me!" Cazador laughed. "You didn't save my life, and I doubt you look as good in dress."

Serving girls appeared with more wine and trays of orange and mango slices that had been dusted in sugar and kept on ice. Asmā watched as one by one her comrades became distracted and made her move. When the dancer began to dance for her Asmā began to dance with her. The woman was game, and their bodies seemed to slip around each other like two silk scarves as they twisted and gyrated to the music. Cazador was captivated his lively eyes drinking in he scene like sand soaked in water. Freeing a candied mango from the tray Asmā dipped it in her wine and popped it in the captain's mouth. The surprise in his eyes faded into delight. Before he could speak Asmā kissed him. His lips were warm, full and inviting. She could feel the rigidity in him melt as he lost himself to their kiss.

When Asmā broke away she found Cazador eying her with an intensity that made her heart race. He seemed to bleed desire and the thin grey material of his trousers hid no secrets from her. "Asmā..." Cazador crooned as he placed a trembling hand on her hips. "I want this. I want you although I should not.

I am your captain, to do so would be to abuse my position, and I respect you too much to ever besmirch your honor." In the face of his earnest expression she could do naught but laugh. "You are my captain and yet you salute me." She said lightly gesturing to his manhood straining against its cloth prison. "Do I look like I'm being abused?" Cazador shook his head dumbly. She kissed him again, this time until she felt as though she would immolate from the inside out. The dancer made to leave but Asmā caught her hand. "Where do you think your going?" She crooned leading both the captain and the dancer by the hand toward an empty alcove.

* * *

The alcove was small and private seeming a world away from the common room beyond. Asmā released his hand and spun to face him the predatory glint of the lioness in the verdurous eyes. Her hands went first to her belt, then to her shoulders and her sword and dress cascaded to the floor. Cazador felt his pulse races as Asmā stood before him in naught but hose and wimple. Her eyes pinned him like spears as she stood boldly before him. "As I said my lady, a goddess whether you wear everything or nothing." He whispered as the world fell away. All there was, was her. Skin like sand kissed by honey, full pendulous breast and a soft stomach that flared to wide hips and shapely thighs. It was all he could do not to fall to his knees. Before him was no willowy wisp of a woman. She was no delicate confection, though her lips were the sweetest thing he'd even known. This was a goddess of earth, iron, and fire, and he was hers. He had run from this. Fought it like any foe. *I can still walk away from this.* He lied to himself. *I am still in control.* He lied again. When he finally dragged his eyes back to Asmā's he saw and inevitability that crumpled his defenses.

The dancer was all but forgotten until Cazador felt her hands on his shoulders before they moved to his belt. No sooner did his weapons fall away with a clatter were the dancer's deft hands working free his tunic and it joined his weapons. Next came his dan ciki. There was nothing lean about him. Broad shouldered with a barrel like torso he was a bull among stags. Old scars and recent bruises told their own tale forcing the dancer to suppressed a gasp. Cazador undid his drawstrings and let his pants fall. Stepping forward into Asmā's embrace the world soon fell away.

* * *

Sabri and the rest of the Monts Des Maures deserters had pushed hard doing all they could to distance themselves from Don Ricardo's host of destruction. They had warned all who would listen. They had swung west to Alameda before aiming south for Teba, knowing the path Don Ricardo and his false goddess had planned. Altogether it left the ragged tired band of men feeling like harbingers of death. As masterless men they were little better than outlaws unwelcome and treated with hostility wherever they went. After Ard Allam they would march on Bobastro.

He wondered how long before the haughty guardians of Teba were just another smudge of smoke on the horizon. When the hints of burning wood carried to him on the wind, he at first thought it was his imagination but when he looked west a column of smoke greeted his vision. Looking around he wasn't the only one to notice. From their camp on a hill several miles south and east of Teba their view of the surrounding countryside was commanding. It would have been impossible to miss it. From the few refugees they had encountered Woodwose and ghul had been unleashed as forerunners to Don Ricardo's main force. Sabri had no clue what their numbers were but with so many troops lost fighting for the caliph none of the towns had been able to resist. With the Almohads in disarray Sabri doubted that would change.

They had been there for two days. Sabri had wanted to rest the men. Both the foot soldiers and the horses were in sore need of it, they were all reaching their limits. The fact that behind them lay a trail of death was grinding them all down emotionally and spiritually. It stank of cowardice. Riding to submit themselves to their true lord was starting to feel a lot like running. As spokesman for their company he would have loved nothing more than to order them to ride for Teba but he was loath to lead his comrades into a vainglorious death. Instead Sabri shouted "Strike the camp, we ride for Ard Allam!"

Chapter 23: Ard Allam

C azador lay amid a tangle of of limbs, cushions and sheets feeling as close to bliss as mortally possible. The dancer snored softly beside him as Asmā lay on his chest. He ran his fingers through Asmā's short curly hair, shorn so that her helmet fit better. "Of all the art made by the hands of God and men, none is more beautifully wrought than women and there isn't one to match you." He murmured softly. Asmā planted a line of kisses along his collarbone. "Its talk like this that got us here captain." Asmā said before kissing the most delightful spot she had discovered where his jawline met his neck. "Then I pray poetry ever falls from my lips when I speak to you." Cazador said finding Asmā's lips with his own. She growled into his lips and straddled him. Cazador looked up wondering how he had lived his life without the vision before him.

It was agony but they disentangled and dressed. They found the rest of their party in the common room. His mensie were all in various states of debauched disarray. Diallo wore only his boots sword belt and his kora, strumming idly singing softly to a trio of utterly enthralled dancers. Alberto was stripped to his trews being fed dates by two very nude women. Maurice was frozen mid stroke torn between finishing and checking for signs of immediate danger. Cazador chuckled. "I'll settle your tabs if you are all kitted and outside in time for us to be back at Bobastro before vespers." He had to suppress a laugh as they scrambled to prepare. Merfynn and Izan unceremoniously dumped dancers from their laps as Jaime and Roland did their level best to quaff the rest of the wine from their respective carafes. Moments later they were all half drunk but fully accounted for, dressed, and mounted grinning like fools. Cazador settled up and they made their way towards the main road which curved to the west around the town before turning north.

In the distance Cazador spotted a pillar of smoke stainining the sky. Heart pounding he desperately tried to recall what lay in that direction. Closer at hand was a column of warriors under a white flag paired with the last banner he expected. He'd last seen them fighting for the ill fated Miramollin and now here they were again. The dejected looking force under the argent and purpure bearing the canes in first quarter and the Moors head and fourth, the arms of Le Cannet Des Maures marched towards Ard Allam like men on their way to the hangman. Many emotions fought for his attention all at once. Shock and confusion were first. Then there was fear that Richard's force had come already. Anger that he had been set aside from his birthright, and men who has served his family for generations had died by his hand with more likely to follow. *And the day had been going so well.* Dismounting Cazador pulled free the lance from his saddle and attached his arms and this of his grandfather. was well known in the area and to any who was connected to the Monts Des Maures clan. His own banner depicting the tierced in fess angled argent azure and sable with the sable lions head in first quarter was less well known but it would be known as his today. Once he remounted Cazador looked at his knights and smiled. "Lets go introduce ourselves, shall we?" With that he led his mensie toward the column at the canter.

They met the Le Cannet Des Maures column a few hundred yards before the town limits at the bridge over the Túron. The column of warriors looked rough, worn to the bone. To look at them was to see a company of living ghosts. Cazador drew himself up in the saddle, "In the name of the Lord of Bobastro I command you to halt!" The Le Cannet Des Maures men froze. "I am Cazador Alfiere Knight of Saint Attillo of the Mont Des Maures, what is your business here!" A single man at arms rode forward. "I am Sabri of Le Cannet Des Maures. We are all that remains of the levy that was oath bound to march with the traitor and usurper Don Ricardo." Sabri paused for a moment a flash of anger and sadness passing over his features. " Don Ricardo is a bad lord. We have left the usurpers service in search of the true born heir of Le Cannet Des Maures to swear our blades and give warning. Even now am army of Woodwose and ghul a thousand strong rampage in Malaga. They are servants of Don Ricardo and the dark goddess he is devoted to. Thy march in our wake. Despite our warnings they sack and kill . The Muslims bar their gates to us and spurn our aid. Even now Teba is under attack and shortly they will set their gaze on Ard Allam." Sabri knelt in the dust of the road, and a moment later the rest followed. "We pledge ourselves to you Don Cazador, we will no longer be men of Le Cannet Des Maures but yours. If you will have us." Cazador felt suspicion and elation swirl. Part of him felt unworthy. He'd cut down men of their number to save Omar. It shamed him that once he'd thought commanding men such as these was his birthright when he had done nothing to truly earn it. Besides bad lord nonwithstanding it was a long way back to Provence and Cazador was wise enough to know that he was their only hope of honor and survival.

There was something forlorn in the man's voice. Something that reached out and begged to not be forsaken, like a weapon that sang to be repaired and turned back to it's purpose. His eyes bored into Cazador's own. *Please don't turn us away.* They said and Cazador knew what he must do. They were clan, and in their hour of need he would not turn them away. Like him they came to Bobastro seeking a return of their valor. So it was with pride, elation, guilt, and emotions he could not name swelling within his chest he said. "Men of Le Cannet Des Maures, I welcome you, rise and be commended to my service." The change in the once deserters was immediate. It was as though when they rose from the dust of the road a pall had fallen away and they were new men. They stood straighter, and the eyes of every man gleamed with renewed purpose. Cazador felt inspired. It was just enough to take the edge off his churning anxiety. "How long do you think we have messire Sabri?" The Moorish man at arms frowned thoughtfully. "Woodwose and ghul are as fast as horses as you know Don Cazador. If Teba holds for an hour then we may have four." Cazador smiled. "Thats more time than we had against the traitor at Belda." Turning in his saddle he looked to his mensie as his thoughts raced. His knights had little armor, no spears outside those born of the fifty spearmen from Le Cannet Des Maures. In short he was woefully unprepared for a fight he could not run away from.

His first instinct was to send Asmā to Bobastro for aid, but she was unknown to many there and she would hate him for it besides. Instead he called for his nephew. "Leonardo ride to your great grandsire and tell him a thousand Woodwose and ghul are rampaging in his valley and he's about to miss the party I'm throwing." The younger Alfiere scion grinned. "Greatfather does love a party." He said before saluting and turning his mount to ride north as if the devil himself was chasing him. Next he turned to Asmā, "We need armor milady." She nodded and favored him with a saucy grin. "Nobody likes being underdressed for a party." She said winking. He tossed her a purse heavy with dinars and she took her carriage back towards town.

Turning to the other Cazador clamped down on his anxiety. "Well gentles. We must be wicked because for the likes of us there is no rest. Woodwose and ghul both fear running water. Therefore we hold this bridge. I will ride for the ksar to rally the emir of the town and his forces." Cazador sent a party of almogovars to watch for sign of the enemy and left Pedro, Pablo, along with Roland, Alberto, and Merfynn to organize the Le Cannet Des Maures men. With his task complete Cazador and the others rode for the keep.

The climb to the looming summit above the town taxed the horses but Cazador dismissed his worry about it as he planned to fight on foot. The ride had at least given him an opportunity to wind his turban, observe the defenses, and most importantly time to think. While creatures like Woodwose were common in France and Provence they were almost unheard of in the south. Ghul on the other hand were something at least those from the desert would understand. Diallo announced him at the gate and they were admitted and the vizier of the city's emir an officious looking Sudanese Moor with a short wiry build draped in a yellow kaftan received them in his garden. The man introduced himself as Abu Ibn Safs. Cazador bowed and smiled. "Peace be upon you. I am Sayyad Ibn Wilayam, Ibn Hamza Al Takruri." The vizier inclined his head. "What can I do for you scion of the Lion?" Cazador took a fortifying breath. "An army of Woodwose and ghul are attacking Teba and will be here before nightfall. How many men do you have to protect the town?" Abu Ibn Safs laughed. "Surely you jest. Wildmen are for firanji tall tales and children, and any fool knows ghul can only be found at night." Cazador felt anger laced with panic spike in his gut.

"I do not jest. Nor am I a fool. The world is a big dark place of mystery and wonder and I have blooded my blade against these creatures before. " Cazador snarled his voice hoarse with menace. "Look to the west, you see the smoke. I swear upon my honor and that of my family and to God Almighty I do not jest or lie. Would you be a vizier of bones and ashes?" Cazador snapped giving vent to his rising anger. *Is this what I have to look forward to as I fight the Suddibe? Will I also have to wrestle with the stupidity of men?* Part of him was filled with rage and the other with disgust. It took all he had not hawk the bitter bile that rose in the man's face.

The vizier looked offended and Cazador knew that he was handling this poorly. "The emir has a personal guard and the town milita. Many including our emir's sons marched to the caliph and never returned but Ard Allam has stood since before the Almoravids and it will stand still." Cazador nodded suppressing memories of the battle in the mountains even as rage sparked to life in his chest. Ignoring the man's excuses he asked, "If the town is threatened will your emir raise troops and fight?" The vizier shook his head. "Our emir is a wise and not one to suffer flights of fancy or fools, even if they are the grandson of a sheikh. If you are such a coward you must turn your foes into monsters to explain his fear that is your problem sir and none of mine." Abu Ibn Safs spat. Cazador inclined his head. *So this is how it's to be then.* A knight he might be but a courtier he was not. Pulaaku demanded temperance, but there was a time and place for all things. His left hand shot out and cracked across the viziers face with a spray of blood, teeth and an outraged cry. "I should leave Ard Allam to its fate. I should take my men and march home, but I will not doom innocents because of ignorance." The guards lowered their spears and Cazador laughed as Jaime, Izan, Alcazar, Maurice, and even Diallo joined him with naked steel. Cazador whipped Alkasaara free from it's sheath at his belt and drew his buckler from L'auxifar's hilt. "I will kill you all and walk from this place with boots wet with your blood! Who would wants to die for stupidity's sake?" Cazador roared like the lion on his arms. "Let them come Caz, I could use the warm up," Alcazar snarled twirling his oversized falchion "It *has* been a few days since we've had to kill anyone..." Maurice hissed with casual menace. Cazador laughed then because by God he loved them. Some corner of his brain whispered that they could butcher the emir declare himself the emir and take control of Ard Allam. The idea seemed madness, but the world had gone mad.

"Enough!" Came a voice loud and sharp enough to cut through the tension in the garden. The Ard Allam warrior froze and Cazador's own tensed waiting for his order. "Who disturbs my hall!" Shouted an older Maghrebi wearing a yellow and white turban with matching voluminous robes. His eyes fell upon Cazador. "I see the face of an old friend staring back at me with weapons bared and my vizier bloodied. What is the meaning of this?" Cazador envisioned himself flying at the old man in a flurry of steel. *Kill the old man, bribe whatever guards that survive the onslaught.* He felt the icy grip of Le Gel fight to take hold in his soul but Cazador wasn't that same man that rode from his aunts camp. Instead he spit at the vizier and said, "You knew who I was before I walked into your garden. I came to warn you of a threat and enlist your aid in defending *your* town. But instead I find myself ridiculed and insulted by the servants of my grandfather's *friend.* I have half a mind to march my people away and leave you to the Woodwose and the ghul. Let you suffer the same fate as Teba." The emir's eyes drifted toward the column of smoke to the west. Cazador turned to go, thoughts of an axe won city still swimming in his mind. "You should, but you won't." The old emir growled. Cazador froze as if slapped, and turned slowly to the old Moor and pointed at him with his axe. "I don't know who you think your talking to old man, but you don't know me." The old emir smiled like a cat. "You are not some simple mercenary . Furusiyya and chivalry will not allow it. You serve a higher purpose. Your are a lion, not a jackal and you will not turn your back and flee to leave innocents to die." Cazador narrowed his eyes and lowered his axe. "You'll fight then." The old man nodded. "If I don't you'd likely kill me and take my town. You've already summoned your grandfather, this place will be swarming with Al Takruris soon and if you don't he will." Cazador couldn't stop the chuckle that escaped. "Let no man say Tariq Ibn Sulieman was a coward or a fool." He took Cazador's arm in a warriors grip. "I have a mounted guard of eighty men, half firanji men at arms half Ishelhien riders from Morocco and then the town milita of maybe another hundred and a half men. Give me an hour and we will join you in the defense of the town." The old man smiled warmly but his eyes remained as cold and hard as mountain ice.

Cazador and his party left the ksar of Ard Allam loaded down with food, water, spears and sheaves of arrows. The bells were already ringing signaling the alarm to the townsfolk. "Ahh that went well!" Diallo said beaming as they rode from the gates. Cazador snorted a laugh. "I don't know." Alcazar said. "I was kinda hoping they pushed Cazador a bit more. We could have taken them. The Old Lion practically owns the governor of Malaga and the way I see it Miramollin owes old Cazador a huge favor. This could have been our town." Izan pulled his mount next to Alcazar's and patted the huge man at arms on the shoulder. "We'll get em next time. The Old Lion is talking empire. We pull this off and we might have entire provinces one day." Izan said mildy. He could almost hear the millstone in Alcazar's head turning. "That would be pretty good." He said, voice tinged with awe. "We'll all be rich as Sudanese kings as soon as we handle our duty in England. Then its likey off to scorching Africa." Cazador grunted. *We have to get there first.* He kept his thoughts to himself but the castle gates shutting behind him said enough.

* * *

Richard stared at Wigberto du Grimaud who fairly crackled with pleasure as he rode beside his lord commander. The man had been useful in the past and had continued to be useful to Richard, especially now that he had been named Captain General of the Militia of Our Lady of the Fountain. Even still the man before him now was a far cry from the frazzled noble who had botched the framing of Cazador. He had drunk deep and stood renewed in the waters of their Lady. Much like the Mozarabs they had pressed into service. They were two men united in their hatred of the Du Maurmonts and now they stood at the precipice of tearing out the heart of their collective enemy. "Once we sack Bobastro and kill the clan leaders the Du Maurmont lands will be mine. With the order and the Du Maurmont feudal forces together with Grimaud and support from Boniface of Castellane we could easily take Draguignan, Ròcabruna d'Argenç, Saint Tropez, and forge the heart of Terra de la Dama." Wigberto nodded with the vigor of the zealot. "We can take the Balearics and then Sardinia and Corsica with control of the Sardinian Sea we control the western Mediterranean and all the trade that goes with it." His eyes shone brightly with the promise of their future. "More land and more wealth means more souls for our Lady's glory." Richard patted his shoulder fondly, "And more glory for the sons of Our Lady." Richard said completing the mantra that had been taught them by the Prophetess.

The lady had grown strong, fattened on blood sacrifice and the worship of thousands of new converts. She had blessed her army and they had marched as if possessed until they were but an hour behind the vanguard of Woodwose and ghul. From the east his Lady had called ogres. They would emerge from the deep ways in the foothills south and east of Bobastro and rampage there. His vanguard force had done well smashing towns leaving the dazed and helpless survivors to fall into Richard's waiting arms. There had been thousands fleeing the towns and cities and he had snapped them up. The order brought them the hope of the Lady and drew them into her worship swelling his numbers. Those with experience became men at arms or almogovars and the rabble were sent to Wigberto to fill the ranks of the militia. Now he had a thousand ghul, a thousand Woodwose, three thousand men of the order, and an equal number of armed peasants. They more looked more like an armed migration than an army. His south western approach to Bobastro had seen his forces go largely unchecked and now they stood poised to rid the world of the Old Lion and his kin.

***

When they returned to the bridge they could see the spearman and men at arms were drawn up in good order and archers and almogovars lined the river bank. Asmā had returned and laid out on blankets were twelve identical sets of kit. Cazador dismounted with a grin. "Milady you are ever a wonder!" He said with a courtly bow. Strolling over to the blanket to examine the simple bar nasal helmets, boiled leather greaves and vambraces, canvass coifs, aketons, maille shirts, and gambosed chausses. "Wherever did you find matching kit like this?" Cazador asked delighted as he examined the Maille haubergon. "It was intended for the emir's guards but it's hard to argue with gold dinars and the threat of angry Al Takruri knights."

"Captain!" Cazador looked up to see the already kitted Asmā tossing him his purse. Catching it with a satisfying clank he grinned. "Asmā if you weren't already knighted I'd knight you again!" He said beaming. The lady knight returned his smile. "I'm sure I'll find some way for you to thank me." The twinkle in her eye sent a tingle up his spine and his confidence soaring. Grinning like a fool he began to arm.

The late afternoon sun beat down on them mercilessly and sweat soaked his new gambeson but Cazador smiled. Armored and helmeted he felt like a different man. Almost. His guts still churned for and hour or more had passed since he left the keep and still no aid had come. Against men he would like his odds far better but against the raw might of the wildmen his lines felt thin. He fought the urge to look north for aid doing all he could to project a confidence he did not feel. Woodwose were like men but stronger and hairier with heavier bones and tough skin like a crocodile's that was like an armor in and of itself. Like many of the Suudibe with the exception of ghul, they could not abide the touch of iron or steel, but it had to bite and draw blood or remain on the skin to prove toxic. Such a weakness was a saving grace because Woodwose took a great deal of killing to kill. His hand fell to Alkasaara a smile ghosted across his lips *grandfather knew I would need you.* Even though L'auxifar and Il Martello hit incredibly hard, they were a sword and a mace, Alkasaara was an axe and he was excited about seeing what the she could do.

When the forms of the almogovar scouts came trotting back into view Cazador knew it was time. One stepped forward a grizzled muwallad marked as a veteran by his grey beard. He shot Cazador a simple salute but his wide eyes gave Cazador pause. "The wildmen are maybe a half hour behind us." Cazador took a deep breath. He had known this was coming and they had prepared for it as best as they could. "Don Ricardo's force is behind them. It's more than doubled since we departed." He finished, voice carrying a touch of panic. Cazador reached out and thumped the man on his shoulder. "Thank you for the report. God and our ancestors shall stand with us. Get some food and water." The man nodded some of the panic drifting from his face as he moved on to find rations. Anxiety beat at him like a thousand spears and he could feel the eyes of his retinue on his skin like hot brands. Richards human army would have very few compunctions about crossing the river making Cazador's force all to easy to overwhelm. This time there was no artillery, no steep hill or ravine to save him.

"What did he say?" Alcazar asked. "He said we are all about to die, didn't he?" A fatalistic corner of Cazador's soul wanted to agree while another corner screamed in defiance. Cazadors mind raced as he grasped for a plan. He scanned the area looking for something that would give them time. Somewhere that would keep them from being swamped by the larger force. His imagination could find no purchase having never spent much time in the town. *Bastard emir I should have taken his castle.* Cazador fumed. It would only be a matter of time before the shaken scout revealed what he knew and morale burned away like morning mist. Cazador had to do something and he was running out of time. The bells of the Mozarab church continued to ring and with them tolled inspiration. "The scouts report that Richard the traitor has joined his advance force boosting the enemy numbers upwards of six thousand." There were gasps, grumbles and even some low whistles. Cazador could empathize, but survival hinged on belief that they could win here. Picking his words carefully he continued. "We cannot stop a force that size from this location, we cannot run, but what we can do is withdraw to the town. The street before the Mozarab church will be our battlefield. There we cannot be flanked and we can use the buildings to our advantage. There we will bleed them, break them! Crush them! They will know defeat and despair and where they die we live!" Cazador roared to the nods among his warriors and growls of assent from his mensie. "This will be a red day, souls will walk to heaven on the pile of corpses we leave here but our stories shall not end here!"

***

The captains words still rang in Roland's ears. "Yeala yeala!" he shouted in butchered Arabic as he chivvied the townsfolk past the makeshift barrier of looted wagons and through the line of Le Cannet Des Maures spearmen. Rodrigo, Maurice, Jaime and himself had been given command of ten men at arms, ten archers, and twelve spearmen to hold the four choke points. Asmā had command of the forty other archers who were not holding the bridge with Cazador. She set them strategically in teams of four to rain death on their attackers. Roland's was the far northeastern flank while Rodrigo held the south eastern approach nearby. Jaime held the center approach and Maurice the east.

There was an air of prepared confidence that was infectious. Roland nodded in satisfaction as he watched housewives on balconies heating kettles of sand fetched by fleet footed youths. Elsewhere men hauled stones and bricks to where defenders waited on rooftops. More used to fighting on the plains of Italia, having his lines anchored by the stone buildings made him feel secure.

He wondered if the feeling would last when the narrow streets filled with enemies. *How did I get here?* He still wasn't sure why he had chosen to swear to the Moorish knight. He paid well, and although his blue eyes and pale skin stuck out amongst his comrades he was as safe as he could be from his debtors and enemies in Palermo. It was as good a reason as any to be here but the irony of a life spent fighting Saracens to now possibly die protecting them was not lost on him. But Roland believed in his lord and captain. Cazador had brought them out of more scrapes in a fortnight than Roland had seen in ten years. He began to wonder how many more he would see if they survived today.

* * *

The sun has begun it's journey west glittered from the enemy column. The white and gold tabards shimmered in the late afternoon glow so that it appeared as though some glittering snake of myth had risen against them. They could be smelled before they could be seen. A bitter charnel stink that carried hints of scorched wood and the pork like scent of human flesh given to the flames. Cazador sat his horse beside the twins Pedro and Pablo only differentiated by personality and build. Pedro was a bear of a man, bluff and loud whilst Pablo was of a slighter build and quiet demeanor. Alongside him sat Merfynn, Izan, Alcazar, and Diallo, twenty archers and ten men at arms from Le Cannet Des Maures including Sabri who insisted on riding with his new sworn lord. They blocked the bridge a wall of horses, leather, steel and men. His plan was as simple as it was reckless, kick the enemy in the teeth bloody and enrage them and then ride like hell for their positions. It was cool proof. Unless they died.

At the head of the column under a cloud of banners was Richard the traitor in all his glory. The enemy was bowel wateringly numerous but the sight of the man who had sought to destroy his reputation as well as usurp his birthright brought forth a banishing anger. When they were four hundred yards away Cazador lifted his axe to the sky and the archers loosed sending a cloud of arrows into Richard's force. Bodies rent by bodkins tumbled to the ground.

Cazador felt fear and anxiety cascade and muttered a prayer. *Lord of all thank you for loving me and if I fall here make it to your glory.* After four volleys the enemy had closed the within two hundred yards and Cazador laid his axe across knees to heft his lance. As the fifth volley launched fear and anxiety fell away like water from waxed leather. Any thought of being maimed or killed evaporated replaced by fury and adrenaline. Battle madness crept up his spine and into his skull as he led his knights and men at arms forward in a wordless charge. The wind screaming past his helmets nasal seemed to say *you are Cazador Alfiere you fight and you kill things. You haven't died before and you won't start today.* The sixth volley fell just before they struck. He felt shock run up his lance shaft as he struck one of Richards knights square in the chest impaling him. The body shot back over the horses rump and taking Cazadors lance with it and he snatched up Alkasaara. He slapped away a questing lance and backhanded the enemy knight with a vicious chop beneath the rim of his pothelm. The maille held but Cazador heard bone snap over the din of battle. Alkasaara was light but hit hard.

Laughing with the sheer glory of the fight he turned and deflected a sword stroke with his buckler before hooking it over his opponents shield rim and chopping into the side of the knights phrygian cap style helm sending blood shooting from the man's nose and across the face of shield. Turning his mount he led his force in breaking contact. As they wheeled for a second charge Cazador saw that they had hit them hard but it was like a sword stab versus an elephant, they had drawn blood but the beast was massive and and angry. For some reason Cazador thought that was funny and laughed again as they crashed into Richard's force again. He slapped aside an attack and lashed out with his axe. The man got his shield up in time but the force of the blow knocked him from the saddle. Cazador turned with a growl as a sword skated across his maille armored shoulder. Spurring his horse and bringing his axe back across his body he chopped into his opponents ribcage as he passed seeing links jump free and feeling the bone give under the enormous pressure of the blow.

Wheeling again Cazador extricated his force winging back to the dubious safety of the bridge each man laying low over his horses neck as a storm of arrows leapt overhead into the enemy. They had killed or wounded at least fifty of the enemy to, two riderless horse and two injured men of their own. Out of the thousands that faced them hit was less than a pinprick but it had been a blow well struck. It had begun.

* * *

Diallo clattered onto the bridge with his lord and the others. Heart pounding with the exertion of the charge he sheathed his saber and dismounted falling into the third rank behind Sabri of Le Cannet Des Maures. His fingers found the twenty one strings of his kora as he began to sing. As his notes hit the air he could feel the nyama moving. He sang to the bows of the archers, the strings and the arrows themselves. He sang to the earth, he sang to the grass, he sang to the river and mountain. The sound of the water passing beneath the bridge changed timbre, the dirt and grass they had so recently ridden across seems to writhe ever so slightly. Diallo felt sweat bead on his brow as he concentrated coaxing, wrestling,cajoling, and shaping the energy of the universe to do his bidding.

All at once the enemy force seemed to stagger. The quick confident strides of man and beast slowed and each step became a struggle. The thunder of hooves and feet muted almost immediately. What had begun as a counter charge devolved into an exhausting slog. The ground fought the enemy with every step, mud and grass grasping foot and hoof like desperate hands. Even the shaggy forms of Woodwose struggled mightily many falling to their hands and knees struggling to free themselves from the sucking morass. The creak and snap of composite bows filled the air around him as the archers made their attackers pay. Bodies dropped to never rise again becoming obstacles to the living. The slow moving horses and their riders made easy targets and even those who did not die struggled to rise from the hungry mud.

Diallo sang and the river sang back. What had begun as a muted sursurration became a steady hum as water thrummed against the stones of the bridge. What was once a lazy summer meander became a river in the full fury of a spring flood. Branches and tree limbs from up stream issued sharp reports as they were pulverized against the supports. Diallo sang working Nyama the way a potter throws clay, guiding the energy with hands of will rather than flesh.

* * *

Cazador looked on in awe as the enemy counter charge fell apart. The ground seemed to swallow footfalls and arrest movement like fetters and arrows fell like rain. The Le Cannet Des Maures archers had been given twelve sheaves of arrows per man, complements of the absent emir of Ard Allam. They seemed as though they would use them all as their shots seemed to fell their targets with relentless accuracy. Bodies became obstacles as man, Woodwose, and horse suffered from the combined effects of Diallo's hermetical efforts and the archers training and conditioning. In the opening minutes of their return to the bridge hundreds had died. By the time the first enemies reached the far end of the bridge over a thousand and a half bodies littered the ground.

Cazador took out raised Alkasaara. "God and our ancestors stand with us! Let them taste our fury!" His warriors roared and he clashed his axe on his shield rim. A knot of wildmen who had made the bridge even ahead of the cavalry panted in exhausted rage as they shambled drunkenly towards Cazadors line. Throwing up his shield Cazador blocked a gnarled wooden club and sank his axe into the the Woodwose where it's neck met it's collarbone. Blood geysered and it's head flopped sideways on a ragged flap of skin. Leaning away from another clumsy swipe he trapped his opponents weapon and shattered the creature's skull with his axe sheering away half the monster's face as it tore its way free of bone flesh and gristle.

He was vaguely aware of Merfynn to his right as he chopped through the lead leg of his Woodwose foe before backhanding his axe across the creatures throat. Izan's bar mace flashed pristine and shining in the late afternoon sun. It fell only to rise slick with blood and matted with hair. Pedro and Pablo struck almost simultaneously meeting their opponents with their shields before their axes rose and fell sending wildmen crashing to the bridge carved open from nipple to hip. His Le Cannet Des Maures men at arms found gaps between the knights to stab their spears as Richards knights mountless and mud slathered tried to fall upon Cazador's thin shield wall.

Because of the morass, Richards forces could only hit Cazador's line in bunches. The bridge was riddled with corpses as the archers protected by the raging river continued to reap them like wheat. All across the field lay the bodies of man horse and woodwose. A hillock of bodies lay before them cut down by Cazador and his warriors. A sensible commander would have broken off the attack, but not Richard. He sat his horse far outside bow range and Cazador could feel his hate like heat from a fire. It was only when the woman appeared beside him things began to turn. Behind him Diallo stopped singing and started coughing. The ground which had been a near impassible swamp firmed, and the once struggling enemy surged forward with alarming speed. His gris gris shuffled violently beneath his armor. He heard wretching and needed no further motivation. "Time to go! Move! Move! Move!" The archers unleashed a final volley and ran for their borrowed horses where their arrows were stored. By the time Richard's force made the bridge they were galloping towards Ard Allam.

* * *

Maurice had climbed to the roof of a nearby house to watch the fight at the bridge. What he had expected to be a five minute engagement had turned into a festival of archery and slaughter. The river had run in full spate and the ground the enemy marched upon had become a ruinous swamp, until it suddenly wasn't. That was all it took. Feeling a wave of relief wash over him he was elated his friends had survived They had been tight since they were ten and it burned him to not be holding the bridge beside his brothers in arms. They had piled enemy bodies deep on the bridge that took time to clear giving the captain ample time to escape. "Make way for sir Cazador and the others!" he shouted and an oxen specifically appropriated for the purpose pulled aside one of the carts looted to form the four barricades.

Cazador and the bridge crew came flying through the gap moments later. "That was brilliantly done!" Maurice said excitedly as Cazador dismounted his black chainmaille armor shiny with spattered blood. His friend nodded but his eyes were far away and he was not smiling. Maurice felt a spike of panic. The only time Cazador frowned when in a fight was when they were losing. "What happened out there?" Cazador shrugged and looked at his djali. Diallo was pale and shaken beneath his helmet "Richard and his witch goddess." Caz growled. His eyes far away for a moment. He seemed to shake himself and looked back at Maurice. "You've done well here." He added eying the V shaped cart wall lined with archers and men with slings for enfilading fire. The balconies above were filled with archers or women clutching stones or heating pots. He had read the same books on siege craft as Cazador and although he wasn't as scholarly as the captain he'd picked up a trick or two. Maurice grinned. "Its like you said. Our story doesn't end here." Cazador smiled then. "Exactly!" He seemed to shake something off and turned to Diallo. "Are you hale?" He asked voice laden with concern. The djali nodded but his face looked stricken. "Richard's demoness is very strong, but now I have her measure." The captain nodded. Maurice watched the exchange wondering what had happened that he couldn't see and frowned

Turning back to Maurice, Cazador clapped a blood splattered gauntlet to his shoulder. "Fear not, we've left you a few to kill." He said with a lopsided grin. Maurice laughed "Well I did decorate for a party..." Some of the anxiety he had felt build, floated away. Whatever had spooked Caz was no longer effecting him. In moments like this he was most like his grandfather. The Old Lion always seemed to have one foot in this world and one foot in another, the gears of his mind constantly turning hidden behind humor and exuberance. He was either a genius or a madman but he was loyal to his bones and Maurice knew that Caz would die before failing them. He was ready to fight and Maurice was ready to fight beside him.

* * *

Asmā watched Cazador ride past her checkpoint with elation in her breast. She had watched the fight at the bridge and could feel the great energy that Diallo had summoned. If she concentrated she could almost see the threads that bound it all together. Asmā had felt darkness take the field, felt it snuff out Diallo's working. The vague impression of running water that had come had filled her with rage and revulsion. She had longed to take her flying command of archers and help the captain flay the enemy at the bridge, but instinct told her the trap she set had to be perfect. After they passed Asmā's people were ready with pitch and lamp oil coating the street while others prepared to rain it down on their enemies.

She hefted the crossbow she had brought while shopping for armor. It was a beautiful thing 9f dark oiled wood and brass fittings that gleamed like gold and she had named it Dhiya for the warrior queen of her ancestors and with it a hundred bodkin tipped bolts and had resolved to use each of them to send her enemies to hell. She watched as the team in charge of prepping the ground finished and retreated to their positions careful to remove the rags from their feet as to not spread the deadly mixture. Hidden in alleys were heavy carts that would block the street. Her goal was to trap as many of the enemy as possible then she would make them a conflagration.

* * *

Richard cast a baleful glance over the battlefield as the last of his force crossed the bridge. It looked like some macabre garden, or washed out graveyard as the bodies of knights, woodwose, men at arms, militia and his almogovars protruded haphazardly in the refirmed turf. He had easily lost two thousand of his fighters, and only his faith in the Lady kept the fear that Cazador would be his doom at bay. *I am her paladin and I cannot fail as long as she has worship I will have life.* The thought comforted him but the obliteration of his woodwose, the culling of his knights and men at arms and with his peasant militia whittled down to a third of their original numbers it was the only comfort he had. That and the presence of the Marwah avatar of the Lady herself. She has stopped the magic that had wrought so much havoc.

He looked to his left where she rode stately and beautiful her gold plated maille gleaming. Her skin seemed to flow and Richard drew strength from her presence. He still retained fifty knights, two hundred men at arms three hundred of his almogovars and all of his freshly augmented crossbowman, spearman. Most of his ghul had survived as well. He had more than enough to sweep whatever paltry defense Cazador could muster aside and strike Bobastro. Contented with the thought he spurred his horse into a trot. The lower town had been abandoned and he knew that Cazador's force was likely hiding out somewhere they couldn't be flanked possibly even the castle. Marwah began to croon beside him. Her voice unearthly and her eyes half closed, arms outstretched as she guided her horse with her knees. He spurred his horse faster feeling the rush of the Lady's blessing descend.

When the crossbow bolt struck, Lady Marwah's blessing was all that saved him as his shield came up with inhuman speed. Others were not so lucky. Her guard the Sleepless fell in around the Marwah muscling Richard aside and protecting her with their shields even as arrows riddled their bodies. Archers and slingers appeared out of thin air occupying the once empty balconies and rooftops. "Shields!" he roared uselessly spurring his mount as it shied away from a brick that smashed inches from its hooves. A rumbling crash sounded behind him and Richard looked down hill to see the street blocked by carts. "Forward!" he cried knowing that it was likely the only option out of the trap they found themselves in. He looked back to see how many of his men followed and his gasped as fifty yards from his position the world burst into flame.

Chapter 24: Hour of the Lion

Omar pushed his mount hard, they would be at the rendezvous point soon. He had volunteered as soon as the reports were made moving with impressive haste. A wounded scout had returned with a report of a large force under Richard the Traitor outside Hisn Qanit just ten miles from Ard Allam. Young Leonardo had also reported that Cazador was preparing to face a large advance force of woodwose. The Old Lion had sent him with the remnants of his company augmented by four hundred La Compagnie mounted archers. Omar would have ridden alone if it had come to that. He'd walked Cazador into manhood and knighthood as a kinsman and mentor there was no way he could abandon him and leave him to die.

The Old Lion had sent a bird to the chapter house of the Knights of Saint Attillo in Álora. They were to meet near the Roman ruins just south of Ard Allam. They were perhaps a half mile off when the horses began to flicking their ears and rolling their eyes. Instincts screaming Omar slowed his column. As they drew closer the wind carried the iron tang of blood and the stink voided bowels mixed with something he couldn't quite place. He loosened his Jile in its sheath and knocked an arrow to his bow. It wasn't long after Omar's instincts began to scream. The forest was quieter than it should be. Even the insects seemed to hide as though the very land itself held its breath. Omar tried to dismiss his paranoia but when his horse a battle trained mount shied away from a human arm covered in maille. The body was perhaps a hundred paces away and beyond that the corpse of the horse. After that bodies were everywhere. Maille torn, horses and riders crushed, sixty men reduced to splinters of bone and smears of blood and maille.

It was all he could do not to be sick as the summer sun and flies had already done their work. The clearing was sheeted with blood and Omar's heart chilled at the thought of what could have wrought such destruction. While not as famous of the Templars, Hospitalars, or the Knights of Calatrava but the Knights of Saint Attillo were all gifted fighters. The only group tough enough to protect pilgrims visiting the shrines and hermitages of the Desert Fathers facing the dangers of man and Sudiibe both. To see so many lay low left him feeling cold despite the heat. Few things could do this sort of damage to armored men. Scanning the area for some sort of track proved useless as Omar could make heads nor tail of it. Everything was blood, bodies and the parts of bodies. Desire to understand what has happened warred with the driving need to be away from this place. Ominous foreboding seemed to seep from the very earth around them. *We don't have time for this.* Omar thought as his plan for a speedy relief mission was falling apart. The horses were baulking and wouldn't go further. Frustrated Omar tried to plan, back tracking would take time he couldn't afford to waste, but going forward didn't seem to be an option either. Compounding matters he had the very uncomfortable feeling that he and his command were prey and not the predator. It was a feeling he did not enjoy.

Omar looked back at his column. Nervous men and even more nervous horses milled behind him. The order to turn around dancing on his lips but he spotted a corpses that looked wrong. The arms and legs too long thick to be human. Forcing his mount closer he realized it was no man. A bone splitting roar split the late afternoon air. The earth rumbled as though hundred of horseman charged but instead two score of horrors stormed from the trees. Omar raised his bow and fired without conscious thought. The arrow took the rust skinned monstrosity in the eye and it crashed to the ground in a spray of earth and limbs. Omar had heard of ogres, kin of giants and woodwose, children of Orchus. They were described in the codex as averaging between six and eight feet tall with bodies as thick as two large men. Said to be immensely strong with skin like that of a woodwose that ranged in color greyish purple or green to a rusty red hue. Each carried an axe with a large knapped stone head. What the Codex of Saint Attillo forgot to mention was their speed. He managed to get off one more shot lancing an ogre's throat the arrow seeming ridiculously small in the beast's bullish neck.

He drew his black bladed sword and charged. Already the fleetest among the Ogres had reached his lines and the stone axes whistled through the air rending man armor and beast like rotted wood. Omar threw himself to the side of his saddle as the stone weapon hummed through the space he vacated, before his attacker could reverse his blow Omar rose and punched his demon killing sword into the ogres neck. Blood bright and hot shot up his arm as the big vein was opened and he withdrew his weapon and cut across his body laying his blade across the base of an other ogre's skull. The creature was too busy trying to free it's axe from the remains of Arsuf to stop him. He watched his loyal lieutenant's lifeless body dissapear under the ogre's bulk with a pang of loss so sharp it could cut the moon from the sky.

Keening, Omar spurred his mount at another ogre. Licking out with his sword again he carved deep into the monstrosity's thigh to hamstring it. The ogre roared and turned it's bulk towards Omar who had already hefted a javelin. The beast lashed out again just as Omar threw his projectile. He tried to turn his mount to flee. The horse got its head around but the burst of speed never came as the back of his horse simply stopped existing as the ogre's axe turned it into a cloud of blood and bone fragment. As he fell he watched his javelin pass through the creatures open mouth to explode from the back of its head. It was small consolation. He hit the ground hard biting his tongue filling his mouth with swollen flesh and blood. Rolling to his feet he spat to clear his mouth and shook his head to clear it. As his vision stabilized he didn't like anything he saw, a nightmare had come to life.

The ogres were intimidating on horse back and downright terrifying on foot.

They rampaged amongst his horsemen that hadn't managed to ride clear of the charge. Those not caught in the maelstrom of stone bladed horror punished the monsters with arrows and javelins. Enraged Omar threw himself at the nearest ogre. He leaped away from the first strike evading the orange shot pale purple head. Stepping forward he slashed the creature arms. The beast roared in pain and Omar swayed punching his blade in the creatures gullet.

The fact that so many good men had died filled Omar with a terrible anger. Sprinting he targeted another ogre. It slashed at him with it's axe, Omar dropped to his knees and slid feeling the wind of the weapons passage as he skated across the bloody morass. Rising he slashed open the ogre's gut and punched his point into his foe's groin. The ogres roar which had been vibrating his chest turned into a strangled whimper. Yelling in triumph Omar scanned the field for a mount. Now that the shock was fading his force was giving as good as they got, pincushioning the ogres from a distance slaying them before they could close. Already a dozen or more of the primordial horrors lay dead. If he could rally his force they could win here and ride on to Cazador. Spying a riderless mount a mere two dozen paces away Omar ran and vaulted himself in the saddle. Guiding his new mount with his knees he retrieved his bow, quiver and a brace of javelins from the remains of his saddle.

Rearmed he spurred his horse into a gallop laying low over the saddle as he rode for his knot of surviving men. There were a few cheers as men that recognized him took heart. Taking arrows in his bow hand and knocking one to his strong Omar began to strafe the ogres attacking his fighters. He put arrows in the backs of necks and behind knees causing the beasts to roar in dismay. He felled two ogres, then another. His men chanted his name and the enemy roared in fury. One ogre a gray skinned brute with skulls plaited in his beard and shaggy hair sprinted towards him faster than a galloping horse and Omar roared in challenge drawing a javelin and hurling it like at the monster. The beast turned but Omar's dart struck piercing the bundle of flesh where neck met shoulder. It staggered twisting showing peppering it's back. The ogres frustrated roar shook the earth causing the horses to whinny and rear. Omar fought to control his mount speaking soothing words to the unfamiliar horse. Trying to think of the words to the spell the old lion taught him long ago. A great whooshing whine filled the air and Omar looked up from his panicked mount to see the great axe tumbling towards him.

He leapt from the saddle. Spinning end over end the great blade struck the horse in an explosion of gore. The haft of the weapon struck the airborne Omar with the force of a onager snapping bone and sending sending his body sailing through the air. He hit the ground and bounced body twisting with unabated momentum to career into a large tree. Omar felt something in his body bend then snap, pain lancing his frame. He could feel everything so he knew his spine wasn't broken but he couldn't make his body work. His breathing rasped and bubbled in his chest. He watched with grim satisfaction as his command killed another of the ogres under a hail of arrows and javelins. He saw their panic stricken gazes fall on his battered body. *Do not weep for me comrades. I go on to glory to be with God and the heroes of my line. You are champions go forth and conquer.* He drew a ragged painful breath. Somewhere in his brain he knew it would be his last. *Here me oh Almighty and honored ancestors.* "Al Takrui Awlnasr! La Takruri y La Victoria!" It was a stern commandment, a heartfelt prayer, and a rallying cry for all who heard him in this world and beyond. Omar imbued it with every scrap of his will and every ounce of his being. *The Takruri and Victory!*

* * *

Cazador listened as the sound of arrows striking flesh and armor mixed with the thud of stones and the breaking crockery. It told him that the rear elements of the enemy had made it past the checkpoint. The din filled the street heralding the arrival of the enemy and Cazador's heart began to race. There hadn't been a single sign of aid from the castle in of Ard Allam or from Bobastro. It had been hours since he had dispatched Leonardo and now he fretted for his nephew's safety. He feared for him, almost as much as he feared for himself. Richard had brought a goddess to war. He'd felt her presence and her power like a cloud of depthless malice. The sky was darkened with a bank of cloud like a storm that rose and refused to break. She was a factor he couldn't account for. *Would she call fire from the sky? Conjure forth demons? Or would she take to the field and scythe them like hay? Was she the equal of this Gladr Odinsblood he would face or was she lesser? If Richard was her paladin, what power would he wield?* They were questions he had no answer to but steel, and so steel he would give them. Shaking off his worry he lifted his voice. "Let it be known that on this day, the oathsworn of Sir Cazador stood with the people of Ard Allam to defend against evil!" He roared. "Let it be known that the few stood against the many, the weak against the strong and by God and our ancestors we shall not flee! We shall not tremble! We will not break! **And we will be victorious**!" Cazador's voice rang like thunder and the cheer that rose up was an almighty thing that dwarfed the battle cry of the enemy.

Arrows and stones punished the enemy lines felling a hundred or more before they got within fifty yards of the barricade. Mounted men tumbled as their horses were shot from beneath them and behind them Cazador could see a column of oily black smoke. "Richard you dog! Fight me! I name you coward and traitor! I name you an honorless cur and demand you meet my blade!" Richard looked up to where Cazador stood on the makeshift wall. Warriors, ghul by their posture and arrow riddled bodies turned and stormed his position. Alkasaara fell like an avalanche sweeping aside a spear thrust and crushing a pothelmed head. He flicked away a sword thrust with his buckler and he chopped into his enemy's neck. The leather scale ventail parted and Cazador felt his axe bite flesh and separate bone and the head leaped free in a jet of black ghulish blood. The others fell to a flurry of furious blows from Maurice, Izan, Pedro and Pablo. "Come now Richard are you afraid to fight me?" Cazador screamed. A knight in the white and gold of the order stepped forward. "I will fight you scum! The Lord Commander shall not sully himself with the likes of you!" The man challenged. Cazador stared at his face something tickling at his memory and then it clicked. He had last seen this man when he'd been accused of banditry what felt like a lifetime ago. Cazador felt a smile tug at his lips. "Ah well now, Sir Soon Dead of Dullards Cunt show me your steel!" The man flushed. "I am Wigberto of Grimaud Knight of Our Lady of the Desert Fountain and I will piss on your corpse!" Cazador laughed. Turning to his comrades he sheathed his axe and said, "This won't take long." With a grin he jumped from the makeshift wall before anyone could stop him.

Life was not a troubadours tale. No space cleared for the two men to duel. Instead arrows and stones reached out to snatch lives and shatter bones as Cazador drew L'auxifar and met his enemy's charge with a high feint and a vicious underhand slash. He'd killed or maimed so many men with that cut he was confused when Wigberto skipped aside, nimble as a goat. Undeterred Cazador hammered at the Fountain knight with his buckler. His enemy cut, the blow coming far faster than it should, and angled his strike to catch his opponents arm before his sharp steal could find a home in his flesh. There was nothing he could do to stop the shield bash that sent him staggering ears ringing as though he'd met a horseman's charge. *What the devil is this shit!* Side burning with the makings of an epic bruise it was a miracle he retained his sword. Arrows and projectiles whipped through the air like a rain of doom and Cazador could feel death or maiming haunting his shadow. Du Grimaud was coming again and Cazador flailed like a rank amateur to ward him off. Wigberto du Grimaud cackled. "And I shall be victorious in my Lady's name!" His eyes gleamed like a madman's. "I'll use your mother's mouth as a chamber pot you Grimuadin cur!" Cazador spat.

Snarling his foe thrust and Cazador sidestepped, guiding rather resisting the immense force of the blow with his buckler. At the same time he punched L'auxifar into Wigberto du Grimaud's maille covered throat. The point bit, forcing itself between the maille links and into his throat. "Du Maurmont forever. Alfiere and victory." Cazador hissed freeing his blade with a savage twist and a gout of bright blood. His people roared and Cazador took a showman's bow. Du Grimaud still hadn't fallen and so Cazador helped him on his way with a thunderous blow from his buckler and sheathed his sword as is enemy's body hit the blood soaked street. He turned to trot back to his lines but his gris gris seemed to grab him by the throat he stumbled and the air was cleaved where his head was only a moment before.

Thanking God and his ancestors Cazador turned pulling Alkasaara from his belt. Du Grimaud was back on his feet the hole in his throat closing as his blood ran backwards into the wound. He thrust again, and Cazador punched the blow aside before swatting his rim at then dead man's face. Grimaud ate the blow rocking back a step mashed lips and broken teeth healing right before his eyes. Cazador felt a trickle of fear that turned to fury as he remember Richard healing. He stepped offline and clawed Du Grimaud's shield down with his buckler as he slammed his axe around from left to right hammering into the base of his foe's skull where it met spine. Bone caved beneath the force of the blow and du Grimaud fell bonelessly.

Two arrow studded ghul attacked. Cazador circled left and ,parried a spear thrust from the first with his axe, reversing the attack to lay a blow across his enemy's temple but the beast raised its shield and warded the blow. Growling with frustration Cazador hooked the ghul's shield and pulled the monster into the path of its comrade's scything axe. The blow caved in the back of the first ghul's helmet and heart racing Cazador swung with a rising blow before the ghul could recover. The poll of his axe smashed into its helmet with enough force to crumple the steel and break the neck beneath even if the steel spike had not done its work. Cazador shuffled back to the wall. His muscles burning and sweat running in rivers down his face and body stinging his eyes. Breathing was agony as his battered ribs protested each ragged gasp. Cazador could see Richard sheltered beneath a wall of shields beside a woman in golden armor sheltered by men at arms in blackened armor. She could be none other than The Lady they served or at least her mortal avatar.

She stared at Cazador boldly, a smile playing about her lips as if daring him to come. He could feel a strangeness that seemed to radiate from her the faint sensation of lapping water brushed against his senses. Arrows and rocks continued to fall the sounds of their impacts all around him and one by one corpses began to rise. Growling behind him made him spin. An enemy man at arms half his body pulped by a large dropped stone jabbed at him from one knee with a spear. Cazador jinked and struck, Alkasaara leaving a bloody crease in his attacker's helmet. Terror trilling in his heart Cazador began slamming his axe into the slowly reanimating corpses. For every one he destroyed, two would rise and lurch towards him. Batting away a sword slash Cazador trapped his foe's shield with his buckler and slammed it into a ghul's neck with vertebrae shattering force. Another thrust at him overhand with a spear, he blocked and snapped the monster's head back with a bash of his shield. Cutting low he shattered the freshly risen ghul's leg sending it to one knee, before reversing his stroke and stoving in the monster's helmet. Instincts screaming he turned to his left in time to deflect a sword thrust. Hacking with his axe he sent hand and sword to the ground. Cutting horizontally from left to right he tore aside the dead man's shield and Alkasaara rose and fell splitting the masked phrygian helmet at the weld to burst the skull like an egg. "Caz we are coming!" he heard Maurice shout. "No! Hold the fucking line that's an order!" He called as he shuffled back. His body desperately fighting the reality that he was about to be surrounded. Hundreds of the still viable dead rose. A slow turn showed him that he had little hope. Only the helmet smashing stones and arrows shot into the base of skulls had kept him alive. Cazador rotated his shoulder and twirled his axe desperately trying to loosen the stiffening muscles. *If I am to die here let me take at least four to ten more with me Lord.* Cazador prayed.

* * *

The Old Lion paced the outer gate barbican like a beardless boy before his first battle. He kept looking south, spirit troubled with grim tidings yet unspoken. Cazador's former Company of Saint Moses now the Company of the Leopard stood under a hastily painted banner with an impatient looking Leonardo at their head. His daughter by law snarled with barely coiled fury like a panther denied prey. The knights, men at arms and archers of her hundred strong retinue stood by their mounts like shamefaced schoolboys. She growled at them as if they were the reason her son was under attack. It was moments like that where she most reminded him of her mother. A good deal of his wisdom and guile had been the result of the precognition he needed to please his second wife. It was a decent distraction from his own frustration.

His kele-bolo of warriors from the Hapullar, Sonninke, and Papel tribes of the Sudan was mounted along with his two hundred man personal guard contingent from the Knights of Saint Attillo. He had sounded the assembly horn and the archers, men at arms, spearman, and almogovars of Bobastro were piling in. Some still shrugging on maille or buckling on swords and gambeson. A hundred La Compagnie knights and a thousand Du Maurmont infantry were marching around the lake to meet them. Altogether he had thirty five hundred fighters. They would be out numbered two to one but they would descend like the hammer to Cazador's anvil. If he would have had just a few hours more warning he could have pulled men from the surrounding towns and met the traitor on equal footing. Instead they would have a real fight on their hands. The fact that evil had entered his lands filled him with a cold anger that he longed to vent in steel. He could feel the malevolence of their foe like a great storm, a storm that had broke over Ard Allam.

* * *

Asmā looked at the section of the traitors army that she'd destroyed with deep satisfaction. Her trap had worked flawlessly. Enfiladed by arrows and projectiles their attackers had become literal fish in a barrel. Then came the fire and the air filled with the stink of charred metal, wood, and human flesh. Using catwalks of stout planks Asmā and her command worked their way across the rooves and balconies of Ard Allam. Despite their panicked charge to escape the flames the barricade held and it's defenders frantically dealt death to any enemy they could reach.

She saw Cazador atop the wall, axe blade flashing as he felled attackers. When he leapt from the barricade, her heart leapt into her mouth. Cursing him for his foolishness she watched horrified as he clashed with one of Richard the traitor's knights. Asmā had watched him fight often and for the first time since she had met him, Cazador seemed overmatched. She thought her heart would stop when his opponent bashed him aside like a toy with his shield, it was a miracle he kept his feet. As enemy knight closed in for the kill Asmā prepared to fire, but Cazador swept aside the man's thrust to punch his sword through the man's maille coif into his throat. Her heart soared with elation but it soon turned to horror as the man rose from a killing blow to attack Cazador again.

She felt the wrongness even before she understood what was happening. A pulse of energy shot along the street. A fortunately time stumble saved his life and Cazador put his foe down, but others rose in his stead. Asmā was already barking orders demanding her ranged troops to target the back of the neck, spine, or the eye. Frantically she poured shot after shot at any of the risen dead who made for Cazador. It was only when she got her grip on her panic did it occur to her. Ghul could only be subdued with a broken skull or spine, or fire. Asmā loosed a final bolt skewering a ghul through the base of its skull as it crept behind her captain. Dropping the crossbow she grabbed a wine bottle filled with pitch and lamp oil that was stoppered with a rag from her satchel. Using a nearby brazier she lit it and with a scream of rage hurled it in the midst of the black armored men protecting the gold armored woman. Barely pausing she retrieved another.

* * *

Cazador heard Asmā scream and watched in elation as the golden clad lady disappeared from view in a cloud of smoke and flame. An unearthly wail shook the street and the ghul staggered as suddenly drunk. Scores had already been set aflame by the eager defenders. Cazador threw himself forward, behind him he heard wood scrape against stone and the roar of familiar voices. He sheathed his axe and pulled free his mace. With a will he slung it battering heads and necks like a farmer cutting hay as he ploughed into the ranks of the risen dead. One moment he was alone in a sea of foes and the next familiar bulk filled his periphery as his brothers in arms fell in beside him and together they began cutting their way toward where Richard cowered with his remaining breathing warriors held a orderly withdrawal as his Lady was bustled away.

Together they pushed steadily forward. The ghul fought, but sluggishly with a lack of coordination that made them easy prey for the veteran killers. They only paused when a wave of crossbow bolts forced them the shelter behind their shields. Peeking over the rim of his buckler Cazador could see the second wave preparing to loose another wave of death only to be met by a wave of arrows and fiery projectiles. Cazador who had thought that he would die only moments earlier felt hope surge. Surrounded once again by his sword brothers anything was possible.

* * *

Without the blessing of the Lady Richard felt bereft. Here Sleepless Guard had dragged her away. Richard knew with the grievous injury Marwah had sustained the Lady's power had been diverted. With a curse Richard drew his sword. Most of his force had been destroyed between the fire trap and the tenacity of Ard Allam's defenders. At best he had a few hundred men. Many of those were cowering in the few dead end alleys that lined the long street. Without the Lady's blessing propping him up making him feel invincible Richard knew he had been a fool and led his force into a devastating trap. Hunkered beneath the shield house built by his men Richard knew the bitter taste in his mouth was defeat. *But losing a battle did not mean losing the war.* He saw Cazador advancing but he kept withdrawing unwilling to engage.

Risking a glance behind him Richard saw the Marwah or her guard had cleared the carts blocking the street. Fresh hope blooming in his chest he hurried onward leaving his column to retreat in good order. He had always been fast, even as a boy and he soon caught up with Marwah and her guard. Elation filled him. As long as he has his goddess and her avatar were secure, he could recruit and rebuild. The divine Marwah and her surviving guards had stopped in the field where the blasted deserter scum archers had butchered his force. As he approached he found her knife in hand sacrificing the wounded. With each flash of her blade he felt her blessing return growing stronger with each soul. Sensing his scrutiny for Marwah locked eyes with him and the voice of the Lady appeared in his mind. *We are bloodied but not beaten and far from done.* Richard nodded feeling his resolve return. He could feel the shift in her power as she began to cast once again.

* * *

Tired of chasing Richard and his fellow cravens Cazador had ordered the mounts brought forward. It was time to end this. They rode out of Ard Allam over the corpses of their would be conquerers. Altogether they were fifty-two having lost a dozen in the earlier fighting. Behind them came the archers almogovars and and spearman followed by the people of Ard Allam. They came armed with cudgels, knives, and slings, armored with nothing but determination. As they spilled out of the town Cazador could see Richards forces drawn up on the far side of the bridge. There was no stopping the feral grin that tugged at his lips. The traitor had slunk away with less than five hundred men. About a hundred crossbowman, eight score almogovars, two hundred men at arms, and twenty knights. His two hundred and fifty angry townsfolk gave him an edge.

Cazador led his force forward slowly. There was no reason to rush. He half expected Richard to bolt. As they drew within range he ordered a halt.

"Archers!" He roared and one hundred bows were raised. "Knock!" Tired fingers put arrows to bowstrings. "Draw!" Creaking filled the air. "Loose!" One hundred arrows leapt skyward sounding for all the world like birds taking flight. Arrows sliced into Richard's forces follows shortly by a hail of sling stones. "Fire at will!" Cazador barked and watched as death descended on his foes.

Richard's men had formed another shield house but bodies still fell. After a minute had passed Cazador raised raised Alkasaara and fifty one weapons were freed from scabbards or belt loops. They descended the slow at a fast walk arrows and sling stones casting shadows on the charging force. "For God and glory! For Alfiere and victory! For Ard Allam!" Cazador bellowed as he formed the point of a three rider wedge. He knew they were a sight to stir the blood. He and his mensie in blood spattered black maille, the men of Le Cannet Des Maures behind them their argent and purpure surcoats nearly indistiguishable for the blood and gore, but their weapons glittered in the late evening sun. Arrows and sling stones arched over them punishing the enemy shield house. Elation and satisfaction banished his exhaustion and his horse devoured the space between Cazador and his targets. Standing in the stirrups he cut low with his axe bashing a shield bearer onto his backside. Bringing Alkasaara around he slammed it into the base of another warrior's neck as he forced his horse into the gap he'd created. Cutting across his body he laid his axe into a helmet with enough force that blood shot through the broken steel. A second ranker stabbed at Cazador's inner thigh he blocked with his buckler pushing the blow wide as he trampled his assailant. Suddenly the pressure against him disappeared as the traitors men turned to run. Cazador smiled a hunter's smile as they bolted like rabbits, Richard's scrawny legs carrying him farther and faster than everyone else.

Panic was a funny thing. A wise man could become a fool in it's grip and he could only shake his head in wonder as the foe broke and ran leaving the cover of the bridge for the dubious safety of the corpse strewn field. Bodies littered the ground from the first engagement making footing treacherous for man and beast. Allowing his mount to pick it's way through Cazador and the other riders struck at the backs of the fleeing enemy. It seemed right that the battle should end where it began. Cazador raised his axe to strike again when his horse whinnied rearing suddenly. The spear that erupted from his horses back nearly impaled him as he fell back and out of the saddle. His helmeted head stuck something harder than dirt and his vision darkened with stars and his ears rang and instant nausea bubbled in his guts. All around him shapes were moving rising from the ground emitting a low growl that had become all too familiar. Horses and men were screaming and Cazador's muddled mind failed to make sense of the scene unfolding around him. Mud slathered bodies were attacking his riders, those with weapons lashing out gutting horses, pausing briefly to gorge themselves on the steaming offal before throwing themselves at the dazed riders. Cazador tried and failed to rise, his body refusing to respond to his commands. A mud slathered shape moved towards him it's body riddled with broken arrows, drunkenly swinging it's sword. Terror like nothing he'd ever felt filled him. His body still sluggish and unresponsive refused to move. *Here dies Cazador Alfiere son of William, Son of Leon Knight of Saint Attillo. Stormer of Byzantium, Hammer of Grimaud, and Defender of Ard Allam.* He thought as the notched blade descended to claim his life. His mind flitted to Asmā and Cazador found himself unwilling to die.

Fighting the numbness with all his worth Cazador managed to roll sideways and the ghul's sword bit dirt. The creature snarled but Cazador's scrambling fingers found Alkasaara's haft as it pulled back for another strike. Swinging his axe he hooked the ghul's leg with its head and pulled, using the attack to pull himself up to a kneeling position as his enemy hit the ground. *Can't do that with a sword.* He thought as he rose and smashed the beast's face like a ripe melon. Looking up everything was chaos. His tightly packed formation of riders was shattered and Richard's fleeing men had turned and had gone from prey to predator. Behind them the infantry and arms townsfolk struggled against monsters from nightmare and myth. The air was filled with the crash of weapons and the screams of the dying. Cazador felt victory dragged ever further away with each of his fighters felled.

With a roar he lay about him with his axe. Rage pounded in his heart and the bitter taste of defeat filled his mouth like vomit. He'd gathered his black clad mensie and what remained of his men at arms and they carved a path to their infantry. They had formed a fighting circle that shrank like an apple being bit from all sides. The bridge might as well been on the other side of the ocean for all they could get to it. Cazador fought his enemy and fought despair. He planted Alkasaara in a reanimated woodwose's face cleaving through the nose bone and and eye socket in a mist of blood. His face was a mask of the stuff with the exception of the band of the nasal and the ragged tracks cut by the bitter tears. Maurice fighting beside him took a blow to the hip from a club and went down. Screaming with rage Cazador chopped his axe into the monster's neck, but was too slow to block the thrust that battered his ribs punching into the maille and only stopped when it his the aketon beneath. Although his armor held fire spread making breathing agony. Cazador fell to one knee vision darkening as he struggled to get his wind. Blows rattled from his buckler as he desperately protected his head. With a grunt he lopped off his attackers foot at the ankle and rose slamming his axe down to mangle his foe's helmet. A reanimated knight slashed at Cazador with his axe. Cazador got us shield up but the block was weak and the axe blow driven by undead hands was strong. It bit into his helmet creasing the steel and gashing his head. Reeling Cazador lashed out wildly taking the ghul in the neck with shattering force born of fear and desperation. There was no hope, no exit plan. Only fury and the desire to kill as many as he could.

Cazador heard the rumble of thunder in the distance and assumed that God Almighty was about to vent his displeasure at the days events with a storm. The sky darkened with a hiss and the three horn blasts that sounded in the distance were so familiar that Cazador dismissed it as the product of his overtaxed mind and imagination. He heard the thud of arrows but his vision had tunneled and all he could see was the enemy in front of him. He blocked the ghul's strike but before he could strike back the monsters unhelmeted head exploded as a lance punched through it. Stumbling back in confusion his brain struggled to comprehend what was happening as a rider bearing the Du Maurmont clan banner and his grandfather's arms from a blood splattered lance swept past him followed by a wall of armored horse flesh and weapon bearing men. Cazador turned to see riders streaming from the north west parting around his beleaguered formation like the tide surging around a rock. Laughter tinged with madness bubbled up from his chest. His kin had come.

* * *

Leon Alfiere had lowered his lance took his grandson's attacker like an eagle sweeping down on a vole. The look of shock on Cazador's face was priceless and the Old Lion laught for the joy of battle and realization his grandson lived. Passing his lance to his squire Leon Alfiere drew his Boa sword it's hones edge like his flowing coat of mail was burnished gold by the late evening sun. He let it sing through the air taking the head from an undead woodwose,before reaching across his body to plant its point in the eye of another. There was joy in righteous battle and he gloried in it. Elation trilled and danced with the anger in his blood.

There was no sign of Omar's column nor the Knights of Saint Attillo who were to join him. Absent also were the banners of the Emir of Ard Allam. Mixed in with his grandson and his men were roughly armed peasants showing that Cazador had rallied the town olif not it's leader. He could feel his ancestors fury rise with his own. It reinforced the need for the empire to face the threats to come. The stink of necromancy hung in the air like smoke. Whatever *deva* or being of power unworthy of worship Richard served was strong enough to have kissed false godhead with full lips. The ghul she had raised fought with rabid ferocity but they were no match for du Maurmont fury. He had expected thousands of foes and there were less than eight hundred. Whatever had transpired here was a bloodletting for the ages. Like a stampeding herd the enemy turned to flee. *Completely unacceptable.* The Old Lion thought reaching for his manna opening a channel to the beings of fire and called it down on his foes. Great comets of flame erupted to life in the sky and rained down on the traitors forces like the wrath of an angry angel.

The fleetest of the the foeman burned except for those sheltered by a dome of pure crystalline manna. The rest were mowed down by the cavalry or cut down by the infantry. Young Leonardo led the charge only a few horse lengths behind his great father. Hours of waiting for a battle that concluded in a masterstroke of violence that took mere moments. Detailing the Knights of Saint Attillo to chase down the fugitives he turned his mount to the blood spattered hero that was his grandson Cazador. He had been seated in the grass but when he saw him approaching Cazador stood slowly. "You know if you wanted to impress me grandson, all you had to do was get me a new bull or perhaps a belt. This looks rather like showing off." Cazador rolled his eyes but couldn't suppress a tired laugh. Leon's old axe was glued to his grandson's hand with dried blood and he had the look of exhausted elation native to victors of hard won battles from time immemorial. "I see men of Le Cannet Des Maures far from home!" He called to the men in the grimy argent and purpure quartered tabards. "Si Don Leon, we came to serve our true born lord. As you can see. Service to the usurper did not suit us.

The Old Lion gazed at Ard Allam, noticing that smoke only came from a single street. Heart filling to near bursting with pride he said, "You've done done well Caz. Better than well. You are a true knight and apparently you fight like a demon." Cazador's smile broadened as he inclined his head. "Three actually." He replied with typical Alfiere cheek. It was the Old Lion's turn to laugh. "Just so boy just so. Now tell me where are you hiding Omar?" The post battle euphoria had banished his earlier foreboding but the look on his grandchild's face brought it crashing back. "I figured he would be riding beside you." Cazador said a haunted look creeping into his eyes. Leon put his hand on the young knights shoulder and squeezed. "Fear not your cousin would never abandon you. The high trails are easily blocked by rock slides and who knows what mischief may have delayed him." Cazador nodded stiffly.

He looked as if he was about to speak when his mother appeared. "Looks like you did well son, but why are you on foot like a peasant?" Leon watched a familiar sigh escape his grandson's lips. "A ghul hiding in the mud gutted my horse and nearly me during the ambush mother. It's good to see you well." Cazador said mildly. Linda sniffed. "Its good to see your reckless and rebellious ways haven't gotten you killed." His daughter by law said falling into the ruts of a well worn argument. The Old Lion could hear Caz's hand tighten on his axe haft, see the fury and the hurt in his eyes. He knew Linda loved her son and Cazador his mother yet they were too much alike in the wrong ways. She tried to keep him behind her skirt and her son had fought to escape from it since he was four years old. Linda had wanted her son to be a great scholar or engineer. Cazador simply wanted to remain true to himself and still have his mother be pleased with him. The two had never forgiven each other for it. She was a hammer and Cazador was meant to stand out. Neither could help who they were. "Still you did a good thing protecting these people. I'm proud of you son." Cazador bowed slightly at the complement, but the Old Lion could see it was too little too late. "If you will excuse me honored mother and grandfather...I must find myself a horse and see to my people."

Linda made to say something else but Leon caught her eye with a hard look and she watched him go. "Papa Hamza," She began but he held up a hand to forestall her. "My son would leave without even embracing me." She said with a crackling anger. He has always found it odd how it was said men had no capacity for their emotions but more often than not it was the women in his life that hid tender feelings behind stony expressions and sharp tongues. "Perhaps you shouldn't have rebuked him. Do not miss the greatness of your child in demand of perfection." He cast his hand around. "Many mothers will mourn sons this day. You could be among them and yet you are not." Her glare was furious but she had the grace to flush behind her freckles. "Omar's column never made it here and I cannot find his manna. Your son's victory here will be as nothing before the pain of such a loss. He will need the support of his family. We will all need each other in the days to come. War like we have never known is upon us and battles like the one here will be as nothing. We must stand firm. We must stand together, and to do so we must not cut each other in words or deeds." Linda nodded. In the distance they could see that Cazador had reunited with his company and found himself a mount. They had already crossed the bridge and were working their way into the town with crowd of Ard Allam's surviving native defenders behind them. He put his heels to his horses flanks. This he would not miss.

* * *

The gates of Ard Allam Castle were predictably shut to them. Archers poked their heads over the crenels peering shamefaced at the men and women who has defended their town while they had hid safely. Cazador was tired. His bones and tendons ached so much he could almost hear his ligaments screaming He could have called forward Bayan and the sappers, but now he understood what Diallo could do. "Djail, would you be so kind as to unbar these doors?" His comrade nodded riding forward a bit and freed a drum from his saddle and began to sing and play. Cazador could feel the energy building like pressure in his chest. If he relaxed his vision just right he could almost see Nyama being drawn to Diallo like iron filings to a lodestone. With a great thump of his drum and a shout the doors burst open in a shower of splinters. Archers were blown away from their posts like leaves in an Autumn storm.

He could feel his warparty gape in confusion behind him but Cazador could only smile as he drew L'auxifar. "For the people of Ard Allam! For Alfiere and victory!" He screamed as he spurred his horse through the wreckage of the gate. A spearman rushed him and he chopped at the spear forcing it down and punched his sword into his attacker's face. Beside him his squire barged a man to the ground with his mount and punched his slim headed spear into the man at arms throat. N'faly of Gao sprayed arrows while Abdul Al Daza killed one man with his lance driving it deep into his body where he abandoned it reaching instead for a throwing knife which left his hand with an angry hum to slam into a bowman's face.

Cazador took in the carnage. The efficiency of his warriors made his heart swell but it was wasted, as was the courage of the castle's defenders. Suddenly he could take no more. "Enough!" Cazador roared. Tired though he was his voice rang from the walls of the courtyard. "Why die for a lord that would not ride down the a hill to protect his home? Why die for a man who made you cowards? Surrender and live." Cazador shouted voice hoarse and trembling with emotion. First a sword clattered to the ground. Then a spear, followed by bows and axes. One by one the defenders of Ard Allam castle threw down their arms and knelt. "What is the meaning of this?" The emir hissed. "You would let yourselves be cowed by this... this... Haratin this descendent of Abid!" He crowed voice shrill with anger as he rushed from his keep behind a flock of guards. Silence filled the air as if even his own men knew he tread on the most dangerous of ground with words that could never be unspoken. Eyebrows climbed foreheads as eyes widened. When the new arrivals saw the blood spattered conquerors and their surrendered comrades they parted before their emir's tirade. Naming Cazador as the descendant of slaves had guaranteed he wouldn't survive this.

Cazador dismounted and stalked towards the emir. The blood trailing from his cut head trickled across his face giving Cazador a savage cast. The older man looked down at the young knight with a sneer of disdain, a look that slowly faded to one of horror as Cazador's deliberate measured steps became a shambling run. The old emir was a warrior and managed to thrust at Cazador who swept the blow aside cutting from high to low with the blistering speed. The emir got his shield down in time to stop Cazador from taking or breaking his leg but couldn't stop the rim of his opponent's shield from crashing into his face. This time Cazador's backhand cut landed. He felt L'auxifar shiver as his weapon already coming around descended from high to low crashing into the emir's neck and collarbone with a snap that echoed across the courtyard. Pivoting he twirled his blade and stabbed it into the emir's gaping mouth. With a savage twist Cazador tore his blade free.

The courtyard was silent except for the sound of Cazador's ragged breathing.

He stared belligerently at the dead emir's guards. "Does anyone else want to die for this sleekit piece of shit?" He asked cocking his head sideways like a curious gull. Even his own knights refused to meet his eye and the mad glint that danced there. Silence. Part of him was disappointed. Pushed past exhaustion something feral stood altogether too close to the surface. He felt a sneer tug at his lips and a growl build in the back of his throat. "Who here disputes my right to rule Ard Allam and the lands thereof?" *Speak, I dare you and may God Almighty dispatch an angel to save you from me.* He challenged with his eyes, with his posture, and the quiet menace of the blood dripping from his sword. The Old Lion stepped forward his maille shining like red gold in the sunset the jangle of his harness loud as a church bell in the stillness. The Old Lion met his eye and smiled something indicipherable dancing in his steady gaze. "All hail Sir Cazador Knight of Saint Attillo *emir* of Ard Allam!" The roar shook the castle as a wild cheer rose to the sky. Cazador strode in the keep with Asmā on his arm and his mensie around him. They crossed the garden where he had struck the impudent vizier and into a stately hall where a large chair of dark mahogany inlaid with gold filagree sat upon a raised dais. Cazador sat slowly, adulation filling his ears.

Chapter 25: Lord and Commander

Twilight had fallen and the purple shot clouds that filled the sky over Middleham disguised the Ruhk and their burden. He hadn't wanted to make war on humans but knew it was inevitable. Their world as a battlefield after all. The market town and eponymous castle were a scant eleven miles from Oddmire. Too close for comfort. Scouts from the castle had been poking around. It was only a matter of time before they spied the unfamiliar fortifications and raised an army. As Legatus of the Seelie Court Oberon had been given precious little oversight and zero direction from on high, which meant noone had told him he couldn't do what he was about to do. Fier and a hundred of his spear hounds were on standby along with King Aeryr who had brought fifty fae heavy cavalry and fifty archers to support Oberon's gambit. They waited a few hundred yards away, Fier's men beyond the east gate and ditch with King Aeryr's all cloaked in manna to hide their presence. All that was left was for him to give the signal.

Putting his foot on the rail Oberon drew his mace and summoned his manna. He imbued his body with the energy until he glowed like a star. He'd told Fier and Aeryr they would know the signal when they saw it. *Hopefully this wouldn't be too subtle.* Pumping his weapon filled fist in the air Oberon turned to his Agema. Twenty three sets of eyes stared back expectantly. "For El and the Seelie Court!" He barked before launching himself over the side of the sky boat like he was diving into the ocean. Moments later Minerva, Farheed and the rest of his agema followed. He fell like a bolt of gold lightening from the purple sky. When only a few hundred feet separated him from the battlements of the castle he drew on his manna once again. The humans guardsman in his shirt of iron links looked up face twisted in an O of suprise. Oberon hit the walkway of the south east tower with the sound like a marching drum. He used his manna to transmit the shock of his fall into a wave of force, energy shot like gleaming smoke to race around the castle walls. The gawping guard and his compatriots were helpless as their bodies were flung from the parapets like screaming rag dolls. Oberon had been trying to keep a low profile, masking his manna, reluctant to tip off the Odinsblood to his presence or power. But tonight he needed to send a message. For too long the Children of Samyaza had been thought mere myth and tale, but now humanity would learn how real the first born children of El were.

Other glowing forms alighted on the walls but Oberon was already moving along the wall for the east gate. Everything was chaos, but the human warriors were rallying and they had to move quickly. Oberon leapt into the courtyard below and was immediately charged by a human swordsman. He could feel the toxic steel like the heat from a torch as it swept towards him in an arc of death. Leaning away like a stalk bending in the wind Oberon let it pass him, before swaying back whipping his weapon around to batter the human's brain inside his helmet as his body pitched sideways. Another human charged with a spear and he sent a pulse of manna at the shaft to push it aside as he sent his mace against the steel of the man's maille standard feeling the shock of his foe's crushed throat.

Oberon shoved the corpse aside and ran for the gate. But a line of humans stood before him iron burning in the night air. Most humans could do no more with manna than a chicken couldn't with an axe. But what they had was manna draining iron, flesh corrupting, soil poisoning iron. It weakened spells, sapped strength, and destabilized channels. Even human magi avoided it when they could. There was one thing it couldn't thwart however. Tapping his reservoir of manna once again he created a channel to Baraqiel focusing on the iron clad killers, their weapons and the iron nails in the gate behind them. "In the name of El, Lord of Hosts God of Adam, I Oberon Legatus of the the

Seelie Court, King of Penume's Reach purge you with holy fire!" Lightning green as summer leaves and forked from the sky blowing the gate apart in a cloud of killing shards. The humans cooked in their armor were thrown in twitching glowing heaps. The air stank of ozone, scorched leather, and the cooked pig scent of too hot man.

Beyond the shattered gate the yellow gold eyes of direwolves and the grey green glint of moose eyes glimmered in the dark. There was a grunted commands and the host of King Aeryr poured into the castle followed by Fier's cynocephali unleashing unearthly howls that chilled the blood. The humans came with fire and steel but it was too late. The fae heavy cavalry lowered their lances as they crashed through the gate and plowed into the human lines who had targeted Oberon's agema holding the east gate. For a moment he pitied the humans. To face down a charge of fae heavy cavalry was uniquely terrifying. It was over in minutes. The fae archers met their human counterparts at the arrow loops while the fae chivalry unleashed their mounts upon their targets. Dire wolves selectively bred for eons to be the size of ponies snapped off arms and legs or crushed heads in powerful jaws. War moose tossed men aside sending bodies to crunch against the walls of the stronghold. None was more terrible than the king. Aeryr rode a cave bear fitted for war in bronze scale armor. It's forepaws reinforced with gauntlets tore a hole in the human lines wide enough to drive a wagon through. Aeryr lay about him a stone axe as his bear bit the head from a charging horse. The knight deprived of half his mount tried to stab the fae king who laughed as he slapped aside the spear blow and buried his axe in the rider's head. The humans broke, and died.

Two days later Oberon sat in a sky boat observing the timber built Potto Castle. It's motte was vaguely square and measured some two hundred feet by one hundred and sixty feet. The whole structure was surrounded by a dry ditch sixty feet wide and almost twelve feet deep. A strong place that could be improved upon. He needed to capture it if he was going to push east to the sea. He had scouted a half dozen or more such places each essential to the defensive network he had planned. The humans might not thank him for it now, but when his wall of castles and marching forts stretched across the neck of northern Albion and stopped the armies of the Odinsblood from destroying the breadbasket of the country they would thank him soon enough. But for now the human lords had rallied their troops and squatted in their castles like chiggers Oberon must root out of the flesh of the land. Already rumors abounded at what has befallen Middleham and Jervaulx Abbey. The curious monks wanting to know about the battle and the beings of light had been worth a taxiarch of fighters. Oberon smiled. He had never felt so much manna in his life.

* * *

Sunlight filtered through the high stained glass windows of Bobastro's church dappling the mourners with vibrant color. The priest a wizened Nubian droned on. He had called back Omar's soul thrice. An echo of their family's service to ancient Rome but his kinsmans chest failed to rise. After that the Hero of Ard Allam heard nothing. Cazador sat with the black bladed sword across his knees as he presided over the funeral of his cousin. As Omar's heir it was part of his inheritance along with the hundred survivors of his company, a sizable pile of coins, and a handful of estates in Nubia, and the Holy Land. Sadness festered in his mind like a sore tooth radiating pain that threatened to overwhelm him. Cazador would gladly have never had it at all, he just wanted his cousin back. Omar had died a warrior's death fighting monstrous ogre like a hero in a chanson. It didn't feel real. Couldn't feel real. His brave cousin was dead and the world was wrong.

Cazador was a warrior and understood that death was a part of life and an integral part of his chosen trade. He had lost comrades and kin and mourned them. He had been to more funerals than birthday celebration. But nothing could prepare the mind for what it had never imagined. Cazador had never imagined a world without his cousin. Already letters had gone to the Pope of Omar the Ogre slayer the man people were already calling a saint for his brave deeds against evil. It was fitting for the man who had taught Cazador to believe in himself. To think big and dream bigger. His cousin looked like a king rather than a just a knight swathed in indigo silk jazerant from Algiers stitched with silver talismans. An arming sword and a beautifulfully inlaid bow with a full quiver rested with him. The people of Bobastro and the surrounding towns turned out and lined the road as Omar's djali Seydina sang praise songs in Arabic. They carried his body in state to the chapel of the Order of Saint Elesbaan where he was interred to join his revered ancestors in a place of high honor.

Only the sadness of Omar's mother and brother eclipsed his own. The lady Taealaa was a picture of dignity and strength and Cazador bowed low to her. Omar's brother Musa's usual smile was absent, his eyes broken as he and Cazador embraced. Together they stood honored in grief. It was a send off worthy of a hero but Cazador could shake feeling as though he had somehow failed. *If only I had been more patient. More responsible. If I had only stayed in Bobastro. Omar would yet live.* There were a million things he wished he would have said or done. Things that had been so important now seemed hollow. Cazador had won a great victory but he couldn't shake the feeling that he had lost. Asmā caught his hand. The sinking spiral of his thoughts stilled. "Your cousin would be proud of you. Proud of what you have done. The few stood against the many and triumphed. Omar gave his life fighting a foe so you would not have to. Don't dishonor him." She whispered fiercely. Cazador turned wondering how she could possibly read his thoughts, but when her intense green gaze caught his own he felt his soul laid bare. It was terrifying yet oddly peaceful. Unable to find any words he squeezed her hand back and held it the entire ride back to Bobastro.

* * *

Pulling the company together for the journey to England had proved a welcome distraction. After a small ceremony retiring the colors of the Company of Saint

Moses to a trophy wall in the main hall of Ard Allam Castle they'd donned their new colors. He had commissioned blackened maille, gambeson, heavy canvas chausses , round topped bar nasals helmets with torses in black and gold, and tabards in the company arms for each man and woman under his banner. Asmā's prediction of looking resplendent in gold and black holding true. The company had grown to a roll of one thousand and ninety two with the addition of forty Knights of Saint Attillo, survivors of the column that had been ambushed by the ogres. They had fled the field arriving at Bobastro too late to deliver a warning. Disgraced they had been stripped of their status and would now ride as paid men with Cazador. His aunt and grandfather had also detached two hundred men to flesh out his ranks with forty more knights bachelor, sixty men at arms, three vintenaries of almogovars, and two of crossbowman. With the eleven score survivors of the men of Le Cannet Des Maures, the nine score of the original company and two hundred and sixty five recruits from the towns around Malaga the Company of the Leopard was more than five times the size of the Company of Saint Moses. He now commanded an army of ninety two knights, one hundred and forty six men at arms, two hundred spearman, one hundred eighty six almogovars, one hundred and forty crossbowmen, one hundred and twenty archers, one hundred cataphracts, sixty sappers, forty armed pages and eight squires. They made a brave show on their march to Marbal'la.

He could see the ocean winking like a jewel as they descended from the Mountains of the Snow, it was a stirring sight. Word of the fight against Richard had already reached the folk of surrounding towns. They came out to see the hero, the kaffir knight who had defended Ard Allam Although his body was a mass of bruises and pain racked his body from his neck to his toes, Cazador straightened under the gaze of the people as they rode through Monda and wound their way to Hoxán. Their gold and black tabards and horse barding shimmered strikingly against the white washed buildings of the ancient towns. Diallo sang of his deeds in Maghrebi Arabic burnishing his reputation amongst the descendents of the people who had once rebelled with Ibn Halfsun. A famous name counted for much whether you be a man at arms, a knight or a mercenary.

They continued on to their destination aiming to enter through the Ronda gate. Marbal'la was a grand old walled town built around a castle as old as the Phonecians. From the hills above the town the harbor had been in full view. His grandfather and aunt had lent him part of the fleet of La Compagnie and the Du Maurmont clan. The largest ships were shows bigger than crusader cogs and equipped with oarboxes. They housed thirty sailors, one hundred and eighty passengers with berths in the triple tiered aft castles and a total of forty horses could be stabled in the hold. Ten of the great ships waited at anchor bobbing gently on the jeweled surface of the ocean just beyond the harbor bows to the beach. Alberto whistled. "The riverboat we took was a good size, but it's naught but a turd of one of those monsters." Cazador could only nod. The side rails were studded with Seljuk panjagans that could throw five arrows at a time while the ships castles were armed with three springalds each. With a draft of only five feet they were cargo haulers and pirate hunters, the backbone of the Du Maurmont clan's over seas trade. Each bore the clan arms proudly on each sail. Beside them was a squadron of oar supplemented mtepi that would carry them and their gear where the large dhow could not reach.

Cazador led his company to the beach where the ships waited. Ramps leaned from the bows leading directly to the horse holds. Once his mount was stowed safely Cazador made his way to the aft castle where he climbed the stairs to the top floor of the superstructure divided into four rooms for the captain and high status passengers. Cazador had no question as to which chamber was his, his arms were painted on the door. Inside he found the room done in his colors with a desk, a plush bed a weapons rack, an armor stand, a chest of draws, a wash table with soaps and mirror of polished steel. Much to his delight beside the desk lay a bookshelf. Yvain, also called The Knight with the Lion by de Troyes. The History of the Kings of Britain by Monmouth. An Arabic translation of The Mabinogion. The Poema de Mío Cid and Rubáiyát of Omar Khayyám. There was also a copy of the Shahnameh, the Persian book of kings.

As much as he hated the very idea of going to England, Cazador was looking forward to the trip. If nothing else it would be a chance to rest, heal, and mourn. He would have anywhere from eight days to a fortnight of nothing more strenuous than light practice and reading. His body had taken a beating and his forehead pounded and itched where a blade had found its way through cutting the rim of his helmet and his skull beyond. He traced his fingertips from his scalp cut to his temple knowing it was only grace that saved him. Grace that had saved them all. What new challenges awaited them in England he could only guess but .Cazador divested himself of his armor and weapons washed himself. He was standing in nothing but fresh braes when his door swung open to admit Asmā. From the look in her eyes Cazador was forced to admit that there would likely be far less reading than he anticipated.

* * *

The mouth of the Thames was so wide it took Cazador time to realize they were no longer on the ocean. His ship the *Raed* now escorted by two English patrol craft. They had been respectfully intercepted passing the great port of Plymouth and told that they had been given orders to escort the Moorish captain to the kings agents in London. Their hosts had seemed equal parts nervous and excited at the sudden arrival of over a thousand men. It was only belatedly that he had realized that that ten warships and a thousand soldiers looked every inch the invasion. Therefore it was with the rest of the company waiting at anchor that they sailed into London. Malaga, Marbal'la, Seville, Quadiz, were all big cities. They were dwarfed by the sheer size and grandeur of Byzantium, but nothing could have prepared him for the crazed warren of timber, thatch, wattle and daub and stone that was London. He had only taken the knights of his mensie, Diallo, Asmā his squire Marco and a dozen pages. They were met by an extremely well dressed knight wearing a rich blue silk surcoat embroided with golden lions rampant that matched his hose and shirt. He seemed to dwarf his horse much the same way Alcazar did evidencing his great height as did the sword he bore. It seemed ridiculously long to Cazador, though dangling from his waist it fit the tall man well. Dismounting he introduced himself as Guillaume Espada Longa, William Longespée and his half brother Ralph Bigod. Cazador fought down a shock of fear. Now that he had a face to put to the name he knew that this man was King John's war leader and half brother. Named for the second duke of Normandy. Cazador had fought under his command against the Capetians and since then he had studiously avoided both England and the Plantangenets for years. Yet here he was standing in the streets of London with one and about to swear an oath to another. He began to wonder what his grandfather was playing at by sending Cazador of all people here.

Summoning a smile he bowed slightly. Many other places this man would be called prince, but he was bastard born and here in England he was merely Lord Salisbury. "I am Sir Cazador, lord of Ard Allam, Knight of Saint Attillo, and heir to the knights fee of Moorhouse." Longespée smiled. "Of course you are." Catching the glint of humor that told of a sharp wit and mayhaps a devilish sense of humor. Cazador made introductions for the others beaming with delight as the Englishman worked out lady Asmā was a knight in her own right. Although he couldn't quite shake the look of wonder Longespée recovered well. "Welcome to London where it *always* smells wonderful!" He continued. Longespée had a long bluff face that was currently split by a genuine smile wisps of the dark red hair shared by King Henry's sons peeking from under his maille coif. Gesturing like a chamberlain the Earl of Salisbury led them deeper into London.

People gave way as they passed knowing nobility when they saw it, even when it was as foreign as Cazador and his retinue. Dressed in a cloth of gold jazerant stitched with black leopards with his head covered by a blackened maille hood and tied with a gold and black torse. The rest of his party wore the livery of the company. They made a bold show even among the riot of color that was London. Every few pages it seemed they came across a blackfriar, or a brownfriar. "A man can't walk ten steps without being blessed or shriven, surely all of London will find themselves in heaven." Cazador muttered bemused. Longespée clapped a buckler sized hand to Cazador's shoulder and laughed heartily. He led them to a renter of horses and proceeded to lead them through the city. As the rode Cazador counted no less than ten large churches and enough men in monkish robes to make him think he had somehow ended up in Outremer. After the first score he had given up counting the smaller churches. As they walked their mounts Cazador could see the scars from the great fire that had struck earlier in the summer. The scent of burning lingered in the air along with he smells of fresh cut wood, sewage, river mud, and the fuge of thousands of people and animals living together in close confines. Longespée led them across London, and out through the Moor Gate, so named for the open heathland where they turned west toward Windsor.

It was late afternoon by the time they approached Windsor Castle. It was laid out it three wards. The middle ward was dominated by a great drum tower on top of a large hill flanked by upper and lower wards. Cazador who had spent his life around castles grunted. "Wouldn't you be a bitch to take." Longespée chuckled. "That's why the Conqueror built it." Despite himself Cazador was warming to the Earl of Salisbury. Tall men usually carried a grating arrogance but Longespée's easy humor and quick smile made his good company and his eyes held no guile. While their dark skin hadn't caused much stir in cosmopolitian London, now, curious eyes seemed to follow them everywhere at the castle. If Longespée noticed, he hid it well or simply ignored it as he busied himself relating stories of his childhood and recent campaigns as he led Cazador and his retinue to the hall in the upper ward. His friendly banter enough to distract Cazador from his worries.

Cazador was less impressed by the interior of the fortification. While as a defensive structure it was a masterpiece, as a residence it was somewhat lacking seeming rustic and drab compared to rich decoration and refinement of Al Andalus or Provence. To Miramollin or the caliphs in Baghdad this was a roomy stable. After they entered royal knights or men at arms divested them of arms and they were promptly announced by Sir Warin fitzGerold the king's chamberlain. It wasn't long before they were brought into the royal presence.

King John sported his dark red hair fashionably, cut and curled below the ear. He was shorter than Cazador but had been blessed with the broad chest of a wrestler. Fairly incardinated with a red silk over tunic and hose accented by gold slippers and cloak. Cazador bowed. "Your majesty does a humble knight too much honor. Your nation is beautiful and prosperous and it will be my honor to serve." Cazador murmured respectfully. Inwardly he wondered why the king of England was meeting with a mere knight and mercenary. Descended from ancient kings an from a respected family he might be, but socially Cazador was so far beneath King John that he should never be noticed. His host inclined his head his expression thoughtful. King John had a reputation for pettiness, treachery, lechery, and cowardice. Cazador knew how big lies from small men could tarnish a reputation, but under the scrutiny of King John he felt distinctly unsafe. *How much better for England would it have been for Longespée to have been born on the proper side of the blanket.* He thought. After what seemed like an eternity the king smiled crookedly but without humor. "I asked the Old Lion for a soldier and a warrior and he sends me a poet and a courtier instead." Cazador smiled cooly. The pasty bastard could think as he liked. No man could ever say *he* ran from a fight. "Perhaps we've gotten two for the price of one milord." Longespée supplied and the king laughed aloud.

John looked at Cazador again, appraising him. "I understand that you lead a company of men over a thousand strong?" The king questioned. Cazador nodded. "His majesty is indeed correct." King John nodded sagely "I will be transparent with you Sir Cazador. Your fief Moorhouse to the north, as does a huge threat to the Kingdom of England. Norse Irish pirates raid our northern coasts, the Scots have trouble brewing, and even the Aos Sí have risen against us and taken eight castles." John fixed Cazador with a glare as if he were personally responsible. "I cannot risk them allying with the

Scots or emboldening the Welsh. There is witchcraft and dark magic afoot and creatures of myth stalk my land. Raiders come with tidings of demon worship. I cannot stand aside. I am putting together an army under Longespée to counter the threat. To that effect your forty days of service shall be spent under his command. I will hire your Company of the Leopard at...." King John waved his hand and fitzGerold also the royal exhequer began. "Pay begins at two shilling a day for knights. One shilling a day for squires and men at arms. Six deniers a day for ranged soldiers, spearmen, and other foot soldiers. After your forty days you would be due six shillings daily as captain." Sir Warin met his eyes with a tired smile as if to say it was the best he could do.

Cazador bowed with a small smile. "More than sufficient, thank you your majesty." John did not look impressed. He snapped his fingers again and servants appeared with a table. "Show him Longespée." The Earl of Salisbury nodded and Cazador joined him at the table where hide map of England lay pinned to the board. He laid a long meaty finger on the map. "You lot will continue north along the east coast and land here at Mydilsburgh." Longespée murmured. "The town is enemy hands the residents either killed, dispossesed, or sided with the Aos Sí. Take it and proceed west The Lord of Annandale William De Brus and the Prince Bishop of Durham have been amassing troops and will be in position to support you from the north. From the west will be the forces of Lancaster and Manchester. Other forces be moving north from here by ship. They will march overland to the Ouse and take a cog up the coast to follow in your footsteps." Cazador nodded. "And where will you be my lord?" Longespée smiled. "I travel with you, we have a fleet ready to sail." Cazador clapped his hands together smiling broadly. "Excellent when do we sail!" He didn't have to feign eagerness, he wanted away from King John. Cazador was happy enough that the English were taking the threat seriously and he didn't have to beg for support.

Sir Warin and Longespée shared a look. "I see your grandfather didn't exaggerate. The king says witchcraft, magic, and fairy creatures. You don't even blink." He looked at Cazador incredulous. "Is it true you came to mastery of Ard Allam as payment for fighting off a lich queen her knights and ghul?" The king asked gaze rapt. Cazador chuckled without humor. "I fought the lich queen and her army because I am a knight of Saint Attillo and such is my duty to send creatures of darkness and their allies to hell. I took the town because the emir promised me aid, watched me bleed and my men die and did nothing. For that, from him, I took everything." A wintry smile quirked his lips until all his teeth showed as he bowed. *"Your majesty."* King John inclined his head his eyes hard. "I too cannot abide being crossed Sir Cazador." Hands itching for want of a weapon he held the king's gaze. "I'm glad we understand each other Your Majesty."

* * *

The splash of the oars biting the ocean and the creak of rigging was there was to interrupt the predawn stillness. Diallo had sung up a fog so thick Cazador thought he might scoop a handful in his palm. Mydilsburgh was nothing but collection of ghostly shapes, gray hulks in an iron grey mist. The horses would need time to recover so the Company of the Leopard would attack on foot and Cazador stood cramped in the horse deck with his original eight lances and Longespée who like Alcazar and Leonardo had to hunch in the claustrophobic space. The horses snorted and stamped as if protesting the presence of humans in their equine world.

He had sent Idris the younger ashore the previous day to scout the enemy position. The almogovar had returned with a report that Mydilsburgh Priority was now surrounded by an unnatural hedgerow as tall as five tall men and as thick as knights tent. It was said to run from the priory grounds, cutting through the town to the river that was blocked by a line of low barges packed with Idris the younger had dubbed strange folk. At the time it had just been a report, but now with battle imminent he wondered exactly how strange.

With a echoing thud that startled man and horse the anchor dropped and the hatch flipped open. For a moment Cazador was confused until a sailor bustled through and began cranking the windlass that would release the ramp. He could hear Asmā's sharp command to the archers in the stern castle. The taste of her lips still fresh on his own as arrows and bolts snapped through the fog laden air in a sheet of covering fire. It seemed awfully loud and took entirely too long but the ramp hit the deck and Cazador drew L'auxifar the blades soft glow filling him with equal parts fear and excitement. He had eschewed his maille for the leather lamellar and aketon. Over it he wore his flashy surcoats marking his status as captain making him instantly identifiable in the cloth of gold fabric with the company arms in eschucheon over his heart. If he died today he would look good doing it and he would not drown. "For Saint Attillo and Saint George! A Alfiere !" He bellowed and charged blade low almost shield to shield with Alcazar and doughty Merfynn.

Arrows snaked out of the fog like deadly ghosts. He could feel them kick and bite his shield even as he hunched further into it's protection. Risking a peek over the rim of his shield spying his target. A short man, no higher than Cazador's chin with a wiry build, a short goatee and hard yellow amber eyes that glowed in the gloom. He got low and went shield to shield with his target expecting to bowl the man over and stab him in the groin. Instead it was like hitting a tree. A tree with deep roots. His enemy spat and screamed abuse in a language Cazador had never heard. His opponent shoved him away like a child and stabbed. Cazador deflected the strike with the face of his shield and punched his opponent in the mouth with the rim. Pulling his shield back he trapped the short man's arms and stabbed him in the eye with L'auxifar. Flicking the man away Cazador just managed to get his blade up and around in time to parry a spear thrust. Stepping forward he cut, his new target a strikingly beautiful woman floating on wings that seemed spun from light and color. Eyes the color of the sunset flashed at him with unbridled rage as he drove his edge into the graceful fingers gripping the spear. Before he could attack again a gold fleched crossbow bolt drove into her helmet snatching her from the sky.

The screams of the wounded and dying mingled with the cacophony of weapons, flesh, and armor being struck. A roar drew him back to the battle. A brown skinned brute with silver hair streaming from beneath his helmet stabbed at Cazador with a sword that seemed a shard of molten gold. It bit his shield with the force of a horses kick before skating away Cazador stepped forward punching his shield into his enemy's pausing it just long enough to punch his sword into the soft flesh of his inner thigh. Blood squirted up his blade as the artery released its supply and the light left his foe's violet eyes and his flesh begin to shrivel. He should have taken longer to die but Cazador didn't have time to think about it.

Turning he saw Longespée roaring like the lion on his shield sweep the rest of the resistance from the barge with his enormous sword. With his lance and the Englishmen in tow he leapt from the barge into the shallows of the river shield high as he slogged towards the bank. Flying enemy archers were torn between contesting their landing or preventing the archers from shooting them from the sky. As soon as enemy resistance formed Bayan and the sappers pounded them with the ship born springalds and pole slings. Their fire knocked men from the wall of shields like piles from a fence. Cazador heard a roar from the barge line and turned to see Sabri of Le Cannet Des Maures pumping an axe in the air as two barges swung apart. Turning back to the river bank he saw enemy reinforcements filtering through the town from the priory running from cover to cover while avoiding bunching up. "Company of the Leopard to me!" He roared and a shield wall formed. Longespée falling in on his right and while Alcazar brooded on his left. "Lets kill them all!" He shouted glorying in comrade's bloodthirsty answering roar.

***

Oberon looked on in dismay. The humans had come out of the unnatural fog like devils of iron and blood. The assault had been led by a Moor in a gold tabard who's sword blazed with manna and charms and wards crafted by the hand of a master. These humans fought well and his people were dying. He had known man would come eventually and he had been on high alert. Now needed a plan and he needed one fast. The human ships had breeched the blockade and poured men onto the river bank covered by archers and killing engines. Aeryr's archers were being shot to pieces. It had been a good first blow from the humans but now it was time for Oberon to hit back. He'd sent the cynocephali forward with orders to spread out and use cover to get to the humans through the town. To strike their left flank. Oberon would get what was left of his taxiarchy mounted and would swing north to hit the right flank from behind his fae heavy cavalry.

It took too long. King Aeryr's force, Fier's, and his own formations bled as they held the human's in place. Samyazan magic was availing them little as the iron clad humans were anathema to all but the most adept and potent manna wielders leaving the average warrior with naught but bronze, stone, and will. Minerva gleaming at the front took her place at the head of the wedge with the other fae knights. Her war moose ready to run swayed it's great rack ominously from side to side like a boxer loosening his neck. His great bronze and leather clad form seemed poised for havoc. From the second rank Oberon blew his horn, a spell already building.

His formation rolled forward and Oberon unleashed his spell clawing a great wheel of fire from the sky. The enemy was turning to face them, but the spell tumbled forward and struck the enemy formation like a hammer. It was met by an indigo dome of pure manna. It simply sprang to life reverberating like ten thousand ancestoral warriors throwing up shields and locking them together. A few men burned, others were thrown to the ground or lost their balance as if struck by a heavy blow. Then they struck. Minerva's moose simply shrugged off hastily raised spear points and tossed men aside bodies cartwheeling through the air like broken toys. Dire wolves bit through maille clad arms like rotten wood. Fae plunged lances like great bronze awls into human flesh. A great hole was torn in the enemy formation. The screams of the dead, broken, and dying rising with a wail of dismay from the enemy.

Oberon expected them the break, to flee back to their ships in horror. Instead a wave of stones and great bolts joined a cloud of arrows in strafing his wedge. Good Samyazans died and he watched in horror as Minerva was thrown from her saddle her mighty mount pierced by a enormous bolt. Frantic Oberon searched for her, finding Minerva crawling on her hands and knees like a drunk. Pulling the dazed fae up into his saddle Oberon warded blows with his lance, arm moving with speed didn't know he possessed as his heart pounded with unabated panic. When the second volley came it was only a reserve taxing wall of raw manna that saved his life and those closest to him. Oberon looked at his force his proud wedge blunted like a bronze spear that had struck stone. He ordered all troops to dismount hoping that smaller targets would make for less casualties. Before he could give another order, the Moor in the gold tabard was on him. Oberon hammered his mace at him but the human got his shield up deflecting the flanges as he pushed his iron clad rim at Oberon's face. He could feel the heat of the man's steel like a branding iron on his skin as he skipped away. The Moor was good. Too good and for the first time in many years he found himself pressed.

* * *

Cazador growled in frustration turning his missed thrust into a low sweep that he turned and arced that for his enemy's legs. Like a hero from a saga he swayed away forcing Cazador to cover as the mace came again like a comet smashing his shield. The strength behind the blow was incredible and Cazador was knocked back half a pace. Arrows and sling stones flayed the enemy and Cazador pressed the attack once more using the distraction to punch L'auxifar into his enemies foot. Violet eyes widened and his foe spat in a tongue he didn't know but bastard translated in tone, if nothing else. With a roar he lashed out with his shield and twisted his sword savagely before yanking it free. His foe screamed and Cazador bellowed as he moved to finish his foe when a screaming man with dirty blond braids and ice blue eyes vibrant in his brown face swooped down on him like a hawk with a flurry of axe blows. Such was the fury of the assault he could do naught but defend.

Cazador sheltered behind his shield spying his other opponent shooting green light from his hand at his stricken foot. Swaying away from the axeman's next strike he pushed out with his shield trapping the axe against his enemy's shield. He brought his sword around in a vicious overhead cut laying open the bronze helmet like a melon and biting into the skull beneath. The man was dead before Cazador kicked him from his blade. They were vastly out numbered and part of him longed to retreat to the ships yet some burning rage pushed him to wipe the enemy from the face of the earth. He hunted for the purple eyed rogue with the mace and found him sheltered behind a ring of warriors. "Who are you human?" His foeman called. Cazador inclined his head. "I am Cazador Alfiere . Knight of Saint Attillo, Lord of Ard Allam and tenant in chief of Moorhouse. Captain of the Company of the Leopard. Surrender what you have seized and you may yet get out of this alive!" His enemy laughed like an adult in the face of a fierce toddler. "I am Oberon, King of the high elves of Penume's Reach Legatus and Taxiarch of the Seelie Court. I seized these lands to protect them from a darkness greater than you know." Cazador spat. "So say all greedy tyrants!" Oberon's purple eyes flared. Before he could say another word a horn sounded to the east. Cazador peered downriver to see flashing oars and sails painted with an odd symbol.

The horn blared again raising gooseflesh across his skin. He turned to the huge and blood spattered Longespée. "Yours?" The Englishman shook his head. He looked back to Oberon to see a great shadow descending even as the Seelie Court forces pulled back. A ship tethered to enormous birds thumped to the earth and Oberon was bustled aboard. "Until we meet again Sir Cazador!" he called. Cazador simply responded with a rude gesture feeling anxious, deprived, and relieved all at once. "Prepare to face whoever comes on those boats!" He bellowed. "Sappers! Fire at will!" The warriors of Gladr Odinsblood had come to England.